survival

By Lizzy Graham

 Survival1992   fb.me/Survival1992   survival_1992

Author's Note:

Any events that involve real, existing companies are fictional, written solely to fit with the storylines and are in **NO WAY** intended as a reflection of the companies or any of their staff.

Chapter 1:

Lizzy's First

Saturday 15th September 2007

'Are you okay there?' a voice asked. I looked up at the owner of the voice that spoke and came face to face with, not just any boy my age, but one I'd met before. Even amidst the embarrassment of my predicament, I still had the headspace to feel surprised to see him.

'Will! Er, yeah, the bag's split,' I said, awkwardly.

We caught each other's eyes. I looked into Will's light brown eyes for five seconds before I came back down to Earth.

Will crouched down and started helping me pick up all the stuff I'd dropped. We finished gathering everything together and put half the items back in the part of the bag that didn't have a massive tear in it.

'Where's all this stuff meant to be going?' Will asked.

'British Heart Foundation,' I answered.

I had made plans with one of my mates, Scarlet, to go round her house in Dorchester, and I deliberately caught the bus up there early, to give myself loads of time to drop off a bag of donations at the British Heart Foundation shop in town, though I was a bit too desperate not to be late at Scarlet's after stopping by at the shop, it has to be said, but who knew I'd end up feeling glad I had? The bag I'd been carrying up Cornhill was really heavy. I should've seen it coming, because the handles looked like they were about to give way any minute, and there were a few pointy items that were straining against the bag. Luckily there hadn't been anything breakable in the bag when it split, but I'd still been embarrassed enough to wish I could've dropped dead at that moment. I'd started gathering everything up, wondering what on Earth I was supposed to do.

Because I was super grateful for Will's help in picking everything up and taking it to the shop, it gave me a really good excuse to ask him, 'Are you interested in getting a coffee?'

'Yeah, that would be brilliant!' he answered immediately, sounding eager, so off we both went to Costa.

'So, you been up to much?' he nervously began the conversation with, once we'd sat down.

'A fair bit,' was my answer. 'I went on holiday to Spain in the summer. I did enjoy it, though God, it was hot! And I was kept awake most nights by dogs barking!'

'Jeez,' said Will, grimacing.

'What about you?' I asked. 'Did you go anywhere on holiday?'

'Yeah, I went to Devon,' Will said. 'Stayed in a holiday cottage with my dad and his girlfriend.'

'Your dad's girlfriend?' I asked, slightly puzzled. 'Are your parents not together, then?'

'Well... actually,' Will began, sounding sombre and slightly awkward, 'my mum died of breast cancer when I was thirteen.'

'Oh,' I responded, crestfallen. 'I'm really sorry. I can't imagine how you must've felt but it must've been terrible.'

'It was,' Will agreed. 'I don't wanna talk about it, though.'

Without thinking, I'd taken hold of Will's forearm in what I hoped was an affectionate, sympathetic way. He looked at me... and I looked at him. He smiled at me, and we gazed into each other's eyes, and that was when I felt a spark, and I was sure Will felt it too.

A moment later, his phone beeped, breaking us out of that moment. He quickly turned his attention away from me and got his phone out.

By the time we'd finished our drinks, it was twenty minutes to twelve and about time I ought to start making my way to Scarlet's place, so we both left.

We turned and faced each other just outside the door.

'Well, it was, er... nice seeing you again,' Will said, nervously running his hand through his short hair of chocolate brown. 'It was nice to catch up and all.'

'Yeah,' I agreed, nodding, feeling a little nervous myself.

'Bye then,' said Will.

'Bye,' I said.

We caught each other's eyes again, before Will turned and slowly began to walk away. And then it happened. He strode back over to me and kissed me on the lips! It sent shivers through my shoulders and down my spine; it made my stomach feel like it was fizzing, it made me feel my heart beating wildly!

Will quickly broke away and quickly said, 'I'm sorry, I-I don't know what made me do that.'

'It's fine,' I said, still totally stunned at what just happened.

We awkwardly said another goodbye and then went our separate ways.

I was finding it really hard to concentrate on the movies me and Scarlet had been watching that afternoon, as I couldn't stop thinking about Will. He was my first kiss ever!

He never got in touch with me after that. No friend request on Facebook, nothing - though I guessed neither of us could find each other even if we did search Facebook because we didn't know each other's surnames - so I couldn't ask him where it left us or where I stood, so I'd never had any answers. I had no way of knowing what he was thinking.

Wednesday 1st September 2010

'Lizzy?'

I looked to my right to see who it was, and saw Will stood in front of me in the queue, casually straightening the collar of his baby blue short sleeve polo shirt.

'Hi Will, um, how are you?' I gabbled. You know that feeling you get when you're thrilled to bits to see someone you haven't seen or heard from for ages, but you don't know how to react because of things that happened the last time? Well, that's how I felt, after what happened the last time we'd seen each other when we were fifteen. After that kiss.

I hadn't immediately noticed he had been in front of me in the queue at the Jurassic Rocks Café at Weymouth beach. I was too busy looking at the board of all the different ice cream choices and trying to make up my mind which one I wanted.

'Not too bad thanks,' Will said. 'It's, er, really good to see you. Been a long time, no see, no speak.'

'Yeah,' I agreed. 'It has been.' We exchanged coy looks, before Will's turn came to order.

I had a brief think about how I hadn't heard from him since seeing him last, and how it made me feel. I was wondering whether to say anything to him about it. I'd been feeling so confused about everything during the first few weeks after that.

Will took his can of Coca Cola but stuck around whilst I ordered strawberry and chocolate ice creams in cones and two milk chocolate Magnums for myself, my mum and dad, my two brothers Alistair and Fraser, and Alistair's girlfriend, Sophie, who I'd come to the beach with. It was like he was waiting for me or something.

'Damn! I wish I'd got Fraser to come with me!' I said when I took my order, and realised I didn't have enough hands.

Maybe it was lucky Will didn't leave with his drink straightaway, because who else would've offered to help me carry the ice creams back to where me and my lot were sitting?

Me and Will went down the steps, carrying the ice creams between us, and brought them over to where Dad, Alistair, and Sophie were sunbathing. I saw Sophie sitting up, clearly having noticed me coming back.

When me and Will reached her and the others she asked, 'Hey, who's your friend?' in that vastly intrigued and slightly jokey manner in which people usually ask that question when getting just a tiny bit excited that the new friend in question could potentially become more than that to the person they're asking.

I introduced Will and Sophie, telling Sophie vaguely how I'd met Will, before Sophie took the ice creams he'd been holding.

I thanked Will, who bashfully replied, 'Don't mention it,' before returning to where he'd been sat with his friends, which turned out to be nearby where we were.

Sophie looked over at Will as she got started on the chocolate ice cream I'd bought her, and then winked at me, smiling.

Dad called for Mum and Fraser, who were swimming back in, and they staggered about as they trod carefully over the pebbles and sharp, broken seashells and both flopped down on their towels to have their ice creams. I got started on my Magnum, which was naturally beginning to melt quite a bit already.

I'd moved on a month after what happened, but now I didn't know whether to feel elated to see Will again, or feel frustrated that I'd be left having to try to move on all over again, since I was starting wonder if everything I felt back then was starting to crawl back to me after those three years. As well as not knowing whether it would be a good idea to say anything to Will about it, I didn't even know whether or not I actually wanted to.

When I finished my ice cream, I decided to go back into the sea for another swim. When the surface of the water was above my shoulders, I lay back and tried to float on my back on the surface, with some difficulty as I was never exactly the best at swimming and I never had much confidence when it came to floating, staying relaxed and believing I wouldn't sink either.

'Having a bit of trouble, there?'

I quickly flipped back onto my feet in the water. Will had swum over. He was smiling.

'I'm not the best at swimming,' I confessed.

'I could tell,' Will teased, with a grin.

'You cheeky bastard,' I said, smirking.

'You don't seem too insulted.'

'Oh yeah?'

I splashed a huge wave of water at Will, who coughed and spluttered. Just then, I was worried I'd been a bit over exuberant, and apologised immediately, but then Will started laughing, thank goodness, and I couldn't help laughing too, then Will splashed me back in retaliation! We carried on having a splash fight.

I caught Will's eye at one point. He looked at me, smile fading slightly. We moved in closer to each other, looking into each other's eyes, our heads tilting towards each others...

But then...

'I can't,' Will said.

'Why not?'

'It just isn't right at the moment.'

Will didn't say exactly why it wasn't right, but I just figured it was because of last time.

'Why did I never hear from you, after last time?' I had to ask, though I was hesitating a bit.

'I just didn't know what to say, ' Will said.

I nodded

'I'm sorry,' he said. 'I need to go. Hopefully we'll bump into each other again some time.'

I began to swim back to shore, giving Will one last look over my shoulder. He gave me a feeble smile, which I gave in return.

I carried on swimming and rejoined the family, who were packing, getting ready to leave.

In the car on the way home, I relived that moment in my head. I was thinking about why Will pulled away at the last minute. Why was it not right? And why did he kiss me before if that had been the case? What was I supposed to think about that?

I'd thought about this a few times at night over the next three weeks.

Monday 20th of September 2010

I woke up at six thirty. I had to get up in half an hour, to get ready for my first day back at college. I was starting a foundation Diploma in Art and Design. I did the two previous levels over the last two years when I had finished at Carrie Mount Academy at the age of sixteen.

I lay on my white day bed, looking around my lilac room. Sunlight shone in my face through the gap in the curtains. I think it was that that woke me.

When it rolled onto seven o'clock, I got up, plugged in my shiny hot pink hair straighteners, sat at my dressing table, got out all my make-up from some of my favourite make-up brands, which are No7, Maybelline, Max Factor, Collection 2000 and Rimmel, and started putting it all on, starting with my Max Factor Hydrating and Illuminating primer, and dabbed on my No7 Essentially Natural foundation with my best blending sponge, and then applied my Collection 2000 eye primer, followed by my Collection 2000 Long Lasting Perfection concealer, which I also like to use as a second eye primer. Next, I applied a beige eye shadow, a black mascara from No7, and last of all, a nude lipstick from Maybelline.

Then I brushed my ash blonde hair, and began straightening it, taking care to curl the graduated ends inwards without frying my hair.

I then put on my indigo, pink and cream tartan blouse and my baby blue jeans with the silver diamante studs, with the hems rolled up below the knees, along with my white and silver wedges and had my daily dose of thyroxine, tablets I've been on my whole life. I have this condition called Congenital Hypothyroidism, which has resulted in me having mild learning difficulties and I'm sort of on the Autism spectrum just a little bit, though people have said they never noticed and would never have known if I hadn't told them.

So, I had one hundred and twenty-five micrograms of thyroxine and then went downstairs for breakfast.

Mum and Dad had already left for work. Mum has her dream career of being a garden and interior designer. Dad works as a cartographer, *his* dream job. They used to work together. That's how they met.

They had Alistair when they were twenty-nine, Fraser when they were thirty-one, and me when they were thirty-four.

The first thing I saw was Penny, our brown and white Springer spaniel we'd had from a puppy. Penny ran over to me and jumped up onto her hind legs. Penny happily licked my hands as I made a big fuss of her before going to the kitchen to grab myself some breakfast.

I brought my drink and jam into the dining room. Fraser was already sat at the table, still in the grey melange Adidas t-shirt and navy tracksuit trousers he wore to bed, with a bowl of Cheerios in front of him. His light mousy brown medium length hair was sticking out at odd angles.

Fraser was twenty. He and I used to hang out at break when we were both at Carrie Mount. But now he just goes around with his two best mates, Adam and Dustin.

'Morning,' I said, putting my drink and the jam on the space opposite Fraser.

'Alright?' he said, looking up.

I went back to the kitchen to get a plate and a knife, just as the toast popped out. I put both slices on the plate, took it to the dining room, put it down on the table by the jam and the apple juice and sat down.

'What time is Alistair coming for us?' I asked, as I began to spread jam on my toast. Alistair, who was twenty-three, has a house with Sophie, who he'd been with for five years. They'd lived there together for three years.

'Half eight,' Fraser mumbled, through a mouthful of Cheerios. Eurgh! Talk about revolting.co.uk!

'Do you have to talk with your mouth full?' I asked my brother, disgusted. 'No one wants to see what your breakfast looks like once it's been chewed up and soaked in your saliva.'

Fraser shrugged. I tucked into my own breakfast.

When Fraser finished his cereal, he stood up and walked over to the kitchen door, leaving his empty bowl and glass on the table!

'Are you having another slice of toast after those two? Cos Al will be here in a minute,' he asked, looking back over his shoulder.

'No thanks,' I said.

'Okay,' said Fraser, and he left the room.

So I had to pick up my lazy brother's bowl and glass and put them in the dishwasher! Fraser is so untidy! I barely ever go in his room if I can help it. He has used glasses, plates and Coke bottles, chocolate bar wrappers and empty crisp packets and pizza boxes lying around on the floor and his desk, his bed's never made, and what's the point in him even having a wardrobe, when most of his clothes seem to be strewn all over his room? Mum's given up trying to get him to tidy it.

At half past eight, the doorbell rang. I knew it would be Alistair. I hurried down the stairs with my small, off-white handbag with the silver charms dangling from one of the handles and opened the front door. There stood Alistair. Penny had already run up to him, excited to see him.

'Hi, Lizzy,' he said, cheerfully, scratching Penny's ears as he came in. 'Is Fraser ready, yet?'

'Coming!' Fraser shouted from upstairs, over the thundering sound of him dashing over to the stairs.

He said 'Hi,' to Alistair, and grabbed his rucksack as soon as he'd come down the stairs.

'Ready,' he said, and we all headed out the door. We got into Alistair's hurricane grey Peugeot 2008 and Alistair began to drive along Bowleaze Coveway.

'Any more happening with the band you and your mates wanna start?' Alistair asked Fraser, as he drove along the esplanade. Just before the summer began, Fraser surprised us all by announcing that he, Adam and Dustin had been talking about starting up a band, as they're all really serious about getting into the music industry, and they can do something together, that

6

makes them happy.

'Well, we've chosen a name at last,' said Fraser. 'Rebel Tour Bus.' I knew they'd had a few disagreements about the name of the band. Fraser and Dustin had been leaning towards Criminal Tour Bus, but apparently Adam wanted to go for Rebel 98.

He talked about the songs he and his mates wanted to do covers of to start with. It was a seriously exciting prospect, one of my brothers in a band! I did hope they got somewhere with it.

We arrived at college, where the campus is mainly made up of buildings built with red brick. Alistair's car pulled over to the kerb outside the London Building, which has a classical style pediment that's held up by a row of four columns, which are made up of the same coloured bricks as the buildings.

Me and Fraser got out, thanked Alistair for the lift, and said goodbye before he drove off.

Fraser said he was heading off to find Adam and Dustin, and then walked off.

I started to walk round to the canteen, when I spotted a familiar red haired, rosy pale skinned boy, Charlie Allen, playing with his phone. He was one of Fraser's mates, who I'd had a major crush on since I was eleven. Back then, I never would've stood a chance with him, obviously, because the fact that Charlie was fourteen at the time meant he would only see me as a little kid. But I'd been hoping things would change as I got older, when a three-year age gap between us wouldn't be a massive deal.

That was another thing that added to the confusion I was feeling. It left me confused about what I wanted, as far as boys went, because what I felt with Will hadn't made me completely forget my crush on Charlie. Though Charlie seemed to be a more realistic option, because at least I saw him loads.

Excited, I decided to take that moment, and rushed over to him. Wanting to be friendly, I started by saying, 'Hi.'

He responded with, 'Hey,' though carried on playing with his phone, but then put it away, looked up, and asked 'You okay?'

'Good, thanks,' I answered, but before I could reciprocate the question, I saw him quickly look over my shoulder. I looked round too and saw Fraser still nearby. Charlie quickly said he was going to look for his mate Stuart, then said, 'See you later,' and rushed off. I looked over to see if Fraser was watching. It was almost as if Charlie wanted to get away before Fraser saw.

Fraser's the type of person who's not keen on the idea of their mates and siblings dating. He said I was off limits to all of his mates, which Charlie knew, but Fraser also knew that I'd fancied Charlie for a really long time, so I liked to think that he'd understand and compromise that Charlie could be an exception.

Out of the corner of my eye, I recognised the familiar sunflower blonde, ear length hair of one of my family friends, Jesse Naerger, walking towards me.

Jesse's mum, Flora, is friends with my mum, because they'd been at college together. They'd stayed friends when they left college, and when Mum married Dad.

'Alright?' he said, giving me a hug.

'Yeah, not bad, thanks. How are things going with Annie?'

'Things are still good. Other than the fact that she made me watch Bambi last night, so I had to pretend I needed the loo so that I wouldn't have to watch the bit where his mum was shot,' said Jesse. 'You won't tell her, will you?'

Really?

'No. I won't.'

'Thanks. Also, I can't help wondering, do you reckon she'd fancy me more if I wore a bit of mascara to make my eyes look sparklier?' Jesse asked, curiously.

'No,' I said, 'that would just make you weird. Seriously, where the hell do you get this stuff from?'

Jesse is a bit of an oddball, and can be dumb at times.

He asked me how things were with Charlie and asking if I'd made a move on him, yet. I told him about the brief conversation we just had, if you could call it a conversation, before Charlie had noticed Fraser still nearby and had to skedaddle.

I still wasn't sure if I actually wanted to make a move under the aforementioned circumstances, though.

'I haven't,' I told Jesse. 'And I don't know, yet, if I'm going to.'

'Why not?'

I cleared my throat and said, 'You remember that guy I told you I'd met before?'

Jesse frowned.

'Yeah?'

'I saw him again.'

Jesse's eyes widened.

'*When?*' he said, stunned.

'On the beach,' I told him. 'I bumped into him when getting ice creams for everyone, then he gave me a hand with them because there were too many to carry on my own and we were in the water together and... and we nearly kissed.'

Jesse's frown came back.

'Nearly?' he asked. 'Why didn't you?'

I told Jesse how Will said he couldn't because it wasn't right at that moment and he didn't say why. Jesse asked why I never tried to get in touch with him.

'Well, even if I had any way of contacting him, if I could've become his friend on Facebook, it wouldn't be a good idea because I would've looked like I was pestering him.'

Jesse looked down, sighed, and then looked up at me again and said, 'Listen, he may have pulled away at the last minute, but you and he wouldn't have come that close if he didn't want it. He must've had a good reason for what he said.'

'Maybe,' I said.

'Maybe there was something he needed to... I don't know, sort out. You just need to decide whether or not you can wait for that.'

But even if Will did decide to come back to me, having changed his mind, he had no way of getting in touch. And neither did I.

Later on, I was sat in my new class, trying to listen to what my teacher, Teresa, was saying, but couldn't stop thinking about Will. I knew Jesse could be right. If Will did not want that kiss, he wouldn't have waited until the last minute to say no. I should've asked him why, because perhaps that would've given me a better understanding of why he didn't feel right in letting it happen. And even if there was something Will needed to sort out, like Jesse suggested, how long would that take? And could I wait as long is it would take?

Though part of me still felt I was being stupid. I hoped seeing Charlie would make me forget about Will, and I'd know what I wanted, but I still didn't.

When I was able to give Teresa my full attention, she was saying she wanted the class to start by going round the room, introducing ourselves to each other and telling each other about our hobbies and interests and that we all had to write down what we learnt about our new classmates. This obviously has nothing to do with Art or Design, but it was just a class activity for us to get to know each other a bit. I remembered doing this last year, only it was bad habits, not hobbies, the majority of which was smoking, mine of which being forgetting to take my tablets, which is really bad because if it becomes too much of a habit, I can get really ill.

The first person I approached was a girl who'd been sat at the same desk as me. She has golden honey blonde hair that was in a French braid. I knew I recognised her, but it was one of those *slightly* irritating moments where you know you recognise someone, but can't, for your own life, think where from. Her name's Isabel Cooper.

At break time, I headed to the student lounge and, as soon as I got there, I caught sight of Charlie and Stuart Hart sat at a nearby table. Being sure to check first that Fraser wasn't about, I walked over to them, hoping that we could have an uninterrupted conversation.

I approached them nervously, and said, 'Hi.' They both looked up.

'Hi, said Charlie. I asked if I could join them. Charlie seemed okay with it, but as I sat down, I saw Stuart give him an anxious look, as if he was saying, 'What if Fraser comes in and sees?' Charlie shrugged.

'So, how have your first days been?' I asked them both, though I admit I wished I'd thought of something more interesting to ask. Stuart looked from me to Charlie, still looking slightly on edge.

'Not too bad, thanks,' Charlie said. 'What course did you say you were doing, again? Art and Design?'

'That's right,' I said. 'What about you? You said you were doing a course in Carpentry or something?'

'Yep. It's a level three Diploma in Site Carpentry. I've, um, always wanted to be a builder so I did courses and stuff in carpentry after I er, did brickwork stuff.'

'That's cool,' I said. I turned to Stuart.

'So, um, what course are you doing?' I asked him, feeling a bit embarrassed that I had nothing more interesting to strike up a conversation about. Neither Charlie nor Stuart seemed to mind, though, and Stuart started talking about how he was doing his second year in the BTEC Extended Diploma in Art and Design, which he said was more based around photography.

'How's things going for your brother on his course?' he then asked. 'I heard that he, Dustin and Adam wanted to start a band.'

'Yeah! That's right. They're really into it,' I said. Charlie and Stuart asked me more about it, so I told them all about the bands Fraser, Dustin and Adam were inspired by and how they wanted to do their own guitar covers of some of Darren Styles and Chris Unknown's music.

'Sounds good,' Charlie had said, looking and sounding impressed, but then he and Stuart suddenly had petrified looks on their faces, looking over at the door I had just come in through. I looked over too, and understood why.

Fraser had come in, and was walking over to us. I saw Charlie give Stuart a warning look, as if he was saying, 'Act natural.'

Fraser reached the three of us and said, 'Hi.'

'Hi,' Charlie and Stuart said together, nervously. Fraser obviously noticed their expressions, because he asked them both if they were okay, telling them that they looked like they were being confronted by the police. They both insisted they were fine. Fraser seemed convinced, though he did frown at them, slightly, and then looked at me.

'All right?' he asked, casually.

'Fine,' I said, trying to sound as calm as I could. Fraser talked to the three of us for a couple of minutes, before saying, 'Anyway, see you later, I only came over for a quick catch up.'

'See you,' said Charlie, and Fraser walked off. I looked at my watch and realised it was nearly time to go back to class.

Charlie and Stuart said goodbye and then just as I started walking over to the door, I overheard Stuart saying to Charlie, 'Seriously, mate, you need to stop shitting yourself every time Fraser is nearby when you're talking to Lizzy. It's beginning to show and soon he'll know so you'll have to tell him!'

I slowed down, that way it would take me longer to get too far away from them to hear what they were saying. I heard Charlie say, 'I don't wanna tell him 'til we're in a position where he's gotta accept it!'

Accept what, though?

During the next class, I kept thinking about the near miss me and Charlie just had with Fraser, and more to the point, what I'd just heard Charlie and Stuart saying as I was walking away. What Charlie said about telling Fraser at a time when he would have to accept it had all but confirmed what I'd been hoping, not that I wanted to over-analyse, of course. Though what else could Charlie be talking about, to do with both me and him, that Fraser would have to accept, than the two of us dating? My head was buzzing.

But still, did I want him more or less than I wanted Will?

I spent the rest of the day thinking about this.

At last, the end of the day came, and now Fred Curtis, another family friend, Jesse and I were in Fred's navy blue Mini Cooper with the Union Jack flag painted on the roof, on the way to Fred and Natalie's.

Fred and his older sister Natalie are the two eldest of the three children Auntie Flora's secondary school friend, Claire, had with her husband, Barry. Flora was the one who introduced my mum to Auntie Claire when they became friends at college, and the three of them became inseparable.

Fred pulled into the driveway of the house. It has a grey brick front, with mahogany windows and front door. There's a big stretch of grass with a fair few bare patches next to the driveway, in front of the living room bay window. Auntie Claire's ocean blue Ford Focus, which had a few scratches in the paintwork on the right hand back passenger door, was parked in the driveway, next to where Fred parked his car.

We all got out, walked over to the front door, and then Fred got out his key and let us all in. We all went to the kitchen, where Auntie Claire greeted her son in her usual motherly way, and then she saw me and Jesse.

'Hello, Jesse, darling,' she beamed, giving Jesse a hug. 'And Lizzy, dear, it's so good to see you.'

Auntie Claire always makes us a hot chocolate with cream and marshmallows as well as for Fraser, Alistair and Jesse's sister Rochella whenever any of us come round. Auntie Flora is just the same with me, Fred, Natalie, Fraser and Alistair, as is Mum, with Fred, Natalie, Jesse and Rochella.

Auntie Claire gave me a hug, and then she did indeed say she was going to make us all a cup of hot chocolate, before calling to Natalie that Jesse and I were here, and then filling the kettle.

I heard the sound of footsteps rushing down the stairs and within a minute, Natalie came walking into the kitchen. She was wearing some dark grey, stone washed skinny jeans, a black, sleeveless, collared, lace top, a skinny silver faux leather belt that was made to look like a ribbon tied in a bow, and a pair of silver drop, beaded hoops. Her eyes are the same misty grey as Fred's, and she had straightened her naturally wavy mid back length hair, which is also the same medium ash brown as Fred's.

'Hey!' she squealed, hugging the boys in turn, before turning to me.

'Hi, honey!' she said, giving me a hug and a kiss on both cheeks.

When our hot chocolates with cream and marshmallows were ready, we took our mugs to the lounge and sat down. I took a sip of mine and oh my God! Auntie Claire had used the Maltesar chocolate powder and had added extra milk! The best!

'So, things have been developing with Charlie?' said Jesse, before adding, 'Me and Fred saw you and him talking at break.'

'Er... a tiny bit,' I said. True, I hadn't had a lot of chance to have a good long conversation with Charlie, but what happened was better than nothing, and I felt that Charlie's worry about Fraser seeing us together was a good sign.

I wasn't sure exactly how long he'd liked me for, if he *did* like me, that was. I didn't think he could possibly have liked me when we were younger. Maybe he'd just recently started developing feelings for me now? Maybe he was feeling something for me now, that wasn't there before? Maybe he's clocked I liked him, and it's given him a taste for me?

'I overheard him and Stuart talking about how Charlie reacted every time Fraser saw us together,' I told the others. 'And Charlie said he didn't want to tell Fraser anything until we were in a position where Fraser couldn't object.'

Natalie looked both stunned and excited.

'You are *in* there, girl!'

I was glad Natalie was obviously thinking along the same line I was.

'But Jesse said you weren't entirely sure about whether you wanted to try to make something happen with Charlie,' Fred said. 'Said you'd seen that other guy again.'

Natalie looked from Fred to me, mouth open in amazement.

'You what?'

'Summer, on the beach' I said. 'We very nearly kissed. I'm just so confused about it all.'

I also told Fred and Natalie what Jesse had reckoned.

'Why don't you just try adding him on Facebook?' Natalie suggested.

'I already thought of that,' I said. 'But I don't know his surname and what if I just look like some desperate stalker?'

At this, Fred just laughed.

'Of course you won't look like a desperate stalker!' he said. 'It's how I go about getting with girls I meet, if I don't get their numbers straight away.'

'Yeah, well you would say that, you haven't been afraid of making the first move on a girl since you were ten!' Jesse said, smirking.

Fred had *always* been such a ladies' man. He'd never had any proper girlfriends, just a lot of flings on nights out and casual dates with girls, where he'd had nothing serious with them. He was very confident when it came to chatting up girls, but could be quite conceited about it. He was very popular with girls and he knew it. At parties, he was always the one surrounded by a whole group of them.

'Speaking of which, I really need to go out on the pull, again,' he sighed, as if going out on the pull was a habit you ought to stay in regularly and shouldn't neglect, which, as far as Fred's concerned, it *was*.

'You must have pulled at least thirty times in the summer, Fred,' I told him, astonished.

'What can I say? All those fitties out there can't resist me,' Fred boasted, before saying that whilst he guessed Jesse could be right, I couldn't keep dwelling on when or if I'd see Will again, especially not if there was a chance of something happening between me and Charlie.

'I really do think you should give Charlie a chance,' he advised. 'After all, you know you've been crazy about him for seven years. You didn't half let everyone know it!'

'But unless we can meet up outside college, how are we meant to interact with each other if he keeps bailing every time Fraser approaches?'

I was starting to realise that Charlie's concerns about Fraser seeing us together had become a barrier, standing in the way of things progressing any further.

Fred had suggested that maybe I should try talking to Charlie about it.

'Maybe,' Jesse agreed, uncertainly. 'I don't know what good that'll do, though.'

'But he did seem like he wasn't going to let Fraser's problem with it stop us,' I said. 'He just didn't know what to do about Fraser knowing about it.'

'So, maybe he just wants to put it off until he's decided what to do?' Fred said.

That was a good point. I hoped Fred was right. He still said I should try to ask Charlie, very carefully.

When I was in Dad's car on the way home, I thought about how I could bring it up with Charlie. Perhaps I should start by telling him I'd noticed him and Stuart getting worried, every time Fraser was about when we were talking, and ask him why. I'd probably have to admit I couldn't help overhearing what he and Stuart had been saying, if that was what it took.

Over the rest of the week and the next, I kept thinking about both Will and Charlie more and more.

It also made me think of the other three times me and Will had met, for three years ago was not the first time.

We'd met at the age of six, when we were playing in one of the swimming pools at Oakdene Holiday Park in Hampshire, and had spent every day there since then, playing together until it was the day Will and his family were leaving.

The second time was at Cherryvale Playfields in Belfast. Will was from Northern Ireland, which I discovered when we met then. Dad took me to Cherryvale one day when we were staying with his older sister and her family. They've lived over there for as long as I can remember. Dad had just finished pushing me on one of the swings, and then I wanted to go on the seesaw, but Dad said he was too heavy to go on it with a little girl like me.

Will came over and offered to go on it with me. We may have been only six the previous time we'd seen each other, but I recognised him instantly. We played on the play equipment together until it was time to go home.

And then we met again, in Tesco after school, when we were eleven. We were both sat on the low window ledge, waiting whilst our mums were at the checkouts. Will told me about how his family had moved because of a promotion his mum had been offered.

I had to admit Fred did have a point, given the rarity of my rendezvous with Will. If Charlie, the boy I'd had a huge crush on for ages did like me, I couldn't throw that away on what had been going on with Will. Truth be told, I did still really like Charlie, and despite everything, it would be great if something happened between us.

Friday 1st October 2010

I woke up in a really good mood. I was looking forward to meeting the whole gang at Dan Hart's party. I would see Charlie then. When we talked over the past two weeks, he said he was coming, and actually asked if I was, in an anxious way, like he was desperately counting on me being there. Result!

Dan's Stuart's younger brother, who I went to Carrie Mount with. He could be kind of haughty at times. He was doing a course in Motorcycle Maintenance and Repair at Euro Capital House College. He's always had a keen interest in cars and motorbikes in particular. He originally wanted to save up for a motorbike, but his mum is dead against them. After five weeks of persuasion on Dan's part, his mum finally compromised that he could get a moped once he had the money for one. His girlfriend Nikki leapt with excitement the moment he told her he was getting one, because she said she looked forward to getting rides on the back of it.

I got ready, had breakfast, had my thyroxine and Mum gave me and Fraser a lift to college. I whizzed through the day, and now I was getting ready to go to Dan's. I picked out my ecru, short sleeved, off-the-shoulder top with spaghetti straps, and my cream skinny jeans.

I sat at my dressing table, applied my usual primer, foundation, concealer and black liquid eyeliner, flicked up and outwards from the outer corners and ends of my top lids, then I chose two eye shadows; dark burgundy for the outer halves of my top lids and a slightly lighter peach for the inner halves. Next, I applied my black soft kohl pencil eyeliner, right the way around my eyes, blending it to the best of my abilities along my lower lash lines and in the outer corners, for a real smoky effect, using a cotton bud. I finished the look with my black mascara and a slightly darker nude lipstick with some shimmery lip-gloss of the same colour. I brushed my hair, before straightening it, put on my outfit and then put on my gold strappy sandals. I spritzed on an Avon perfume named Far Away, one of my favourites.

Mum gave me a lift to Dan and Stuart's house in Littlemoor, and Dad would pick me up. I do feel lucky that Mum and Dad are so chilled out about parties!

'Hey, Lizzy. I'm glad you came,' said Dan, when he opened the door. 'You want a drink? We have Smirnoff Ice.'

'Yeah, please,' I said. Smirnoff ice is one of the very few alcoholic drinks I actually like the taste of. Jesse once let me try some of his beer. It was *horrible*! Fred and Jesse cracked up at the face I apparently pulled when I tasted it.

Dan led me to the kitchen, where Nikki was, and went to pour me a glass of Smirnoff Ice, then I went to the lounge, where I saw Scarlet Doherty, one of Dan's stepsisters-in-waiting, sat down by the window, and went over to her.

Scarlet's dad is Dan's mum's live-in boyfriend. She's a year older than me. Mr Doherty's also very good friends with Fred and Natalie's dad, Barry, which is how Scarlet knows Fred and Natalie, and then me and Jesse through them.

'How's things with you?' Scarlet asked.

'Well, I like to think I'm beginning to make headway with Charlie,' I began, before Scarlet said, 'No, I don't mean with boys! How's college so far?'

Scarlet is the total opposite of Natalie, who places just as much importance in pulling blokes as her girl-crazy brother places in pulling girls. Dating, however, is not the top of Scarlet's priority list. She's the more career-orientated type.

Even though I obviously did choose to apply for the course I was doing this year, I couldn't get too worked up when telling Scarlet how my first couple of weeks in my course were. Don't get me wrong, I do enjoy Art, and designing things is always one of my favourite hobbies, since I've always loved creative activities, and back then I was actually hoping that it could lead me to a job as *some* kind of a designer, but it just wasn't easy to elaborate when all I could tell Scarlet was that we hadn't done much practical art work.

'Have you seen Charlie, yet?' I asked.

'He is here,' Scarlet said, casually.

I hoped I'd spot him soon. Who knew what could happen by the end of the night?

Out of the corner of my eye, I could in fact see Charlie nearby. He was looking resplendently handsome, in a pale grey, short-sleeved shirt and light washed jeans.

He caught my eye and a few seconds later, he started walking in my direction! Thank God Fraser hadn't come to the party, nor had Adam or Dustin, so hopefully they wouldn't find out.

Scarlet noticed him too, and said she'd leave us to it, before getting up and leaving the lounge.

'Hey,' Charlie said when he came over. He gave me a smile that made me go weak at the knees! Oh my God!

I said, 'Hey,' back.

'Um... I just wanted to say, I, er, I'm sorry about the way I've been acting, lately,' he said.

I was quite taken aback that he actually came and apologised. This was proving easier than I thought.

'I know it's kind of awkward when Fraser nearly catches us, because of what he thinks of his mates dating me or Alistair.'

Charlie looked at me, like he was taken by surprise, and then said, 'Uh, yeah, course.'

He then said what I'd been half-expecting.

'Fraser will get suspicious that something's going on.'

'But there's nothing wrong with us being friends,' I told him.

'Well, no of course there isn't. But that's not what this is about,' was his reply. This was getting exciting. He obviously meant more than friends. It didn't stop there, though.

'Do you want to meet up sometime?'

What did I just hear? Was Charlie asking me out?

'Well, um, I would like to go for a drink,' I said, hardly able to believe it, and then we arranged to meet at the William Henry on Sunday.

'Probably best not to tell Fraser about that one,' he said, smiling. 'I had hoped to ask if you wanted to meet up before. It was just because of him.'

I was over the moon!

'You don't think...' Charlie began, sounding unsure. 'Do you reckon he would mind?'

I opened my mouth, wanting to answer, but then realised I didn't really know what to say.

'Er... I don't know for sure,' I said at last. 'He did say he'd rather I didn't date any of his friends, so like you said, I won't tell Fraser about Sunday.'

I said I'd just pretend I hung with Natalie if Fraser asked. I can trust Natalie with my life, so she would back me up for sure!

Isabel Cooper then came over, asking if she was interrupting anything. Charlie said he would leave us to have one of our girl talks, that he was going off to find Stuart, but he'd talk to me later and see me on Sunday. I couldn't believe what had just happened!

'Looks like you've got something going on there!' said Isabel, excitedly. 'Do tell me more!' So I told Isabel everything, the seven year crush I'd had on Charlie, our worries that my brother wouldn't like it, because of his issues with me dating his mates, our hopes that Fraser might possibly be okay with us dating in spite of that, our arrangements to go and have a drink in Wetherspoon's, and Charlie's preference to keeping it a secret, which suggested it was a date, or we wouldn't have to.

After agreeing with me that perhaps it did mean something, she asked, 'Fancy joining in some shots a group of us are taking in the kitchen?'

'I'm in!' I said, eagerly. I followed Isabel into the kitchen, where Scarlet, Natalie, Jesse, Fred, Nikki, Dan, Stuart and Charlie were.

'C'mon, guys! Let's get that bottle of Sourz open!' Isabel yelled.

Sourz turned out to be a bottle of bright green alcohol. It was apple flavoured. I'd never had it before. I expected it to taste like cider, but that was just because of the apple flavour. I didn't actually know you could get it in other flavours too.

We all picked up a shot each, and downed them. It tasted *nothing* like cider. It was nicer! I asked Dan if I could have a glass of it, but he went bananas at the idea.

'No way, Liz! You'll be vomming all night!' he'd said. 'And you're a lightweight, so it'll be even worse for you. You can have a glass of W.K.D Blue, if you want?'

'Awesome!' I said, so I had a glass of W.K.D Blue. I was getting *well* hammered as the evening went on. I flopped onto the sofa, next to where Fred and a girl with ginger hair were all over each other.

Everything was feeling distorted, like none of this was actually happening, like it was all a dream.

Natalie suggested I should try to sober up. Scarlet asked if I wanted some food to sober up.

'What do you fancy?' she'd asked. 'We have some Cornettos that really need eating up.'

13

Cornettos! It was a bit random, but the only thing I could think of that I actually wanted was ice cream.

Dad came to pick me up at eleven o'clock.

'Had a good night?' he asked, as we drove home. Luckily, I'd sobered up a bit, and I no longer felt sick, so I reckoned Dad probably wouldn't notice.

I was woken up late next morning, by the most terrible headache! The first thing I did when I got up was go to the bathroom, fill one of the cups with water, get the box of paracetamol out of the cupboard above the sink, and gulp down two caplets with water. I was famished! I had a real craving for sausages, but I felt too tired cook any.

I had my tablets then went down to the kitchen to find Mum filling the kettle.

'Morning, hun,' she said. 'Would you like me to make you a cup of tea?'

'Yes please,' I yawned. Mum asked if I was hung over at all. I said had a really bad headache, and was hungry for some sausages, which she said she was going to take as a yes.

'Have you taken anything for the head ache?' she asked.

'I had a couple of paracetamols before I came down,' I told her.

Mum cooked me some sausages, which I enjoyed immensely. I had a shower after breakfast to freshen up, and then picked out what I was going to wear tomorrow. As we were just going for lunch in the William Henry, I didn't think I needed anything too dressy. I chose my floaty, salmon pink, v-necked, three-quarter-length sleeved top, light blue jeans and my gold strappy sandals.

The next morning, I wore my make-up the way I usually do as my every day look, but added some lip-gloss and put my hair up in a high bun before spraying with some VO5 hair spray to keep it in place.

I caught the bus into town, listening to "Complete" by Jaimeson on my MP3 player on the way.

Charlie was already waiting, just inside the door to the William Henry.

'Alright?' he said. 'Nice top.'

'Thanks,' I said, grinning, as we both went to find a table.

Once we were seated, we both had a look at the menus.

'So... I heard you were pretty pissed at the party.'

What?! He knew about that? Should I be embarrassed or... what?

'Er... yeah, I did have a lot of W.K.D Blue,' I admitted, sheepishly.

'That's all right,' Charlie said, in a relaxed voice. 'People go to parties, get drunk, they throw up. Nothing to be ashamed of.'

That made me feel a bit better.

'What you having, then?' Charlie asked when we'd finished looking at the menus.

'Steak, as usual,' I said. Every time I eat out, I nearly always have a sirloin steak with peppercorn sauce, and everything it comes with, except the peas.

'"As usual"? Must be your favourite thing, then,' said Charlie. 'I was torn between the pork ribs and the chicken burger. In the end, I went for the ribs.'

'Not bad,' I said, before we took turns going up to the bar to place our orders.

'So...' I began, desperately trying to rack my brains for a good conversation topic, when Charlie returned from the bar, 'what movies have you been into, lately?'

'I'm more into T.V series, personally,' Charlie said. 'I like stuff like N.C.I.S, C.S.I, 24 and Heroes.'

'Oh?' I said, trying to sound interested, even though I'd never watched any of those shows. N.C.I.S, C.S.I and 24 never honestly sounded like the sort of thing that would be my cup of tea, but I asked Charlie to tell me more about Heroes, since I always thought I should give it a try at some point.

'I'll have to lend you the D.V.Ds,' he said. 'I've got the entire box set if you'd be interested in borrowing them at some point?'

'That would be cool,' I said, gratefully.

'Awesome,' said Charlie. 'So, um, what do you hope to do next, after you complete your course?'

14

'I don't really know, come to think of it,' I said. 'I s'pose I just want to see how this year goes, before I decide what I'm gonna do after that. I take it you're planning on doing the next level up from your course?'

'Nah, there is no next level up from Site Carpentry level three,' said Charlie. 'Maybe I'll go to university, or go straight into employment.'

'Cool! Well, you don't want to rush these things,' I said.

'S'pose not,' said Charlie, shrugging.

When our meals arrived, I tucked my plum paper serviette into the neckline of my top and got started on mine right away. I did feel like a bit of a pig, finishing so quickly compared to Charlie, who was still halfway through his lunch.

When Charlie finished eating, he pushed his plate towards the middle of the table and said, 'Anyway, one of the reasons I wanted to meet with you, as well as just wanting to spend time with you, was to talk about... well... us.'

I felt my heart skip a beat. What was Charlie going to say?

'I know Fraser's your brother, but I really don't give a toss what he thinks,' Charlie went on. I nodded, unblinkingly, desperate for him to carry on, which he did, saying, 'Though if it is important to you, we can be careful not to let him find out. I can handle that. But I wanna be your boyfriend either way.'

I had to pinch myself to check I wasn't dreaming because it all felt too good to be true. Charlie seriously wanted to be my boyfriend?

'Honestly?' I said, weakly.

'Yeah. Honestly,' said Charlie.

I looked at Charlie, dumbstruck, lost for words.

'*Great!*' I managed to say, finally. 'Awesome!'

Charlie grinned at me, as broadly as if I'd just accepted a marriage proposal from him.

'Cool,' he said, 'um...' Charlie awkwardly leant in and kissed me, slowly, for twelve seconds then broke away.

I couldn't believe it! Charlie Allen, the boy I'd fancied since I started at Carrie Mount, was now my boyfriend! I was way too overjoyed to be worrying about what Fraser had to say about it, but Charlie was right. As long as we were careful, Fraser wouldn't find out we were an item. Though if he didn't like it, stuff him. It was his problem, not mine and not Charlie's.

Chapter 2:

Ruby-lynn's First

Friday 8th October 2010

Zellweger's, the hair and beauty shop I work at in town, was due to shut in thirty minutes. I finished restocking the shelves with hair removal products, then jumped back onto the tills, where a customer was getting very angry at Gemma, who'd been on the till next to mine, just because the card reader had declined her card.

'How can it keep coming up, saying that my card has been declined?' the lady was saying.

Gemma stayed calm and said, 'It might be because you don't have enough money to pay for the items you want to buy.'

This did not calm the lady, who then said, 'That is absolute nonsense! I have *quite* enough money!'

Gemma suggested that the lady should go to an A.T.M to check her balance, only for the lady to demand to be allowed to speak to the supervisor.

'I'll go and get Bev,' I said. I went to find the shop manager, Bev, who was near the heated appliances section with Jacqueline, one of our newbies, and said, 'Bev, a customer's card has been declined and she's taking it out on Gemma.'

Bev said she would come straight over. She told Jacqueline to carry on whilst she went to see to the customer, and then I led her over to the till.

I decided to see what else could do with restocking. I went to the same aisle where I'd been replenishing stock, to see if the packs of wipes and make-up remover could do with restocking.

I've been working part time in Zellweger's, this independent hair and beauty shop since the start of the summer, working sixteen hours, four afternoons a week. I've loved working there since day one, and it's fair to say that the staff discount comes in very handy.

I finished at Fleetview sixth form in July after completing my A-levels in Fashion and Textiles, Economics, Psychology and Chemistry, but I decided to go into employment after that rather than go to uni.

'Ruby-lynn?' said a voice. I looked up and recognised the auburn haired, gemstone green eyed, slender girl stood at my three o'clock. I knew Scarlet Doherty from Our Lady of Wyke. We weren't in the same tutor group or classes, as Scarlet was in the year above me. We hadn't seen each other all summer.

'Hiya!' I said, thrilled to see Scarlet again. 'How have you been?'

'Not too bad thanks,' said Scarlet, merrily. 'I didn't know you worked here.'

'Yeah, I started in the summer,' I told her, before Scarlet asked if I was free to come for a coffee with her after my shift had finished, which I said yes to, instantly!

I looked at my watch. It was now twenty past five. Ten minutes before closing time. I was pleased I now had coffee with Scarlet to look forward to, as really I wanted to have a proper catch up with her. I went back to join Gemma at the till.

'Has Bev sorted that lady out?' I asked.

'Yeah. She told her that she would have to leave the shop if she carried on speaking to me in that way,' said Gemma. 'When are you next in, again?'

'Tuesday.'

'I'm back in tomorrow. Just how I love spending a Saturday!' Gemma sighed, sarcastically. I said nothing. I didn't want to rub it in that I was off the next day.

We both stayed behind the till until Bev came over and said we could go.

'I'm meeting with Chandler later,' said Gemma, as we both went to get our things out of our lockers. 'You wanna come?'

'No, thanks, Scarlet's just asked if I want to come for a coffee,' I said. 'I've not seen her for ages.'

'Fair enough,' said Gemma.

Scarlet was just outside the door when we came out. Gemma went off to meet her boyfriend, Chandler, whilst me and Scarlet walked up St Mary's street.

'Costa Coffee okay?' Scarlet asked.

'I'm good with whatever,' I said. 'So, what you been up to since finishing your A-levels?'

'I'm doing a two year course in Health and Social care at Fleetview,' Scarlet said.

'Sounds good.'

'Have you ever thought about going back into education?'

'I might do, some day,' I said.

Costa luckily wasn't too busy. Scarlet ordered an Americano with no milk and I ordered a cappuccino. Scarlet carried both coffees on a tray over to a table at the back of the restaurant and we both sat down.

I asked her how things were with her mum and dad's new families. Scarlet's dad's now with a widowed mum of four, who she doesn't see eye to eye with, and her mum has remarried and has two children with her new husband, as well as a stepson and daughter from her husband's previous marriage.

'Leslie is still being a nightmare!' groaned Scarlet. 'I seriously don't know what Dad sees in her.'

'Well, I hate to say I wouldn't know anything about that,' I said.

'Nah, you're lucky, your parents are still together,' Scarlet agreed, enviously. 'Though Dan and Stuart can't stand her either, and she's actually their mum, so they have to put up with her more than me!'

'My mum can drive me up the wall sometimes!' I admitted.

'Well, maybe mine can too, some times,' said Scarlet. 'But, God, the twins are spoilt, and Dan's not that much better, either. He keeps acting like he's cooler than everyone else, just because he's getting a motorbike. Oh no, my mistake, his mum's only letting him get a moped!'

I looked down, feeling a bit awkward and not knowing what to say. I must've looked a bit uneasy, because Scarlet quickly apologised, before saying, 'Hey, are you working tomorrow? Only... well, I know this is short notice, but I'm going bowling with my mates. Would you be interested in joining us?'

I was more than flattered to be asked, and accepted the invite straight away. Scarlet said she was meeting her friends at Lakeside at eleven o'clock.

'And then afterwards, me, Lizzy and Natalie are going shopping for our Halloween costumes if you'd like to come with us?' Scarlet asked, also inviting me to come out with them for Halloween.

'Sounds awesome!' I said. 'What are you all going as?'

'Posh, china dolls,' said Scarlet.

Posh china dolls. I definitely liked the sound of that idea! I had some very long false eyelashes, and I still hadn't used them, and now I had no excuse because they were just the thing to wear with the costume! I said I was definitely up for it. This would be the first time I'd met Scarlet's friends.

And speaking of friends...

'Have you heard from Becky at all?' I asked Scarlet.

Becky Perry's a year older than Scarlet and two years older than me. She also went to Our Lady of Wyke. Becky was away at university, though I can't remember which one, or what course she's doing.

'I did see her over the summer,' said Scarlet. 'Also, can I just say, I really like your hair.'

Shortly after finishing at sixth form, I dyed my shoulder length hair hot pink. At first, I doubted whether it had been a wise choice, given my job at Zellweger's, but I guess I was lucky. Either that, or they just see me as a good advert for the brightly coloured hair dyes they sold!

'Thanks,' I said, grinning.

I caught the number one bus home after another hour of catching up.

The first thing I heard when I arrived home was Mum's voice from the kitchen, saying, 'Ruby, where have you been? Your supper's getting cold!'

Ruby-lynn isn't actually my Christian name. Lynn is actually my middle name. I was named Ruby after my mum, Rubianne. It was Dad's choice, but I prefer to be known as Ruby-lynn.

I took off my coat, hung it up, and went to the breakfast area to see Mum and Dad sat at the table, already eating their plates of the lasagne that Mum had cooked.

'I was having coffee with Scarlet,' I told them, as I got myself a class of Ribena from the kitchen.

'Scarlet Doherty?' said Dad, enthusiastically. 'It's been weeks since you've seen her. How is she?'

'All well,' I said, sitting down opposite Mum, before getting started on my tepid lasagne.

'Scarlet's invited me to come bowling with her and her mates tomorrow,' I enlightened them.

'Oh, that'll be nice!' said Mum, sounding pleased.

'Yeah, I was thrilled that she wanted me to come along too,' I said. 'And then afterwards, we're going shopping for Halloween costumes. Scarlet said I should come out with them. We're all gonna dress up as antique dolls and stuff.'

'How very original!' said Dad, sounding fascinated.

'And how was work, darling?' Mum asked.

'All fine, apart from a customer getting rowdy with Gemma, just because her card kept getting declined,' I said. At this, Dad tutted, and started grumbling about customers who always blame the cashiers for things like the card readers declining their bankcards and their vouchers expiring.

Mum shook her head and said, 'The customer is *not* always right.'

After dinner, I had a bubble bath. I sat in the bath and laid back my head. Such bliss! I had such a busy afternoon at work. I was *well* glad I didn't work Saturdays!

I washed my hair with L'Oreal Elvive colour protect shampoo, then after rinsing, I massaged my Herbal Essences Ignite My Colour conditioner onto my hair, before washing myself with Body Shop strawberry scented shower gel.

When I got out of the bath, I caught sight of my hair in the sink mirror, which was mottled with watermarks, and noticed my roots needed redoing. I'm thinking of maybe dying it violet at some point.

I wrapped my hair in the dark teal hand towel that was folded up on top of the grey toilet seat lid, then wrapped a purple bath towel round my body like a sarong, picked up my clothes, and left the bathroom.

I pulled on a pair of tracksuit trousers and my cosy Pineapple hoodie, grabbed my lime green Lenovo laptop, and carried it out to the lounge, where Mum and Dad were sat on the cream leather three-seater sofa, watching Emmerdale. I sat down on the matching two-seater sofa in front of the window, logged onto Facebook and spent most of that evening playing some more of Candy Crush saga.

I had a thought about the porcelain doll costumes when I went to bed later. What could I buy to wear? Maybe I could get a curly synthetic costume wig, with some little bows to go in my hair?

What would Scarlet's mates be like? Would they be easy to warm to? Would they warm to me easily?

I got up at eight, Saturday morning. I picked out my bright orange skinny jeans, lilac converses, then searched my top drawer and found my Innocent Lifestyle Cartoon vest top and my black and white striped hoodie, both of which I bought off Blue Banana, my number one online clothing shop. I've always been into the emo style, hence the bright pink hair!

I chucked everything down on the bed then took my make-up bag and Tresemme hair straighteners all to the lounge. It was empty. Dad usually works Saturday mornings, and Mum likes sleeping in at weekends.

I did my make-up in front of the T.V, then straightened my hair, got dressed back in my room, grabbed my baby blue holographic backpack and keys, left the house, and then decided I'd walk to town, seeing as it was such a beautiful day.

As soon I reached the town bridge by the harbour, I had to wait for it to go back down after it let a boat through.

I checked my watch, afterwards. It was quarter past ten. I'd left the house early on purpose so that I'd have time to stop by at MaccyD's, and grab a bacon and egg snack wrap and a mocha.

MaccyD's was pretty busy when I entered. Downstairs looked full so I hoped there was room upstairs.

I sat on one of the stalls at the high table by the front windows upstairs, where I was in danger getting my face melted by the sunlight blazing in, admittedly, but I liked being able watch everyone in the street below. It had been ages since I had a MaccyD's breakfast.

I left and made my way to Lakeside as soon as I finished. I walked inside Lakeside and looked around for any sight of Scarlet. From my one o'clock, I suddenly heard a voice, which I recognised as Scarlet's, call out, 'Ruby-lynn!' I looked over and saw Scarlet on a sofa, beckoning me over to her. I walked over to her and her girl mates, grinning.

'Hey!' she said as we hugged. 'This is Lizzy,' she added, waving her hand in the direction of a small skinny girl with fair skin, green eyes and mid back length ash blonde hair that had a full fringe cut in, before adding 'and Natalie,' waving her hand towards a tall girl with elbow length medium ash brown hair and cloudy grey eyes, 'and girls, this is Ruby-lynn.'

'Hi,' said Lizzy and Natalie, together.

'Hey,' I said, sitting next to Scarlet, on the sofa opposite Lizzy and Natalie.

'So, is it just us four, or are there more coming?' I asked.

'We're still waiting for the boys,' said Scarlet. 'There are three of them.'

'So, how did you two meet, then?' asked Natalie.

Me and Scarlet both explained to Lizzy and Natalie about how we'd known each other at Our Lady of Wyke, and how both our mums would insist on taking us to church every Sunday, when we were at junior school, just so that we could get into Our Lady of Wyke, before I asked Lizzy and Natalie how they knew Scarlet.

'Scarlet's dad is mates with my dad,' said Natalie. 'As is Dave's dad, and Dave is one of the guys we're meeting, along with my brother, Fred, and his best mate Jesse.'

'I grew up being friends with Natalie, Jesse and Fred,' Lizzy said.

'So, you're all each other's parents' friends' sons and daughters, and that's how you're all mates? Because you seem like you all hit it off well,' I asked.

'We didn't immediately see eye to eye,' Scarlet confessed.

'Yeah, you always used to think Fred had a big head after all the girls who'd been into him,' Lizzy said.

'Yep!' said Scarlet, nodding. A ladies' man, by the sound of it.

We heard the door open at that point and Lizzy and Natalie, who were both sat on the sofa, facing the door, were the first two to see who had come in.

'What time do you call this?' Lizzy teased, pretending to be cross.

'Sorry we're late, boss,' said one of who I assumed were the three boys who were meeting us.

'Boys, this is Ruby-lynn,' said Scarlet. I looked up at the three boys. They looked over at me.

'I'm Jesse, and this is Fred,' said a blonde boy, clapping his hand on the shoulder of the boy who I guessed was Natalie's brother, going by the colour of his hair and eyes.

'Hi,' said Fred, looking at me like he was transfixed.

The tall, dark boy, who I figured was Dave, said he, Fred and Jesse were going to get drinks, and asked if we wanted anything as well.

'Four Fantas,' said Scarlet. 'For me and the girls.'

When the boys returned with the drinks, the seven of us went to get our bowling shoes and got set up on one of the alleys.

As Jesse took his turn, I caught sight of Fred out of the corner of my eye. He was looking at me! I gave him a smile and he did give me a bit of a feeble smile back.

As Jesse threw his ball down the lane, I heard the most horrible thud! What the *fuck*?! It turned out that Jesse had thrown his ball straight up in the air! It landed in the lane to the right of ours. Fred, Lizzy, Natalie and Scarlet were pissing themselves! Figuratively speaking, that is, not literally!

The noise had also attracted the attention of the man that served us, not to mention that of a group of thirteen-year-olds on a lane, two lanes to the left of ours.

The man came up the steps and walked over to Jesse.

'Can I just say, that it might be a good idea to use the slides,' he suggested, sternly.

Jesse went cherry red. Jesus, he must've felt just as much as a moron as he looked!

'Okay,' he said, sheepishly, and the man walked back to the counter.

Natalie teased him, saying not to feel bad and reminding him that Lizzy still had to use the barriers on every go, which made Lizzy, say, 'Oy, shut up!'

My turn next. I grabbed a ball, stepped up to the start of the lane, fixed my eyes on the middle skittle at the front, focus, focus, focus, swung the ball back, then swung it forward and released it. I watched as it sped down the alley, towards the skittles and knocked over all of them! *YES!!*

I heard the other three girls cheer.

Next, I watched Lizzy have her go. Lizzy, who admitted she'd never been that great at bowling, went to fetch the slide. She lined it up, placed her ball carefully at the top, and gave it a very hard push down the slide. It rolled down the lane, edging slightly over to the right as it went, and rolled into most of the skittles on the right hand side. It was a good shot, for someone who had to use the slides.

'Yay, Lizzy!' cheered Scarlet.

Natalie had her turn, followed by Dave, Fred, Scarlet, Jesse, and then it was my turn again. I chose a bright pink ball that matched my hair - haha - stuck my fingers and thumb into it, and swung it down the lane. But the next thing I knew I very nearly went flying! I heard laughter from behind, then realised, the ball hadn't even come off my hand! I tried to lift my hand, but my fingers were stuck tight in the holes! Shit.

'What's wrong, Ruby-lynn?' said Lizzy.

'My hand's stuck! The ball won't come off!' I moaned, in that sort of mock-frustrated way people do when they're sort of half laughing, half pretending to cry. Lizzy held onto the ball and pulled at it as I tugged my hand out, well, at least I tried to, but it wouldn't budge. Lizzy said we were going to have to get someone. She spotted an assistant and we went over to her, before I asked if she could help because my hand had got stuck in the ball. She led me over to one of her colleagues and asked her to fetch some hand cream. She came back a minute later, with a tube of hand cream. She squirted it round the edges of the holes and rubbed it into my fingers. I tried to move my fingers around in the holes. Oh God damn it! I still couldn't free my hand! The lady said she was going to get some W.D 40. She sprayed it at the holes. I wriggled my fingers again, and halle-fucking-lujah! I could finally pull my hand free!

'Thanks,' I said to the ladies, and took the ball back to the lane. Maybe I'd better use the slide, like Lizzy had? Just to be on the safe side.

I lined it up, placed the ball at the top, aimed, and pushed the ball.

This time, I wasn't so lucky. The ball was edging over to the left as it went. It only knocked over two of the skittles.

'Ah!' said Natalie, disappointed.

None of us fancied having another round, so we sat and had another drink.

'So, what are you doing now, Ruby-lynn? Are you at college?' asked Jesse.

'No, I'm working part time, in Zellweger's,' I told everyone, and I elaborated on how I started working there in the summer, and how I really enjoyed it, and how I liked the discount I got from working there.

'Sounds good,' said Dave.

'Are you lot working at all?' I asked.

'Nah, only Natalie,' said Jesse. 'The rest of us are still at college.'

I asked Natalie about her job, so Natalie talked about her travel agent job, as she said she'd always had a very dedicated interest in Travel and Tourism, and how she did an extended diploma in that subject for two years at Euro Capital House College, before she abruptly turned the talk to relationships.

'So, are there any boys in the picture?' she'd asked.

'Typical Natalie,' Scarlet sighed.

'No, I don't have a boyfriend,' I said. The most I'd ever had with a boy was when a large of group of us were round Penelope Walton's house on a Saturday night when I was at Our Lady of Wyke. We were playing Truth or Dare, and one boy, Henry Drew, chose Dare, and was dared to snog me for two entire minutes! Tongues and everything! In front of everyone! When I came into school on Monday morning, it was plain that half the school already knew about it, and let me tell you, it did *not* go down well with Frances Hale, a girl who Henry was casually "seeing," as opposed to actually being her boyfriend.

'What about you lot?' I asked.

Lizzy launched into an explanation about her crush on one of her brother's mates, how she fancied him since she was eleven, and how things had developed with him.

She fancied him for seven years! About time *something* happened between them!

Natalie then told us all about the exciting man she had started seeing, who was known as V.

'He lives in this *awesome* house, he drives a *Mercedes* and earns *loads* of money!' she said, ecstatically. She then started boasting about how she never had to pay for anything, as he always covered it whenever they went out, and he would spoil her with clothes and jewellery.

'Gold digger,' Scarlet called her, and she was right. Sure, the idea of being spoiled rotten by a boy seemed fantastic, but was that the only reason Natalie was with him?

Dave took his turn to start boring everyone about the progress he claimed to have made with Alyssa, the teacher he liked.

'I'm on fire!' he'd said, ecstatically. He told everyone about the phone call his mum said she had from Alyssa about how pleased she was.

'Though on the downside, Stuart is being a real cock brain about it,' Dave said.

'I wonder why,' said Jesse, sarcastically.

After we finished our drinks, we left Lakeside, and yay, shopping time! Dave, Fred and Jesse said they were heading off to do their own thing, and the seven of us agreed to meet again, later, at Radipole Park Drive. I caught Fred's eye before I followed Scarlet, Natalie and Lizzy in the opposite direction to him, Dave and Jesse.

We decided to look in some of the charity shops for some old-fashioned looking dresses. We headed to the British Heart Foundation and looked at the dresses in there. I thought I'd see if I could find some black buckled shoes to wear with my costume, but I couldn't find any. I looked at the skirts to see if there were any I could wear with a top. I caught sight of a duck egg blue, layered fifties style skirt with pink and yellow roses. What top could I wear with it? I checked the label. It was a size ten, my size. Perfect! I went to the back of the shop, just in time to see Lizzy coming out of the changing room, in a peach, slash necked, empire lined and short, puffy sleeved chiffon dress, dotted with dark red cherries.

'What do you think?' she said, grinning. How I wished I could find something like that. I suggested Lizzy could wear her hair in loose curls with a ribbon in her hair.

Scarlet came over with a green and navy tartan, sleeveless, skater dress.

'How about this, with a white shirt underneath?' she asked us.

'Great!' Natalie grinned.

Lizzy said she was definitely getting the dress she was trying on. I began looking at the tops. How about getting a white shirt to wear, tucked into the waistband of the skirt I picked out? Just needed a top in a size ten and, luckily, I found a white silk button up shirt with short, puffed sleeves and a Peter Pan collar. I also found a similar one with long sleeves, which I reckoned Scarlet could wear. I showed the short-sleeved shirt and skirt to the others to ask what they thought.

'Wear this with it,' said Lizzy, and she handed me a black bow tie. I held it up to the collar of the shirt.

'It looks brilliant,' I said, before thanking Lizzy for picking it out, and showing Scarlet the long sleeved shirt.

'You said the skater dress you chose would look good with a long sleeved blouse.'

'Oh, awesome!' beamed Scarlet. 'Thanks Ruby-lynn.'

Natalie went into the fitting room with three dresses, wanting each of us to tell her which one we preferred. The first one she showed us was a rose pink lace, empire line, three-quarter-length sleeved dress with a gathered knee length skirt. That was Lizzy's favourite, naturally. Scarlet preferred the second dress, which was a double breasted, pleated, navy dress with three quarter length sleeves, a white Peter Pan collar and a white lace trimmed hem, which Lizzy also said she liked. The one I liked best was a violet silk lace up bodice dress that had long sleeves which were puffed from the shoulder to the elbow, but slim-fitted to the wrists, and a short, layered skirt. In the end, the navy dress with the Peter Pan collar got the vote.

We decided to go to Zellweger's next, so that Scarlet, Natalie and Lizzy could buy some false eyelashes, similar to the ones I was wearing.

'Good thing you mentioned about the eyelashes, as those china dolls do have really long eyelashes,' said Lizzy. 'I may need a bit of help putting them on, on the night, as I've never used them. I've always worried I'd get eyelash glue in my eyes.'

'I'll help you,' I offered.

'Thanks, hun.'

She, Natalie and Scarlet chose some eyelashes and went to pay, then we left the shop.

'I wanna go to a fancy dress shop,' said Lizzy. 'I can buy a curly synthetic wig!'

'Yeah, I might think about getting one too,' Scarlet agreed. So me and Natalie joined Lizzy and Scarlet in running along to Christopher Robin, the fancy dress shop on the seafront. Scarlet took an instant liking to a curly chestnut brown wig. Lizzy was a little more indecisive. Okay, *much* more indecisive. Jesus Christ, who needed half an hour to decide on a bloody wig? I felt like saying, 'For fuck sake, just pick one, will you?'

We were all bored stupid, waiting for her, but, at last, she chose an equally curly wig of blackest black, which she said went perfectly with the dress she'd bought. That made me even more annoyed because why couldn't she have just picked it out straightaway?

As we had more or less found everything we needed afterwards, we decided to start walking to Radipole Park drive to meet the boys.

It was a long walk to the park. On the way, we talked about what else we could wear with our costumes.

'What make-up could we wear, to make our faces look more doll-like?' said Natalie.

Scarlet said she had some pale powder which we could all use, and wear some pink or red blusher, and I thought some dark red lipstick would be ideal.

When we arrived, we saw Dave, Fred and Jesse by the half pipe with Dan, one of Scarlet's stepbrothers-in-waiting, and another boy I didn't know, who Fred introduced as Tom, who was skinny with bleach blonde hair in a number five cut. Dan, on the other hand, is short and stocky, with hair of the darkest brown in a side fringe.

'Fuck me, who blew bubblegum in your hair?' Dan asked, staring dumbfounded at my hair.

'He's just joking. *Aren't* you, Dan?' Scarlet said, with a look on her face like she was saying, 'You'd fucking better be, or I'll come over there and pound you one!'

Dan didn't say anything, but he did tut and roll his eyes in an exasperated way. Stuck up prick.

I joined the girls, who were sat on the low wall around the football ground, whilst the boys played football.

'Everyone's coming round mine for seven, to get ready and have pre drinks,' Scarlet said.

'Which one will that be? As I know you have two houses,' I asked.

'I think I'll be at my dad's that week,' said Scarlet. 'That'll make it easier for Dan, as he will be there too.'

We started talking about what drinks everyone would be bringing round, but our conversation was cut short when Jesse kicked the ball in our direction. All four of us screamed and ducked, and the ball flew over us, narrowly missing Scarlet.

'*Jesse!*' shouted Natalie, very annoyed.

'*Sorry!*' Jesse called, not actually sounding very sorry at all.

I looked over and noticed the swings in the distance, and saw they were both empty. I didn't know why, but I felt like having a good swing.

I stood up and asked the girls to look after my bag, and then walked over to the swings. I sat down and pushed off. I felt the breeze whip through my hair, as I swung to and fro. I tipped my head back as I swung forward and up, and closed my eyes. It felt incredible.

After a few swings, I saw Scarlet coming over.

'Hey,' she said, and sat on the other swing. I let myself down, carefully, and eventually stopped.

'Hi,' I said.

'You enjoyed today?' asked Scarlet.

'Yeah, I did, thanks,' I said. 'I got on with Lizzy and Natalie.'

'They are really good friends, to me as well as each other,' said Scarlet. She explained that, whilst Lizzy had a tendency to be naïve, and Natalie could be quite catty at times, they were, deep down, good people.

I was slightly envious. I'd never been that close to any of my friends at Fleetview Sixth Form, and I hadn't had much contact from my friends at Our Lady of Wyke after finishing there. My mates at Fleetview were just sort of, "at school" friends. I didn't really do a lot with them outside of school, and I explained all of this to Scarlet.

'They're those types of friends if you know what I mean.'

Scarlet nodded, then we both heard the boys laughing and saying, 'Go on, do it!' and Lizzy shouting, 'Oy, *no*, Fred! *Don't*! That's Ruby-lynn's bag!'

I got up off the swing. I could not believe what I was seeing. Fred was running around with my bag! What the fuck did he think he was doing? Me and Scarlet ran over to stop him from doing whatever it was he was going to do. He stopped just below the branches of a tree, and threw the bag up in the air, and it was hanging by its strap on one of the branches. All five boys were laughing their heads off. Scarlet, Lizzy and Natalie were blaspheming. I was fuming. How *dare* he?!

I stormed over to the tree and jumped up to try to grab it, but I couldn't reach it. I turned on Fred.

'For Christ sake, what the fuck?!' I raged. 'How am I supposed to get it down?'

'It's okay, I'll get it,' said Lizzy. 'Nat, give me a leg up, will you?'

Natalie gave Lizzy a leg up, so she could reach up to grab my bag. As Lizzy raised her arms to try and get it down, Fred reached up and started tickling Lizzy under her right armpit.

'Oy, piss off!' she said, annoyed. She managed to get my bag off the branch, Natalie put her down, and she gave it back.

'Fucking moron,' muttered Natalie to Fred, 'she's only just met you. She probably thinks you're a right bell end!'

Bell end was right.

'*Chill*, sis! It was only meant to be a joke,' said Fred, only for Natalie to say that the joke was over.

'Don't let Fred get to you,' Scarlet said, as we all walked back to town, not long afterwards. 'He probably just wanted to get your attention.'

'Well, I guess I can now see what Natalie has to put up with,' I managed to joke, but I still felt irritated with him.

When we got to the seafront, me, Scarlet, Lizzy, Dave, Tom, and Dan said goodbye to Fred, Jesse and Natalie, who were driving home in Fred's Mini Cooper, then the five of us said goodbye to each other before Lizzy crossed the road to catch the number five zero three bus to her house, Dan headed for the Littlemoor bus stop,

Scarlet and Tom ran to catch the number ten bus, and I waited at the Portland bus stop.

On the bus, I thought about what Scarlet said about Fred trying to get my attention. It didn't make me feel any less annoyed. Why did he do that? Boys are so weird. Why do they do silly things like that for female attention? Because Fred's actions did *not* make me like him! But I knew that, as much as I wanted to, I couldn't really avoid him all the time, as we were now in the same group of friends.

But I didn't let my annoyance at Fred spoil the excellent day I had. I enjoyed bowling, except for when my hand got stuck in the ball of course, and I was pleased I bought something to wear for Halloween, and shopping with the girls was fun. Though I didn't know what Dan's problem was. I knew he could occasionally be a real dick, but most of the time he wasn't that bad.

When I got off the bus at Ford's Corner, I decided to go down to Daniel's and buy some cheesy chips.

As soon as I came home afterwards, I noticed Mum seemed a bit preoccupied, sat at the kitchen table, staring into space, not acknowledging me or asking if I had a nice time. I'd seen her like that, before. It was when Dad had to go to hospital to have his appendix removed. She'd been bricking it that he'd get worse, and not better. But as you can see, my dad's alive and well, now.

'Hi, Mum.'

'Hi,' Mum said, still not looking up at me.

'I had a good day today. Met someone who took a bit of a liking to me, so we had a quickie in the park.'

Still nothing, however shocking that would be if that *had* happened! What the hell?

'Are you okay?' I asked.

'It's fine, I've just been a bit busy with stuff today,' Mum said, sounding shifty. I shrugged it off and took my chips over to the table, unwrapped them, and started eating. I was *sooo* hungry, I ordered a large portion, as I hadn't eaten much, if anything, since that snack wrap in MaccyD's. Usually, Mum fusses about me bringing home food for just myself, as she does prefer that we all have a meal together, as a family, but she didn't complain much this time.

After I finished, I took everything to my room. I took all the parts of my costume out of its bag, grabbed a coat hanger, hung my costume on it, and hung it on the back of my door. I stood back and admired my outfit. It was going to be one great night!

Suddenly, there was a knock on the door. I opened it, and saw Dad stood there.

'Darling, I've had a thought,' he began. 'As your mother seems in a bit of a state at the moment, I was thinking it might be nice if we could watch a nice light-hearted film together, as a family, this evening?'

I was starting to get slightly concerned.

'What's going on, Dad?' I asked.

'Oh, I don't know,' said Dad. 'I keep asking her but she won't tell me. I shouldn't worry about it.'

I nodded. Dad invited me to come and help choose what film we could watch that evening.

Later that night, the three of us were all sat down in the lounge, watching Notting Hill. I'd only seen it once before, but I did sort of enjoy watching it the second time round. I went straight to bed afterwards, but I couldn't sleep. I was still worried. What was going on with Mum, that she was hiding from Dad? It couldn't have been anything major, or I would've been told, but it was just odd that Mum wouldn't even tell Dad about it.

I felt myself drifting into an uneasy sleep around one o'clock in the morning.

I didn't wake up until ten o'clock. I had a banging headache. My phone suddenly beeped. I picked it up, unlocked it, and looked at it. It was a Facebook notification. I opened my Facebook and saw a friend request from Fred. I sighed, still slightly cross about what happened yesterday, but I knew that if I stayed annoyed at Fred, it would make any times we all met up as a group awkward, so I decided I ought to accept his friend request.

I put down my phone, searched the middle drawer in my bedside cabinet for the paracetamol, got up, walked over to the window, and pulled back the curtains. It was a cloudy day, with a hint of sun. I went to the bathroom, got a cup out of the cupboard above the sink, filled it with water, got two tablets out of the packet, put them on my tongue, and took a big gulp of water.

I downed the rest of the glass, as I knew that would help, then refilled it, took it to my room, left it on my bedside cabinet, and went to the kitchen for some breakfast. Dad was sat at the table on his own, with a plate of toast and marmalade. No sign of Mum, so she couldn't tell me off for not drinking enough water because of my head ache.

'Slept in, did we?' Dad said, as soon as he looked up and saw me.

'I couldn't sleep,' I said, walking over to the cereal cupboard, to get out the box of Crunchy Nut Clusters. 'Where's Mum?'

'She said she had to run an errand. I didn't ask what errand that was, but I'm not going to pretend I'm not starting to suspect anything,' said Dad, off-handedly.

This made my worry about what Mum was up to even worse. When had she ever had any *errands* to run? This wasn't making any sense.

I got out a bowl, poured some crunchy nut clusters into it, did the box up, and put it back. As I got the milk out of the fridge and poured some onto my cereal, I asked Dad when Mum would be back, but he said he didn't know.

'Like I said,' he explained, 'I don't know exactly what it is she's doing, so I can't really say how long it's likely to take her.'

I sighed. I put the milk back, got a spoon out of the cutlery drawer, brought everything over to the table, and sat down next to Dad. I could tell he was just as worried about her as I was.

After I finished my breakfast and put my bowl and spoon on the worktop, I went to my room to get dressed.

I heard the front door opening. I heard Mum's voice. I then heard Dad say, 'Why won't you tell me where you were going?' sounding slightly frustrated, before I heard my name mentioned.

'Ruby has noticed something isn't right!' he'd shouted, then I heard Mum say, with rather a short-tempered tone, 'I don't want either of you to worry!'

This was definitely a bad sign. I had no idea what was going on, but I knew it was something serious, no matter how hard she tried not to worry me and Dad. What was I going to do?

I worried about it all day. At one point, I feared the worse, thinking Mum had a terminal illness, and burst into tears. Dad must have heard me crying, because he poked his head round the bedroom door and asked what was wrong.

'What if Mum's got cancer?' I sobbed. 'What if that errand she said she was running was a hospital appointment?'

Dad sighed and came over.

'Hey,' he said, giving me a hug. 'It's all right. I know it's weird that your mum isn't telling either of us what's happening, but if it was something that bad, she would definitely have told us, okay?'

'Okay,' I sniffed. I felt Dad kiss me on the top of my head, then he asked if I fancied helping him repaint the garden bench.

I did feel better after that. I knew Dad was right. It was probably just a minor thing Mum was trying to sort out and maybe she didn't want to make anyone else worry whilst she was trying to fix whatever it was.

Painting the bench with Dad was quite fun. Usually, I find things like that quite tedious, and a bit tiring, but that's usually when I do it on my own. I do enjoy painting, though it sort of depends on what I'm painting. I'm not that great at art, so paintings are not one of my strengths. But when I made things in Arts and Crafts classes, I enjoyed painting those. I've never really enjoyed painting walls and stuff, so I'm not so fussed about D.I.Y.

Mum did seem calmer at dinner, so I felt a bit more at ease.

I decided to have an early night, as I slept so badly last night.

I woke up bright and early Monday morning. I thought I'd go for a walk, and get some fresh air. I got dressed, and left the house.

I decided to walk along Rodwell trail. It was peaceful, but it was quite cold and windy, so I'd wrapped up warm. I hadn't planned on going too far, but it was a nice long walk just the same. There were people going for runs in the opposite direction, and others were walking their dogs or riding their bikes. I wish I hadn't outgrown my old violet and yellow one. I'd played on it every day of every summer when I had it, until I was eleven. I attempted a sharp turn, making the bike fall to its left and I fell off it and ended up dislocating my left arm. I went right off riding it after that, because I was desperate not to let it happen again. By the time I got up enough courage to give it another try, I realised I was too big for it and had to sell it. Gutted!

As soon as I reached the sloping path up to Buxton Road, I headed up there and started walking back home.

As soon as I got indoors, I went to my room and got out my laptop, as I felt like going on iTunes and adding some more songs to my turquoise iPod mini. As soon as I logged onto my laptop, I fetched my iPod cable from my bedside cabinet, and connected my iPod to the laptop.

About seven minutes after I opened up iTunes, I heard the wa-*ching*! sound that my Samsung smart phone makes whenever I have a message on Facebook. I opened my Facebook conversations. The message was from Fred. It said, 'Hey, how r u? Thanks 4 accepting my friend request x,' so I thought for a moment. Deciding to build bridges with him, I replied with, 'That's okay. I'm not too bad thanks. How are you?' then went back to iTunes.

I began deleting some songs that I barely listened to anymore from my iPod, then got another message from Fred.

'I'm good, ta. im sorry about what I did in the park x,' it said.

I'd almost got over the bag in the tree incident, but I was grateful that Fred had the decency to apologise for it. Before I'd decided what to write in response, though, I got another message from Fred, saying, 'I was being a real asshole x,' to which I replied, 'it's okay.'

I got a reply back, saying, 'R u sure? I don't want u pissed @ me x.' I replied to reassure him that it was all right, and then I stayed online to chat with him. I noticed some of the messages Fred sent me during that conversation were a bit flirty. Is Fred like that with most girls, or just some in particular that he likes? Should I perhaps ask Scarlet what he's like, or maybe Natalie? As she is his sister.

Me and Fred spent another hour getting to know each other more, until he went offline.

I'd been so busy chatting with Fred, I hadn't done as much as I planned to do on iTunes. I added a couple of songs by Marina and the Diamonds, then closed down iTunes, ejected my iPod, and turned off my laptop.

I went to the kitchen to make myself a latte. Mum was doing some washing up.

'Did your little morning stroll do you any good?' she asked. I could tell she was trying to sound cheerful, but she sounded tired, too.

'Yeah it did, thanks,' I said. I put the kettle on, grabbed a tea towel, and dried the items Mum had just washed up. She was really happy. I made both her and Dad a cup of tea whilst making my coffee.

I took my coffee into the lounge, followed by Mum, who was carrying both cups of tea. Dad was sat on the sofa, reading the paper.

I sat and read one of my chick lit books. I planned to take it easy for the rest of the day and just relax anyway and I spent the rest of the day doing exactly that.

I had work, Tuesday afternoon. As it was a weekday, it wasn't as busy as it was in the weekend, as most people were working and the children and teenagers were at school.

I spent most of the afternoon restocking the shampoos, conditioners and hair dyes, only working on the till when Gemma went on her afternoon tea break.

It was around four o'clock when it was very quiet in the shop. I'd almost finished restocking the hair accessories and brushes when a group of six men, who looked like they were in their mid to late twenties, came in. They looked kind of rough, and they seemed really aggressive, and were swearing rather a lot. They reminded me of the type of men you'd see in one of those really dark, gritty movies full of characters that carry guns and knives and deal and use drugs.

26

That was when I started to feel uneasy.

I was really shocked by what happened next. One of the men went behind the counter, and moved up really close to Gemma, practically invading her personal space! I knew something really bad was going to happen.

'Alright beautiful?' he said to Gemma. She looked more petrified than I felt, if that was possible. I started to walk over to the till to help Gemma, but I felt a pair of hands grab my arms and saw that one of the other men had grabbed me by the arms, holding me back. The other men went over to do the same with some of the other shop assistants and even a couple of the customers!

The man who had gone behind the till went on to say, 'Now, I don't want this getting unpleasant, so if you're willing to co-operate, then we can part on good terms. All you need to do is open the cash drawer and let us have the money. I'm sure you guys make loadsa money out of all the fancy shit you sell here, so I think you can afford to let us have what's in the till. What do you say?'

Gemma shook her head, looking down, not wanting to say anything. She was shaking like a leaf, and I could see her eyes were filling with tears.

'Aw. Don't cry,' said the man. He laughed, and then, putting his face right up close to Gemma's, he said, 'You're a very beautiful woman, not one I'd wanna hurt outta choice.' He pulled out a pistol, and then said, 'You've got such lovely long hair,' as he ran the tip of his gun through her long, chestnut brown hair. Tears ran down her face.

I didn't know what to do. I wanted to help Gemma, and I was so angry at how frightened the man was making her.

'Leave her alone,' I snarled, angrily.

The man behind the till turned his head sharply to look at me.

'*Shut* it, *you!*' he spat, viciously. He turned back to Gemma, and said, 'We just wanna take what we came for and be gone, so how about you just humour me and my men here, and nobody gets hurt. Obviously your little friend here doesn't know what's good for her. Why don't you show us that at least you're a bit smarter? You wouldn't want your friend to pay the price for your refusal to oblige, would you? You wanna spend the rest of your life, knowing that she died, 'cause you had to be so stubborn?'

Gemma shook her head. She unlocked the till drawer and opened it. No, no, no, no! The man grabbed the notes, folded them neatly, and put them in the inside pocket of his coat. He then took out the coins and put them in his trouser and jacket pockets.

'Smart girl,' he said. He backed out from behind the till, the men who had hold of me and the others let go of us all, then all six men left the shop.

I could feel fury, like never before, boiling up inside me.

'The *bastards*!' I cried, through gritted teeth, almost in tears with uncontrollable anger. 'I'll *kill* them for this!'

Gemma was sobbing hysterically. I pressed the alarm so that the police would come. Bev came out. She came over, took one look at Gemma and, alarmed, she asked, 'What on Earth is wrong?'

But Gemma couldn't say anything.

'We've been robbed!' I shrieked, furiously. 'The police are coming.'

Bev looked absolutely horrified. She told one of the sales assistants to mind the till for Gemma, and took her and I to the back so I could tell her what happened.

'They had guns, and they had hold of some of us, including me, so we couldn't even go for help!' I said to Bev.

The police arrived a few minutes later. They took statements from everyone who was present, including me and Gemma, once she'd calmed down, then asked to see the C.C.T.V footage.

After the police left, Bev told me and Gemma we could go home.

We both walked up St Mary Street, both very shaken. I looked round at Gemma. She was breathing heavily, and fresh tears were running down her cheeks.

'Are you okay?' I asked. Gemma nodded. I had never ever seen her like this before. But then I'd never seen her being threatened before, of course.

When we got to Bond Street, I gave Gemma a hug goodbye, as she was going down Bond Street to the Hereford Road bus stop.

Even though I felt terrified on the way home, it wasn't until I got to my room that the reality of what happened hit me full on and I broke down in tears. My workplace was just robbed! One of my colleagues was threatened! By men with guns!

I hoped Mum and Dad didn't hear me crying, as they'd only come in and ask what was wrong, and I would have to tell them then.

When I'd eventually been able to stop crying, and had dried my tears, I came out and went to the lounge where Mum and Dad were watching the news. I hoped the robbery wouldn't end up on the news, as I didn't think I could bear it if anyone I knew found out that I'd been there at the time. I did not want people fussing over me about it, constantly asking if I was okay. And Gemma had been so traumatized by the whole ordeal. I felt so sorry for her, and I didn't blame her, either. *I* probably would be in that state if that man had been threatening me and sleazing all over me like that.

I lay awake in bed that night, thinking, and worrying. What was going to happen at Zellweger's? Would it be shut the next day if the police needed to investigate or what would happen? What if they came back to rob the shop again? The very thought of it petrified me. I had no way of knowing what was going to happen. Should I not go in to work the next day? I didn't feel safe and I didn't want to have a wasted journey if it turned out I needed to not be there.

The next day, I decided to ring the shop.

'Good morning, Zellweger's stores, Chloe speaking, how can I help?'

'Hey, it's Ruby-lynn,' I said.

'Hi, Ruby-lynn, you okay?' asked Chloe.

'Yeah, thanks, I'm just calling as I'm a bit unsure of what's happening in the shop today, after what happened last night, so I don't know if Bev's still expecting me in this afternoon,' I explained.

'Ah, yeah, I heard what happened,' said Chloe. As Chloe doesn't work Tuesday afternoons, she wasn't been present during the robbery, so she obviously hadn't known about it until that morning.

She asked if I was okay, and I truthfully said I was a bit shaken.

Chloe went on to say that she reckoned, as the store was open, I probably was expected in.

'As long as you're not *too* shaken by the events,' she added, as she heard Gemma wasn't expected to come in, given the state she'd been in.

I thanked Chloe, we said goodbye, and hung up.

Phew! If the shop was still open and people were still going in, at least I could get on with my job there as normal and try not to think about what happened.

I got ready for work, had breakfast, and then left the house, trying as hard as I could, not to worry about the day before's events.

Chapter 3:

Dave's First

Friday 15th October 2010

I couldn't get Alyssa out of my head. I'd never had such an unbelievably sexy teacher. She had the most gorgeous brown glossy hair, the most incredible pair of jugs, and don't get me started on her arse!

I couldn't believe how fucking lucky I was that I was actually looking at a whole year of being taught by her. Just enough time to get to know her better, and make her want me too. She wasn't my teacher during the first year of my course. The guy that taught me last year had to leave his job for medical reasons.

I didn't give a shit that Alyssa was a teacher and I was a student. I had to make her mine, no matter what.

Whenever Alyssa passed me in the corridors, she'd grin and say, 'Hiya.'

'Hey,' I'd say, with no doubt that she would've had to have liked me too, or she wouldn't have said hello.

I'd get home every day, sit up in my room, and start working, with Alyssa still at the back of my mind, phone on silent, only leave the room to use the loo, until tea time.

I could not wait to hand in all my coursework, and Alyssa would name me her top student. That would be amazing!

I said to her I'd been really knuckling down, evening after evening.

'Well, I'm very pleased that you have, as it shows how serious this is to you!' she'd beamed. She also said I'd worked the hardest out of all the class, so far, and told me to keep up the good work.

Stuart had grilled me about this, and even had the cheek to say that I'd never worked that hard in my life!

I didn't let it bother me. He was just jealous, the sad prick.

I worked as hard as I could in class for the rest of that week. But by Friday, I realised that and the way she'd see me and say 'Hi,' in the corridors, was the only attention I was getting from her, so I decided I needed to up the ante.

I arrived home from college that day and went to my room. I needed to think. First thing I needed to do was make myself look smarter whenever I went to college, so I'd look more grown up. But what if that wasn't enough? What if I wanted to charm her a bit? But how could I do that?

Love letters! Though I'd have to make it anonymous. I didn't want to be the laughing stock of the class. If only I had a stationary set, instead of just scrawling it on a sheet of paper from my refill pad, as that didn't look very romantic or sophisticated. I knew Mum had a stationary set on her desk in the study area. I didn't dare ask her if I could borrow one of the letters. I didn't want her knowing what I was doing, even though I'd been pretending it was another student I fancied. That was a story I came up with when Dad noticed that I had, not only been working harder than usual, but also used too much Lynx and asked me if I was just trying to impress a girl.

'Yeah, that's right!' I'd said. 'Cos she's really into photography too, and I want us to match up.'

Dad seemed convinced. Not so sure about Mum, though.

I crept downstairs and into the lounge and dining room. There was no one in either of those rooms, luckily, except Clover, my Border Collie. She was curled up on the sofa. I tiptoed quickly over to the desk in one of the alcoves. Clover raised her head and looked up at me. Mum's letter rack was on the desktop. I grabbed a letter and an envelope and ran back up to my room. I sat down, grabbed a pen and sucked the end of it as I tried to decide what to write. I'd never done anything like this before. I'd never really been into anything romantic. I found all the overly romantic stuff a bit wet, to be honest. Whenever I went on a date with a girl, it was never anything fancy, like an evening in a posh restaurant, just a trip to the cinema or having a coffee.

I started the letter with, 'Dearest Alyssa,' hoping that wouldn't sound too soppy. I thought about what to write next. I went with, 'Roses are red, violets are blue, both are so beautiful, and so are you.'

Before I'd had a chance to decide whether or not that was enough, Mum came in, telling me to tidy my stuff out the lounge.

I went down into the lounge, and started tidying all my stuff away, and brought it all up into my room wondering if maybe I'd also send Alyssa a gift with the love letter?

I planned to go into town the next day, as it would be Saturday. I'd buy her a present, wrap it up, and leave it on her desk on Monday morning.

I overslept Saturday morning. It was ten o'clock when I did get up. I went to the kitchen in my pyjamas. Clover came in, so I fed her first, before pouring myself a bowl of Shreddies, grabbing a spoon, taking my bowl to the lounge, flinging myself down onto the sofa, grabbing the remote and switching on the T.V. I flicked through the channels, and decided to watch the Jeremy Kyle Show.

I left my empty bowl and spoon on top of the dishwasher. Then I went up to get dressed.

I left the house and started walking to town. It was a nicer day than it was yesterday. It was cloudy and the temperature had dropped over the last few weeks, but it wasn't raining.

I couldn't wait to get my own car. I don't know what type of car I want in the future but for the time being, my uncle was going to bequeath his old orange Volkswagen van. I passed my test two years ago and I didn't want to be dependent on public transport forever.

I decided to buy Alyssa some nice jewellery. But I didn't want to get anything too expensive, but none of the sort of stuff they call costume jewellery, either.

Hang on! I remembered this necklace Mum had from a friend, last Christmas. I remembered her saying it was from Debenhams.

When I entered, I strode right over to the jewellery section. I saw Fred and Lizzy, stood by the counter, looking at a rack of pearl necklaces. Exactly why Fred was looking at jewellery with Lizzy would be a mystery to anyone who doesn't know him that well, but Fred's marketedly interested in fashion.

I looked at the pearl necklaces too. Would Alyssa like something like that? I went over to have a better look at them, as well as to say 'Hi,' to Fred and Lizzy.

They looked round and Fred said, 'Alright? What are you up to?'

I had to lie and say I needed to buy Mum a birthday present. Thankfully, her birthday was only next month, so it didn't take much convincing.

'What about you two?' I asked.

'Shopping for more jewellery,' said Lizzy, before making a joke that Fred got stuck with her because Jesse was seeing Annie.

'Fair enough,' I laughed.

I looked at the pearl necklaces Lizzy had been looking at. They had different colours of pearls. I wasn't sure what colour pearls I ought to get for Alyssa, that was if I was going to buy her a piece of jewellery that had pearls on it. I saw Fred and Lizzy out of the corner of my eye. They were walking past the stands displaying necklaces and earrings in their boxes. I went to look at them.

I spotted this one set of earrings and a necklace that looked like it was made of bronze or copper, only nicer. I think they call it... rose gold? Something like that.

Anyway, I didn't want Fred and Lizzy seeing what I was doing, because I knew that they, like everyone else, would ask questions, so I watched as they walked towards the perfume section. I picked up the box to look at the necklace more carefully. It was perfect. I went to pay for it, then left the shop.

I remembered I also decided, last night, that I needed some clothes to make me look more grown up. The clothes I usually wear are casual t-shirts, hoodies and jeans. I reckoned maybe getting some buttoned shirts and smart trousers would do the trick.

I went into Peacocks, grabbed a basket and went to look at the shirts. I picked out a navy and orange, long sleeved, check shirt, a green and white, long sleeved check shirt, a grey, short sleeved shirt, and a white short sleeved shirt with a blue collar. I put all four shirts in the basket, and then browsed through the trousers. I grabbed a pair of black skinny jeans, dark grey slim leg chinos and some smart navy trousers. Finally, I went to look at shoes and went for a pair of grey lace up boots and some shiny black brogues.

I tried everything on, paid, and left.

Now I just needed to head to WHSmith to look at paper to wrap the present in. The problem with wrapping paper with romantic patterns it on it is that they only have it out when it's coming up to Valentine's Day, which it wasn't, obviously. Never mind. I chose a set of two sheets of pale blue paper that had birds on it.

I was in such a good mood! I popped into Subway before heading home, and bought myself a chicken and chorizo melt. The sun was coming out as I walked along the esplanade.

Great. Fucking Stuart, he was outside the Rock and Fudge and I really didn't want to see him, because he was only going to ask me what I bought, he wouldn't believe me if I lied about why I bought the things I had, I knew that! And I couldn't just walk away like last time. I looked away so he wouldn't recognise me.

'Alright?' he'd said. Fucking great. I turned around, slowly, and faced Stuart.

'Had a bit of a solo shopping trip, have we?' he said. I was feeling a bit uneasy. I nodded. Thank God I'd hidden the necklace and paper in the Peacocks bag.

'You gonna show me what you bought?' asked Stuart. I slowly got out my new clothes to show Stuart. Stuart frowned.

'But you never wear stuff like this, Dave. I know you, you're usually dressed *way* more casual than that,' he said. 'Why have you - ' then his eyes suddenly went very wide. He sighed, annoyed, then said, 'Fuck sake Dave!'

I was *really* pissed off!

'I really don't want to be near you right now,' I said.

'You're going to make yourself look a right knob, one day,' said Stuart, then he walked off.

My good mood had been ruined, right there and then! What was his fucking problem?! He was being such a child. But I was not prepared to let Stuart make his jealousy *my* problem. That was all it was.

I was still in a shitty mood when I got home. It must've shown when I came in through the front door, because Dad said, 'What's up, son?'

'Just bumped into Stuart in town and he's still being a cock!' I said, grumpily, and went up to my room, then dumped my shopping on the bed. I didn't get up to much that evening, as I'd got all my coursework done. On Sunday, I took Clover out for a walk to get some fresh air. I took her to Radipole Park Drive and played fetch with her.

When we arrived home, I remembered I still had the present to wrap up. I taped the letter to the present, and put it in my rucksack ready for the next day, then got out the green and white shirt, and the black jeans and grey lace ups.

I set my alarm half an hour earlier than usual when I went to bed early, because I wanted to get to class before anyone else did, so no one would be around to see me leaving the present on Alyssa's desk.

I got up at six thirty, yesterday morning, and dressed.

Damn it! It suddenly occurred to me I should've bought some perfume in town as well! Oh well, I decided just to borrow some of Dad's. I went into Mum and Dad's room to look on the shelf under the bedside cabinet on Dad's side of the bed and chose Joop! Por Homme. I sprayed it on my wrists and rubbed them together, then on both sides of my neck. Then I went downstairs and had a couple of chocolate pop tarts for breakfast.

It was raining when I left the house, so I caught the bus. It was packed so I had to stand up. I held onto the bars as the bus drove along the esplanade, watching the raindrops streaming down the windows, distorting the view of all that was on the other side of the window.

I got off the bus at Westerhall and legged it up the back footpath, across the car park, and through the automatic doors to the Belfast Block, which is the name of the building the photography classes are in. I was knackered as soon as I got indoors.

I went straight to the classroom, opened the door, looked around to make sure no one was in there, and walked in, quietly. I shut the door behind me, walked over to the desk, opened my backpack, got out the present, and put it somewhere on the desk where only Alyssa would see it.

I headed to the student lounge to see if Fred, Lizzy or Jesse would be there. The college had been decorated throughout in black, orange and purple paper chains and fake webs with black plastic spiders stuck in them for Halloween.

There weren't many people in the student lounge, and Fred, Lizzy and Jesse weren't there, either.

When I returned to the classroom, I saw Stuart sat at the back of the room. He was still blatantly annoyed with me. I didn't care. I wasn't going to try and make up with someone who was being a twat and wouldn't admit it.

Alyssa came in, greeted us all in her usual way, sat down at her desk and I could tell she'd seen the present when I saw her stop in her tracks!

As per normal, Alyssa was as pleased as ever with my work. And then, after class, I took as long as I could, packing up all my things, because I wanted to see her reaction when she opened her present.

I was the last one out of the classroom. I walked out very slowly, then stayed outside the door. I peeped round the door and watched. I saw Alyssa reading the tag, and a big smile spread across her face. She unwrapped the present, then opened the box. I saw her mouth open and her eyes widen in amazement. I watched as Alyssa took the necklace out of its box and held it up to get a better look at it. She then grinned. Then I saw her look over at the door. I quickly hid. Then I walked down the corridor as quickly and as quietly as I could.

I was *well* psyched! I literally could not concentrate on anything else. I kept remembering Alyssa's face when she saw the necklace. She looked so touched. Now I knew for sure that the necklace had worked, I needed to think about the next present I could leave for her. For a split second, I *had* thought of sending her some flowers. Nah, it would probably be a better idea to start subtle. Flowers would be too much.

So what other presents could I leave for her, other than jewellery?

Oh yeah, I suddenly got reminded of when I was looking at that necklace back in Debenhams, when I had to make sure neither Fred nor Lizzy were about. They were walking towards the perfumes.

Yeah, good idea, I'd get Alyssa a nice perfume. But where from, though? Oh yeah, I remembered the Avon representative that served our area was coming round with the new Avon book tonight. Mum ordered loads of stuff, including perfumes, so yeah, I'd have a look and see what nice perfumes I could buy, and maybe buy myself a perfume too, so I didn't have to keep borrowing Dad's.

'I must say, you have been mystifying me lately,' said Mum, when I asked if I could look at the book to buy myself some perfume. 'It's not like you to suddenly care how you smell. Still, it would be nice if you could have some nice perfume and Avon does do some pretty good ones.'

I sat on my bed, trawling through the pages. I came across some of those patches that you rub and then sniff the perfume. I came across a ladies' perfume in a hot pink bottle. It was called Secret Fantasy. I rubbed the rub and sniff patch and sniffed it. That one was quite nice. I sniffed the patch for another perfume, called Perceive. That one I really liked. That one was the one. Should I maybe get her something else in addition to the perfume? No, the perfume would be enough.

Next, I started looking for some perfume for myself. First one I looked at was called Christian Lacroix Noir for him. There was no rub and sniff patch. I wasn't that keen on buying a perfume where I couldn't check what it smelt like first. I kept looking. The first one I was able to sniff was called Avon Life for him. Not bad. The next one I sniffed was called, One Pulse for him. Definitely that one!

I wrote both perfumes down on the order form and took it back downstairs to give back to Mum, and asked when the lady was picking up the book and orders.

'Next Monday.'

'And how long do the orders take to get here?' I asked, hoping it wouldn't be too long.

'About a week. It shouldn't be more than that, hopefully,' said Mum.

A week. So I was guessing, if the Avon lady didn't pick up the orders for another week, and the orders took a week to arrive after that, then I'd have to wait two weeks for it. I'd better think about what other presents I could buy for Alyssa until then, and what other things I could do to make her like me. In the meantime, I kept doing well in class and with my coursework.

Wednesday 20th October 2010

Doing well on my course wasn't getting me the attention I was aiming for. I started thinking about how else I could get what I wanted, whilst I sat in Fred's car on the way into town with Lizzy, Fred and Jesse to meet Ruby-lynn, Scarlet and Natalie. We'd made plans to meet in the White Hart for a quick drink.

Though I often felt like the odd one out because I didn't really have a best friend in the gang, hanging out with them didn't make me unhappy.

Jesse asked us if we definitely were all coming out with him for Halloween on Saturday the thirtieth of October. Halloween was actually going to be on Sunday, but, as most of us, me included, had college the day after, it had to be the night before instead.

'Definitely! Anywhere there's a chance of pulling, I'm up for it!' said Fred, ecstatically.

Scarlet rolled her eyes and said, 'Is that all you think about?'

'Can I invite Charlie along?' Lizzy asked, eagerly.

At this, Scarlet said, 'I refer you to the question I just asked Fred.'

Obviously I couldn't ask if I was allowed to bring Alyssa along! Though I honestly *did* like the very thought of her coming out with me!

The others started talking about what costumes they were going to wear. I didn't know what I wanted to go as. Maybe dress as a gangster? But I couldn't put as much thought into this as I should've done, because my mind kept wandering off to the prospect of Alyssa asking to see me after class. She would tell me she knew it was me who left her the present, and then we would have a moment where we would look into each other's eyes, and she would hopefully feel a spark, then we would kiss...

'Penny for your thoughts, Dave?' asked Jesse. I looked over at him. The others were looking at me like I was on crack or something. Must've been obvious I'd been miles away, just then.

'I was thinking, maybe I should go as a gangster?' I said.

'Good idea,' said Jesse, who then told the others how he'd already bought his Willy Wonka costume. Fred sniggered.

'I was with him when he tried it on. He looked hilarious,' he said.

'Well, thanks for boosting my confidence,' said Jesse, sarcastically.

Lizzy, Natalie, Ruby-lynn and Scarlet started on about how they'd already bought all their curly synthetic wigs, false eyelashes, and posh, old-fashioned frocks.

On the way back home, afterwards, I caught sight of Alyssa, whilst walking up St Thomas Street. She was walking towards Lloyds T.S.B. I watched her. She reached the entrance to the bank and I saw her talking to a man her age. He looked like he had a bit of a wild side to him. He was tall, with short dark blonde hair and tanned skin.

I saw Alyssa give the man a kiss and a hug. I felt my heart sink like a stone. I couldn't believe it. I never stopped to think that Alyssa might be married or have a boyfriend.

I know I shouldn't have, but I kept torturing myself on the way home with the memory of what I'd just witnessed. But I couldn't give up now! I'd win her over, even if I had to beg, borrow or steal! Yeah, that's right, steal her off another man! And she was fucking *well* over the moon when she opened that first present I left! I was going to stick at it, and I'd have all of half term to think about what else to do.

I didn't have a lot of time to think of what more I could do. I had to be at Scarlet's dad's house around seven, for pre drinks whilst getting ready to go out. What was I supposed to do about Stuart being there too? I had half a mind to say to the others that I'd meet them in town, but Dan and Scarlet were keen for me to come round, even if Stuart wasn't.

I started getting everything ready to go round. I grabbed my gangster costume, and went downstairs and put it in one of the bags containing the drinks I was bringing to Scarlet's.

Mum gave me a lift to Dan's at six forty. Scarlet's dad, Kevin, answered when I rang the bell. Kevin has always been great mates with Dad, as well as Barry, Fred and Natalie's dad. Whenever they go to the pub with Mum, Claire, Lizzy's parents, and Jesse's mum, our dads usually get completely fucked out of their brains, which annoys the mums.

'Alright?' said Dan, coming out of the lounge when I brought my stuff in. I saw Scarlet come down the stairs, already in her costume.

I went into the lounge, where Charlie, Stuart, Dan and Tom were changing into their costumes. The television was on, and it was on one of the music channels.

I got an annoyed look from Stuart as soon as we saw each other. I could only give him an awkward shrug back.

A few minutes later, Fred, Jesse and Natalie arrived, not long before Ruby-lynn, Lizzy, Fraser, Adam and Dustin had.

'Oy, Jesse! Where's the chocolate?' Tom teased. I looked round at Jesse, smirking, to see how he would take this, but he just looked confused.

'I didn't know I was meant to be bringing chocolate,' he said.

'But you're Willy Wonka, though!' joked Dan. 'I would've thought we'd be entitled to free chocolate.'

Jesse rolled his eyes as the rest of us laughed.

Dan said the drinks could go on the table in the kitchen, before I walked past him with Fred and Jesse and the drinks. All three girls went upstairs to change, whilst Fraser, Adam and Dustin came in to join the rest of us in the lounge after we all helped ourselves to Kopparberg, Sambuca, Budweiser, Guinness, Stella Artois and Coors Light.

Me, Fred and Jesse changed into our costumes, Jesse already had his orange top hat perched on his blonde hair. Fred was dressed as Spiderman, Charlie was dressed as a ghost buster, Stuart was dressed as an air force captain, Dan was dressed as a zombie cowboy, Tom was dressed as a policeman, Fraser was dressed as a ghost pirate, Adam was dressed as a SWAT commander and Dustin was dressed as Superman.

Shortly after, the girls, who had changed into their costumes and had come downstairs, joined us in the lounge so they could do their hair and make-up whilst having drinks.

Whilst they were in the kitchen, getting drinks, I asked Fred if he fancied Ruby-lynn and was hoping to pull her later, since I could guess he probably did like her, from the way he acted around her the first day we all met.

'Isn't that obvious?' Fred said.

'Doesn't matter who Fred pulls when he goes out, whoever it is, she's nowhere near as hot as *my* girl!' Dan bragged. Was he fucking serious? Why did he have to be such a bigheaded wanker?

Before either of me or Fred could say anything, the girls came back in with glasses of W.K.D.

We got two taxis into town because there was a massive group of us, and we were dropped off at the back of Debenhams, and headed to Yates, first.

'Boys' round!' Fred yelled, which meant all of us lads had to buy the girls' drinks as well as our own, whilst they went off and danced.

Half an hour later, Dan's girlfriend Nikki Jones, her mate Isabel Cooper and her boyfriend joined us at the table we were sat at by the window, having our drinks. Nikki was dressed as a nineteen-twenties Coco flapper, Isabel was dressed as an imperial empress and her boyfriend, Ellis, was dressed as a khaki toy soldier. Fucking hell, he'd even painted his hands and face the same colour as his costume!

'Things still not great with Stuart?'

I turned and Scarlet had sat down on my right.

'Obviously I'm not going to ask why,' Scarlet said, 'partly because I already know, but also because we're obviously going to have a row about it, because I know we'll just disagree with each other.'

What made her think that?

'Well, why don't you just listen to me, unlike everyone else?' I said, looking round at her. 'And just agree with me, yeah?'

Scarlet was looking at me in that annoyed way that you'd look at someone who'd kept doing something you'd already told them a gazillion times not to do.

'I am not going to argue with you, Dave,' she said, firmly. 'That is all I'm saying.'

She got up and walked off. Well, she clearly didn't agree with what I thought about my chances with Alyssa. God sake, she was just like everyone else, just not taking any of it seriously.

I wasn't going to let anyone get to me. It was their problem that they wouldn't listen to me, but they'd change their tunes once I'd worn Alyssa down. They'd see!

But tonight, there was only one thing for it! We came out to have a good time, and that was exactly what I was going to do!

I was going to get completely off my head and forget about everything else! Yeah!

We left Yates, except Tom and Dan, because they said they were staying behind with Nikki, Isabel and her boyfriend.

'I wanna go to Rumshack. Annie said she'd be there,' said Jesse.

We went upstairs to the bar in Rumshack, and, sure enough, there was Annie. She had come out as, what she referred to as a Bavarian wench. As soon as she saw Jesse walking over to her in his Willy Wonka costume, she cried, 'Oh my God! You look *so* hilarious!'

'Yeah, thanks, babe,' said Jesse, sarcastically. Annie grabbed the rim of Jesse's hat, took it off his head, placed it on her own head, and they shared a kiss.

Amongst the crowd, I could just about make out Fred and Ruby-lynn. They were *all over* each other! They weren't kissing but what was happening was a sure-fire sign that things were hotting up!

I joined the other lads in a load of jagerbombs. I downed shot after shot after shot until I was plastered enough to really let myself go on the dance floor. Charlie had to practically drag me away when we were leaving. On to the next club, wherever that was!

We left Fraser, Adam and Dustin behind because they'd said they weren't coming with, as they'd seen some friends from their course, who they wanted to join. The rest of us headed off to Cellar Bar.

We entered and went downstairs into the club. I went to talk to the rest of the boys during the girls' round of buying the drinks.

'She kissed me!' Fred was saying to the others, ecstatically, sitting next to Jesse, who then held up his hand for Fred to high-five him.

'So, you gonna ask her out, then?' I managed to slur.

'Well, I can't *not* ask her out,' he said. I looked round at Ruby-lynn. She was talking to Scarlet and they were both looking at Fred, smiling, excitedly.

'Mate, you'd better at least try to look sober or they'll kick you out!' I heard Jesse warn me. I pretended not to hear him. I didn't care if I went home reeking like a brewery.

The girls came over with drinks for everyone.

'What a night!' Scarlet exclaimed. 'Tom and I were having a good chinwag, back in Yates! He'd been telling me all about his course, because of what he wants to be, later on in life. He's always been a very sporty, active person.'

Tom was in his first year of his level three course in Sport, Development, Coaching and Fitness. He wanted to be a fitness coach. He was really into sports as well, especially football.

Tom was from Liverpool, so obviously he was a Liverpool supporter. He was your typical footie mad scouser.

'So, where are we heading next?' Natalie asked, excitedly. 'I definitely don't wanna go home after this!'

'Well, I definitely have no intention of calling it a night after we finish here!' said Stuart, ecstatically.

I downed more jagerbombs before getting up for another dance. I could barely keep my eyes open. Fuck it if I looked like a zombie or whatever, I was having a bloody good time!

The rest of the night went by in a haze. I honestly can't remember anything until waking up in bed on Sunday morning.

God, I was so hung over! It was worth it though. Dad got pissy because he said he needed my help with sorting through everything in the loft and taking some things to the tip. Well, excuse me for having a good time the night before, for fuck sake.

I got dressed and sprayed on loads of the perfume I bought for myself on Monday morning. My plan was to do what I did with the necklace; go into college early, leave the perfume I bought Alyssa on her desk and then secretly watch her open it.

The perfumes had arrived last Monday. I didn't need to attach a love note or anything when I wrapped it. I still had plenty of the paper left from the last present.

As soon as I arrived, I went straight to the classroom, again ensuring no one else was there, opened the door, checked no one was in there, crept in, shut the door behind me, went over to the desk, put the present somewhere on the desk, and left.

I looked over at Alyssa's desk, subtly as I could when I came back in just before class started, but the present was gone!

Alyssa wasn't at her desk, though I could tell she'd been in the room that morning, because her bag was down by her desk, so thank God she'd probably picked it up and put it in her bag. She hadn't left it unzipped, so I couldn't see if it was in there.

I'd come up with the perfect plan. Instead of working well, I'd been doing the exact opposite, since finding out Alyssa had a partner, partly so she'd offer me a bit of one-on-one help, but also because I'd look cool and edgy.

I kept on fantasising that Alyssa would ask to see me after class, saying, 'I've left my partner. I'm all yours,' and then she would kiss me...

'Um, Alyssa?' I said. Alyssa looked up at me.

'Yes?' she said, smiling.

'I was wondering if you could help me?' I asked. I explained there was a part of my coursework I couldn't decide on and asked if she could talk to me about it and give me some ideas. I came up with a story about the troubles I was having.

'Thanks,' I said, after she had. Well, that didn't work out how I planned. I thought about what to do during break. I needed to keep on pretending to struggle with it, and then maybe ask for a one to one session.

I was in the dark room, dousing my photos in the developing chemicals, having another think about other things I could do. I wanted to buy more gifts to leave for her. I thought again about flowers, even though before, I'd thought they'd be too much, but now I knew that Alyssa was in a relationship, I had a lot of competition, so maybe flowers could be the best idea for the next gift I'd leave her.

But how was I meant to bring a bunch of flowers into college without being noticed by anyone? There had to be a more subtle way. I knew that you could order flowers and other gifts to be sent directly to whom they were meant for. I had to look into it tonight on the Internet.

Also I knew I shouldn't just stop at leaving her gifts, especially as I'd make sure they were anonymous and hadn't thought it through exactly when I planned on letting her know they were from me. I needed to do things that would show her I could be a gentleman.

But before I could think any further on the subject, Stuart came in.

'Dave, what the actual fuck?'

What on Earth was wrong now?

'What?' I said.

'What kind of saddo sends their teacher some lame-arse love letter saying, "Roses are red, violets are blue, both are so beautiful, and so are you,"?' shouted Stuart. 'Just when I think you can't get any sadder than changing the way you dress, you start sending her presents and playing dumb! I'm not fucking blind, Dave, and I'm not a retard either! That present I saw left on her desk a few weeks back *had* to be from you!'

'Yeah? *Fuck* you, Stuart! I've had it with your jealousy,' I snapped back, angrily.

'You think I'm jealous?!' said Stuart, in disbelief. 'You think I want to make an idiot of myself, trying to get with someone who is off limits, by making myself look like some pathetic, lovesick spaz?!'

I glared at him, then barged past him, out of the dark room. I didn't give a bloody fuck what it looked like to everyone else! I didn't care that it was illegal to have personal relationships with your teachers! I *especially* didn't fucking care that I was knowingly trying it on with someone else's wife or girlfriend! Alyssa was the girl for me and I'd never find anyone like her ever again!

I went outside of the building and let out an angry scream, throwing down my fists.

I knew I couldn't rise to the bait, though. I knew I had to keep calm and try and appear more laid back, because Alyssa wouldn't fancy me if she thought I was hot headed with a short fuse.

I returned to the studio after collecting my photos from the drying room. I saw Alyssa's handbag, down by her desk. It was open. I remembered this one time, when I'd been walking around college with my bag not done up properly and my folder had fallen out. Someone had spotted it and had been kind enough to pick it up and give it back. What would happen if Alyssa forgot to close her bag before picking it up? What if something had fallen out of her bag? Would someone notice and have the decency to pick it up and give it back to her? I knew I would. If only something did fall out of Alyssa's back.

I noticed her keys through the opening of her bag. Some one could easily... stick their hand in and take them! That was it!

Before I could stop myself, I found myself doing exactly that! I'd stolen from a teacher! And not just any teacher either, but the one I liked. I don't know what made me do it, I just thought I could catch her after class, and give them back to her, saying she'd dropped them.

I carried on doing as badly as I could. At the end of class, I asked Alyssa if I could maybe have a one to one time with her so she could help me. Unfortunately, she didn't sound so sure.

'I'll see when I can spare some time, but I have got a hectic schedule this week,' she had said, 'but if you could try and stick at it in the meantime, that would be great. I know you can do it,' she added, giving me an encouraging smile.

'Right,' I said, disappointed. Damn it!

I went to lunch. Things were not going to plan at all. My chances of getting some quality time with Alyssa weren't looking good.

But I still had the "returning the keys" plan up my sleeve, so not all hope was lost.

I knew Alyssa wasn't likely to leave the room with the class. I hung around by the stairs near the entrance to the building, and waited. I checked now and again if I could see her coming out. I ended up waiting a good half an hour for her to come out! I hid round the corner, right next to the lift. Her footsteps were growing nearer. Just to be on the safe side, I tiptoed over to the stairs, quick as I could, and ran up them, just before Alyssa came past the lift. I watched from the top of the stairs as she walked through the automatic doors and out of the building. Then I quickly ran down the stairs and exited the building.

I saw her at my one o'clock, walking across the car park to her silver Toyota Yaris. I wasn't that far behind her.

'Alyssa!'

Alyssa looked over her shoulder.

'Dave?' she said, sounding surprised, coming back over. 'Are you all right?'

'You dropped something,' I said, and held out Alyssa's keys.

'Oh,' Alyssa said, sounding puzzled. 'They must've fallen out of my bag.'

I watched, hopefully, as she took the keys and put them in her bag.

'I'm glad you noticed,' she said, sounding grateful, then, with a smile, she added, 'That's really nice of you, thank you.'

I grinned back, and told her she was welcome any time.

I went home in a much better mood that I had been earlier. I shouldn't have let that knob Stuart get to me. When I won Alyssa over, he'd have no choice but to admit he'd been totally in the wrong.

Back at home, I switched on my computer and opened up the Internet. What was I going to type into Google? I tried, 'flower delivery service,' and looked at the results. I looked at eflorist.co.uk and scrolled through the different flowers. There were so many choices. I had no idea what sort of flowers Alyssa liked. A bouquet of white roses and lilies grabbed my attention.

Brilliant! I could choose the delivery date, and I could pay by PayPal, which was good because I have an account with them. I did, however, need to create an account with eFlorist, before placing the order, making sure I set it to arrive the next day. I addressed it to Alyssa, with the college's address. Wait, should I add the Belfast Block to the address? No, there wouldn't be anyone for the guy delivering the flowers to give them to. But then, if it was handed in at reception, whoever was on the front desk would probably know what to do.

Another gift order done and dusted!

I got myself dressed in the white and blue shirt, my grey chinos and black shoes Tuesday morning.

I walked to college, anticipating what would happen when a bouquet of beautiful white lilies and roses arrived for Alyssa, what she'd say, what she'd think!

I didn't know what time they'd arrive. I didn't know if I'd be able to make sure I was close by for when Alyssa got the flowers. Something else occurred to me. I needed to make sure Stuart wasn't there to see, or he'd only give me another hard time.

I was just on my way out of the dark room to hang up my photos, when I heard Alyssa's voice in the corridor, as well as another lady's voice. I peered down the corridor, taking care not to let them see I was watching. Alyssa was talking to one of the receptionists, who was giving Alyssa the flowers. Yes! Alyssa appeared astonished and mystified at receiving them. I watched and listened as Alyssa said that this was the second present she'd had this week, and that she was flattered by who ever had sent them, but she didn't want her partner to start getting funny about it, adding, 'You remember me saying what he's like.'

So, Alyssa's significant other was the jealous type. The type who would get queer about his girlfriend receiving presents from another man. That was sure to cause problems in the relationship.

I went to the drying room to hang up my photos. Definitely going to be keeping at it.

I still made sure that I did as crap as I could. Maybe I'd have another go next week at trying to get some help for her on a one to one basis? Hopefully she might have a bit more time, then.

That night, I Googled 'gift ideas for women.' I came across a picture of a silver and crystal ornament from a company called Swarovski Elements. I did think of buying that exact one at first, but then I noticed it said, 'To my beautiful wife,' written on it.

I searched for Swarovski crystal ornaments on Amazon. I'd been scrolling and scrolling through the results, looking at gold and silver ornaments that had crystals in every colour, then I came across a silver ornament of a rose with a lilac crystal in the middle of the petals. Engraved on one of the leaves were the words, 'For Someone Special.'

Perfect. It was eligible for Prime. Brilliant, because I could get it with free one-day delivery. I ordered it right away. I'd do what I did with the necklace; go into college early, leave it on her desk and then secretly watch her open it.

On Wednesday, it was waiting for me on the hall table as soon as I got home from college. I took it straight up to my room to take it out of the little white box it came in and unwrapped the bubble wrap so I could have a proper look at it.

It was gorgeous! Alyssa was sure to love it. I wrapped it back up in the bubble wrap, put it back in the box, and wrapped it.

Thursday morning, I got up, had breakfast, got ready and left for college.

As soon as I arrived, I went to leave the present on the desk.

When I returned to the classroom later, there weren't very many others there. Stuart wasn't there, luckily.

Alyssa was looking at the present, though she didn't unwrap it. At least she'd seen it.

As I went to grab a chair and sit down, I saw her leaving the room with it still in her hand. She came back in a few minutes later, when some of the others came in, looking slightly uneasy and didn't greet us in her usual way. What was wrong? I did think of asking her, to show I cared, but didn't think it was a great idea. I'd hoped it was something to do with her other half; maybe things weren't going right between them?

Also, I didn't think it was a good idea to ask again about having a one to one session with her, either, as she obviously wasn't in the right frame of mind right now.

But I carried on going out of my way to fall behind; that way, she'd have to give me at least a bit of mentoring. I didn't really like failing on something I loved, but it was the only way to get her attention.

And now I knew what car she had, and where she'd usually park it, I loitered around near it at home time, and started a quick chat with her when she came over to get in and drive home. I was hoping she'd offer me a lift, not that I knew whether she lived in my direction.

Friday morning, she asked me to see her after class.

My plan worked!

I couldn't wait for the end of class. I knew why she wanted to see me. She *had* felt the same way! When the lesson ended and the rest of the class left, I walked over to her desk, grinning.

'Okay,' Alyssa began.

'Before you start, can I just ask, did you like that necklace you got the other week?' I asked. Alyssa looked up at me, frowning.

'I did,' she said, confused.

'What about the flowers? And the other presents?'

'Yes,' Alyssa said, sounding hesitant. 'Why do you ask, and how do you even know about those?'

'It was me,' I told her, and I smiled. 'I left them for you. And I sent you the flowers.'

Alyssa looked down, uncertainly. It didn't look promising, but this was the moment. I had to tell her.

'Listen,' I said, 'I know what I'm about to do is insane, but I really like you. I know it's kind of wrong, because you're my teacher and I'm a student, and I know you're with someone, but I really do think we could have something special, like, really incredible. And I know you feel the same way about me, because that was why you wanted to see me after class, to tell me you like me, wasn't it?'

Alyssa looked down, her mouth open and her eyebrows raised in surprise, then said, 'Dave, I am not going to lie to you. This is *very* inappropriate.'

I couldn't believe what I was hearing. I didn't *want* to believe it.

'Yes, I *am* with someone,' Alyssa continued, 'but how did you even know that?'

I confessed to seeing her with her other half outside Lloyds T.S.B. At first, she was horrified, until I said it was when I was walking home from meeting the gang and promised I wasn't stalking her.

'But do you know I've actually had to call the police about all this?'

She what?! She'd called the fuzz?!

'I was flattered at first, don't get me wrong, but, as far as I knew, I thought it was a stalker from outside of college, who knew more about me then I would've thought they should have. I wasn't to know that it was a student who had a school boy crush on me.'

I didn't know what to think. I was so frozen with fear, I couldn't pay proper attention to what Alyssa was saying. Would I be arrested?

'And do you not know what could happen if anything were to happen between us?' Alyssa went on. 'If we got caught, and there would be a very big chance that we would be, I could lose my job and even get arrested. And I'm really, *very* sorry, Dave, but I don't like you in the way that you want me to, and if anything I have ever said or done has led you to believe that I do, again, I apologise.'

But I was not giving up. How could she not return my feelings? And who was to say that we'd be very likely to be found out?

'Why do you think we'd get found out?' I asked. 'And why don't you like me like that? I know I could make you fifty times happier than your boyfriend ever could!'

'I am *very* happy with my partner, Dave.'

Alyssa sounded like she was protesting. I was getting desperate now. I did *not* want to back down.

'I'm sure you are, but I could still make you much happier!' I persisted. 'Why settle for second best when you can have... um, first best?'

Alyssa looked daggers at me. I was still not going to take no for an answer. I strode round her desk, bent down and kissed her on the lips.

'Dave! Dave! Stop it!' Alyssa yelled in horror. 'I think you'd better leave the room this minute!'

'But what about what you really wanted to see me about?'

'I am *not* in the right frame of mind, now! *Out!*'

'Okay,' I said, glumly.

I left the classroom, absolutely heartbroken and humiliated. I didn't know what to think at that moment. I'd just told the woman of my dreams that I fancied her, only to be told that she didn't feel the same way, was in a relationship, and would get into huge trouble with the law if we did have a relationship. I'd tried to kiss her and she pushed me away!

I'd hit an all time low. I couldn't believe I let my crush on Alyssa get out of hand.

Even worse, I didn't know what the police would do, now that Alyssa had found out it was me who'd sent the presents. And would she tell them I tried to kiss her?

I needed to talk to Stuart. I went to look in the Learning Gateway, to see if he'd decided to catch up on some coursework, but couldn't see him in there as I crossed the room to the other door, and then went up the stairs to the library, but I searched and he wasn't there either.

I went back down the stairs, left the building and went across the grounds to the canteen. Nope, still no sign of him.

I went up to the student lounge and Stuart was sat at one of the computers by the wall. I went over to him and sat on the empty stall next to him.

'Hi,' I said. Stuart looked round and sighed.

'What do you want?'

I took a deep breath.

'You were right about everything,' I admitted. 'You only tried to help me.'

'What changed your mind?'

I knew I had to tell him what had just happened.

'Alyssa asked to see me after class, and I thought she was going to tell me she fancied me,' I explained, 'but she was shocked when I confessed my feelings for her, and told me that it was inappropriate and that nothing could ever happen between us because she was my teacher and was with someone else, and that she'd told the police because she thought it had been some creepy stalker who'd sent those presents. And then I kissed her.'

Stuart glared at me.

'You absolute bell end!' he said, angrily. 'I tried to warn you but you wouldn't listen to me! You just kept making me out as the one in the wrong, like I was jealous. You could get chucked off the course for this at the very least, you know that, right?'

I nodded, looking down.

'I really was sorry,' I said, 'can we just forget it ever happened.'

'What, just so you can feel better about it, just so you can pretend like it's not such a big deal?' Stuart interrupted.

'Please, Stuart, I'm feeling really shit about it,' I tried to say.

'That's not my fault, or my problem for that matter, and I'm not going to forgive you, just so you can stop beating yourself up for something you knew was really stupid and naïve,' was all Stuart had to say in response.

It was no good. I'd apologised to Stuart to the best of my abilities, but I knew that it wasn't Stuart's fault he wouldn't forgive me. I only had myself to blame.

I walked back over to the door, left the student lounge and walked down the steps, thinking about everything I brought upon myself. I was the top student and Alyssa had been so impressed. But now I'd frightened her off. And my mate wouldn't talk to me.

I will never let myself develop a crush on a teacher ever again, and if I do, I'll make sure it does not get out of hand.

Chapter 4:

Fred's First

Friday 5th November 2010

I was planning my third attempt at asking Ruby-lynn out. I was sat in the back of Flora's car on the way to the seafront, thinking about how to go about asking her. I needed to decide how to word it. I didn't want to go with just, 'Hey. Wanna go out?' I wrote that when I texted her on my second attempt. No wonder I got a 'No' that time round!

Six of us, her and me included, were meeting up for Bonfire Night. I hoped to sit with her when we'd watch the fireworks then. She'd said no the first time I asked.

I'd been amazed, not horrified, or disappointed. She was trying to play hard to get, which just drew me in even more!

Over the week, I'd asked her out a second time, by text, but still, her answer was 'no thanks.'

I've fancied her the first moment I saw her, but things hadn't got off to a good start, after I really annoyed her in the park. But I hoped, after we'd talked on Facebook, I'd made things better with her.

She has the most amazing blue eyes, just like sapphires, and I love her pink hair. *Very* daring!

We'd spent most of the Halloween night out together. I'd been looking forward to seeing Ruby-lynn in her Halloween costume. I knew what she was going as. She looked unbelievable, and in a way, she sort of looked like one of those Japanese cartoons with her pink hair, blue eyes and the clothes she was wearing. And wow! Her false eyelashes!

We chatted when we were in Yates.

'Will I get to see your face properly at all, this evening?' she asked, since my Spiderman costume obviously included the Spiderman mask.

'I may take the mask off, later,' I'd said, and then added, 'if you're lucky,' to which Ruby-lynn replied, 'I'd like that.'

When we'd gone to into Rumshack later, Ruby-lynn had invited me for a dance! Get in there!

My stomach had somersaulted as Ruby-lynn placed her hands on my shoulders. I'd nervously put my hands on her hips and we'd danced. I'd felt the warmth of her body as she moved in closer, putting her arms round my shoulders and resting her head on my shoulder. I'd moved my hands over Ruby-lynn's back. I'd suddenly felt her move her left arm, and put it down through the gap between my torso and right arm. I'd felt her run her hand down my back, and down over my arse. Then she'd grabbed it! Cheeky!

When we'd left Rumshack afterwards and walked to Cellar Bar, we'd walked a little way behind everyone else.

'I believe you said you'd remove your mask later on tonight if I was lucky,' Ruby-lynn had said, giving me a smile. I'd smiled back and said, 'So, I did.'

'Am I lucky now?' Ruby-lynn had asked, grinning. We'd both stopped walking and I said, 'I dare say so.'

I'd taken off my mask, Ruby-lynn had looked into my eyes, and I'd looked into hers. She'd leaned in, and kissed me!

It was like nothing I'd ever felt with any other girls I'd kissed. And she has the most amazing lips.

After twenty seconds, she'd broken away and smiled at me.

I knew I *certainly* had to ask her out, now she'd kissed me, and I most definitely wanted to!

I'd laid awake in bed that night, thinking about Ruby-lynn, and wondering how many times I'd have to ask her, before I'd get a yes. Maybe she'd say yes the very next time? Maybe I'd have to ask her a thousand times before she'd say yes? I do love her playing hard to get.

Ruby-lynn's nineteenth birthday was Sunday the seventh of November, so I'd bought her a gift set from the Body Shop because Scarlet told me Ruby-lynn liked their stuff. I saw one that contained British Rose body butter, Fuji green tea shower gel, vitamin E night cream, moringa body scrub, and shea hand cream. I knew it was the one, since I didn't know exactly what flavours she liked, so I thought it was a good idea to have a bit of a mix. I intended to give it to her along with the card I bought for her.

Me, Jesse and Natalie met Lizzy, Scarlet and Ruby-lynn at the Alexandra Gardens.

'Hey,' I said to Ruby-lynn, grinning.

'Hi,' she said, smiling. Maybe I could be in with a chance tonight?

'They've just lit the fire,' Scarlet said. 'We have got plenty of time to kill before the fireworks start.'

'Okay, so what should we do until then? Anyone got any ideas?' Natalie asked.

Lizzy said she wanted to go on some of the rides that were outside the pavilion.

They had the Waltzers, and there was the Miami Dance, the Orbiter and the Twister, all of which we went on, multiple times, since we all had plenty of change between us.

Afterwards, we went down onto the beach to find somewhere to sit. I took care to make sure I was walking closely to Ruby-lynn so it would be easier to sit down next to her.

'Alright?' I said, when we sat down.

'Yeah.'

'Is the ice queen starting to melt yet?'

'She's started melting, just not quite enough, yet,' said Ruby-lynn, smiling.

'So... if I asked you out again, right now,' I began, 'your answer would be...'

'No thank you.'

Damn! I was so sure I was going to get a yes this time! Oh well. Things were looking up, at least.

I rummaged through my shoulder bag and pulled out the card and present. I saw Ruby-lynn look round.

'Here,' I said, holding them out to her. 'For your birthday.'

'For me?' she said, sounding touched.

I nodded.

'Aw, thanks,' she said, grinning. Man, I really hoped it would be a yes the next time I asked.

After we watched the fireworks, we went to K.F.C afterwards.

'Are you doing anything nice for your birthday?' I asked Ruby-lynn.

'I'm having dinner with my parents at Enzos,' Ruby-lynn said. 'It's one of my favourite places to eat.'

Enzos. Maybe I could ask her if she wanted to go there, next time I tried asking her out? Although, if she was already going with her parents, she might not want to go again, too soon after, even if it was one of her favourite places.

'What other places do you like to go to eat?' I asked.

'I like going to the Swan,' said Ruby-lynn. 'And Rendezvous. Oh, and also the Gurka.'

Quite a mix, then.

I went home wondering when I should have my fourth attempt at asking her out. Not the next day, that would be too soon. My second attempt was two days ago, so I wanted to allow more time. Not on her birthday, as that didn't seem right, some how, though I definitely planned to text her to wish her happy birthday. She texted back in the evening to say thank you for her card and present and that she loved it.

Tuesday 9th November 2010

'Hey, how's you? xxx' I typed on Facebook messenger. I sent it and then put my phone in my phone holder on the dashboard before starting up the engine.

I drove round to Jesse's to pick him up.

'Getting any further with her yet?' he'd asked, once we were on our way to college.

'I can only hope she'll relent this time round,' I said. 'I was so sure she'd say yes when I asked her on Bonfire Night. I think she's on the verge of cracking though. I like to think the birthday present I gave her had helped in the mean time.'

Jesse asked what I said so far, so I told him I just started by initiating conversation and was still waiting to hear back from her.

It wasn't until I was parking the car that my phone beeped. I stopped the engine and lifted it from the phone holder and opened the message, which I knew was Ruby-lynn. It just said, 'Fine thanks. how are you? x,' so I typed back, 'Not too bad thanks. you at work today? xxx,' and sent it.

We messaged each other throughout the morning, secretly messaging her in class, hiding my phone under the desk.

It wasn't until afternoon break that I thought it would be a good idea to bring the subject round to going out together.

'So has the ice queen been sufficiently thawed, yet? xxx,' I asked.

She came back about five minutes later with, 'I dare say so xx,' so I replied with, 'you fancy going to dinner at the swan? xxxx'

I didn't hear anything else from her until home time. She replied, asking if I was free Wednesday evening, which I was, so I said I'd pick her up at seven.

She was wearing a Hell Bunny dress with Irregular Choice heels, which she said were birthday presents from her parents.

'You smell nice,' said Ruby-lynn, smiling, once we were seated.

'Do you say that to all the boys?' I joked.

'I'm not as chilled out as you are when it comes to chatting up the opposite sex.'

'Nah, I know.'

Ruby-lynn asked what perfume it was I was wearing. I'd chosen my Paco Rabanne Million, which I'd bought in Debenhams.

'So how did you know I liked Body Shop products?' asked Ruby-lynn.

'Scarlet and I had words,' I told her. 'I needed a couple of hints about what would make an ideal birthday present for you.'

'I see.'

After having dinner, we had a stroll through town.

'So, do you treat every girl you meet to something like this?' asked Ruby-lynn, smiling. 'I just want to know if I'm the latest of a million girls you've also done this with, or if tonight should be leaving me feeling special.'

'Both, really,' I said, grinning. 'Because even though I have done this with other girls, I'm enjoying it more with you.'

'So, I'm... different from the others?' said Ruby-lynn, as we both stopped and turned to face each other.

'Yeah... a good kind of different,' I said, gazing into her eyes. She looked into mine.

'Good.'

She moved in closer, tilting her head inwards, and I found myself doing the same, and we kissed for three seconds before Ruby-lynn broke away again and looked into my eyes.

I looked into her eyes and then kissed her again.

Being Ruby-lynn's boyfriend had given my confidence a massive boost. During my time at Fleetview, both secondary school and doing my A levels, I'd got to know lots of different groups of girls. I'd even hung out with a few of them, and flirted with them as well, without it actually meaning anything. And even now I was going out with Ruby-lynn, I hit on certain girls at Euro Capital House College, where I was doing my I.T BTEC level two Diploma; ones I sat near in class, ones I passed in the corridors, ones I was next to in the canteen queues, just to see how they reacted.

Saturday 13th November 2010

I got changed, grabbed my Men in Black D.V.Ds from my room, and Mum gave me, Jesse and Natalie a lift over to Lizzy's at quarter past five.

'Hi,' Lizzy greeted us, when she answered the door.

'Hiya, Lizzy!' said Natalie, giving her a hug and a kiss on each cheek as we all piled in.

Penny came to greet us too, bounding over and jumping up onto her hind legs, looking up at all three of us. Dogs are cute, the way they come running over to you, all excited to see you. I've always been more of a dog person. I don't mind cats, but I used to be allergic to them. Nothing a couple of anti-histamines couldn't help with. I grew out of it, which I discovered when I sort of accidentally came into contact with one and didn't suffer any kind of reaction, but Mum and Dad don't want to risk getting a cat for a pet, you know, in case my allergy might come back.

I scratched Penny's ears, then we followed Lizzy into the lounge, where Scarlet and Ruby-lynn were sat on the two armchairs near the television. I wasn't at all surprised to see Dave wasn't there. He'd been suspended from college for two months, and was on probation, which meant he had to stay well away from his teacher until he went back to college after his suspension, and Susan - that's his mum by the way - was so angry with him, she'd grounded him until January. I mean, Jesus, what was he thinking?

'Hey!' said Ruby-lynn, as she and Scarlet got up, grinning.

'Hi,' I said, before Ruby-lynn gave me a hug and a kiss.

Natalie sat on the armchair at the far end of the room. Lizzy was laying down her dance mat, near her Playstation 2, which she had brought down from her room.

'S'cuse me,' came Fraser's voice from behind me. I stepped out of the way. Fraser was carrying his red P.V.C bean bag into the lounge and had put it in front of the coffee table between Scarlet and Lizzy's chairs, before dashing out to answer the door as the bell rang.

Me, Ruby-lynn and Jesse went to sit on the new, pale grey, three-seater sofa that Lizzy's mum, Jane, had bought from Dunelm, to match the armchairs.

'Hey!' Adam said when he and Dustin followed Fraser into the lounge.

'Alright?' I said.

'Having a movie night?' said Dustin. 'Us lot are going for a lads night out. Charlie and Stuart are coming too.'

'Dave would've been coming too but...' Adam grimaced, 'given, you know...'

'Yes, we do,' sighed Scarlet. When she'd found out about the load of trouble Dave had got into, she'd gone, 'Oh Dave, you are *such* a tard!'

Probably just as well Dave couldn't join us. He got completely blotto when we went out for Halloween and didn't give a damn that he was making an absolute prat of himself.

Fraser, Adam and Dustin had left, and then we went to the kitchen to help ourselves to drinks.

I was opening a Budweiser when I felt a pair of arms round my waist from my right. I put my arm round Ruby-lynn. I felt her head burrowing against my shoulder, her smooth, shiny pink hair brushing against my chest, before smiling up at me and asking if we were sharing a pizza. I agreed we'd get a large one, before giving her a kiss. Ruby-lynn then asked Lizzy where we were ordering the pizzas from, as she let go of me and poured herself a glass of Kopparberg's strawberry and lime cider, and Lizzy said we were getting a Dominoes takeaway, with sides and desserts, too.

'Nice!' I said, grinning. 'So, what's the plan, Liz? You're the host.'

'We're going to have a night packed with movie marathons, console games and drinking games,' Lizzy said, grabbing the Dominoes menu and leading us back to the lounge. 'Let's decide what pizzas we want first.'

Me and Ruby-lynn returned to our previous positions in the lounge and waited while Lizzy and Scarlet looked at the menu and decided what pizza they wanted to share. When me and Ruby-lynn had our turn, we both agreed on a large Texas Barbeque pizza.

We watched the first Men In Black film while we waited for our pizzas, as well as whilst we ate, then we were all stuffed, afterwards.

'Are we gonna play a drinking game now?' asked Natalie. Wizard Staff was what she'd most been looking forward to about tonight. Thank God we had plenty of beer! Turned out Natalie had bought loads of cans of Budweiser, Foster's, Amstel Beer and Carlsberg, as well as five rolls of duct tape. Wow, she was really desperate to play it!

Unsurprisingly, Jesse won, him being the beer fiend he is! And Lizzy hadn't even finished *one* can by then, so it was safe to say she lost!

Whilst being the drunkest out of the lot of us after winning Wizard Staff, Jesse then got even more drunk playing Pyramid, the Ring of Fire, and especially Fuzzy Duck, because of the number of times he kept buggering up, naturally from being pretty smashed already. He'd got so tanked up; in fact, he'd actually started blubbing!

Lizzy put on the second Men in Black film, whilst I sobered Jesse up on the Dominoes leftovers

'Oh God!' he cried. 'It's so sad!'

What? In what way is Men in Black 2 possibly a tearjerker?

'What's sad?'

'The Lion King!'

What?! Why was he suddenly talking about the Lion King? We were watching Men in Black!

'What are you talking about, you weirdo?' I said.

'His dad dies and he never sees him again! Except in the sky!' Jesse sobbed, drunkenly.

Sorry, did I say Dave acted like a prat when he was drunk? Well, that was nothing compared to this!

'You are completely off your face!' I said.

'Talk about stating the obvious,' said Scarlet.

It was past midnight when we decided to call it a night, after playing on the Xbox games that Scarlet had brought round, then playing on some of Lizzy's Playstation games, including Dance Edition, Test Drive 6, and Dynasty Warriors 3.

As Fraser was staying over at Dustin's, me and Jesse could sleep in his room. Ruby-lynn, Scarlet and Natalie were sleeping with Lizzy in her room, and no, *not* in a naughty, lesbian way, as I know how that must've sounded.

I gave Ruby-lynn a kiss goodnight and was just about to go into Fraser's room when I felt her grab my hand and pull me back for more!

'Get a room!' shouted Natalie, who was stood in the doorway to Lizzy's room. Me and Ruby-lynn withdrew from each other, then she went to Lizzy's room, giving me a cheeky smile over her shoulder. I said goodnight, before going into Fraser's room.

I can't help feeling slightly envious of Lizzy, Fraser, and Alistair. They have a big house with a swimming pool in the back garden, and hardly have to pay for anything. I won't go as far as to say they're spoilt, not even bordering on that, but Colvin and Jane do give them more than you'd expect.

I was just about to get into Fraser's bed, in just my Calvin Kleins, because I hadn't brought anything else to sleep in, when Jesse ran out of Fraser's room and into the bathroom. I ran after him. I really wished I hadn't, because Jesse had chucked up all over the bathroom floor and *eurgh!* Fucking hell it was rank! I warned the girls not to go in the bathroom because of the stench.

'Oh God, Mum and Dad are gonna go mental! Thank God the floor's made of tile,' Lizzy cried, running in and grabbing the loo roll. She yanked a large wad of it off the roll.

'Help me wipe it up,' she said, handing me another load of paper.

Damn you, Jesse, you owed me for this!

Luckily we were able to wipe up most of Jesse's upchuck. Lizzy had wiped up the remains with one of Jane's citrus scented floor wipes, before she fetched Jesse a bowl in case he was sick again.

The six of us had breakfast in the lounge on Sunday morning, so we were all watching the television with plates of bacon, fried eggs, tomatoes, mushrooms, sausages, hash browns and baked beans.

Me and Ruby-lynn sat together on the sofa. I asked her if this had been the first time she'd been round Lizzy's, and Ruby-lynn said it was and that it was nothing like she'd expected.

'What do you mean?' I asked.

'Well, for some reason, I expected her house to be a bungalow or something like that,' said Ruby-lynn, admitting with a smirk that she didn't know why and that it did sound really weird and random.

I wanted to ask if Ruby-lynn fancied meeting up later on today, but thought it probably best to take it easy, as I was still slightly hung over from the night before, and I imagined Ruby-lynn would be, too. I knew she couldn't meet me after college tomorrow, as she had plans.

Dad came to pick me and Natalie up at eleven o'clock.

As soon as we arrived home, I had a shower and put on some clean, fresh clothes. Luckily I'd recovered from my hangover by the evening. I don't know if the same could be said for Jesse, though.

On Monday, I didn't know what I wanted to get up to after college. I ended up going into town and having a little browse around Gamestation. I usually went there with Jesse, but Jesse was seeing Annie today, so I went on my own.

There was one particular shop assistant, who had darkish skin and ebony black hair and was extremely fit. We'd become rather chummy in the past times I'd come into the shop on days she'd be working there, as me and Jesse were regulars. Her name was Gabrielle.

It started off with her asking if we needed any help, as you should do with customers when you're working in a shop, adding, 'Come and get me if you need anything.'

It then went from the regular, professional offers for help to friendly conversations about console games, then, when I got to know her very well, I started chatting her up a bit, to which she would roll her eyes and smirk, which I could tell it had shown she'd seen the funny side of it.

This time, when I was looking at Playstation three games, Gabrielle sidled up to me.

'So, what's drawn you here today? The new Fifa game, or the shop assistant you enjoy coming to chat up?' she said.

I looked up at Gabrielle, grinned, and then said, 'Half and half.'

'I see,' said Gabrielle, smiling. 'Guess your wing man couldn't make it, this time.'

'Who, Jesse? Nah, he's seeing the other half, so I'm on my tod.'

'So you don't have a girlfriend yourself, then?'

'No,' I answered, without hesitation. 'Why you've not yet been taken off the market either, I will never know,' I added, smirking.

We chatted some more, throwing in a bit more flirty talk, before Gabrielle asked if I wanted to hang out some time, so we exchanged numbers.

I waited for Gabrielle as the shop was closing, and we walked up St Mary's Street together.

'When do you want to meet up?' asked Gabrielle.

'I'm free on Saturday,' I said. 'Do you fancy going to the cinema?'

'Definitely!' she'd said, eagerly. 'Would you be interested in seeing The Tourist?'

'Yeah, I'm cool with that,' I said, so we both agreed we'd meet at five o'clock next Saturday.

We continued up St Mary Street, towards the seafront, and said goodbye there, as Gabrielle was heading in a different direction.

I looked into her eyes and Gabrielle moved closer, and I knew she was leaning in for a kiss, and I didn't try to stop her. It felt amazing. When we broke apart, we said goodbye and I started walking down St Thomas Street, towards Bond Street.

In the car on the way home, I felt *so* guilty for letting Gabrielle kiss me, but there was no way Ruby-lynn would ever find out, was there?

Saturday 20th November 2010

I went on a cinema date with Gabrielle, after which we shared another kiss. I double dated her and Ruby-lynn for two weeks, and then I began to go out on dates with a few of the girls I'd made friends with at Euro Capital House College, including Abi.

On the first day at college, I'd made a remark on how short her skirt was.

'Did half your skirt tear off on the way to college this morning?' I'd asked her.

'It was that short when I bought it.'

'So you accidentally bought it several sizes too small, then?'

'Are you drunk?' she'd asked.

'I'm just intoxicated with you,' I replied.

'What's the deal?' she asked. 'Do you get showered with cards every Valentine's Day, or something?'

'And the rest!' I'd told her, proudly.

'You've never been on one night out without pulling at least one girl?'

'You've got it in one.'

She'd given me a smile, said, 'I'm impressed. And if you carry on impressing me, you might get lucky.'

Every day in class, me and Abi exchanged chat up lines. Like Ruby-lynn, Abi played hard to get, but she was taking longer to relent than Ruby-lynn was.

Tuesday 7th December 2010

At college, I asked Abi if she fancied going for a drink after college. We went to Moby Dick's, on the seafront. I bought both Abi and myself a Magner's pear cider each and we grabbed a table that had a sofa either side of it and sat down next to each other and talked.

'So, what's changed then?' I asked, curiously. 'Why am I lucky now, when I wasn't before?'

'That's for me to know, and for you to wonder,' was Abi's answer. Wow! I was truly taken aback by this new mysterious side she was suddenly displaying!

'You are full of surprises! This is obviously another part of your charm, that I've never seen before,' I told her before asking her with a grin, 'Exactly how lucky am I, tonight?'

'I'd have thought you'd have worked that one out yourself,' she said, smiling.

I looked into her eyes, and then Abi leaned towards me and kissed me for five seconds before breaking away.

'Now I have,' I said, before kissing Abi again. Another one in the bag!

We went back to her house and we were alone together in her room. Abi let me inside her mouth. I was amazed! I'd only just started dating her that night, whereas I'd been out with Ruby-lynn for a month and I hadn't even got that far with her yet!

I went home afterwards with my ego at a high.

I was powerful and popular. It was a free country, and there was no shame in what I was doing, as I wasn't hurting anyone. None of these girls knew anything about each other and what they didn't know wasn't going to harm them, was it? It wasn't like I'd shown any of these girls any indication that I was serious about them, and I made myself a rule not to go with more than one girl from each group of friends, so that none of them got jealous of each other or fell out over it, and I just wanted to have some fun and there wasn't anything wrong with that!

But I knew the others wouldn't agree, so I'd kept it from all of them, as Scarlet would only rat me out to Ruby-lynn, especially.

I was kind of out of control, I admit, barely thinking about what would happen if Ruby-lynn, Gabrielle or Abi found out I was also seeing two other girls at the same time, but keeping all three of them from each other had appeared to be surprisingly easy. For a start, Ruby-lynn and Gabrielle weren't at Euro Capital House College, like Abi was, and both of them had jobs in different workplaces and, whenever we arranged to meet up, we met in quiet places where we wouldn't be seen by anyone we knew, that or I just had Ruby-lynn round, or went round either hers, Gabrielle's or Abi's house.

I saw Abi the most, because we were both at Euro Capital House College five days a week, and I dropped in to visit either Ruby-lynn at Zellweger's, or Gabrielle at Gamestation.

I made excuses, telling Ruby-lynn I had to spend the weekend with the family, but then I met up with Gabrielle or Abi.

Monday 20th December 2010

We'd all broken up for the Christmas holidays on Friday. I didn't know whether or not I'd be seeing much of the three girls I was now dating. I knew Ruby-lynn and her parents were going away for Christmas, but I didn't know about the other two.

My lot, on the other hand, were staying at home, and my Uncle Robert, from Mum's side of the family was coming round on Christmas day, with Auntie Linda and cousin Diane, who's a year older than me, and a year younger than Natalie. This meant that Natalie and I were strongly needed to help with all the preparations.

I'd been so busy with my Christmas shopping, during the time I'd been three-timing Ruby-lynn, Gabrielle and Abi, and I had little time on my hands to wrap up all the presents I'd bought for the rest of the gang. We were all going round to Jesse's house to see each other for the last time until New Year's Eve and exchange presents. It had also been Dave's idea to do a Secret Santa, so I also had to buy a secret present for Lizzy as well. I'd bought her 'Money Tree' pot plant. It was meant as a joke. Even though Annie would be round Jesse's too, she wasn't involved in Secret Santa.

Me, Natalie and Annie were the first three to arrive at Jesse's, as we live the closest to him.

'Hey! Happy Christmas' he'd said, cheerfully, when me and Natalie arrived, with a plastic bag containing a drum of cheese footballs, a bag of Kettle Crisps, another drum of Twiglets, and a packet of cheese savours. We followed Jesse into the lounge, where Annie was sat, surrounded by Jesse's family's four cats; Tommy, a chubby brown tabby, Toby, a tail-less calico, Lucy, a feisty grey tabby, and Daisy, a mixed breed between a Persian and a black and white medium hair.

A Christmas tree stood next to the T.V, twinkling in bright white lights, and was decked out in gold and silver tinsel and gold and white baubles. An angel in a white and silver gown and white feathery wings was perched at the top of the tree. Tail-less Toby kept batting at some of the baubles. There was a compilation C.D of Christmas songs playing on the D.V.D player, and on the coffee table were plates of mince pies, stollen slices and slices of Christmas cake, and a bowl of mixed nuts, including Brazil nuts, walnuts, almonds and hazelnuts, with a nutcracker laid just next to the bowl.

'We've brought round a few snacks ourselves,' I said, as Jesse came into the room.

'Awesome!' said Jesse. 'Bring them to the kitchen, and I'll get bowls to put them in.'

We followed Jesse into the kitchen, where Flora was getting out all the drinks that she and Jesse had bought for his get-together. No alcohol, as it wasn't meant to be that kind of party this time. They'd bought bottles of Schloers, J2Os, Pepsi, Fanta, lemonade and cherryade, with some cartons of orange juice, to mix with the lemonade.

'Hi, you two,' she said, happily. 'Are you both looking forward to Christmas?'

'Really excited!' said Natalie, grinning.

'Jesse tells me you have a new woman in your life, Fred,' said Flora, sounding intrigued.

'Oh, er, yeah, I do,' I said, starting to feel a bit bad.

'Have we got any more bowls in the cupboard? Fred and Natalie have brought some snacks,' said Jesse.

'So, Fred, tell me more about this new girlfriend, then,' Flora said, getting out some more bowls.

If you've ever been in this situation, which I hope you haven't, you'll understand the struggle I'd felt to sound happy, and not guilty, as I told Flora all about Ruby-lynn, how we met and what I liked about her. Flora said she was very happy for me.

'So, it's still going well, then?' Jesse asked, as we put some of the snacks into the bowls.

I confirmed that we were still getting on great, which we were, with the exception of my secret infidelity.

We brought the snacks back to the lounge, and put them on the table.

The doorbell rang just before we heard Flora answer the door, say, 'Lizzy! Come on in!'

'Hi!' said Lizzy, as she came into the room. Judging by the bag Lizzy was carrying, she also appeared to have brought some snacks. She put the bags down and all five of us had a group hug. I could not wait for everyone else to arrive. I did really want to see Ruby-lynn again before she went away.

Lizzy and Jesse went to the kitchen for more bowls for the snacks Lizzy brought, which turned out, as she and Jesse brought the bowls back in, to be Peking spare rib and five spice flavour crackers, caramelised red onion and balsamic vinegar flavour crisps, and roast chicken and thyme flavour crisps. Lizzy had also brought some large packets of Maltesers, Minstrels, and Milky Way magic stars.

Twenty-five minutes later, I could hear another ring of the doorbell.

I rushed over to the window. I felt my stomach somersault. Scarlet and Ruby-lynn were outside the door!

I followed Jesse out into the hall to let them both in.

'You look gorgeous, as usual,' I said to Ruby-lynn, as I gave her a kiss. She wasn't very dressed up, just casually dressed, but that didn't matter to me.

'Likewise,' said Ruby-lynn.

We followed Jesse back to the lounge, where we got settled and all got ourselves drinks and were ready to start exchanging Secret Santa presents.

'Eldest gives theirs, first,' Jesse said, 'so that means Dave, who unfortunately couldn't be here through his own foolishness, but he did give me his present to give to the intended recipient, which is... Scarlet!'

Scarlet grinned, delightedly. Jesse picked up the present from Dave, got to his feet and walked over to Scarlet, wished her happy Christmas, sat back down, pulled his phone out of his pocket and held it up, no doubt planning to record Scarlet's reaction.

'What. The. *Fuck*!' Scarlet said when she opened them. Oh my actual God! It was a pair of mermaid style boob tassels! Lizzy let out a scream of laughter, and everyone was in hysterics!

'They suit you, actually,' Natalie teased.

I saw Scarlet had caught sight of Jesse holding up his phone, laughing his head off.

'Are you videoing all of this?!' she shrieked.

'Dave was looking forward to seeing your reaction!' Jesse said. 'He was gutted he couldn't come!'

Next was Natalie's turn, but her present was for Dave, which she said she'd give to him the next time she saw him.

Next came Scarlet's turn. Oh awesome, it was for me! She'd wrapped it black and gold wrapping paper. I gave her a hug to say thank you, before she went back to her seat. I unwrapped it. It was a pack of different coloured shot glasses.

'Nice!' I said, grinning. 'Cheers, Scarlet!'

Next was my turn. Yes! I stood up and gave Lizzy her present and a hug, and sat back down and everyone watched her unwrap the pot plant I bought for her.

'Oh!' she said, taken aback.

'Don't get excited, you can't grow *legitimate* money on it,' I joked.

'Oooh!' groaned Lizzy, pretending to sound disappointed.

Lizzy had given Jesse a collapsible pint glass. Jesse gave Ruby-lynn a unicorn mug and Ruby-lynn had given Natalie a set of wooden letters painted gold, spelling the word 'Love'.

Afterwards, we all distributed the rest of the presents and then had a marathon of Christmas movies.

As this was the last time I was going to see Ruby-lynn until she came back, I wanted some time alone with her, so, after we all finished watching the National

Lampoon's Christmas Vacation, I asked Jesse if me and Ruby-lynn could go up to his room, just so we could talk.

Me and Ruby-lynn entered Jesse's black and red room, and sat on his bed to talk. I still felt really, *really* bad for going behind her back, but the problem was, I also liked Gabrielle and Abi, just as much.

'So, as this is the last time I'm going to be seeing you before you go away, I wanted to say goodbye to you properly,' I told her, nervous as hell.

'I was intent on doing the same thing,' said Ruby-lynn. I looked into Ruby-lynn's eyes.

'I will get to see you on New Year's Eve, won't I?' I asked.

'Of course you will,' Ruby-lynn reassured me.

'When are you going away?' I asked her.

'We're going the day before Christmas Eve. We come back the day after Boxing Day,' Ruby-lynn told me. She went on to tell me about what she'd be doing in Wales, which was where she said her dad's parents lived.

'Well, it's nice that you'll be spending Christmas with your grandparents, as you probably don't get to see them a lot, what with them living in Wales,' I said. I then enlightened Ruby-lynn on what me and Natalie would be doing at Christmas.

'It sounds good,' said Ruby-lynn. We looked into each other's eyes. 'I'll miss you, Fred,' she added.

'I'll miss you, too,' I said, feeling worse than ever, now. Here she was, thinking I was the loveliest, sweetest guy, and I was lying to her!

'I know things didn't really start out that great when we first met, after the way you annoyed me, but I managed to get over it, when we became friends online and talked on Facebook,' she went on.

'I was so nervous the first time I met you,' I told her, honestly. 'I'd never been like that around anyone before. So, I guess that's why I did such silly things for your attention. But I regretted it later on, though.'

'I do hope we can stay together for a long time, because I really like you,' she said. I was so touched by this, and I told her, 'I feel the same,' and it was true, I *did* feel the same. But then I felt that way about the others. I was so confused.

'You're beautiful,' I told Ruby-lynn, gazing into her stunning sapphire eyes. She smiled.

We shared a kiss, and then we went downstairs to rejoin the others.

When the evening came to an end, and it was time for everyone to go home, everyone said goodbye to each other and wished each other a merry Christmas.

The next few days were bloody manic at home. Mum was under a lot of pressure with some very short notice preparations for Christmas Day, so me and Natalie were up to our eyes, helping her with it all.

Mum had put in an order for a turkey, over at Chilcott's farm, so we all drove out there to pick it up, the day before Christmas Eve.

On Christmas Eve, we were going out for lunch at Vaughan's. We caught the bus there, as both Mum and Dad wanted to be able to drink, without having to worry about driving, and then walked through town to the restaurant.

I had an awesome afternoon. Dad ordered a bottle of white wine, which I tried a glass of. Usually I prefer beer to wine, but I did like this type of white wine a lot. We ordered our food, then we pulled our crackers and all five of us kept our hats on throughout the rest of the afternoon.

As we were all full up after our main courses, none of us felt like having pudding, especially as we were having homemade eggnog and mince pies later on when we got back home. Me, Natalie and Mum and Dad went shares on the bill and we stayed for another hour before heading home. Even Max, who usually gets bored very easily whenever we eat out, had a whale of a time.

We arrived home and Mum made the eggnog, leaving out the spirits in Max's, as, being only seven, he's too young for alcohol, and we all drank our eggnog and had puff pastry mince pies.

As we'd had such a big lunch, we just had dips for dinner, in front of the T.V, whilst we watched White Christmas, and then Max came in with his Christmas list and asked if he could post it up the chimney to Santa.

'And don't forget the glass of milk and mince pie! And a carrot for Rudolph, too!' he kept reminding Mum and Dad, excitedly. Max is always very excitable at Christmas, bless him.

On Christmas morning, I woke up to Max bouncing up and down on me, squealing, 'Fred! Fred! Wake up! It's Christmas! Santa has come!'

I sat up, laughing, and got out of bed. Even though I was eighteen and Natalie was twenty, Mum and Dad still liked to fill our stockings as well as Max's.

The three of us brought our stockings full of presents downstairs to the lounge, where Mum and Dad were sat with cups of tea, and we took turns opening a present from our stockings. I had a desk top tin in the shape of a Stormtrooper, a packet of Marmite popcorn, a hand held fan, a pair of silver cufflinks that had a turtle on each of them, a new mobile cover for my Nokia, a pack of Marvel Top Trump cards and a silver hip flask.

We were all in stitches when Natalie saw that the price was still on one of her stocking presents.

'I didn't know Santa had to buy all the presents from the elves,' Dad joked.

After me, Natalie and Max finished unwrapping our stocking presents, we all took turns unwrapping one of our presents from under the tree.

I texted Lizzy, Jesse, Dave, Dan, Tom, Scarlet, Ruby-lynn, Gabrielle and Abi to wish them Happy Christmas. I probably wouldn't have got many replies until much later, because of the signal.

Uncle Robert, Auntie Linda, and my cousin Diane would be coming round at half past eleven, so we went upstairs to get dressed before they came round. I'd chosen my baby blue shirt, smart navy trousers, my smart black shoes and my black belt with the silver Gucci buckle.

Me and Max came down and I helped Mum put all the vegetables in the oven for roasting.

Natalie came down, all dolled up in a black sequined dress with a matching shrug and shoes, about a minute before Uncle Robert, Auntie Linda, and Diane arrived.

'Tell me about what you've both been up to!' Diane said to both me and Natalie.

'Well, Fred's got a new girlfriend!' said Natalie, proudly. Diane looked round at me, her eyes wide and her mouth open in amazement.

'No way! What, like a *proper* girlfriend? Who are you, and what have you done with Fred Curtis?' she cried. She knew I only ever had flings and not serious relationships with girls before.

I told Diane everything about Ruby-lynn, as we went to the lounge, once again trying to sound like everything was as it should be and I was doing nothing wrong. If I wasn't still feeling so damn guilty, I would've been able to go into greater detail with more enthusiasm.

We all went into the dining room where, laid out on the table, there were dishes of roast potatoes, carrots, broccoli, cauliflower, Yorkshire puddings, pigs in blankets, parsnips, and red cabbage. There were bowls of cranberry sauce, bread sauce, and stuffing, a jug of rich, dark gravy, and, in the middle of a table, was a large, oval plate with a roast turkey.

Eight shiny, red and gold Christmas crackers lay on the table. I was looking forward to sitting down, and started piling my plate high with some of everything on the table!

As soon we were all seated, Dad began carving the turkey and then we all began filling our plates with potatoes, stuffing, sausages, sauces and vegetables, topping our plates with gravy, and then I dug in immediately. It was all scrumptious, every bit of it!

After dinner, we pulled crackers, exchanged all the same jokes we'd heard countless times every year, and wore our cracker hats all day! My phone beeped four times, to say I'd had text messages. I got my phone out, secretly, as I knew Mum didn't like phones out at the table at any time of year, but at Christmas especially, and looked at the texts. They were from Lizzy, Jesse, Tom and Gabrielle, all wishing me happy Christmas. Nothing from Ruby-lynn or Abi yet. I put my phone back in my pocket.

We had Christmas pudding for dessert, with single cream, before going back to the lounge and exchanging more presents.

I'd had an absolutely fabulous Christmas. When Diane, Uncle Robert and Auntie Linda left at half past five, we were all too bloody knackered to do much. We'd cleared everything off the table, put all the leftovers in Tupperware containers and put them in the fridge, and left all the cutlery and crockery on the kitchen work tops, agreeing we'd tidy it all away the next day.

My enjoyment of the day made me forget about how awful I felt for all the girls I'd been seeing at the same time.

When I went to bed, my phone beeped again. I picked up my phone and looked at it. It was a text from Ruby-lynn. It said, 'Happy Christmas xxx.' I smiled, put down my phone, snuggled down and felt myself falling into a deep sleep.

As agreed, we spent most of Boxing Day tidying the house, especially the kitchen, because of all the debris from the day before. The day whizzed by because we'd been so busy. I was really looking forward to New Year's Eve, as me and Natalie would be seeing the rest of the gang then. And I'd missed Ruby-lynn *so* much, as well as Gabrielle and Abi. I'd been texting them all every day, telling them about what I got up to on Christmas day and, in return, finding out what they did at Christmas. Gabrielle had spent Christmas day with her brother, who had a house and started a family of his own. Abi's family had been lucky enough to get a lunchtime reservation at the Trumpet Major in Dorchester on Christmas Day.

Gabrielle asked if I fancied coming out with her on New Year's Eve, so I had to make an excuse, saying I was going to be away.

The next few days snailed by. We'd been out for walks and gone round to see my gran and grandpa from Mum's side of the family.

Friday 31st December 2010

At long last, New Year's Eve came.

Me and Natalie had arranged to meet Jesse, Lizzy, Ruby-lynn and Scarlet in the William Henry and we'd have drinks there, first. When we arrived, the others were already there, sat at a table near the back.

'Oh my God, hi!' Lizzy squealed with excitement, the minute she saw us. I saw the rest of them look round and they saw us too.

'Fred!' cheered Jesse.

'Hi,' Ruby-lynn said, smiling, shyly, when me and Natalie had come over to the table they were sitting at.

'Hey,' I said, grinning, before we kissed, and then I sat down on the seat Ruby-lynn had saved for me, before Jesse started telling us all about how he, Flora and Rochella had spent most of the holidays seeing their extended family.

No matter what the occasion is, Flora always invites her very large extended family, as well as all her friends, whether it's an anniversary of any sort, or a birthday party to celebrate a special age, like eighteen, twenty-one, thirty or forty. This extended family includes a vast number of not just first cousins, aunties, uncles, grans and granddads, but also first cousins once, twice or thrice removed, second cousins, some of which also removed once, twice or thrice, great aunties, great uncles, I could go on. I've met them so many times and still can't remember who's who.

Scarlet had been at her mum's for most of Christmas Eve, before going to her dad's and spending Christmas Day with him.

After we had a drink, we headed off to the Lazy Lizard. We got some more drinks there, and sat down at a table by the window.

'Are we gonna go on the bridge for the countdown to the New Year?' Ruby-lynn asked, eagerly.

'God, yeah! We have to!' said Lizzy.

Every year, on New Year's Eve, we'd planned to go up to the town bridge and countdown the last ten seconds until the New Year, but, either we missed it when we went out, or we didn't even go out for whatever reason.

My phone beeped. I got it out and looked at it. It was a text from Abi.

'Im in Aura. You nearby? xx' it said. I did want to see Abi, but could I get away long enough, without being caught?

53

Before I had a chance to change my mind, I told Lizzy I'd just seen someone I knew just walk by and that I was going to go and say hi. I got to my feet, and ran out the door. Outside the entrance to Aura, I texted Abi to say I was outside, then waited. A minute later, she came out.

'Hey,' she said, grinning. 'Had a good Christmas?'

'Yeah, great, thanks,' I said. 'You?'

'It was good, thanks,' said Abi. 'I've missed you over Christmas.

'I've missed you too,' I said.

'Do you want to join me and my mates?'

I quickly made an excuse that I wasn't going to stay out all night, as I wasn't fussed. I hated lying but there was nothing else I could do.

'Could we maybe meet up next weekend?' Abi suggested, looking hopeful.

'Yeah, sure,' I said.

'Great,' said Abi, grinning.

We looked into each other's eyes. Abi gave me the sweetest smile. My God, I did love her smiles!

I couldn't hold myself back. I leaned in, cupped Abi's face and kissed her for fifteen seconds, before breaking away.

'I'll text you,' I said, then went back to the Lazy Lizard.

My head was a fucking mess. I was crazy about Ruby-lynn, Gabrielle, and Abi. What was I going to do?

I seriously hoped I wouldn't bump into Gabrielle whilst we were out, especially after the lie I'd told her, as well as if she saw me with Ruby-lynn.

We still had a few more hours before the countdown, so we went onto a few more clubs, meeting Annie along the way, until, at half past eleven, we made our way to the town bridge, where Stuart, Charlie, Tom and Dan said they'd meet us. We all stood by the railing on the bridge. I stood between Ruby-lynn and Jesse.

'Hey, let's start at the last minute!' shouted Tom, jokily. 'Sixty! Fifty-nine! Fifty-eight! Fifty-seven!'

'Tom, shut up! You know you're not as funny as me,' laughed Dan.

I looked round at Ruby-lynn.

'Have you ever done this before?' I asked.

'What, do the countdown on the bridge?'

I nodded.

'I've never really though of it before,' Ruby-lynn said.

'I'm glad we've finally got round to doing it this year,' I said.

'It does sound more fun than staying at home and watching it on the T.V,' Ruby-lynn said.

'I look forward to seeing what the New Year brings us,' she said.

'Me too,' I said. Both me and Ruby-lynn looked at each other, and then up at the sky. It was dotted with stars. It was a perfect night.

At ten seconds to midnight, we all shouted out the countdown to the New Year, at the tops of our voices.

On the stroke of midnight, we all cheered. All the couples, Ruby-lynn and myself included, kissed, and we were all crying 'Happy New Year!' as we hugged each other.

'HAPPY TWENTY ELEVEN!' shrieked Natalie, as she and Lizzy threw their arms around each other. I broke away from Ruby-lynn and hugged all my mates.

This was the best New Year's Eve I'd ever had. I'd never forget it. And I looked forward to seeing what things the new year would bring me.

Chapter 5:

Natalie's First

Saturday 8th January 2011

I reached New Look, and V was already stood outside.

I met him at the White Hart in September. I went there for a quick drink after work with some of my mates from work. We started talking, then V asked, 'Can I add you on Facebook?'

We talked online for four weeks, then started dating in October. I wanted a boyfriend who was cool and exciting, and, as far as I was concerned, V fit the bill perfectly!

He was going to take me on another shopping spree. He sometimes would treat me to whole new outfits at a time, complete with a new handbag and some jewellery to go with it, most weekends. I didn't have to pay for *anything*. I felt so lucky to be with him.

I would always want to make sure I was nicely done up, so I wore my white, long sleeved, bat wing top with the black corset bodice which has gold buttons, my ruched, magenta pencil skirt, gold hoop earrings, some black, patterned tights and my black shiny ankle boots. I'd chosen to wear all that with my magenta snake skin cross body bag with a gold chain strap, my faux leopard print fur coat, and a selection of gold jewellery to match. I'd backcombed most of my t-section and secured it at the back of my head, leaving out my side swept fringe.

'Hey, tasty!' he said. I loved it when he called me that! I grinned.

V gave me a kiss, and then said, 'Ready to be spoiled again? I want to buy you some jewellery, to go with those sexy dresses I bought you before Christmas.'

'I'm always ready to be spoiled,' I said, smiling, and we both went inside. We went upstairs, where the jewellery was, V grabbed a basket, and we both started looking at the jewellery.

I was looking at the chokers. The first one that caught my attention was a pink, diamante choker. I decided I'd have that one, and put it in the basket.

'How about this one as well?' said V, holding up a silver charm choker.

'I like!' I said, eagerly, and V put it in the basket.

Next, we looked at earrings. I showed V a pair of rose gold, hexagon hoop earrings that I wanted.

'You'd look very sexy with a nice pair of hoops,' said V, so into the basket they went.

I also went crazy over a pair of gold orb and tassel drop earrings, a pack of five gold charm bangles, a pack of six gold rings, a gold diamante Taurus star sign pendant necklace, a crystal cubic zirconium square pendant necklace, a pair of silver layered hoop earrings, a silver diamante sweetheart collar necklace, and a pack of five silver embellished glitter rings.

When I'd finished looking at the jewellery, we started looking at the handbags. V showed me a grey, leather-look ring handle tote bag, which was definitely going in the basket. I also spotted a round, black and beige faux snakeskin shoulder bag that I liked, not to mention a rose gold flat clutch bag, a brown leopard print suedette cross body bag with a gold ring and handle chain strap and the coolest black leather-look, bowler bag with gold studs I'd ever seen!

Finally, we looked at the shoes. I picked out three pairs; some grey suedette, bow side stilettos, some strappy leopard print sandals and a pair of dark red espadrille wedges.

We joined the queue and V paid.

'That's two hundred and seven pound, eighty-five, please,' said the lady at the till. Fucking. Hell.

'Are you sure you're okay to spend that much on me?' I asked.

'This counts for nothing against the eight hundred pounds I make a day,' V said.

Eight hundred pounds a day?! I knew he did earn a lot, especially as he dealt drugs, but did that really make him that much money?

We went to have a drink and something for lunch in the White Hart, then, after visiting a couple more shops, we walked back to the multi-storey car park, where V had parked his car. It was a fire opal red convertible Mercedes E-Class. Every time we went out, we would drive with the roof down, as long as it wasn't raining, and I loved every second of it!

We drove back to V's house, which was on Bowleaze Coveway, so not far from Lizzy's house. It was a white, poured concrete, terraced, three-storey townhouse, with doors and floor length windows, all of which had black frames.

V parked round the back of the house. We got out, unloaded all my shopping, and went inside.

'Let me take your coat,' he said.

'Aw, thanks, you're so sweet,' I said.

We went upstairs to the first floor, where the open plan lounge, dining area and kitchen were. The walls were painted white with European oak effect flooring.

The lounge had darkest brown leather sofas with a matching armchair, and a forty-nine inch screened Samsung T.V stood on a T.V stand in the corner, near the doors to the balcony, facing the open sea. I could *not* believe how lucky V was, to have been able to find such a big, funky, modern house with an amazing view of the sea!

V sat down on the sofa and invited me to sit next to him.

'Anything you fancy watching on the telly?' V asked. 'Or shall we just talk?'

'Let's talk,' I said. V smiled and kissed me. We carried on kissing as I felt V pull me up onto his lap and run his hands up my back.

After another thirteen seconds, he broke away, suddenly.

'I meant to ask, I need you to do me a favour, if that's okay?' he said.

'Yeah, sure, what is it?' I asked.

'I have some cannabis that I can't keep in the house,' V explained. 'Can you keep a hold of it for me?'

He trusted me with something this important?! I did not hesitate to say, 'Yeah, of course I can!' I was so flattered, though I knew it was wrong, but I didn't care.

'Tell me more about your gang,' I said. He often talked about them, and I liked hearing about them.

'I doubt I've actually got much left to tell you about the times we get up to stuff together,' V chuckled.

'But you guys do everything together,' I said.

'I've only told you about the good times,' said V.

'What do you mean by that?' I asked.

'Well... things don't always go great when I'm with the gang,' he said. 'It's not like we just get totally fucked and have a laugh every time we see each other. I did once go to jail for armed robbery, a few years ago, when I didn't have very much money.'

He'd been to jail?! For armed robbery?! I was alarmed!

'Why did you do it?' I couldn't help asking him.

'I know it's bad,' he said, 'but back then, I would do whatever I had to do to eat.'

I started to feel a bit frightened. I was beginning to realise I could get seriously hurt if I did anything to upset him or anyone in his gang.

But, equally, I knew that if ever I needed their help, I could call on them, and that made me feel safe. And that was why I was with V, because he protected me and spoiled me rotten. He looked after me. And I loved dating someone who most people respected and feared. I felt lucky he'd even spoken to me on the day we met.

I stayed at V's house for four more hours, most of that time we spent together in V's bed, until he drove me home at half past seven in the evening.

'Guard the weed with your life,' he reminded me, when we said goodbye. I promised I would, then we kissed, and then I got out and V drove off.

I was in such high spirits to have found such a fucking mint, awesome boyfriend. I looked forward to showing Fred and Mum and Dad all the presents he'd bought me.

But, when I got in, Mum did not seem in the mood.

'Where on Earth were you, young lady? Your supper's been getting cold!' she said, the minute I'd put my foot through the doorway. I was really fucked off at this. Was I just not allowed to spend time with my boyfriend?

Fuck, I must've said that out loud, because Mum said, 'Of course, I don't have a problem with you seeing your boyfriend, but I just wish you'd let me know.'

I said I was sorry for not texting her, then went to the dining room, to eat my cold sausage casserole, mash and cabbage.

Oh yeah, and I suddenly remembered I had a bag of cannabis I was meant to be hiding for V. As soon as I finished my dinner, I got up, rushed out to the hall, ran up to my room with my handbag, went to my room, shut the door, and rummaged in my handbag for the drugs.

I hid it at the very back of the top drawer in my dressing table, where no one would ever think to look. I knew it was unlikely that anyone would come round here, looking for it, but I just wanted to be on the safe side.

On the way back downstairs, I saw Fred.

'Hey,' I said. 'How's things with Ruby-lynn?'

I'd been ever so excited when Fred and Ruby-lynn started dating. She was his first proper girlfriend, and they made an awesome couple. Lizzy said that too.

'Yeah, I saw her today, actually,' he said. 'I was round her house, and we watched the Matrix films.'

What was going on there? Fred wasn't even into the Matrix films, and they didn't sound like the sort of films that Ruby-lynn would watch.

'I didn't think she was into that sort of stuff,' I said, confused. Fred's eyes widened.

'Er...' he said, sounding awkward. He then said, 'Um, I dunno, maybe she used to not like them.'

But I wasn't sure I believed that. But why on Earth would both Fred and Ruby-lynn waste their time, watching films they weren't even remotely interested in? It didn't make sense.

'Okay,' I said, uncertainly. There was no point in asking any more questions. If he were hiding something, he would've started being defensive.

'Being spoiled by your boyfriend again?' said Fred, following me down the stairs. God, I hoped he wouldn't start grilling me.

I played it cool. I stopped in the hallway, turned around, and casually said, 'Yeah. He likes to do that,' and carried on walking to the kitchen.

'Sure he does,' he said. I heard his footsteps as he followed me. What was that supposed to mean?

'Well, yeah. He does. He looks after me; it's called *love*, Fred. You should understand that, you're in a relationship,' I said.

'Of course I understand,' said Fred, 'enough to know that love isn't just based on how much money a man spends on you.'

I glared at him. Of all things to ruin my mood! I got out a can of Strongbow, walked past him, out of the kitchen, through the dining room and went to the lounge, wanting to get away from him before he could say any more. I sat down on the sofa in the bay window.

Mum and Dad were watching Deal Or No Deal. I drank my cider, pissed off about Fred. He was doing it again. Questioning whether V actually cared about me, just like he'd done with the other boyfriends I'd been with, who *did* care about me, but were just bad influences! Fred just didn't get it.

I couldn't wait to see V again. We'd arranged a date on Tuesday. Just a casual one. We were going to go and have dinner at the Marquis Granby, which is walking distance from my place.

I was meeting the girls for coffee tomorrow. The four of us like to go to Costa, to have a girly chat. I was going to wear some of the new jewellery that V bought me, along with one of the new bags and pairs of shoes. He'd bought me a new pair of boots in Priceless. They were wine red suede ankle boots with gold zips and I could not wait to show them off. I could think of the perfect outfit V bought me before Christmas that would go with them.

I took all my shopping upstairs and, before I went to bed, I chose my gold bangles, the black bag with the gold studs, my gold and diamante stud earrings, my red and black sleeveless leopard print peplum top, black leggings with leopard print down the sides, a skinny leopard print belt and my other faux leopard print fur coat, the one with the black faux leather sleeves. I do love my animal prints. Hope you can tell.

Just as I'd finished brushing my teeth, I saw Fred stood in the doorway. Oh, what the fuck did he want now? I spat the water and toothpaste out, then turned to face him.

'What's up?' I said.

'Are you still meeting Scarlet, Ruby-lynn and Lizzy tomorrow?' Fred asked. For some reason, he sounded anxious. When I said I was, I noticed Fred turn white in the face, looking absolutely terrified. What was wrong?

'Are you all right?' I asked, frowning.

'Yeah, I'm fine, just... don't tell Ruby-lynn I told you we met up today. She... doesn't like... doesn't like me going on about it too much, okay?' said Fred, nervously.

'Er, okay,' I said, confused. I went to my room, starting to get suspicious.

Fred had been acting very weirdly since the Christmas holiday ended. Ruby-lynn said that whenever she asked if she could come and meet him after college on a Monday, he'd say she couldn't and make some random excuse. Jesse also said that whenever he finished in his class first, he would come to meet Fred after his class, and that Fred would always be the first one out of the classroom, and would always hurry Jesse away.

I still didn't want to pry, though. I got into bed and went to sleep.

I started getting ready for my coffee morning with the girls as soon as I got up the next morning. I did my make-up, got dressed, then went down for some toast and marmalade with a glass of orange juice for breakfast.

After I'd finished, I brushed my teeth, grabbed my chosen handbag from my room, and brought it downstairs, and put my purse, iPod, and mobile in it.

'Another new handbag?' said a voice. I looked over my shoulder. It was Mum.

'V bought it for me,' I told her.

'Why do you call him V?' she asked, curiously.

I just shrugged it off by saying it was a nickname.

'Be careful with this one,' Mum warned me, kindly, and she gave me a hug, adding, 'Have fun with the girls.'

I caught the bus into town, and then walked to Costa. None of the others were outside, so I went inside and looked around to see if any of them were there. They obviously hadn't arrived yet. I chose a table not too far from the counter, so that they would see me as soon as they came in. I didn't have to wait very long, before they arrived.

'Girlies!' I called over to them. Scarlet was the first to look round and see me.

'There she is,' she said to Lizzy and Ruby-lynn. They came over and all four of us exchanged hello hugs, then me and Scarlet went to get the coffees, whilst Ruby-lynn and Lizzy waited at the table. I saw Scarlet notice my awesome new boots whilst we were in the queue.

'*They're* nice!' she said, enthusiastically. Yay, she was impressed!

'Yeah, V bought them for me yesterday,' I said, pleased, but then I noticed the smile fading slightly from Scarlet's face. Not so much "Yay!" after all then. Obviously Scarlet thought I was only after him because of all the money he spent on me. Typical.

'I'm not with him just because he spoils me,' I said. 'I love him.'

Scarlet leant back in shock.

'It's a bit early to be using the L word, don't you think?' she said.

'Not when you just know you feel that way about someone,' I told her. I did not want this leading to another argument. I was still annoyed about what Fred said last night, and I did not need someone else questioning me about it!

'What can I get you?' asked the lady at the till, so I ordered Lizzy a hot chocolate with cream and marshmallows, and myself a latte, and Scarlet ordered both Ruby-lynn and herself an Americano, each, with milk for Ruby-lynn and without milk for herself.

'Things still good with Fred?' Lizzy asked Ruby-lynn, as soon as me and Scarlet had come back to the table with the drinks and sat back down.

'Brilliant, thanks,' said Ruby-lynn, joyfully. She didn't say anything about the day before, though. Maybe Fred was telling the truth when he said that Ruby-lynn didn't like talking about it too much. Maybe she wanted to keep it quiet for a bit. But she did seem very happy, so I didn't worry about why Ruby-lynn would want it kept quiet.

I showed Scarlet, Ruby-lynn and Lizzy the new jewellery, handbag and boots that V bought me.

'Did I mention he drove a Mercedes and lived in a three-storey townhouse?' I gloated. 'I think I did mention it, once.'

'Yeah, once every time we hang out,' said Scarlet, smirking.

'Whatever, at least I'm with someone exciting, who protects me,' I retorted.

'You *do* know his gang runs our area, don't you?' Scarlet said, in a warning tone, looking at me with her eyes wide in that cautious way people usually did when trying to make you aware of something important and serious.

Anyway, as a matter of fact, I did *not* know that his gang ran our area, but now that Scarlet had said it, wow! I felt even more delighted at my luck at the man I got to be with. How was I meant to resist boasting about how, everywhere him and me went, people would talk to him with the utmost respect?

'Do you know who you're dealing with?' Ruby-lynn asked, frowning. For fuck sake! Now Ruby-lynn was being dismissive about it as well.

'I *do* actually, and I'm *proud* to be dating him, thank you very much!' I came back with. What was so terrible? V was a great guy and really cared about me! Yeah, he'd been to jail before, but Scarlet and Ruby-lynn were just jealous, and I was *not* going to let it get to me! *They* had the problem, not *me*!

Only Lizzy said nothing, I noticed. I knew it was because she didn't really want to get involved in an argument when she knew we were supposed to be having a joyful, gracious girly coffee and catch up.

Ruby-lynn and Scarlet seemed to have given up. Lizzy, blatantly wanting to make light of the situation and avoid any arguments, changed the subject and asked Ruby-lynn, Scarlet and me what we were all getting for Fred for his birthday, as it was in a couple of weeks.

'Damn, I totally forgot it was so soon!' said Scarlet.

'I would've said he'd want to go clubbing,' I said. 'Except he only ever did that to go out on the pull, which he clearly doesn't need to, now he's got you, Ruby-lynn.' I smiled at Ruby-lynn, and she smiled back.

'Maybe he'll want to go out and have drinks?' Scarlet suggested. 'But maybe we should probably wait and see what he invites us out to do.'

We talked about a few other things, such as how our jobs and courses were going and how Lizzy's brother's band, Rebel Tourbus, was coming along.

'They're looking for a place where they can practice, where they won't disturb anyone, at the moment,' Lizzy told us. Ruby-lynn asked if they'd written any songs yet, but Lizzy said that they were just starting off doing covers of other songs, and would take it from there.

'They're practicing their cover for "Outta My Head," by Darren Styles. The only downside is, both verses in Darren Styles' version are exactly the same, so I don't know what Fraser and the boys plan on doing about that,' said Lizzy.

We talked more about where and when Rebel Tourbus might perform, before Scarlet asked what we wanted to do after we'd finished our drinks.

'We could just have a walk around town and, you know, look at all the funny people?' Lizzy suggested with a grin.

"Look at all the funny people." An expression Lizzy got off her dad. Uncle Colvin always says that, as well as his own dad, even if there isn't actually anything funny about the billions of other people walking through town.

When we all left Costa at two o'clock, we did indeed walk down St Mary Street, though we were too busy talking about other matters, like how things were at home for us all, to be looking at all the "funny people."

'Money's really tight for my mum,' Ruby-lynn said, 'like, *really* tight. She's not had money problems like that before. Well, not ones this bad. I don't know what's going on but she seems like she's getting really frustrated by it.'

Ruby-lynn told us that her mum had asked her to increase the monthly standing order to her account, as she really needed money at the moment and left all the food shopping to her dad because she didn't have much money.

I didn't say anything. I felt so guilty. There I was, bragging about the amount of money that V had spent on me, and yet, poor Ruby-lynn was left with hardly any because of some unexplained money problems her mum was having!

'I'm so sorry, Ruby-lynn,' I said. 'I wouldn't have bragged so much about V if I'd known.'

'It's okay,' said Ruby-lynn.

I heard a shout, coming from ahead of us. It sounded like someone was calling Lizzy's name. I looked round at Lizzy and saw her looking straight ahead, grinning. I looked down St Mary's Street, and saw Charlie hurrying over to all four of us, waving.

'Hey, Lizzy,' he'd said, as soon as he reached us. He and Lizzy kissed.

'Alright, girls?' he said, acknowledging the other three of us.

'Yeah, we're good,' I said.

'Don't mind if I steal Lizzy away do you?' Charlie asked us. We all said it was fine, before Charlie asked Lizzy if she was okay to come to the Harbourside Grill House. Lizzy let out a groan.

'We *always* go to the Harbourside Grill House!'

'It's my favourite place!' Charlie protested, before Lizzy retorted that Charlie had said always said he hated it there, but caved in when Charlie insisted he wanted to go.

That was a bit weird. Charlie insisted on going to a particular place that he didn't even like, every time he met up with Lizzy? But hey, maybe Fraser knew Charlie hated it there so he reckoned it would be the last place Fraser would think to look for him and Lizzy, if Fraser was starting to suspect anything and decided to start poking his nose in where it didn't belong, that was. If he actually did, he'd probably think to look somewhere he knew Charlie liked to go, though I wasn't entirely sure whether Fraser had got suspicious at all, never mind to the point where he'd stalk his own sister and one of his mates!

'See you later!' Lizzy called to us, as she let Charlie take her by the hand and lead her away.

I did sort of have a good time, despite the argument I had with the girls about V, and I didn't mean to get so snappy at Ruby-lynn about him, I just didn't get what everyone's problem was, that was all.

On the bus back home, I thought some more about V. I could hardly believe he wouldn't have turned a corner and decided to turn his life around after going to prison, though he did deal drugs. As he was driving me home last night, he'd even asked if I fancied coming on a night out with him when he planned to sell some of it. I'd jumped at the chance. I'd be entitled to some, totally free, as I *was* his girlfriend after all!

I had a shower and hair wash when I got home. I had work on Monday, so, when I finished in the shower, I decided to paint my nails.

I sat in front of the T.V, filing my nails before I painted them. I'd chosen plum red. Fred came into the lounge and sat with me.

'Ruby-lynn still seems happy with you,' I said, happy for my brother. Fred frowned.

'Yeah? Why wouldn't she be? Things are still great between us,' said Fred. I told him Ruby-lynn had seemed coy and hadn't mentioned yesterday, to which Fred said, 'See? I said she wanted it kept discreet.'

'You definitely weren't lying there,' I said, applying base coat to my nails.

'Why would I?' asked Fred, starting to sound slightly defensive. Was he hiding something?

'I wasn't saying you would,' I told him, truthfully. 'It was just s'posed to be...' I couldn't think of what to call it, but Fred nodded, looking down, which proved he understood.

I blew my nails dry, and left them for a bit, before painting on the first coat of nail varnish.

'Had a good time with the girls?' said Fred.

'I did, actually,' I said. I knew better than to tell him about the row I almost had with Ruby-lynn about V, as I knew Fred would only go on about how right she was and how I should listen to her and not argue.

I decided to tell Fred about the latest news Lizzy gave me, Scarlet and Ruby-lynn about Rebel Tourbus, as he was just as interested in how things were going as I was.

'I will definitely go and watch them when they perform,' he said. 'Lizzy's probably hoping we all will, and I definitely will be.'

I was looking forward to Rebel Tourbus's first performance, whenever and wherever that would be. I hoped we could all go as a big group to watch.

I applied the next coat of nail varnish. My phone suddenly beeped, making me jump out of my skin. I ended up getting nail varnish all over my left middle finger nail, which I'd been painting at the time.

'Crap,' I said. 'Fred, please can you fetch me my cotton buds and nail varnish remover from my dressing table? They're in the top drawer.'

'Sure thing,' he said, standing up. He left the room, and I heard him climb the stairs. I was just about to pick up my phone to read my text, which I knew would be from V, when I suddenly remembered...

'Shit!'

...I'd hidden the bag of weed in the drawer I'd just asked Fred to rummage through!

'Fred!' I shouted, frantically, quickly getting to my feet and racing up the stairs to my room to stop him. 'Fred, don't worry, I'll get -'

Too late. Fred was already stood by the dressing table, holding up the bag of cannabis, and he was giving me the most unimpressed look ever.

'Did *he* give it to you?' he said, very angry. I was shocked, unable to say a thing.

'First you go for a truant, then you date a thief, now you're with a drug dealer. Has he ever been to prison?' Fred questioned me. I knew I couldn't tell him the truth about that.

'No,' I said, though I knew I didn't sound the least bit convincing. 'No, he most definitely hasn't.' Fred glared at me. He clearly didn't believe me.

'You're lying,' he said. 'Natalie, gangs are violent and what you see as his glamorous lifestyle is just cruel and shallow.'

I marched over to Fred, snatched the bag of cannabis, threw it back in the drawer, grabbed my cotton buds and nail varnish remover out of my drawer and rammed it shut.

'I don't have to explain myself to you,' I said, storming out of the room, 'not when I know you're hiding something from Ruby-lynn, I mean why the fuck would you two watch the Matrix when you're not even into that film? I will ask her, myself!'

'Please don't!' Fred said, suddenly sounding desperate.

I stopped. What was he hiding? I slowly turned around to face him.

'I will,' I told him, slowly, 'if you tell Mum or Dad about the weed.' Fred looked down and nodded. He seemed to have got it.

'If you keep schtum about the weed,' I went on, 'I will keep schtum about the Matrix, and I won't ask you another question about Ruby-lynn. Deal?'

'Deal,' Fred agreed. I went back to the lounge and began to clean up the mess I'd made with my nail varnish. Whilst I let it dry, I remembered I had a text. I read it. It was from V, just as I expected.

'Hey sexy! Looking forward to seeing you on Tuesday. Did you hide the weed? xxxxx.'

It was a good thing my mobile was a touch screen, as texting on a phone with buttons would've smudged my nail varnish. I texted back, saying I'd hidden it as soon as I got in and it was safe and sound, and no one would ever find it, though this obviously wasn't true, because someone *did* find it.

I applied a third coat and let it dry.

We had a dinner of jacket potatoes with salad, coleslaw and mayonnaise at six o'clock. Luckily my nail varnish had dried by then, but I hadn't put a topcoat on yet.

When dinner had finished, me and Fred had to help Mum and Dad clean up in the kitchen. I dried up whilst Mum washed up, and Fred and Dad loaded the dishwasher. When the kitchen was clean, we all sat down in the lounge, and Mum and Dad wanted to watch Homes Under The Hammer, whilst I topped my plum painted nails with top coat.

When I went up to bed at ten o'clock, I was still shitting myself that Fred knew about the cannabis. *Why* did I have to hide it in that drawer? And *why* did I have to send Fred up to go ferreting about in there? At least I found a way to keep him quiet. But what the hell was Fred hiding, that he was so desperate to keep a secret, he wouldn't rat on me about the drugs? I lay awake in bed and thought about this.

I had work at nine the next morning. I got up at seven, went down for some breakfast, then went back upstairs to do my long, straight, light brown locks up into a backcombed French twist, do my make-up and got dressed.

I went downstairs, where Dad was waiting, grabbed my bag and coat, then said goodbye to Mum.

Dad dropped me off at the back of Debenhams. I thanked him as I got out, we said goodbye, and then I grabbed my bag, shut the door, and started walking to work.

I arrived at work at ten minutes to nine and, as per usual, went to hang up my coat and stow my bag in my locker. My colleague, Martin, was in the staff kitchen, his head buried in the fridge.

'Pete better not have drunken all the bloody milk again,' he mumbled to himself.

'You are actually looking for it the proper way, this time, aren't you?' I said.

Martin straightened up and saw me. He never looks for things properly. If it's something in the fridge or a cupboard he's looking for, he'd open the door, have a quick glance and say, 'I can't find it,' without even moving anything out of the way!

'Hey, Nat,' he said.

'Hi,' I said, walking over to the fridge. I saw the pint of Tesco's semi-skimmed milk in the fridge door. I got it out and held it up.

'Is *this* the milk you were looking for?' I asked, smirking at Martin. Martin thanked me, and took it, giving me a sheepish look. He offered to make me a cup of coffee, as he was making himself one. I accepted immediately, since I hadn't had any coffee this morning.

'How's things with your man?' Martin asked, getting out another mug.

'Great, thanks,' I said, still left unsure by the argument I had with Fred. 'He splashed more money on me on Saturday. I'm seeing him again tomorrow night. How's things with yours?'

Last time I'd been at work, Martin had told me, happily, how he and his boyfriend Rod, who he'd been with for eighteen months, had moved into their new rented flat.

'Still good,' he said, putting a spoonful of coffee into my mug. He made both cups of coffee, then we carried our mugs to our desks.

I had a busy morning, arranging travel for various business and vacation customers and setting up and organizing trips.

My tea break was at eleven, so I went and had a fag out the back of the shop, whilst Martin covered for me, until I had to go back in and get back to work at twenty past eleven.

I could barely concentrate on my work. Even though I didn't want to let Scarlet and Ruby-lynn get to me, my mind was whirling with everything they said.

I was so lost in wonder about what to do that I very nearly made a mistake with a reservation I was booking.

At lunch, me and Martin decided to go down to Subway. I ordered a chicken tikka sub with a bowl of melted cheese nachos and a bottle of Oasis.

'You been alright?' asked Martin taking a bite out of his barbecue beef sub when we'd sat down and ate. 'You seemed distracted earlier. What's up?'

'I'm fine,' I said. 'Just been a busy morning.'

'Yeah, fair enough' Martin agreed. By the time Martin had finished, we had fifteen minutes before our lunch hour ended. Martin's the slowest eater I know.

We were walking back down St Mary's street, when I really wanted to talk to Lizzy. I knew Lizzy hadn't been as judgemental about V as Fred, Ruby-lynn and Scarlet had been, and I just wanted to tell her about my concerns after Fred told me about V's "shallow and cruel" lifestyle. I got out my phone and called Lizzy's number. Lizzy answered immediately.

'Hello?' she said.

'Hi, Lizzy!' I said.

'You okay?'

'I'm not too bad thanks, babe,' I said. 'I was just wondering if we could talk about something later, when I finish work?'

I told Lizzy what time I finished, then Lizzy said she was coming to town around that time anyway, to take Penny for a walk on the beach, so she suggested I could walk with her. I looked down at my shoes. Yeah, they'd be okay on the sand, though I wished I'd worn more sensible shoes, not that I had any way of knowing I'd be walking along the beach with Lizzy. At least I wasn't wearing kitten heels, or worse, stilettos.

'I'll definitely be up for that,' I said, before saying I had to go and we both said goodbye to each other.

I had just as much a busy afternoon as I had a busy morning. I'd had a fifteen-minute tea break at three o'clock, then, finally, it rolled onto half past five.

I retrieved my belongings from the back room, sent Mum a quick text to say I was meeting Lizzy on the beach, left the shop, and walked up St Mary Street, towards the beach. When I got there, I saw Lizzy playing fetch with Penny, who was splashing around in the sea, trying to find the ball that Lizzy had thrown.

I walked carefully down the sloping ground towards the beach, and over the sand, over to Lizzy. At that moment, Penny was running back over to Lizzy, dripping wet, carrying the ball in her mouth.

'Hey, Natalie!' Lizzy said, looking round at me, grinning. We hugged.

'Looks like Penny's having a lot of fun,' I said, as Penny dropped the ball onto the ground in front of us and looked up at Lizzy, wagging her tail in an excited, expectant sort of way. I watched as Lizzy scooped the ball off the ground with the ball thrower she'd been using, and threw the ball as far she could. Penny shot off like a cannon ball over the sand, and picked the ball up with her mouth again.

'You want to have a go?' asked Lizzy, offering me the ball thrower. All right, why not?

'Yeah, okay then,' I said, eagerly, taking the ball thrower. Penny dropped the ball in front of us and kept nudging it towards us with her nose, looking up at us, hopefully. I picked the ball up with the ball thrower and gave it a good throw into the sea. Penny whizzed over the sand, very narrowly avoiding knocking into a middle aged couple who were walking past with their own greyhound.

As me and Lizzy watched Penny search the water for the ball, Lizzy looked at me and asked, 'What did you want to talk to me about?'

'I'm a bit concerned about something Fred told me about V,' I began to explain, but I was interrupted by Penny running over to us with the ball, dropping it down in front of us and vigorously shaking herself dry.

'Eurgh!' said Lizzy, as we both backed away from Penny to stop her drenching us. I scooped up the ball, threw it again and then told Lizzy what Fred said about gangs being violent. When I finished, I waited as Lizzy thought.

I did not like the uncomfortable look on Lizzy's face when she looked down and then said, 'Well, I do happen to have heard about a guy known as V who is in the type of gang that carry knives and guns, has loads of money and deals drugs. Do you even know how he earns so much money?'

My stomach lurched. His lot still did that kind of stuff?

'No,' I admitted. 'I just thought he'd had a really good job that paid loads. And he seems so nice.'

Lizzy gave a very disbelieving laugh.

'Oh he *seems* nice? They *all* do, Natalie, but they're all trouble. Except "trouble" is an understatement,' she said. 'When are you seeing him again? Have you made any more arrangements with him?'

'I'm seeing him tomorrow, we're going to the Marquis Granby,' I told her.

'Just be careful,' Lizzy warned me.

As we walked across the sand, my heels kept getting stuck in the sand. Lizzy looked down at them.

'Jesus, they're covered in *sand*!' she told me.

'I know,' I sighed. 'If I'd known I'd be doing this, I would've worn more sensible shoes, *and* gone for trousers rather than a skirt!'

'It's okay, you weren't to know,' said Lizzy.

We walked as far as the Pier Bandstand, then turned around and started walking in the opposite direction, towards the Pavilion, my shoes still sinking into the sand. It was a nightmare.

By the time we reached the Pavilion, I couldn't bear it any longer, and said I was going to head home.

I didn't know what to do about V. Even after what Lizzy had said, I refused to believe he was still capable of that stuff. I didn't want to believe my boyfriend would do that!

I had work again the next day, but only from nine to one, which I was glad about. I was meeting V at six o'clock in the evening.

I'd managed to get through the morning, and then when I finished, I went straight home, and decided to unwind before I got ready, as we weren't meeting up for hours yet.

I was still determined not to say anything about any of the things Fred, Ruby-lynn, Scarlet and Lizzy said.

When the time came for me to start getting ready, a comforting thought occurred to me. Even if V hadn't changed from what he'd been like before he'd gone to prison, he'd never want to hurt me. He loved me. Well, he didn't say that, but I was sure he did.

I wanted to make myself look extra pretty and sexy for that night. I was going to wear my hair down, as I'd had it up all morning, though I'd have it backcombed and in a hair band, and wear the most stunning clothes that V had bought me. He bought me mostly tight tops with low, revealing necklines, and very short skirts, but I knew I'd be freezing if I'd worn one of those skirts in January. So, I put on the sexiest top I could find, a burgundy peplum top with straps and a plunging neckline, with my white flared jeans with dark gold details, and a peach lace blazer to wear over my top, to keep me warm when I took off my coat in the pub.

I also wanted to use a different bag that he bought me, and I picked out a black quilted faux leather handbag with the gold chain strap, before picking out some jewellery. I put on a pair of grey suede and gold ankle boots, put on my coat, and I was good to go.

I started walking to the Marquis Granby. It's a twenty-six minute walk from where I live. It was so cold, as it was only January. At least it wasn't windy.

I was nearly there when I'd reached the end of Yarlands, which meets with Chickerell Road, when two men who looked the same age as V came over.

'You must be Natalie, right?' said the first one. I nodded, nervously.

'Nice to meet you,' said the second one. 'I'm T and this is F.'

'Nice to meet you too,' I said, then asked where V was. Why hadn't he come to meet me himself? Was he not able to come, and couldn't text me for whatever reason?

'He's back at the pub,' F said. 'He doesn't want you on your own, out in the dark, so he sent T and I to go out and meet you.'

Phew! At least he hadn't cancelled.

As I walked to the Marquis with them, they were very friendly and they talked and joked with me and I liked that I got on with V's friends and they made me feel protected, especially as I knew V had sent them out, specifically so I wouldn't be alone.

We were just passing the turn to Everdene Drive, when three more of V's friends showed up.

'So, *you're* V's sexy lady!' said one of them, smiling.

'V's a lucky man,' said another, walking closer to me. I began to feel uneasy. He got right up close to me and ran his fingers through my hair, asking if I fancied a "quick one" before we met V in the pub. What the fuck?!

'Are you *insane*?!' I screamed, pushing him away, horrified that one of V's mates would actually ask his girlfriend for sex.

'All right! Calm down, we're only having a laugh,' said the third man, as all five of them circled round me. There was no one around so no one could help me. T pushed me down to the ground and tried to make me let him inside my mouth.

'GET AWAY FROM ME!' I screamed, crawling through his legs.

I ran down Chickerell Road. I looked over my shoulder. They were chasing me, shouting after me! I didn't stop. I couldn't or they'd get me! I carried on up Cumberland Drive, not wanting to stop. I turned right and carried on up Cumberland Drive, I kept on running until I got to Radipole Lane then ran North, towards the roundabout, not daring to look back.

I'd almost made it to the roundabout, but they'd caught up with me.

'Trying to get away, were you?' said one of them.

I cried out as I felt the five men push me down to the ground and held me down as one of them forced himself inside me. I screamed and cried, but they didn't care how scared or upset I was.

After ten minutes, they all got up and, laughing, all five of them ran off and left me.

I lay on the pavement, breathing heavily in the dark and cold. I was so weak with shock I couldn't move. Did that really just happen?

When I eventually could move, I got to my feet, and started staggering back home. It was a longer journey back than it had been on the way to the Marquis, as I was going a lot slower than before, but, to my relief, I finally arrived home.

I knew Fred and Mum and Dad would still be up, but I didn't want them asking questions. Hands shaking, I got out my key, pushed it into the keyhole very slowly, and turned the handle, carefully, as it was a bit squeaky. I opened the door slowly, and not too wide, so as not to make the hinges creak, squeezed through it, then shut it carefully, turning the handle so that the catch wouldn't click. Then, I tiptoed up the stairs and into my room. I was still so shocked I hadn't even remembered to turn on the light. I took off my shoes and coat and was just starting to undress, when I passed out on the bed.

I awoke the next morning to my phone ringing. I looked at my clock. It was eleven in the morning. I was so dazed with shock; I didn't even know what day it was. Did I need to be at work? Because if I did, would it be Miriam, my boss, wanting to know where the hell I was?

My phone stopped ringing.

I had this horrible dream last night. I dreamt I was gang raped by V's gang...

I saw what I was wearing. I hadn't even undressed the night before! Oh God, I remembered passing out... Oh my God, I really was raped!

My phone started ringing again. I picked it up. It was V. He was obviously angry I hadn't shown up. He must've thought I'd stood him up. He was phoning to ask me what the fuck I thought I was playing at.

I knew he had a right to know what his friends had done to his girlfriend the night before, when I was supposed to be meeting him. I answered my phone before it stopped ringing again.

'Listen, V–' I began, desperately, but he cut across me, sounding very angry.

'You don't have to tell me anything! I've already seen a video of you slutting around with my mates!' he'd shouted from the other end of the phone. 'How fucking dare you! You got a lotta nerve going behind my back like that!'

I couldn't believe it! V thought I was cheating on him? And what made it even more sickening was that I'd just found out now, from what V said about seeing a video of it, that they had been filming the whole thing!

'No! V! Listen, I didn't cheat, they raped me and one of them asked me for quick sex and another one of them forced me to give them a blowjob!' I tried to explain, desperately, but all he said was, 'Oh I don't have time for bullshit! Just come and see me later at my place!'

What? He wanted to see me, after he thought I'd been cheating on him?

'Well, why should I?' I'd managed to ask.

'Cos I have the video of you and my mates shagging and I'll release it if you don't come round,' he said, instructing me to bring the weed and be round his place at five o'clock and no later.

I was terrified. What was he going to say? What was he going to *do*? But nothing made me feel more sick than the idea of that video of me, screaming and pleading with his gang as they pinned me down, being posted, on the Internet, and going viral, for *everyone* to see; my friends, everyone at work, and, worst of all, *Mum and Dad*! I was so ashamed; I didn't know what else to do. So, I had no choice but to do as he said.

I had a shower, put some different clothes on and went downstairs to have something to eat. Dad came out of the kitchen.

'You were back very late last night,' he said. 'You clearly had a good time.'

I nodded and went to the kitchen. I was so nervous about seeing V later, I realised I wasn't actually that hungry, but I knew I had to eat something.

I didn't do very much during the day. I didn't have work, so I'd been lounging around. Luckily, Mum and Dad thought it was because I'd had such a great night with V, so they weren't worried, and I wanted it to stay that way, whatever would happen later. I let Mum know I was going to see him again at five and wasn't sure what time I'd be back.

I left the house at four, as I had two buses to catch and would need more time to get to V's house.

I walked along Bowleaze and over to V's front door, rang the doorbell and waited for him to answer, fully expecting to him to grab me by my hair and drag me indoors, calling me all the names under the sun.

Nothing of the sort. Obviously, he didn't greet me his usual way. He had opened the door, said, 'hey,' in a way that showed he still wasn't happy with me, and let me in. I followed him upstairs to his lounge.

'You got the weed?' he asked. Not saying anything, I got the cannabis out of my bag, and gave it to V, who then told me to sit down. I sat on the armchair near the door to the balcony. V himself sat on the sofa nearest the chair.

'Right,' he began, 'I need you to do me some favours with some guys I know.'

That was random. He accused me of cheating, then asked me for favours?

'You'll be coming round my house, whenever I call you, and you're gonna go to my room, and let one of these guys do whatever they want with you, okay?'

I sat back in horror. V was expecting his girlfriend to go to bed with other men?

'Why would you ask me to do that?' I asked. 'I'm your *girlfriend*!'

V's mouth curved in a smile. 'That was just what I wanted you to think,' he said, standing up. He started pacing the room, in a superior and careless sort of way. 'I knew you, like all the previous girls I'd turned into prostitutes, wouldn't go out with me, unless I impressed you with rides in my Mercedes, and presents to gain your trust, then I could take cash from any man that would sleep with you.'

I couldn't take it in. V was a *lover boy, as well* as a gang boy?

'I've made eight hundred pounds a day, selling my previous so-called girlfriends for sex,' he went on. 'How do you think I was able to afford all those clothes, jewellery and fancy handbags, eh?'

I felt so humiliated. I trusted V, but all he saw me as was just another innocent, unsuspecting girl he could trick into prostitution.

'I should've listened to my mates before I got into this mess,' I snarled at him. 'As for the sleeping with various men in your bed, there is no way I am doing that!'

'Oh, you're not, are you?' V sneered, walking closer to me. 'I was quite serious about that video I have. The video of you having sex with my friends and sucking them off. The video that I have already said I'd release if you don't do what I want.' He put his face right up close to mine. 'Do you really want people seeing that sort of video of you?' he went on. 'What would Mummy and Daddy say if they saw it? And what would your friends say? And I do feel you're being very selfish, you know. After all the money I spent on those lovely clothes and shoes and handbags and jewellery, all the rides in my Mercedes, and you won't do this in return? Very ungrateful, don't you think?'

I nodded. V ordered me to be back round his place at ten o'clock, the next day, to start.

'I have work from nine until half five,' I argued.

'Well, fucking call in sick then!' V just said, angrily.

I was powerless. I was scared. I still didn't want to tell anyone, out of worry that it would only make things worse. I didn't want anyone getting hurt.

So, the next morning, I called Flyaway Paradise and said I had an upset stomach, and then went off to V's house, reluctantly.

There, I was introduced to a man named Q, who V allowed to go up to his room with me, where I had to let him do what he wanted, as V had instructed.

Afterwards, I watched from the window as Q gave V some money, down on the driveway before walking off, then I was told to stick around for another two men that were coming round.

I went home at half five, pretending like I'd had just a normal day at work, then I went back out to be back at V's house for nine, then I went home at ten at night, and sneak in whilst everyone else in the house was asleep.

That had now become my daily routine. I hated myself for it, but I was trapped. V had me under the thumb, and there was nothing I could do about it. V sent flowers and gifts to my house so Mum and Dad believed that he was my boyfriend. I deeply regretted not listening to Fred about V, and now my refusal to do so had got me into a mess I couldn't get out of.

Chapter 6:

Jesse's First

Friday 14th January 2011

'Mum, what is the point of tidying tonight?' I asked, in the middle of picking up all my Kerrang mags, and my hoodie, backpack and trainers. 'It's just going to get untidy again, before we go to bed.'

Mum sighed.

'No, it won't, Jesse,' she said. 'Because anything that you get out this evening will not be left lying around when you've finished. You'll tidy it away once you've finished with it.'

I reluctantly went back to my tidying. Mum would want my help cleaning up the kitchen after I'd finished the lounge, only to then make dinner, then lunch for tomorrow, then tidy up again, then wash up afterwards! Before then, I'd been busy helping Mum to bake a pomegranate cake for tomorrow's dessert.

At least this distracted me from how I felt about tomorrow. Mum had arranged with Christian that he would come round to meet me and Rochella, and then, after that, they would arrange when we could go round to meet Jamie.

Rochella had been writing a letter one Friday evening. When she'd left the room, I'd picked up the letter, and started to read. She hadn't written very much. She'd only got as far as, "Dear Jamie."

Who could Jamie be? Why had she been writing to him all this time? I'd asked Rochella who he was, on the way up to bed, but she'd just said he was a pen pal, but then I woke up next morning to voices on the landing. Rochella and Mum were arguing about Jamie and the letter.

I'd gone down to breakfast. Mum said she 'needed a word with me about something,' and I knew that was it, so we went to the dining room and sat down at the table.

She asked how much of the letter I'd seen, so I told her I'd only seen the "Dear Jamie," part.

Mum told me about the time when Dad left and then went on to explain that Jamie was mine and Rochella's brother and, when Mum and Dad split up, he'd left with Jamie, before any of them even knew she was knocked up a third time. She'd gone on to say that she hadn't seen either of them since, because every time she tried to go round there, nobody answered.

So now I knew. But I wanted to know more about Jamie, and what he was like, but I knew it was unlikely that could happen. I also wondered what Dad was like, apart from what Mum had said. Maybe he just wasn't the ideal husband or boyfriend, as he made Mum so unhappy, but a good father, just like she'd said.

I wondered if Mum had any photos of Jamie, as well as Dad. I hoped she'd at least have some photos of Jamie when he was small, hidden away somewhere, so I asked if she had any photos that she could show me. She showed me some photos of her on the hospital bed, holding baby Jamie. Then I saw some photos of Jamie, that were taken during his first Christmas, some of which Rochella was in, when she was four, including photos of them unwrapping Christmas presents, draped with tinsel, and wearing cracker hats.

Even though they were very old photos, it did give me a very rough idea of what Jamie looked like, because he looked a lot like what I looked like at that age. I know siblings do tend to look similar when they're little, then begin to look less and less alike as they get older, or the other way around, but I did wonder if me and Jamie did look anything alike now.

I didn't think I could hold out much hope of meeting Jamie, but the more I learnt about him, the more I wanted to.

But it wasn't until I was having breakfast on the first Saturday morning of December, and heard the phone ringing out in the hall that there had been any more developments. I had got up to go out and answer it myself, but Mum beat me to it. She'd said hello when she picked it up. There was a long pause, and then...

'Hello Christian,' she had said.

And after some private discussions between Mum and Dad, and Mum meeting Jamie alone, here me and Rochella were now, preparing for the next day, when Christian, my long lost dad, would be coming round to meet us.

I never told anyone about any of this, not even Lizzy, Natalie or Fred.

I took my stuff up to my room, and then returned downstairs and entered the kitchen, where Rochella was tidying and Mum was getting out all the ingredients and equipment needed to make dinner, to tell her I'd finished.

Whenever Mum asks us to tidy, she *always* inspects, to make sure she's satisfied. She's one of those mums who still talks to her grown up children like, well, children. Even though I was eighteen and Rochella was twenty-three, Mum would be like, 'Don't forget to make your bed!' and 'Have you brushed your teeth?' and, in my case, 'Remember your coursework for college!' She means well, in way that can irritate the hell out of you, that is!

She checked the lounge, and said there was still a pile of D.V.Ds, near the T.V, that needed putting away. For fuck sake, they weren't even mine! I didn't argue though. I put the D.V.Ds on the shelf where they belonged.

I joined Rochella and Mum in cooking dinner. We were having this pork and mushroom casserole thing.

We had to wash up and dry up whilst we left the casserole to simmer for thirty minutes., before Mum asked if I'd lay the table, so I fetched some cutlery from the drawer and laid the dining room table.

'So, your dad will be here at ten thirty,' Mum explained, as we sat at the table and had dinner. 'And I must warn you both not to expect a tearful reunion, because he wasn't exactly emotional at the idea of meeting you two.'

I wasn't too surprised at this, as what I knew about Dad made him come across like he wasn't that fussed. Part of me didn't know why Mum was even bothering to arrange for me and Rochella to meet Dad, if I should even be calling him that, though it was still important, nonetheless.

'How did he react when you asked about us meeting him?' asked Rochella.

'He took a frustratingly casual approach to it when he agreed to it. It was like he didn't even care, either way, to be honest, and he's supposed to be your dad!' she said, sounding livid.

'I thought you said he was a good dad?' Rochella queried, confused.

'When we were together,' said Mum, in a cynical tone that suggested she suspected he might not have been treating Jamie in a way that would win him the Best Father Award after they broke up, if there were such a thing.

I wanted to believe that it would mean more to Jamie to meet Rochella and me and I was rather positive that it did, because I knew both Jamie and Mum were emotional when they met for the first time.

'Any idea at all when we might meet Jamie?' I asked.

'Probably next weekend in theory, darling,' said Mum.

I was pleased I'd get to meet my long lost brother, even though I'd only found out about him a few months ago.

Ever since Mum had received that phone call from Christian, she'd been meeting with him, to talk about her meeting Jamie, and me and Rochella meeting Christian, and then eventually meeting Jamie.

They agreed to arrange things this way, rather than me, Rochella and Mum meeting both Jamie and Christian all on the same day, because Mum thought it would be easier for me, Rochella and Jamie to take baby steps.

After dinner, Mum told us to put our dirty plates, cups, knives and forks in the dishwasher to be run.

The next morning, we had to be up and ready for Christian. Mum was rushing about like a mad one, no doubt feeling on edge about Christian meeting his two children, one of whom he hadn't seen for years, the other of which he didn't know existed, for the first time.

I just hoped there wouldn't be any unpleasantness between Mum and Christian. I didn't want Mum getting reduced to tears.

'Jesse, can you get dressed, please?' she nagged. 'We've got to be ready for your dad to come at half past ten!'

Nag, nag, and nag! I went upstairs to change.

The doorbell rang at thirty-three minutes past ten. Mum went to answer the door. A tall, slim man with brown hair entered. He was wearing grey jeans, a blue shirt, and a black jacket.

'Jesse, Rochella, this is your father,' Mum announced. 'Christian.'

Rochella and me looked at Christian. Christian looked at us.

'So, you've grown, Rochella,' said Christian. No shit, Sherlock!

'Yes, Dad,' said Rochella.

Christian turned to me.

'And you're Jesse?' said Christian. 'I left with Jamie before any of us knew your mother and I were expecting a third child.'

'That's what Mum said,' I mumbled, feeling awkward.

'Christian, why don't you follow your children to the lounge and have a nice chat with them, whilst I make drinks,' said Mum, obviously trying to lighten the mood and keep things friendly. 'Tea or coffee?'

'Black coffee. No sugar,' said Christian, without even bothering to say 'please.'

Me and Rochella went into the lounge with Christian in tow. Rochella nervously invited Christian to sit down as we sat together on the sofa. Daisy came running into the lounge, giving a small meow, and jumped up onto Rochella's lap.

'Ow!' Rochella said. Daisy was probably digging her claws into her thighs.

Christian pulled a slightly disgruntled face at Daisy.

'I hate cats,' he mumbled in an uncertain tone, like Daisy was riddled with a deadly and contagious disease. 'So... what's been going on in your lives?' he then asked. I had a feeling Christian didn't have a clue how to talk to his own children.

Rochella told Christian about the advanced Business and Administration apprenticeship she was doing at Fleetview College, though Christian didn't show very much interest.

I told Christian about how I was close friends with Lizzy, Fred and Natalie, through Mum's friendship with all their parents.

'Oh, yeah, Jane and Claire, the women that married Colvin Graham and Barry Curtis,' said Christian, casually.

'When I finished secondary school, Fleetview had the prom at Portland Heights Hotel,' I told him. 'And a small group of us went in one of those yellow New York taxis! It was me, Fred, my girlfriend Annie and another mate, Matt.'

'You got a girlfriend, then?' asked Christian. The way he asked me and Rochella all these questions made him sound like he was just doing it to sound like he was interested, and didn't actually care! Though that might have been the case, going by what Mum said the night before about Christian not caring. But I was still shocked.

I told him about how Mum worked with Annie's mum and they were close friends, and that was why me and Annie were so close, that and the fact that we both went to Fleetview. We'd been together for three years. We started dating when we started in year eleven at Fleetview.

'What's been happening in your life?' Rochella was interested to know, but Christian just shrugged and said, 'Not a lot.'

I tried asking Christian if he was with anybody at the moment, or if he'd been out with many women, if any, since he and Mum had split up, and his only response was, 'a fair few.'

'Rochella and her friend Sarah went to their prom in a sports car with the roof down,' said Mum, coming in with a tray bearing the teas and coffees and placing it on the coffee table, obviously having heard me telling Christian about my prom.

Sarah is Lizzy, Fraser and Alistair's cousin. She's the daughter of Colvin's sister and brother-in-law. She, too, became friends with Rochella through Colvin and Jane's friendship with Mum.

'And was your prom at the Portland Heights Hotel as well?' Christian asked, sounding bored.

'No, it was at the Portland and Weymouth Sailing Academy,' said Rochella, picking up her coffee. 'And neither of us had dates. But we were both happy being single then.'

Rochella doesn't have anyone in the pipeline, though she does have a bit of a thing for Dominic Woods, who's the fraternal twin brother of Alistair's girlfriend, Sophie.

'I see,' said Christian. He didn't ask Mum what she'd been doing with her life. Either it was something he'd already done, or he wasn't interested.

'What have you found out about your long lost son and daughter?' Mum asked Christian as she sat down next to me.

'Jesse has a girlfriend and Rochella's doing an apprenticeship,' he casually said.

'I'm sure Rochella and Jesse told you more than that,' Mum politely said.

'Jesse was telling me about the taxi he went to his prom in,' Christian told her, sounding reluctant to elaborate about the conversations he'd had with his own son and daughter.

I saw Mum raise her eyebrows, then she looked round at me, Rochella, and then down at Daisy, who was still on Rochella's lap, purring, her eyes shut in a contented way. She smiled at Daisy, and then looked over at Christian.

'Right, now that I'm here, and you've had a civilised conversation with Jesse and Rochella, I thought we could discuss when they could meet their brother,' she said.

Me and Rochella looked at Christian, determinedly. Christian looked from Rochella, to me to Mum, then back again.

'Okay,' he said. 'Right, well, I was hoping that maybe you could come round to meet Jamie a week today?' he then suggested, gruffly. 'And when you do, providing everything goes well, I have something else I need to discuss with you, that I think will benefit all of us. It's about what you'd asked me to think about when you came round to meet Jamie.'

I saw Mum look down, uncertainly. I could tell she was wondering what Christian wanted to talk about. She said Saturday was fine and asked what time to be round.

'How about eleven o'clock?' asked Christian.

'That's fine, that's doable,' said Mum.

She asked Christian if he would stay for lunch, saying that she was making avocados stuffed with crab and dressed with buttermilk. Christian said he would, but that he'd have to be heading off after that.

Mum went back to the kitchen to make lunch, leaving me and Rochella to talk to Christian some more. I pursed my lips, wondering what to say, and then...

'How is Jamie?'

'He's alright,' Christian shrugged. 'Hoping things will work out okay when he meets you two.'

We might as well have given up trying to bond with him, as it was obvious he didn't want to know. Why did Christian even want one of his children coming with him, if he wasn't interested in getting to know his other two?

'Lunch is ready!' Mum called from the kitchen.

We went into the kitchen. Mum handed Rochella the jug of elderflower cordial we would be drinking with our lunch, and asked me to bring the tray into the dining room, bearing the tumblers and cutlery.

Christian sat down as I placed the tray in the middle of the table, and Rochella placed the jug next to it. I placed one of the tumblers on each of the coasters, then placed the knives and forks either side of each placemat and then me and Rochella sat down.

Mum came in, carrying two plates, each of which had half an avocado on it, with salad leaves, cherry tomatoes, and drizzled with the buttermilk dressing.

'I hope you like crab meat,' she said to Christian, placing one plate in front of him, and the other in front of me, and then went back to the kitchen to fetch hers and Rochella's plates. The avocado was filled with crabmeat, lime zest, chopped shallots and coriander.

Mum placed hers and Rochella's plates on the table, and then sat down.

'Dig in, and help yourselves to the elderflower cordial,' she invited everyone, cheerfully.

I poured myself a glass of the elderflower juice, and then tucked into my lunch. I wouldn't say crab was my favourite food, but I did like it enough to not want to pass on it.

'What's Jamie up to, today?' asked Mum, after finishing a forkful of crab and shallots.

'Sat at home, probably,' Christian mumbled through a mouthful of avocado and tomato. Rochella asked how Jamie reacted when he was told he would get to meet her, me and Mum, and Christian just said he seemed fine about it.

That didn't really give me much idea as to whether or not Jamie was fussed about it, but I hoped he would be.

After lunch, we had the homemade pomegranate cake, before Christian said goodbye, seeming like he was in a rush to leave.

After Mum shut the door behind him, she turned to face me and Rochella.

'Well, you've seen what I mean, then?' she said. 'About him not being fussed.'

'He looked like he would much rather be somewhere else, rather than here,' Rochella pointed out. 'Do you reckon Jamie really does want to see us?'

'He did seem very keen,' Mum said, clearly noticing Rochella was a bit worried that Jamie would feel the same way about meeting us that Christian did.

'So, we're going round theirs next Saturday, then?' I asked, just wanting to confirm.

'Yes,' said Mum. 'Will you two help me clean up?'

So me and Rochella helped Mum clear the dining room table, clean up the kitchen, wash up and dry up.

Mum had Michael, her other half, round that evening, so that she could tell him all about it. Michael's quite tall and muscley, with tanned skin and black, tousled hair, whereas Mum's fair and blonde. He's from California and had moved to England a couple of years before he and Mum starting seeing each other.

I hadn't been part of the conversation about Christian. I went upstairs to get on with my coursework for the first Diploma I was doing in Travel, Tourism and Events.

I didn't get as much done as I would've liked to, but it was still enough, I thought.

The next morning, I was all set to leave for Fred's at twelve.

As I walked to Fred's house, I realised I was early, but didn't think Fred would mind. Claire was quite surprised, but not in a disappointed way.

'Hello Jesse,' she said in her usual cheery way. 'Fred has a friend from college upstairs, but I think she must be going soon, if he's supposed to be spending time with you this afternoon.'

She let me in. But who was this friend from college, that Fred had up in his room? It couldn't have been Ruby-lynn, because she wasn't even *at* college.

'Natalie in?' I asked.

'No, she isn't,' she said, reprovingly. 'Gone to see that boyfriend of hers. They really are spending too much time together. But I shan't worry you about that, now. I'll make you a drink if you like?'

'Yeah please,' I said. I asked for a black coffee and Claire put the kettle on and said just to go on up to Fred's room.

'Sorry I'm so early, by the way,' I said.

'That's all right,' said Claire, before I reached the top of the stairs. I knocked on the door. I could hear Fred say 'Ssh!' though the door. What was going on?

'Hello?!' I heard him shout through the door. I know I should've waited for Fred to invite me in, but I opened the door. Fuck, I really wished I hadn't.

What I saw was fucking shocking! Fred was in his bed with another girl! Who was she?

Fred gave a very annoyed sigh.

'Well done, Jesse!' he said, irritably. I was speechless. Fred really liked Ruby-lynn! How could he do this to her?

'Sorry, Catriona, he wasn't s'posed to be –' he started to say, before Catriona cut across him, crossly, saying, 'You said he wasn't coming until one!'

'Why are you so early?!' Fred angrily asked.

'I didn't think I'd walk in on this!' I argued. Fred sighed. I could tell he knew he couldn't really blame me.

Luckily I was only twenty minutes early, and it turned out they'd both lost track of time and that Catriona was supposed to have left ten minutes ago anyway.

I waited outside Fred's room, whilst Fred and Catriona got dressed.

'Wait up here while I say goodbye to Catriona,' Fred said, walking over to the stairs with Catriona. I went back into Fred's room. I heard the sound of the footsteps down the stairs, before Fred said goodbye to Catriona and they arranged to see each other again, at her place, tomorrow night! Then I heard them snogging!

I waited. After the sound of the door opening, and then shutting again, I heard Fred bounding up the stairs, and he came back in, shutting the door behind him.

'If we'd kept an eye on the time it wouldn't have mattered if you were early,' said Fred, sounding harassed. 'I hoped I'd be able to have her in and out again before you got here.'

'What the fuck were you even doing –,' I asked him, not realising how loudly I'd said it. Fred had to hiss at me to keep my voice down.

'What Ruby-lynn doesn't know won't hurt her,' Fred said. I couldn't believe what I was hearing! Fred's my best mate, but what he was doing was wrong!

'I'm not going to grass you up, but why would you do this to Ruby-lynn?'

'I've been going on a few dates with other girls, but I never acted like I was serious about any of them,' Fred said. 'It probably wouldn't have started if I hadn't got so chummy with Gabrielle, from Gamestation. I'm not saying it's her fault. I didn't *have* to say I didn't have a girlfriend when she asked me, but I'd just become a whole lot more... up myself than usual, since me and Ruby-lynn started going out, and I'd hit on other girls, but I never thought of going behind her back like that until that day when I went into Gamestation on my own. But I really like Ruby-lynn, and the other girls just as much, so I have been finding all this really confusing now. And when I let Gabrielle kiss me, as bad as I felt, I kept telling myself Ruby-lynn would never find out.'

I swallowed. I didn't understand exactly, but in a way, I sort of knew where Fred was coming from, if you get me.

We started finalising our plans for what we were doing on Fred's birthday. The whole gang were coming round for pre drinks whilst we got ready.

Hang on, though. What if we bumped into any of the other girls Fred had been seeing when we were out? That would ruin Fred's birthday entirely, especially as Ruby-lynn was obviously coming too.

Luckily, it was a themed night out; Masquerades, so maybe, even if Fred did see any of the girls he was seeing, they wouldn't recognise him, hopefully. It was Fred's idea. I did have a sneaky suspicion that he decided on that theme, just so he wouldn't be recognised, but it's just a thought.

I'd already bought my Devil Masquerade suit. Fred was wearing a Zorro Bandit costume, which included a hat as well as an eye mask, so I reckoned Fred wouldn't be recognised. I knew what Fred was doing was wrong, but we were best mates, and I was not going to rat him out to anyone.

'Can't *wait* to see what Ruby-lynn's wearing!' said Fred, excited. I nodded, awkwardly. Fred looked up at me, with a grateful look on his face.

'Thanks for not blabbing about my relationship with Ruby-lynn in front of Catriona,' he said, before abruptly going back to talking about his birthday and adding that, miraculously, Natalie was able to come out for his birthday.

Whoa! What made Fred think, for a moment, that Natalie wouldn't be able to see her own brother on his birthday?

'Well, she *is* your sister!' I pointed out. Fred lowered his voice and told me not to tell anyone, especially not Natalie herself that he told me this, but he found a bag of weed in her dressing table drawer, that she said she was looking after for V.

'Shit!' I'd said, starting to get more concerned. 'I knew he was trouble!'

'I said I wouldn't tell Mum and Dad about the weed if she didn't snitch on me to Ruby-lynn,' said Fred. Did Natalie know what Fred had been up to as well?

'But what does Natalie know about what you'd been doing?' I asked.

'Oh, it's something Natalie got suspicious about, that she threatened to ask Ruby-lynn, which would get her asking me a load of questions, and she could find out everything, it's a long story,' Fred explained, making it clear that he didn't really feel like going further into the matter, so I dropped the subject.

'How come you couldn't see me yesterday?' Fred asked.

I took a deep breath, and decided Fred might as well know now.

'I have something I want to tell you,' I said.

'What is it?' Fred asked.

'Well... the thing is, I have a brother,' I told him, slowly. Fred looked astonished. I could tell he wasn't sure he heard me right.

'You have a brother? Like... like a long lost brother do you mean?' he asked, sounding like he was having trouble taking in what I just said.

'Yeah,' I said, and I told Fred all about the letter I'd seen Rochella writing to someone named Jamie, and that I'd over heard her and Mum talking about my right to know about it, and Mum's intention of telling me when I'd turned eighteen, and her struggles to find the right opportunity to tell me.

'Mum also said that she and Dad split up before I was born,' I said. 'Jamie left with Dad, so neither of them even knew about me, because even Mum hadn't found out she was pregnant with me until after they'd left.'

Fred looked shocked.

'Fucking hell!' he said. 'Do you think my mum and Jane know about Jamie? They're both very close to Flora.'

'I do wonder, now that you said it, if they did know, because how can they not know?' I said.

'I know you have a point,' Fred said, but me, Natalie and Lizzy would've known, if Claire and Jane had told is, that is. So, what happens now?' he then asked, sounding curious. 'Will you get to meet him?'

I told Fred about when Mum had that phone call from Christian.

'I met him yesterday,' I told Fred. 'And we're gonna meet Jamie next Saturday, before we go out for your birthday.'

Fred frowned.

'So... all this has gone on for a while, if I'm right?' Fred said, slowly. 'Christ, why didn't you tell me before?'

'I'm sorry, I would've told you sooner, but we hadn't hung out much since then. And I just didn't know when or how, especially when I was still trying to take it all in,' I told Fred, truthfully.

'How does it make you feel? That you're going to meet your brother?' Fred asked.

'I do feel nervous about meeting Jamie,' I said, 'just like I'd been nervous about meeting Christian, but I've really wanted to meet them just the same, as I want answers.'

'Why's this happening now?' Fred asked.

'I don't know. Out of the blue we just had a phone call from my dad, about a few weeks ago, saying Jamie wanted to meet us,' I answered. 'Mum went to meet him the day after Boxing Day.'

'That's a bit random,' Fred said.

'Mum didn't sound happy when she talked on the phone to him,' I went on to say.

'You've always said your mum hated his guts after they broke up,' Fred said. I said maybe everything would come clear when we met Jamie.

'So how did it go, when you met your dad yesterday?' Fred asked, as we drove along Abbotsbury Road.

'Well, it went okay but Christian wasn't fussed.'

'What do you mean by that?' Fred asked.

'Well, every time he asked a question, you'd think someone had forced him, the way he spoke,' I told him, 'like, he sounded kinda bored, and then when Mum came in and asked what he'd learned about me and Rochella, he just said that Rochella was doing an apprenticeship, and I had a girlfriend.'

'An apprenticeship in what, though? He didn't even specify that,' Fred agreed.

I went on to tell Fred how Christian didn't really care to tell us much about his life, even when we both asked. Fred, sounding cautious, agreed that Christian didn't sound like he could give a toss about us. I said that, luckily, Mum seemed positive that Jamie wanted to meet us, as he was apparently very happy when he met her.

'As glad as I am to meet him, there's no point denying that it will still be weird for all three of us,' I said. 'Hey, also, when we discussed when we could go round to meet Jamie, Dad said he wanted to talk to Mum about something that would "benefit us all," but he said he wasn't going to say it until the day we meet Jamie, and it was on the assumption that everything worked out.'

Fred frowned. I could tell he was wondering what that could be, and then Fred said that at least we would find out, as long as it all did go well, that was.

We sat and ate in Subway, before we met with Lizzy at the Alexandra Gardens.

'Hey, Liz!' I said, giving her a hug. 'You not seeing Charlie today?'

'Nah, he's with Stuart today,' said Lizzy. 'Shall we have a play on the games, then?'

So the three of us went inside. I had to change the money I'd just drawn out for coins before I could play on any games, as did Fred.

I watched Fred and Lizzy play a manic game of air hockey, which reduced Lizzy to fits of giggles, then I played against her, and then Fred, to both of whom I lost, mainly because I kept scoring for them both. By accident, obviously.

'I'm gonna go on Ice Ball,' said Fred, dashing over to one of the one of the alley roller games and inserting some coins. Me and Lizzy stood and watched, before I decided to have a go on Down

The Clown, a ball toss game, after which I then had a go on Ice Ball myself. I was better at both this and Down the Clown, than at air hockey.

After that, I joined Fred in watching Lizzy playing a midway styled game called Gold Fishing. She squealed as one of the balls came flying back out at her, and then the three of us were pissing ourselves as she had to run to fetch the ball as it rolled away across the carpet. The fun I had did numb the nerve of meeting my long lost brother next Saturday.

After a few other games, we went to get milkshakes from Shakies, before me and Fred gave Lizzy goodbye hugs, before walking back to the car park.

On Monday, I sat through my first lesson, then, as usual, I went to go and meet Fred in the canteen. He was sat with a girl with camel coloured hair that grew down to her hips.

'Alright mate?' I said, sitting down opposite him. 'Who's this?'

'I'm Abi,' said the girl. 'I'm on Fred's course. I'm amazed they haven't arrested him yet, for being a bit too gorge!'

'I might say the same about you!' said Fred, smiling at her, and they kissed. I looked down, starting to feel uncomfortable about what I knew Fred was doing to Ruby-lynn. I still didn't want to expose him, but I really didn't know how much longer I could keep quiet for. At least Natalie was the only one who suspected anything. But what if Lizzy saw? I hope Lizzy wouldn't dob him in, as she'd known Fred a whole lot longer than she'd known Ruby-lynn.

But that was given a violent shove out of my mind by Fred saying that Natalie's boss had called last night, wanting to know why Natalie had been off sick so much and if there was anything seriously wrong with her, when she'd been leaving the house every morning, in her work uniform.

Something was definitely up with her.

Saturday 22nd January 2011

Me, Rochella and Mum left the house at ten to eleven. In the car, I had time to go into my Facebook on my phone and write on Fred's wall, wishing him a happy birthday.

It was a forty-two minute drive to Christian's house in Beaminster.

Mum had a bit of difficulty finding where to park the car. When she eventually did find a space and parked, she stopped the engine, but didn't open the door and get out. Neither did Rochella. Neither did I. I could tell Mum was thinking, anxiously, about what would be happening in a few minutes time.

'We're still a few minutes early,' she said. I saw Mum's reflection in the rear view mirror. She was looking down, nervously.

'What's a few minutes early, Mum?' asked Rochella, reassuringly. 'Dad was three minutes late, to be exact.'

I saw Mum look round at Rochella. I saw Rochella look at Mum.

'Come on, then,' said Mum, and then the three of us got out.

I could hear my heart beating fast as I followed Mum and Rochella to the front door and waited after Mum rang the doorbell.

The door opened and there stood Christian.

'Alright?' he said, casually, as he stood back to let us in. 'He's just here in the lounge.'

'Thanks,' said Mum, as Christian shut the door, which was opposite the staircase in the lounge, behind her, me and Rochella.

The three of us looked into the lounge. There, sat on the red sofa, was a boy in his early twenties. His hair's in the exact same length and style as mine, but exactly the same colour as Rochella's, and he's a spitting image of me. He was wearing a t-shirt and jeans that looked much too big for him.

'This is your brother,' Mum said to me and Rochella, 'Jamie.'

Jamie peered at us both.

'Do you remember Rochella, Jamie? Your sister?' said Mum, her hands on Rochella's shoulders in a proud way. She then moved round behind Rochella, to stand by me. 'And this is your brother, Jesse.'

Jamie slowly stood up and walked over to us. He stood in front of me and looked at me.

'Jesse?' he said. I nodded. Jamie then walked over to Rochella.

'You're Rochella?' he said, as if he could barely believe it.

'Yes. Rochella,' said Rochella.

Jamie looked down, eyes wide, eyebrows raised, as if he was unable to take any of this in. Mum said she knew how big it was for everyone, especially because of what Jamie had been led to believe about her and Rochella.

I could tell Mum had blurted out something she didn't mean to say, because she looked down, her hand over her mouth, her eyes suddenly widened with shock as soon as she said it. Rochella frowned at her.

'What was he led to believe?' she asked. Mum sighed and said that she would tell her and me, but now wasn't the right time.

'Dad told me -' Jamie started, but Mum held up her hand and said, 'I will tell them, Jamie.'

She then suggested Jamie took me and Rochella up to his room to talk, whilst she spoke to Christian.

We nervously followed Jamie up the stairs. Jamie invited us to sit down on his bed, as he himself sat at his desk. We both exchanged uneasy looks.

'So, er, tell us about yourself,' I said. 'What was your school life like and all that?'

Jamie slowly began to tell us that he didn't have very many mates at school, and that he'd lost contact with the mate he did have, because of certain things that had happened, but he didn't go into any detail as to what those things were, only that they resulted in him being taken away from school. I was mystified as to what that could be.

'Did you have any girlfriends at all?' Rochella asked.

'Nah, not really interested in having a girlfriend, if I'm honest,' Jamie said. 'I never was. '

I asked Jamie what Christian was like, and if he was the fatherly type.

Jamie lowered his voice as he said, 'No, he wasn't. He wasn't very nice.'

Mum came bursting in, looking slightly irritable.

'Get your stuff, you two, it's about time we were leaving,' she said to me and Rochella.

'Mum, what's going on?' asked Rochella, concerned, as we all followed Mum down the stairs, but Mum said that nothing was wrong, and that it was just something Christian had asked of her, that she said she would do, but she still wasn't happy. I tried to ask what it was.

'Just get in the car, I'll tell you later!' she snapped. I caught Jamie's eye. I then saw Jamie give Christian an alarmed look.

I did as I was told after we said goodbye to Jamie, but I was worried. And what had Christian been telling Jamie about us? More secrets I'd have to wait for "the right time" to find out and I was fed up of it!

I didn't know how I got through the next couple of hours with that playing on my mind, before I had to leave for Fred's.

I was the last person to arrive at Fred's place. It was decorated with blue, white and silver balloons, even though we were all going out for Fred's birthday. I'd bought him the complete Heroes box set he'd asked for.

Us lads got changed into our costumes in Fred's room, and girls in Natalie's room. Exactly how Natalie was able to spare some time, amongst whatever she kept running off for, Fred said my guess was as good as his.

Dave was wearing a black and gold vampire Venetian costume, Tom was wearing a white and gold satin Casanova Renaissance suit with a white pony tailed wig and a gold mask, Dan was wearing a Phantom of the Opera costume, which he kept bragging about how 'fucking buff' he looked in it, Stuart was wearing a black suit with a black eye mask, and Charlie was wearing a white, gold and burgundy storybook prince costume, with a white, gold and burgundy eye mask to match.

We went downstairs to the lounge. The girls weren't there yet, so we went to the kitchen to help ourselves to drinks.

When we returned to the lounge, we saw the girls parading around in their costumes. Lizzy looked like an angel with her white eye mask and her short, strapless white dress. She'd even added wings and a halo. Natalie had gone for a short purple and silver dress with a sparkly purple and silver eye mask with diamante, Scarlet had chosen a black eye mask with a large black corsage at one side of it, which I guessed was to pick out the black bust on her otherwise blue dress and Ruby-lynn was wearing a black corset and a black tutu with a black cat masquerade eye mask. She also had some very long black lace gloves with claws on the fingertips. Annie looked incredibly sexy in her black velvet eye mask with turquoise swirly patterns and a short black dress with gold and blue peacock patterns. She'd even added a black feather boa to match.

'So, where you been, Natalie?' Dave asked, when the girls joined us after getting some drinks.

'Just... spending time with my boyfriend,' she said, shiftily. I still didn't get it. I really hoped V hadn't been giving her drugs, like the weed that Fred said he found in her room. I looked over at Fred, who I noticed was narrowing his eyes at Natalie suspiciously. Natalie hadn't noticed, however.

'So, Nikki couldn't come then?' I asked.

'Nah, she's not well,' said Dan.

'How did it go when you met Jamie?' Fred asked.

'Nerve wracking,' I said.

'Thought as much.'

'But it was better than when we met Dad,' I said, and I told the gang how me and Rochella got to know Jamie, and how he seemed more interested in what we had to say than Christian.

'He looks just like me,' I said. 'I think we both take after Dad in the same way, whereas Rochella takes more after Mum.'

I went on to tell them that we'd gone upstairs with Jamie to talk in his room, and Mum had come in, looking and sounding really hacked off, but wouldn't say why.

'Do you know what it was that your dad wanted to talk to your mum about yet?' Natalie asked.

'No,' I said, 'and to top it off, I think Dad's been telling Jamie some stuff about Mum and Rochella, which Mum said she'd tell us, but she still hasn't. I'm just so sick of all this secrecy.'

'Maybe you'll find out everything tomorrow?' Natalie suggested.

'Hope so,' I said.

I could suddenly smell candles, coming from the kitchen. I knew what was coming. A moment later, Claire was bringing in a very large chocolate cake with white and milk chocolate curls encrusting the sides, and nineteen candles stuck into the top, all alight.

'Okay, everyone?' she said, and she sang, 'Happy Birthday to you...' and the rest of us joined in and Lizzy sang, 'Happy Birthday dear Freddie Fred...' and we all finished singing as Claire put the cake down on the coffee table. It had a thick layer of milk chocolate frosting with the words 'Happy Birthday,' written on it in what I guessed was white chocolate icing.

Natalie took a photo of the cake on her phone, before Fred blew out the candles. Then, Claire cut everybody a piece, taking care to give Fred an extra large slice, as he was the birthday boy.

Annie came and sat with me, asking about going on a double date with her best friend Sherri and her new boyfriend.

'Ah nice, have you met him?' I asked.

'Not in the flesh I haven't,' said Annie. 'But I've seen what he looks like because Sherri's shown me loads of pictures of the two of them together, he's got dark brown hair and brown eyes. His name's Will and he's from Northern Ireland.'

Dark brown hair, brown eyes, and his name was Will and he was Northern Irish? All the things Lizzy said about the guy she'd met. Was it the same Will? Not that it couldn't have been a coincidence, but at least Lizzy was with Charlie, the guy she'd had it bad for since she was eleven, so she wouldn't care either way.

'At least we'll be drinking on tummies full of cake!' said Scarlet, eating her slice, neatly with one of the cake forks Claire brought in. Us boys hadn't bothered using the forks and were taking big bites at a time out of our slices.

'Especially me!' said Fred, proudly, munching on his piece.

After some more drinks, Claire gave Fred some money for taxis and called for two taxis, as there were twelve of us.

We were dropped off outside the New Vic, we all went along to Dusk, where we bought drinks and sat down, and took photos on our phones.

Suddenly, Swedish House Mafia's "Miami to Ibiza" came on.

'C'mon, you guys! I love this song!' said Fred, ecstatically, and the couples got up to dance, leaving Dave, Dan, Tom, Stuart, Natalie and Scarlet at the table.

As I was dancing with Annie, I caught sight of Gabrielle, from Gamestation. Buggeration, she could not catch Fred with Ruby-lynn! I watched her nervously as she and her friends made their way to the bar for drinks. I looked over at Fred, who I could tell had seen her too, and I was not surprised to see him looking massively terrified. I caught his eye. He looked like he was mouthing something at me. He looked like he was trying to say, 'Act natural!' I then saw Fred give me a nod. I nodded too, to show I'd got the message.

Both me and Fred watched as Gabrielle and her friends began walking straight towards us. Oh, fuck, fuck, fuck! Gabrielle glanced in Fred's direction. I was ready for her to do a double take when realising exactly who that was, all over another girl, but luckily she couldn't have looked less bothered, and she and her mates walked straight past him and sat down.

I saw Fred and Ruby-lynn break apart and she started walking towards the stairs. I broke away from Annie and said, 'Just need a word with Fred, babe, yeah?'

'Course, hun,' said Annie, and she sat back down with the others, as I went over to Fred.

'Talk about super close!' said Fred, sounding breathless with relief. We agreed we should keep our masks on all night, in case we ran into Gabrielle again, or any of the other girls that Fred had been seeing behind Ruby-lynn's back, who would recognise me too.

As soon as we all arrived in the Lazy Lizard, where we moved on to after we left Dusk, I saw Lizzy and Charlie rush up the steps and began to dance together. We all watched, bemused as Charlie kissed Lizzy multiple times as they danced.

Out of the corner of my eye, I saw a slightly plump red haired girl, who looked about Charlie's age, stood by the bar, watching Lizzy and Charlie. She had a jealous look on her face. Who was she?

I nudged Dave.

'Alright?' said Dave, looking round.

Pointing the girl out to Dave, I asked, 'Do you know who that is?'

'That's Priscilla Atkinson. Stuart said she was in his and Charlie's tutor group at Carrie Mount.'

I looked over at Priscilla. She looked as though she might run off crying shortly. She obviously had it bad for Charlie.

I looked round at Fred, who hadn't noticed Priscilla.

'C'mon, we can't let *them* two have all the fun! Let's get our girlfriends up there!' he said.

We took our girlfriends by the hands, onto the dance floor and we joined Lizzy and Charlie. Twenty-two minutes later, Dave, Stuart, Dan, Tom, Scarlet and Natalie joined us.

We'd gone to a couple more clubs, and then decided to head to Rendezvous.

I walked with Dave, who looked like he was feeling left out. I felt sorry for him. He was the only one who hadn't made any success with the woman he really fancied, whilst the rest of us had exciting things going on in our love lives.

'You alright?' I asked him.

'Yeah, sure,' said Dave, but I didn't believe him. I knew Dave really meant, 'No, I'm not, I'm just pretending I am, just so I don't have to talk about what's bothering me,' although not saying those words.

'You still sore about your teacher?' I asked, hoping I wouldn't end up wishing I hadn't.

'I'm still embarrassed, but I've finally made up with Stuart, he's forgiven me, Dave said, 'and my coursework's beginning to get better, which Alyssa's pleased about, and I know that does not mean she fancies me, because I've learnt to accept that.'

'I'm glad to hear it, mate,' I said, patting Dave on the back. He gave me a weak smile.

As usual, when we entered Rendezvous, we got drinks and, because most of the music that was playing was some of our favourite songs, we spent most of our time dancing.

Us lads had such a great time on the dance floor; we'd barely noticed where the girls got to.

I caught sight of Ruby-lynn and Annie bringing out Scarlet, who had her arms draped round the backs of their necks, and she was breathing very heavily, and she was sobbing. All three of them had taken off their masks.

Me and Fred rushed over to them.

'Is she okay?' Fred said.

'She's really, *really* drunk, that's all,' Ruby-lynn explained. Annie told me and Fred how she had gone into the ladies' toilets to find Scarlet knelt on the floor in one of the cubicles, with the door wide open, hyperventilating, with vomit round her mouth, all over her chin, and down her front.

'She can barely stand up, she's had *way* too many jagerbombs!' Ruby-lynn had said. It's okay, Scarlet, I'm here.'

'Omigod, Scarlet, are you okay?' cried Lizzy, rushing over.

'Too many jagerbombs,' said Annie. 'She'll be fine, though.'

I took off my mask. We needed to get Scarlet home and sober her up, so me and Fred helped Annie and Ruby-lynn take her outside.

'Bee Cars is just round the corner,' said Ruby-lynn. She said she should go home with Scarlet and that she would be fine with her. So, when Fred, me, Annie and Ruby-lynn took Scarlet to the taxi office, Fred, me and Annie said goodbye to Scarlet and Ruby-lynn.

After that, we decided to head home. Me, Fred, Natalie and Annie got a taxi home, together, as we were all going in the same direction. We said goodbye to the others.

Annie was the first to be dropped off. I got out of the taxi, walked her to her door and gave her a kiss goodnight.

I was the second to be dropped off. I said goodbye to Fred and Natalie, told Fred I hoped he'd had a good birthday, and went to let myself in. I didn't turn on any of the lights. I crept upstairs, quietly, so as not to wake Rochella or Mum. I went to my room, shut the door, undressed, and got into bed.

As I hadn't got so drunk, I wasn't hung over on Sunday morning. I got up and went down to breakfast. I fixed myself a nice big bowl of Rice Crispies to fill myself up. I wanted to ask Mum what she and Christian had spoken about, the day before, but worried she might still be a bit too huffy about it to tell me.

Rochella had been out with Sarah, but she came home at two o'clock. Mum didn't seem to be in a rush to tell her and me about what Christian had said, unfortunately, but later on, when we were sat in the lounge with cups of tea and coffee, she carefully brought the subject round to Jamie.

'Okay, now, the first thing I want to get off my chest is not going to be the easiest part to say,' she began. 'It's about what Christian had been telling Jamie about me and you, Rochella.'

I looked round at Rochella, who nodded, seeming to have understood.

'And this has a lot to do with why he never replied to any of your letters,' Mum continued. 'Here's the thing. I'm afraid Christian has been telling Jamie a couple of untrue stories about us.'

Untrue stories? As in... downright *lies*?

'The truth is... the truth is, he told Jamie that me and Rochella were, well... dead.'

My dad faked my mum and sister's deaths?

Rochella looked affronted.

'What do you mean, "He told Jamie we were dead"?'

'Christian told Jamie that Rochella died of a blood clot to the brain, and that I committed suicide out of grief, by overdosing myself,' Mum explained, her voice catching

I couldn't believe it. Christian hadn't just shut us out of his life; he'd wiped us out of existence. Well, Mum and Rochella, anyway, since he didn't know I existed. I knew Christian turned out to be a bit of a twat, but I never thought he'd do a thing like that.

'The next thing I want to talk about, which we are going to need to discuss together, is what your father said that he'd wanted to talk to me about, yesterday,' Mum said. 'What he'd asked of me whilst the three of you were upstairs.'

Mum took a deep breath, said, 'I understand if either or feel it's too much, or things are happening too fast, but how would you feel about the idea of Jamie coming to stay with us?'

I didn't know what to say. I didn't know what to think. I'd only known my long lost brother for a few minutes, and Mum was already talking about him staying with us?

'Like I said, I know it feels too soon at the moment, but I don't mean immediately,' Mum explained. 'Your father was hoping, maybe in a couple of months time. I had said, myself, that I wanted him living with me when I had found out how he had been treating him, but your father said that it was madness, the idea of my taking Jamie away from him just like that, when this was only the first time I'd seen him, but I compromised, saying that maybe it didn't have to happen eventually, and told him to think about it.'

'I was angry because, even though he said it would help everyone, which I think it will, he's only doing it to be shot of Jamie,' she went on to explain,' and he changed his mind and decided he did want Jamie living with us when it had occurred to him that that would be his chance to wash his hands of Jamie.'

'So, in other words, he was just being selfish?' I guessed.

'That's right,' said Mum.

She went on to say we could both go away and think about it, but maintained that it would be a good idea, that Jamie seemed quite keen, and she wanted him to come.

'But why would Christian pretend we were dead, then dump Jamie on us?' Rochella asked, confused.

'He'd only taken Jamie with him to use him as leverage to get more money after the divorce,' Mum said. And he's been treating Jamie very badly throughout his childhood, and has actually been making his life a misery. He lied to him to keep us apart, because I would find out he'd been mistreating him and insist on taking him away with me and he'd lose that leverage. When Jamie had found out Christian had been lying to him, he knew he'd been caught out, and had to tell him the truth and let him meet me. Jamie told me all of this when we met.'

I felt fucking terrible for Jamie. I didn't know how far the 'making Jamie's life a misery,' part went, but I didn't get why Christian bothered keeping Jamie in the dark about our mum and sister, and lying about their deaths. And Jamie had had to spend his whole life, living with someone who abused him, and believing there was no one alive that loved him. Why hadn't Jamie been taken away by social services and gone into care? He would've been better off then, probably. He needs freedom from the abuse.

I did indeed go away to think about the idea of Jamie coming to live with us. I went to my room, where I could think about it in peace.

Mum did say that it wasn't going to happen immediately, and I did hope a couple of months would be long enough for me to come round to the idea. And maybe me and Rochella would see Jamie a few more times over those months, and get to know him more, so that it wouldn't be weird when the time came?

But what if it didn't work out? Then what? But I supposed Mum might have already taken that into account, and was willing to do what she could to make it work, and would try to encourage me, Jamie and Rochella to do the same and make some effort.

All in all, whatever decision was put forward would partly rest with me. I needed to give it some more serious thought, and maybe discuss it further, with my mum and sister.

Chapter 7:

Scarlet's First

Friday 28th January 2011

When were Dan and Tom going to get called up to the stage? Me and Dave had set them up to sing Aqua's "Barbie Girl" for a laugh, but they hadn't been announced yet.

I was in the New Vic with Dave, Dan, Tom and Stuart. They often have karaoke nights there. I thought it probably best to go easy on the alcohol, after what happened when we went out for Fred's birthday. I'd remembered what had happened, and I couldn't be more embarrassed.

'So, Scarlet, what song are you going to sing next?' asked Dave, handing me a folder that was full of lists of songs they had on the karaoke sound system. I looked through them. I was spoiled for choice. I'd only sung a couple of songs so far; Martine McCutcheon's "I've Got You," and "Rise" by Gabrielle.

I eventually decided on Sophie Ellis Bexter's "Music Gets the Best of Me." Some of the boys had put their names down for a few songs, too. Tom had chosen "Shake It," by that band, Metro... something or other, Dave had chosen Jason Mraz's "I'm Yours," Stuart wanted to sing the Backstreet Boys' "Larger Than Life," and Dan had chosen "Shine A Light" by McFly and Taio Cruz. I took the pieces of paper with our names and song selections to the front. When I sat back down, I saw Dave and Stuart writing another song on another piece of paper.

'What song are you thinking of?' I asked them, interestedly.

'Not saying!' said Stuart, teasingly. He gave me a cheeky grin. I was sure it was a prank. I saw Stuart get to his feet and take the note up to the front. I looked round at Tom, who shrugged his shoulders.

Finally, the man who'd been announcing who was singing which song said, 'Next up, we have Dan Hart and Tom Harris, with "Barbie Girl," by Aqua!'

Lots of people in the bar laughed.

'What?!' yelled both Dan and Tom, together.

'Go on up, boys!' teased Stuart.

'Nope! No! No fucking way, I'm not doing it! Sorry!' Dan said.

'Aw c'mon, don't be such a spoilsport!' said Stuart, pulling Dan out of his chair by his arms.

'C'mon, it'll be a laugh!' Tom cajoled him, grabbing his left arm.

'Fuck you lot!' Dan shouted, angrily, as Tom and Stuart frogmarched him over to the stage. Normally Dan's tendency to take himself too seriously to take a joke when he was the butt of it really got on my nerves, but this time, I couldn't help finding it funny.

I watched as Dan and Tom stepped up onto the stage and picked up the microphones. The song began and, as much to my amusement as everyone else's, Dan sung all Ken's lines, and Tom sang Barbie's lines, including the part where they were talking at the beginning and the end! Dan sounded unenthusiastic and Tom was having trouble singing clearly whilst laughing his head off at the same time, and everyone had cracked up. Some people were crying with laughter.

Everyone was laughing so hard at the very end, mainly because, right after Tom realised what he'd just had to say to Dan, he shouted, '_What_?!' They both walked back to their seats, strawberry red in the face, Tom smirking, Dan looking properly sulky!

'So gonna fucking get you all for this!' he said through gritted teeth, flinging himself back down in his seat. Jesus Dan, lighten up!

An hour later, after we'd sung our songs, the man had announced that the next song would be me and Tom, singing, "We've Got Tonight," by Lulu and Ronan Keating.

'Oh, very funny!' I said, looking over at Dave and Stuart, remembering Stuart being so secretive about what he and Dave were writing down. Reluctantly, I followed Tom up to the stage and we picked up the microphones.

I watched and listened as Tom started with Ronan's lines. Just as he began singing the third line, I saw him look sideways at me, nervously, and then at the audience again. I could tell he sounded a bit embarrassed too.

I sang Lulu's lines, feeling a bit awkward about singing a romantic duet with a friend who was a boy. But when it got to the chorus, we suddenly caught each other's eyes, and then quickly looked away again. People were cheering.

At the end of the song, we sat back down, smiling shyly at each other.

'*Nice!*' said Dan, nodding at us, grinning.

The boys were still teasing Dan and Tom about having to sing Barbie Girl when we all left. We were walking along the esplanade, with Stuart putting on a girly voice, mimicking Tom.

'Fuck off,' said Tom.

'Aw, do you two love each other, now?' teased Dave, putting on a high voice.

'Just give it a fucking rest, will you?' Dan spat, still failing to see the funny side.

'Oh, get over yourself, Dan! It was a laugh!' Stuart said, and I noticed he sounded a bit irritated.

I caught Tom's eye as he looked over his shoulder at me.

'You go on, Dan,' I heard him say. Dan walked on ahead as Tom and I hung back to talk.

'You put us up for it, didn't you?' said Tom, smirking

'Me and Dave did, yeah' I said, and Tom and I laughed.

'It was classic prank,' Tom admitted. We caught each other's eyes again. We looked into each other's eyes, still smiling, and then Tom looked down, the smile fading, slightly.

'You were really good in there,' he said. I felt myself blushing. 'You have a really great singing voice, you know,' Tom went on.

'Thanks,' I said, looking down, bashfully. This was the first time I'd ever felt shy around a boy. What was wrong with me?

We caught up with the others, before Dan, Stuart and I said goodbye to Tom, who was getting a different bus, and Dave, who was walking home, then went to the number two bus stop.

The three of us went to bed as soon as we got home. I have quite a big bedroom, as I have to share it with my sister, Crimson.

Crimson and I both have names that are different shades of red because red was always our parents' colour when they were together. It was the colour of the dress our mum wore on their first date. It was the colour of the ruby in the engagement ring our dad had presented her with when he proposed. It was the colour of the tie our dad wore on their wedding day, and the colour of the bouquet of roses our mum carried, as well as the dresses that all her bridesmaids wore, whilst carrying bouquets of white roses.

After finishing her A Levels, Crimson took a gap year in Russia. Now she's studying Biological and Forensic Science at university.

I, on the other hand, was in my first year of the two-year course in Health Social Care I'm doing at Fleetview College, as I want a job in social work, or something similar.

I got into bed and turned off the light. But I did not go to sleep. I felt very weird about tonight. Not *bad* weird, it's just that when I caught Tom's eye, I was unsure of whether or not I felt something. Maybe I did feel something ever so slightly, but I didn't know for certain.

I went to the kitchen and made myself a coffee in the morning. Emily and Kathryn, my ten-year-old identical twin stepsisters-in-waiting almost knocked into me from behind as I entered. My stepmum-in-waiting, Leslie, came in.

'For goodness sake, Scarlet,' she said, irritated, without even bothering to say good morning and ask me if I slept well. 'Why can't you put your bag and shoes away in the cupboard when you arrive home? Someone could trip over them!'

I sighed, impatiently. Since the start of Leslie's relationship with my dad, she's been my enemy. And Emily and Kathryn aren't any better. Leslie always spoils them. At *my* expense! And my dad never takes my complaints about it seriously! Whenever this happens, I feel like Leslie has corrupted him.

'Hallway's looking a bit untidy,' my dad said, out in the hall.

'Maybe if a certain person hadn't left her stuff lying around, it probably wouldn't be,' said Leslie, looking over at me. I looked at her, evilly. I wanted to answer back, but I knew that would only lead to another argument. Another one of the arguments I've had with Leslie in the past. She's the sort of person who only ever looks at her own children through rose tinted glasses. She lets the twins get away with murder. If anyone else tries doing one bad thing under her nose, then, not only does she give you a big lecture for it, but also she goes on about it at any opportunity she can.

The twins were both sat side by side at the kitchen table, looking all sweet and innocent.

'It's okay, Leslie, it's done, let's just let it go, shall we?' said my dad, hesitantly.

'No, it's not okay!' said Leslie, crossly. 'It just isn't good enough! My daughters never leave their things all over the floor!'

The only person I get on well with in my dad's new family is Stuart, as Leslie's snooty attitude hasn't rubbed off on him like it had on Dan. No, he must've got more of his dad's nice nature. Well, I don't know that for sure. I never knew him. Stuart said he used to work as a chef in a restaurant somewhere, I can't remember what it was called, but then there was a fire in the kitchen and he didn't make it out.

Leslie sighed.

'I don't know why your daughter can't be like my two angels!' she said. My dad, sounding very defensive, told her that I had always done very well at school.

'She never got a certificate for doing so well in swimming though, did she?' said Leslie, proudly, walking over to Emily and giving her a kiss on her forehead, smiling. Well that was where she was wrong!

'Actually, I got three, when I was younger than Emily was,' I retorted. So *there*!

'Mum, Scarlet's saying I'm rubbish at swimming!' said Emily. She and Kathryn have many ways of getting me into trouble, and twisting things I say, to make it look like I'm being conceited and unkind is one of them.

'Scarlet, Emily is not rubbish at swimming!' said Leslie, crossly.

'We all know that I did *not* say that,' I protested, annoyed.

'Tell Emily you're sorry and that Emily is very good at swimming, at once,' Leslie ordered me.

I sighed. 'I'm sorry for telling you you're rubbish at swimming,' I said, reluctantly.

'She didn't say I was good at swimming! She was supposed to say I was good at swimming,' demanded Emily.

'Say it, Scarlet,' said Leslie, with that warning tone in her voice, so, as disinclined to do so as I was, I told Emily that she was very good at swimming.

'That's better,' said Leslie. 'Kevin, you want to have a word with your daughter. She can't go around telling everyone that she's better than them.'

I gave Leslie another evil look, and helped myself to some breakfast.

My mum has remarried, and it's fair to say that I like her new family, the Sparks, better then Leslie, her superior son, and her two bratty daughters, although I feel that my thirteen-year-old-stepsister, Katie, from my mum's new family, can be irritatingly nosey at times.

I went upstairs to get dressed. Stuart came out of his room.

'Mum having a go again?' he asked.

'How did you guess?' I asked, sarcastically. Stuart reminded me that at least I only had to put up with it half the time he did.

I left the house at quarter past ten, now here I was in Dolce Vita with Dave, Lizzy, Ruby-lynn, Fred and Jesse, sat at a table near one of the bay windows. I was not surprised to see that Natalie couldn't make it.

'Had a good time last night, then?' asked Fred, once I joined them all. Dave and I wasted no time in telling Lizzy, Jesse, Fred and Ruby-lynn about the karaoke at the New Vic and Dan and Tom's singing Barbie Girl. Both Fred and Jesse fell about laughing.

'Did you sing any songs?' asked Ruby-lynn.

'Yeah, I sang a few,' I said.

'So did I,' said Dave.

I then told the others how Dave and Stuart had set Tom and I up for a duet, before saying I was going to get a drink and asked Lizzy and Ruby-lynn if they were coming.

'Sure,' said Lizzy, as she and Ruby-lynn stood up and followed me to the bar.

Whilst we waited to be served, Lizzy picked up on the fact that Natalie hadn't been able to come, yet again. I was getting fed up of it. I had no idea what was going on and I knew that Fred was getting worried.

'I wish Natalie had just listened to us all about V because I knew he was trouble!' I ranted, crossly. 'But every time we try to warn her off about a boyfriend she's seeing, who's bad news, she accuses us of being jealous that she has a boyfriend and we don't and I've had enough of it!'

I looked round at Lizzy and Ruby-lynn, who were looking at me, their eyebrows raised.

'Sorry,' I said.

We ordered our drinks and sat back down to talk to the boys about it whilst we viewed the menus.

'Have you noticed Natalie behaving any differently when she does come home?' I asked Fred.

'I have noticed her looking shaken, yeah,' he said. 'Why?'

'Have you tried asking her what's wrong, when she behaves in that way when coming home?' I asked him.

'Natalie just gets snappy at me,' Fred said, before a waiter came and asked us if we were ready to order.

'V lives near me, actually,' Lizzy said, after we'd all ordered. 'That's what Natalie told me.'

'Have you ever seen V before?' I asked Lizzy, and Lizzy said she hadn't.

I tried not to think about it as I tucked into the gammon steak I'd ordered.

Ruby-lynn enlightened us about how she and Fred were planning to go to Longleat together, the following weekend. I've been to Longleat before, a few times with my mum's new family, but I'm not that fussed about it.

Funny though, I noticed Fred looked a bit uneasy. I didn't know why. There's nothing discomforting about a lovely day trip with your girlfriend.

'I'm hoping we can go on the safari boat trip!' said Ruby-lynn, excitedly. Jesse said it sounded good and Lizzy asked how they were getting up there.

'I can drive, can't I?' said Fred, sounding slightly calmer. Lizzy started talking about Longleat house, and all the other attractions there.

'I am looking forward to it,' said Ruby-lynn, smiling.

We decided to look at the menu to choose what to have for dessert, but I wasn't that hungry.

I walked through town after I'd said goodbye to the gang. I didn't feel like going home just yet. It was quite a sunny day, though not very warm, so I felt it was a shame to let it go to waste.

I got myself a black coffee from Costa. I've always preferred my teas and coffees black. I'm just not that keen on white teas or coffees. I normally prefer to drink coffees like Americano and Espresso, or even just a regular coffee without milk will do for me. Without sugar as well, as I don't exactly have a sweet tooth either. I'm the complete opposite of Lizzy, who likes lots of milk and as many sugars as it takes to make her teas and coffees sweet enough.

I drank my regular black coffee as I walked to Radipole Park Drive. As I walked along the pavement, I looked over at Radipole Lake. It was such a picturesque view.

When I reached the park, I saw Tom and Dan playing football with some boys I didn't recognise. I walked over to them and found somewhere to sit where I could watch.

I had been sat watching them for fifty minutes, before Tom looked round and noticed me there. As it was a split second before one of the boys kicked the ball in his direction, Tom could only manage a quick wave before he began dribbling the ball.

After another thirty-five minutes, the boys stopped.

'Alright?' said Tom, coming over to me with Dan and the other boys.

'Hey,' I said. Dan expressed surprise to see me, saying he wasn't expecting me to be here, and I told him how I'd felt like coming to chill in the park after having lunch with the gang.

As the boys were about to leave the park, Dan asked Tom if he was coming with, but Tom said he thought he'd stay and chat with me.

We sat and talked about how our courses were coming along and what we had been up to, lately. Tom told me how he'd gone away to New York for Christmas.

I was so envious. I've always wanted to go to New York, but I know how expensive it is. I would love to stay in the Plaza Hotel, take horse and carriage rides in Central Park, visit the Metropolitan Museum of Art, tour the Statue of Liberty, go shopping in Rockafeller Centre and eat in the Hard Rock Café in Time's Square.

'We went ice-skating there,' Tom told me. 'We also visited China Town and went to Madame Tussauds, and Central Park Zoo.

'Sounds amazing!' I said. 'I didn't go anywhere for Christmas. I was at my dad's place. It was quite good, though. My stepmum-in-waiting's parents had joined us for Christmas Day.'

Tom started rummaging in his rucksack.

'Red Bull?' he offered.

'Sure,' I said, so Tom handed me a can and we both drank.

'My stepmum-in-waiting doesn't approve of this sort of stuff,' I said.

'I hope I won't get you into trouble later,' Tom joked.

'I don't really care what she thinks. She's so annoying,' I said.

'Yeah, I see where Dan gets it from,' said Tom. He and I laughed.

''You're lucky your parents are still together,' I told Tom.

'Well, I'm certainly lucky to have an older sister, as I don't think I could stand the idea of having two annoying *younger* sisters like Emily and Kathryn.'

'They're brats,' I agreed.

We both finished our drinks and put our empty cans in the bin.

'C'mon, let's go on the swings,' said Tom, standing up and running over to the swings.

'Want to see who can swing the highest?' I asked, catching up with him. We sat on the swings and started swinging.

'Bet you can't swing higher than me!' Tom yelled.

'Bet I can!' I teased, and I swung with all my might.

Tom let go of the chains.

'Whoa!' he shouted, as he went flying onto the grass.

'SHIT!' I yelled, but to my relief, he rolled over onto his back and propped himself up onto his elbows and called to me that it was okay and he meant to do that and tried to persuade me to do it too.

'It doesn't hurt! You have soft landing!' he called to me, reassuringly. 'Just leap forward when you swing forward and let go of the chains.

I braced myself and when I swung forward, I let go and found myself flying forwards, towards the grass, where I landed, sprawled on my front a second later on Tom's right. Tom and I laughed. That was fun, I had to admit.

'See?' said Tom. I turned onto my side so that I was facing Tom. He looked at me, and I looked at him, then he leaned in, cupping my face with his left hand, and kissed me on the lips for about five seconds, before breaking away again. I looked into his eyes, and then leaned in to kiss him again.

After I broke away, I was surprised by what just happened. Tom looked at me.

'You all right?' he asked. My surprise had clearly shown on my face.

When he walked me to my bus stop and said goodbye, he kissed me again.

I sat on the bus, thinking about what happened, still unable to believe that it hadn't been a dream.

Dan was in the lounge when I got home. I went in and joined him. Dan acknowledged me and asked if I'd had a good time with Tom after he and the other boys left, which I said I had.

Dan put the T.V on mute, then asked, 'What happened, then?'

I swallowed, hard.

'Well...' I said, uncertainly, 'we kissed.'

Dan looked at me, eyebrows raised, mouth hanging open.

'Fuck me!' he said. 'I never imagined something would happen between you two! I knew Tom had liked you for a while, but I never thought you'd feel the same! How did it happen?'

'I can't explain it,' I said. 'It just sort of... *did*.'

Dan gave a very bewildered laugh then sat back, took the T.V off mute, and carried on watching. I watched too.

The next few weeks had been some of my best. Hanging out with Tom was always so exciting. He was very spontaneous. Most of the times when we had arranged to meet, Tom didn't tell me what we were doing, he always surprised me.

He took me on the most amazing dates. The first time, we took the train up to Bournemouth, where he surprised me with a trip to the ice skating rink.

The best time was two days before Valentine's Day, when he took me on a surprise trip on Bluebird Coaches up to London, where we went sight seeing. We looked round Trafalgar Square, the National Gallery, the Tower of London and we went to see the Crown Jewels. And then we'd gone to take photos of Buckingham Palace. After that, we went to take a tour on H.M.S Belfast. He gave me the most gorgeous No7 gift set as a Valentines' present. I love their stuff. He also gave me a Me to You teddy bear, holding an S for Scarlet. I was so touched.

I never got bored of him.

Saturday 19th February 2011

I was in the lounge with Stuart, who had Dave round. I heard a car pulling up outside the house, and then I heard Dan and Tom's voices from outside, followed by the sounds of two car doors slamming. Finally, I heard Dan letting himself and Tom in through the front door.

'Hey, what's up, you guys?' he said, when he came into the lounge with Tom.

Tom came over and gave me a kiss hello as he sat down next to me. He then started bragging about how he had a Range Rover.

'Fuck me!' said Dave, before Stuart cut in.

'Where the hell did you manage to get a Range Rover?'

'Does it matter?' said Dan.

The five of us went outside to the driveway where a silver Range Rover Sport was parked.

Tom asked us all if we fancied a ride. All of the boys were up for it, but I said I wasn't so sure.

'Ah, don't be *boring*, Scarlet!' Tom teased me. That got to me, so I went along with them.

'Front passenger seat's for the missus, of course,' said Tom.

'Not if I'm calling shot gun!' Dan insisted.

'In you get in the back, Dan!' I said, getting into the front with Tom, who then started up the car and turned out onto the road and we sped off up the road. We drove through Littlemoor Road and onto Dorchester Road.

'How, where and when did you get the car?' Dave asked Tom.

'Ummm...' said Dan and Tom together, awkwardly. I noticed Tom sounded nervous when he said he got it second hand. I didn't know Tom had taken any driving lessons, let alone had a licence to drive, but I didn't ask any questions.

Tom made a sharp turn down Monmouth Avenue. He was driving so fast he was making the car swerve all over the road! The boys were cheering, like we were on a roller coaster.

We drove past the roads that turned off Monmouth Avenue, and then we reached the Rugby Club. There was a gate barring the entrance to the car park. To my horror, Tom drove right into it, and went crashing right through it! Tom then drove onto the big stretch of grass to the side of the car park and started speeding all over it.

The boys were all screeching, 'WHOOOOOOOOOOOOOOOO!!!!' and I was screaming as the car raced over the grass. Then, Tom started doing hand brake turns, making the car spin round so fast, I thought the car was going to topple over!

Tom slowed down and Dave and Stuart were blaspheming in shock. Dan, on the other hand, was in stitches with laughter.

'That was awesome!' he'd said, eagerly. I glared at him in shock. What?! We could've all been killed and he thought it was awesome?

'It don't stop here!' said Tom. 'Next, we're going through those nearby trees and other the fields behind them!' he added, pointing to the trees at the edge of the field.

I had my mind made up. I undid my seatbelt, opened the door and got out.

'Hey, where you going?' said Tom, as I stormed off.

I turned round to look at Tom again and shouted, '*HOME*!'

'I'm out of here, too,' said Dave, as he and Stuart got out the back.

'Get out of the car or I'll tell Mum,' Stuart told Dan.

'All right, you tell Mum, and I'll just move out and live with Tom!' spat Dan, but I told him not to be stupid. Dan told me that Dave, Stuart and I were the ones being stupid and that neither he nor Tom needed scaredy cats like us, but I didn't care. The five of us could've been killed, and if Tom and Dan didn't care then stuff both of them.

But I was still hurt that Tom saw me as a boring, scared, goody-goody, and I was especially shocked that Dan had gone along with it as well. Lizzy and I knew both Dan and Tom tended to be reckless, but I never dreamt it would go as far as reckless *driving*!

Dave, Stuart and I stormed off and Dan and Tom drove off.

It had been a very long walk back up Monmouth Avenue. Whilst Dave and Stuart were fuming about Dan and Tom, and how Stuart was going to tell Leslie everything, I spent that entire walk thinking of what we'd been a part of. I was shaking.

At last, we reached Dorchester Road, crossed and waited at the bus stop near the Spa.

Worst of all, I didn't know what this meant for my relationship with Tom. When this suddenly occurred to me, I burst into tears and was glad no one else but Dave and Stuart were at the bus stop.

I'd managed to fight back the tears when the Littlemoor bus arrived. I didn't want the driver or other bus passengers to see me crying.

As soon as I got home, I went straight up to my room. I didn't hear Stuart telling Leslie what had happened, but I did hear Leslie go ballistic.

I wouldn't leave my room until teatime. Dan hadn't come home all night. I wouldn't talk to him when he had come home on Sunday, when the twins and I were the only ones who were in. Tom was with him, wanting to see me.

'I'll leave you to it,' said Dan, when they had come up to my room, and then he left the room. I waited nervously for Tom to talk. I had no idea what he wanted to tell me. Was he going to dump me? Or was he going to say I was right for walking off, because he and Dan had been so stupid?

'I have no idea how you managed to pass your driving test,' I said at last.

'I haven't even taken any driving lessons, never mind pass a driving test,' Tom said, 'and it wasn't even my car we were in.'

'Whose it was then?' I asked. 'Have you borrowed it from a friend? Because I know it's not Dan's.'

But Tom said, 'Me and Dan stole it.'

I gasped. I was horrified. They'd been joyriding!

I felt red-hot anger inside me.

'YOU'RE *ARSEHOLES*!' I screamed. '*BOTH* OF YOU! Just get out, okay?! I don't want to see you *ever* again! We're done!'

Immediately, I noticed Tom's eyes were now shining with tears. But I wasn't going to cave in, not after how stupid he'd been.

'Scarlet, please,' Tom said.

'Just go, Tom, you heard what I said,' I said, starting to cry myself. Tom turned and, after one last look over his shoulder at me, he opened the door and left the room. I heard him thundering down the stairs, fling open the front door, then slam it again. Then, I flopped down onto the bed and sobbed and sobbed and sobbed.

I heard footsteps, then the sound of someone pushing the door open and coming into my room. I looked up and saw Dan, stood in the doorway.

'Leave me alone,' I sniffed, and hid my face in my pillow, but Dan didn't leave.

'You two broke up, then?' he asked. I looked up at him, angrily. He was really trying my patience.

'Go away!' I yelled. 'You're just as much of an idiot for going along with it as he is!'

Dan sighed and left the room.

I'd spent the next week in total misery. I could barely concentrate in college, and my coursework was suffering. I sat up in my room every evening and never went out. I didn't want to answer any texts, calls or Facebook messages I received. Tom kept texting me, saying he was sorry, but I didn't want to talk to him.

Friday 25th February 2011

Ruby-lynn came round to see me in the evening. I had lots of texts and calls from her, but never answered them, so I knew Ruby-lynn was probably getting worried about me.

I was lying on my bed, very depressed, when my mum, whose turn it was to have me this week, brought Ruby-lynn up to my room and then left us to it.

'I am really sorry that you and Tom had to break up over what happened,' she said. 'But you did the right thing.'

I sat up and told her, 'I do, truthfully, want to make up with him, but I know that hanging around with him will only put me in more danger.'

'You're a wiser person than Natalie, you know,' said Ruby-lynn. I nodded.

'But I still really miss him!' I said, starting to cry. Ruby-lynn gave me a hug and I cried into Ruby-lynn's shoulder. After I stopped crying and started to dry my tears, Ruby-lynn drew away.

'Are you still coming round Lizzy's on her birthday? It might cheer you up,' Ruby-lynn persuaded me.

'I'll think about it,' I said, but then I thought about something else. 'Hang on, she hasn't invited Dan and Tom has she?' I wanted to check, cautiously.

'What, knowing they nearly got you, Dave and Stuart killed?' said Ruby-lynn, giving a disbelieving laugh. 'Lucky Charlie hadn't been in that car, cos if he got hurt, Lizzy never would've forgiven them! Lizzy's made it plain that she doesn't want them at the party after how reckless and stupid they've been.'

Ruby-lynn was right. Maybe it would cheer me up. Maybe I'd have a fabulous time at Lizzy's birthday party. I always do, round at her place. And I couldn't stay sat at home, moping around forever. And I knew that, despite her knowledge of what happened with Tom, Lizzy would be extremely disappointed if I didn't come round.

So, after Ruby-lynn left, I started getting things ready for Sunday. I'd already bought Lizzy some presents, which were some toiletries from Ted Baker, and make-up from Collection 2000.

I still needed to wrap them up, but I still hadn't done that, yet. So, I got busy with all of that. I chose some pink paper that had pictures of cupcakes on it. Then I found a nice, baby pink gift bag with a picture of a Dalmatian puppy on it, to put the presents in. Then, I planned what I was going to wear.

When I arrived at Lizzy's house on Sunday, Lizzy was overjoyed to see me and gave me a big hug.

'Happy Birthday, Lizzy,' I said, and then gave Lizzy the bag of presents.

'Ah, thanks so much,' said Lizzy, happily, 'I love the puppy on the bag, and I'm so glad you were able to come!'

I followed her in. The hallway was decorated in balloons of ice cream colours, which I know are Lizzy's favourite. As I went through the dining room, Mr and Mrs Graham were laying the table with cupcakes in various flavours and topped with icing of lots of different colours. There were sandwiches, Pringles in many flavours, slices of garlic bread, quiche and pizza, popcorn chicken, pork pies, sausage rolls, and chocolate brownies.

Lizzy and I went to the lounge, where Dave, Fred, Natalie, Jesse, Annie and Ruby-lynn were. There were more pastel colour balloons, and a big pink and silver banner saying 'Happy Birthday!'

Both Ruby-lynn and Natalie rushed over to me and gave me hugs in turn. Even Penny seemed happy to see me. She had come rushing over to me and started licking my hands, affectionately.

Lizzy had brought her Playstation 2 down from her room, which had music playing on it, and her dance mat was laid out on the floor in front of the T.V, and her Dance Edition Playstation game that came with it. She had some Tomb Raider games, and a couple of car racing games, one of which her dad used to enjoy playing with her and her brothers. There was also a multi tap on the floor by the Playstation, for if we wanted three or four player games.

Lizzy added the bag of presents I gave her to the heap of presents next to the fireplace.

I also noticed that, for some strange reason, there was a big desk fan propped up on the floor. I wondered what it was for as, being February, it was nowhere near hot enough for anyone to need a fan, but then I saw Fred and Jesse opening bags of confetti and decanting them into a large bucket, and I realised what it was for. On the coffee table there was a box of party poppers.

We had drinks of Pepsi, Sprite, Fanta, Lilt, Schloers and J2Os and started by playing on Lizzy's Playstation. We all took turns having multiplayer races on her Crash Bandicoot game; Crash Team Racing, then we had two player races on her other car racing game, Test Drive 6.

Next, we watched as Lizzy opened all her presents, before we played on Lizzy's dance mat. Ruby-lynn danced to S Club 7's "Don't Stop Movin'", Jesse danced to the Bloodhound Gang's "Bad Touch," and Natalie danced to Kylie Minogue's "Can't Get You Out Of My Head."

We went to the dining room to get some food and ate it in the lounge whilst taking turns playing some more Playstation games. I sat with Fred and Jesse.

'You okay?' Jesse asked me. I nodded.

'I'm glad Dave and Stuart had the sense to walk away when I did,' I told them both. I told them how Leslie had a fit when Stuart told her what happened, and that Dan wouldn't come home.

'I don't know what that's gonna mean for Dan and Nikki,' said Fred.

I didn't know if Dan and Nikki would break up. I knew Nikki was sensible, but I also knew she loved Dan, so she wouldn't know what to do.

After we'd eaten, we let off some of the party poppers and made a confetti blizzard by tipping the bucket of confetti that Fred and Jesse had prepared, into the fan. All the girls, including me, squealed.

Finally, we had a marathon of some of the D.V.Ds Lizzy had for her birthday, and I was enjoying myself so much, I forgot all about Tom!

We finished off with Lizzy's birthday cake, which was a white chocolate and strawberry sponge cake. It tasted okay, for something that would usually be too sweet for me.

Everyone went home at half past six. When I said goodbye to Lizzy, I told her I hoped she had a good evening with Charlie.

'Thanks,' Lizzy had said. 'And thanks for coming. I know you've been really downhearted but I hope you enjoyed today as much as I did and I really appreciated you coming.'

She gave me a hug, and then I left. My mum came to pick me up, as I didn't want to get two buses home. My mum asked me how the party went, but I wasn't very talkative, despite the marvellous time I'd had. I was starting to remember the amazing times I'd had when Tom was my boyfriend. But I fought back my tears.

Once I returned home, I went to my room, and set about, trying to fix where my coursework was failing.

On Monday at Fleetview, my tutor was pleased that I was starting to make progress again.

Afterwards, I thought I'd get the bus into town and have a stroll along the seafront. I thought of maybe dropping into Zellweger's to see Ruby-lynn, until I remembered Ruby-lynn didn't work Mondays.

When I arrived in town, I walked up Bond Street, then, as I started walking up St Thomas Street, I bumped into Dan.

'What's up?' he said.

'All right,' I said, still annoyed with him. I was hoping he would admit that he and Tom had been absolute morons, but I was so wrong! To my horror, he started on about how awesome and hilarious it had been and how I had really missed out.

'You would've enjoyed it if you hadn't walked away,' he said. 'Me and Tom drove through a field of sheep!' he added, ecstatically.

I glared at him, furiously.

'Are you actually serious in telling me I would've enjoyed endangering the lives of, not only my friends, but also innocent creatures!' I shouted at him, making people passing us stare, but I didn't care. Dan jumped back, shocked.

'Whoa! Calm down, there! Why are you getting so angry?' he asked me, as if he'd done nothing wrong. 'None of them got run over.'

'That's not the point; you still took that risk, didn't you?' I replied, angrily.

'Worth it, though!' laughed Dan. 'Seeing all them dumb sheep shitting themselves and whizzing out of the way! Never seen anything so funny!' and he fell about in hysterics. I was livid.

'You are an actual dickhead, Dan,' I said.

'Er, now, hang on, you really are being a bit of a hypocrite, lecturing me about killing innocent farm animals,' said Dan, smirking.

What? How on Earth was I being a hypocrite?

'How?' I snapped, furiously.

'Well, I've never known you to be a vegetarian,' said Dan.

What the hell? Why did Dan start talking about vegetarianism? What did it have to do with joyriding?

'And that's supposed to mean what?' I asked.

'What about the steaks, burgers, sausages and mince that you eat, that were originally cows, sheep and pigs that were killed, just to be made into food that you buy and pay for?' Dan asked. I was speechless. How and why was this relevant?

'Don't try to twist morality, Dan, you know you've been beyond careless!' I barked, and stormed off. I couldn't believe it. He and his best mate had stolen a car and gone driving around in it, recklessly, without a licence, putting so many lives in danger, and he thought it was funny, and even had the audacity to accuse me of overreacting and being a hypocrite.

That was the thing with Dan. He never thought what he was doing was wrong. He was an arrogant tosser and screw Tom if he was going to side with him.

I reached the beach. Something did lighten my mood. Lizzy was there, playing fetch with Penny. I went down to join her. I called Lizzy's name. Lizzy looked round and saw me.

'Hey Lizzy!' I said, smiling. We hugged.

'You all right?' said Lizzy.

'Yeah, I'm okay,' I said. I joined Lizzy whilst she continued to walk Penny, then, when we both became hungry and thirsty, we went to get chips and hot drinks from the Boat Cafe.

We sat at a bench on the deck overlooking the beach.

'I've bumped into Dan, who's still acting like he hasn't done anything wrong,' I told Lizzy.

'It's an outrage,' Lizzy agreed.

'Ruby-lynn said that you wouldn't answer any of Tom's texts,' she said. 'Wise move. He's just as much of an idiot as Dan is.'

'And Dan called me a hypocrite for telling him off about the field of sheep he'd been driving around in,' I told her.

'Why are you a hypocrite?' asked Lizzy.

'I got annoyed because he nearly ran over the sheep,' I told Lizzy,' and Dan told me that I paid to have animals like sheep killed and made into food that I ate.'

'Like that has anything to do with how he stole a car and went speeding and had gone off road in it!' said Lizzy. 'If he's trying to turn all this around to look like it wasn't him that was in the wrong, it will. Not. Work.'

'Why have you always been friends with Dan and Tom if they're like this?' I asked Lizzy.

'Well, in their defences, the reckless stuff they have done in the past has been quite harmless in comparison to what they've done now. I thought Dan had more sense though,' she told me. 'I know it won't be easy, and it will be miserable, especially because Tom was tons of fun to be around, but you'll move on and it'll all get better, and you can have all those good times with another boyfriend.'

I knew she was right. And I knew I didn't need a boyfriend. I wasn't miserable before I got together with Tom.

When Lizzy and I finished, I decided to make my way home. I caught the number ten bus back to my mum and stepdad's house. My mum and Hudson were going out to a leaving party for one of Hudson's colleagues, so my stepbrother Norman and I had to baby sit our five-year-old half sister Megan, and baby half brother George, who I unfortunately had to change before putting him to bed.

I had the most tedious evening. Megan didn't want to play any games. She was happy just sitting in the lounge, watching some of her Barbie D.V.Ds, which bored both Norman and I to tears. She has loads, which she keeps in a Peppa Pig D.V.D box.

I had also been left in charge of cooking her a supper of fish fingers, peas, carrots and chips.

'I'm allergic to vegetables,' Megan said, when her dinner was ready. I rolled my eyes. Megan always comes up with an excuse not to eat the healthiest parts of her tea, but I *know* she isn't allergic to all vegetables.

'Don't be silly, Megan,' I told her, using the same tone our mum uses whenever Megan won't finish her tea. 'You eat it all up, or you don't get to have any Smarties afterwards.'

Hudson and my mum always give Megan packets of Smarties, Maltesers, Minstrels, and other sweets whenever she's good and eats all her dinner. She won't get anything after tea if she insists she's full up, even if she also insists she has room for pudding.

'If you've got room for pudding, you've got room to finish your supper, otherwise you're too full up for anything else,' they tell her.

Megan sighed and ate all her vegetables, along with the rest of her dinner, and I gave her a box of Smarties.

I *also* had to get Megan ready for bed at eight o'clock, but Megan had other ideas. She was still wide awake and, when I had undressed her to put her night dress on her, she went running out of the room before I had a chance to put it on!

'Megan! Come back in here!' I called after her, crossly. I got up and ran out after her, still holding Megan's lilac and turquoise My Little Pony nightie. I saw Megan run across the landing, stark naked, towards Katie's door, open it and run in.

'Megan! Get out!' came Katie's voice, sounding very irritated. Three seconds later, I saw Megan running back out, followed by Katie.

'Why is she starkers?' she demanded to know. 'She was waving her bare bum in my face!'

'She ran off before I could put her nightie on her,' I said, before chasing Megan, who had gone down the stairs, squealing and giggling. I saw her running into the kitchen.

'Scarlet's chasing me!' I heard her say. I ran into the kitchen where Norman was.

'Norman, help me,' I begged, seizing hold of Megan under the armpits and hauling her out of the kitchen and into the lounge.

'What do you want me to do?' said Norman, following me into the lounge. I told him to shut the door and stand in front of it to stop Megan escaping. I was able to put Megan's nightie on her, even though she tried to wriggle free. Norman said he'd take Megan up to bed.

'But I'm not tired!' I could hear her protest from the hall, as I heard Norman's footsteps fade as he carried her up the stairs.

I sat and lay back on the sofa. It's very annoying, how Megan's usually so well behaved when either Hudson or my mum undresses her, and yet she starts being naughty if anyone else tries. It's just because I'm not her mum she thinks she doesn't have to do as I say.

I didn't feel much like doing anything else, and now that Megan had gone to bed, I could watch what I wanted to watch on T.V. I was feeling glad that I'd met Lizzy on the beach. What she said made me feel better. I would move on from Tom, all I needed to do was try, and whilst I missed the good times I'd had with him, I could always have them with another boy, like Lizzy said.

And having a boyfriend is not the be all and end all. I wanted to try to remember that that had been how I saw things before I developed feelings for Tom.

My mood had lightened over the next few days, mainly because I'd able to concentrate a lot better on my coursework and now it was back on track.

Friday 4th March 2011

I was still dreading going back to my dad's, because I didn't want to be anywhere near Dan. But when I arrived, I'd found out that Dan had been deadly serious about his threat to move out if Stuart told on him.

A certain someone, who was not wanted, had shown up, asking to see me. I had just come downstairs after unpacking when I'd seen my dad, speaking sternly to someone at the front door, telling him he had a lot of nerve showing up, especially because of the amount of trouble he and Dan had got into. I looked over his shoulder and saw Tom stood there. I was so irritated that he hadn't taken the hint and had the nerve to come round again.

'What do you want now?' I asked him.

'Just go, she doesn't want to see you and Leslie is in the bathroom, and is not going to want to come out of there to see you,' my dad told Tom. Tom gave me a pleading look. My dad looked over his shoulder at me, exasperated.

I sighed.

'Let him in. He won't be staying long,' I said.

My dad sighed and let Tom in, evidently reluctant to do so, then went to the kitchen.

Tom walked over to me.

'So?' I questioned him.

'I've sent you a *heap* of texts, saying that I am *sorry*!' he said, annoyed. 'What more can I do?'

I rolled my eyes.

'Have you returned the car yet?'

'Are you mad?' Tom asked me. 'There is no way I'm returning the car.'

'Then there is nothing more you can do. I'm sorry,' I said, 'but if you've come here to win me back, you've had a wasted journey.'

'Please, Scarlet, I really want you back!' Tom begged.

I wanted him, too, obviously, but not if he was going to keep driving around with Dan in the stolen car.

'Don't make this harder for me, Tom,' I told him. 'You and Dan put us in a lot of danger, and it's all very well *saying* you're sorry, but the fact that you're still doing exactly what you said sorry for just proves you're not.'

Before Tom could say another word, I heard the click of the bathroom door handle. I looked up and saw that Leslie had come out of the bathroom with a towel secured round her body, and another towel wrapped round her hair. The moment she'd seen Tom, her face contorted into an expression like she wanted to break every bone in his body.

'What the bleeding hell do you think you're doing here, you stupid boy?' she yelled, furiously.

Tom looked up at her. His expression also changed, into a petrified one.

'M-Mrs Hart, I'm sorry, I, I, I, j-j-just wanted to -,' Tom stammered.

'*GET OUT*!' she screamed, so violently that the twins, who had come out into the hall to see what had been going on, became scared and ran back into the lounge, crying.

Tom legged it over to the door, flung it open, and ran out, too desperate to get away to properly shut the door behind him.

92

I had to admire my stepmum-in-waiting for managing to get rid of Tom just like that. She was just as angry with him as I was, if not more, and Tom wouldn't dare argue with her.

She was in the lounge now, apologising profusely to the twins for shouting, and reassuring them that she didn't mean to frighten them and there was nothing to be worried about.

Chapter 8:

Jamie's First

Sunday 6th March 2011

'Jamie, you ain't got time to be faffing around on the computer, we've gotta load up the car,' Christian said. 'Start bringing your stuff down from your room.'

Playing a computer game on Christian's computer in the lounge was one of the few things I did to make my life fun. I never went out. I didn't have any friends to go out with.

I did have one friend. My best friend who went to secondary school with. Dave Fox. But we hadn't seen each other seen since I had to be taken out of school halfway through year eleven.

I got up from the computer. For the first time, Christian was right. We needed to load everything into the car that night, because we wouldn't have a lot of time in the morning.

I went upstairs, where there were boxes and plastic rubbish sacks, as I never had a proper suitcase or overnight bag. The wardrobe and chest of drawers were emptied and the desktop and bedside cabinet cleared. The only thing left to do was for the bed to be stripped, which would have to wait until the next day, when I wouldn't be sleeping in it any more. The only clothes that hadn't been packed were the ones I saved for the next day.

I started bringing my stuff downstairs. Me and Christian loaded up the car.

When we finished, I fixed myself some dinner. Neither me nor Christian made anything fresh, apart from homemade sandwiches, nor did we ever have takeaways or fast food. We only ever ate canned foods and frozen food. I hoped it wouldn't be like this at Mum's.

I cooked some fish fingers, potato waffles, carrots, peas and sweet corn and sat and ate in front of the T.V as usual, because me and Christian never ate at the table.

I reckoned it would different to this at Mum's, because she came across as a much more civilised person than Christian, and would be the type of parent who'd want everyone sat round the table, eating dinner together as the proper family they most likely were.

When Christian came home from meeting Jesse and Rochella for the first time, he said he'd been roped into having lunch with all three of them.

'I'd tried to leave after main course, but they'd even made a dessert,' he'd said.

Well, Christian was being fucking ungrateful! The meals I had at my mate Dave's were much nicer than what Christian cooked me, and he still left me starving.

I knew better than to hope he'd plan a meal for Mum, Jesse and Rochella to have with us when they'd come up to meet me.

I went to bed early, as me and Christian had to be up and about quite early. This was the very last day of my old life, and I'd be greeting a whole new life the next day, when I left my so-called dad's.

As soon as I got up the next morning, I dressed, stripped the bed and, with some difficulty, stuffed my dirty sheet, duvet cover and pillowcase, along with my pyjamas, in the overflowing laundry basket containing the dirty clothes waiting for the next rare time Christian could be bothered to do any of it.

I pulled on my socks, tied my shoes, and then went downstairs to cook some beans on toast and joined Christian on the sofa.

'How do you plan on spending your new life without me on your hands?' I asked.

Christian sighed and said, 'Jamie, can you not keep going on about it, please?'

I gave up. Christian knew he was in the wrong, but wasn't going to admit it. Not wanting to start an argument about it, I didn't say anything else. I carried on with my breakfast, until I finished, and left my dirty plate on the table next to the sofa.

'Go upstairs and brush your teeth,' Christian ordered. 'And stop leaving your bloody plates in the lounge.'

But after he said that, he did the exact same thing!

I took both plates out, not that I wanted to, and left them on the worktop. Christian could fucking put them in the dishwasher!

I really was looking forward to getting away from that inconsistent hypocrite!

At nine, I grabbed my jacket and rucksack and followed Christian out the door for the very last time.

He told me to get in whilst he locked the door.

Christian got in, started up the engine, and drove away. Even though I had seen my mum, brother and sister, I'd never been to their house, so I didn't know where they lived.

It was just a forty-two minute drive. We reached the house and pulled into the drive. We got out the car and started unloading.

'Jamie, make yourself useful and ring the bell then come back and help me,' said Christian.

I went over to the front door, rang the bell, and rushed back to help Christian bring all my stuff over to the door.

Just as I was heaving one of the two sacks of my ill-fitting clothes out of the seat behind mine, I heard the door open and Mum's voice cry out, 'Jamie!'

She came over to me and gave me a hug and a kiss. She then said she would start bringing in all the boxes and bags that had already been placed at the front door, and take them up to the room where I'd be sleeping from now on.

Once we'd unloaded everything, I started helping Mum take all the boxes up to my room, when she showed me where it was.

When everything was up in my room, Christian turned down Mum's invite to stay for coffee. I knew he wanted to be out as soon as possible.

As soon as Christian said a very gruff goodbye, he left, shutting the door behind him. Mum looked at me and sighed.

'I know he wanted to get rid of me,' I told her. 'But I don't care. I'm fed up of him.'

'Oh, Jamie,' said Mum, giving me another hug. 'It's okay, you're with us now, and I really think that you are going to get on brilliantly with Jesse and Rochella. Obviously I don't know very much at all about what you eat nowadays, so you'll have to tell me if you have any preferences or allergies, or if you follow any specific diet.'

I nodded. Mum asked if I drank tea or coffee, and if so, what kind. I normally just have a regular coffee, so I asked Mum for a white coffee with no sugar. She then asked how I fancied having pasta with salmon and peas for dinner.

'I don't think I've ever tried salmon,' I said. 'But I like fish, so I should like salmon.'

'Would you like to help me, Jesse and Rochella make it later?' Mum asked.

'I'd like to try,' I said.

'Have you ever done any cooking before?' Mum asked. I told her I'd cooked things like fish fingers and oven chips, but that was it. She said she'd show me what to do, as this was going to be the first time I ever did any proper cooking.

'Christian said you made lunch when he went round to meet Jesse and Rochella,' I said, and Mum went on about the effort she'd put into the avocado and crab meat lunch they made, followed by a pomegranate cake, and how Christian would clearly rather have been doing something else than having lunch with them.

I didn't think I'd never tried crabmeat or avocados, but it all sounded nice, especially as mum talked about how the avocados had been stuffed with crabmeat, shallots and lime zest and dressed with buttermilk. I couldn't believe Christian didn't want to stick around for lunch.

I asked if we could make it again at some point, so I could try it.

'Oh, of course we can make it again! I'm sure Jesse and Rochella would be honoured to muck in with making it, and they enjoyed it, just like I did.'

I was right in thinking dinner with Mum would be nothing like dinner with Christian.

Mum showed me around the house after we finished our drinks. Obviously, I'd already seen the kitchen and the lounge. Mum showed me the dining room, which is just off to the left of the kitchen, at the back of the house, behind to the lounge.

I saw some photos on a cabinet, and went over to look at them. There was a photo of Jesse and Rochella when they were little. They were surrounded by birthday wrapping paper.

'Ah, now that was on Rochella's ninth birthday,' said Mum. 'Jesse was just two or three years old.'

I looked closer and noticed that the pink and orange badge Rochella was wearing in the picture did indeed say, '9 today!' on it.

I looked at some more photos. I noticed one photo of what I thought looked like the three youngest of seven children sat, cross legged, at the front row of the group of them, with Jesse, who I reckoned was about seven, at the end of a row at the bottom of the photo, with the others, including Rochella, who I reckoned must've been twelve or thirteen in this one knelt up behind them. I asked who the other children in the photo were.

Mum picked it up.

'See the little girl with the blonde hair, sat next to Jesse? Her name is Lizzy.'

'Who's the other boy sat next to her?' I asked Mum, who then talked about Fred, who she said was Jesse's best friend.

'Do you remember the first day we came round to meet you?' she asked. 'That was Fred's nineteenth birthday, and Jesse had gone out with him, Lizzy, and some other friends, including Fred's older sister Natalie, who is the one knelt up behind Fred.'

'Who are the other two boys between Natalie and Rochella and behind Lizzy?' I asked.

'They are Lizzy's older brothers, Alistair and Fraser,' Mum told me, pointing to them as she said their names. 'I went to secondary school with Fred and Natalie's mum, Claire, and then stayed friends with her when we left school and started college. I made friends with Alistair, Fraser and Lizzy's mum, Jane, introduced her to Claire, and the three of us went around together as a trio and shared everything, and never stopped being friends when Jane and Claire got married to their husbands, and had their children with them.'

This made me really resent the fact that I'd gone with my dad, because of the friends I missed out on all that time.

'When you've settled in with us, you will be able to meet them,' Mum promised. I didn't know how long it would take for me to settle in. Whilst I was glad to be where I now am, there was no ignoring the fact that it would still be a huge impact on everyone's lives.

I looked at another photo of Jesse, Fred, Lizzy and Natalie, a more recent one, by the look of it. Other photos were school photos of Jesse and Rochella in their uniforms, in front of an abstract background, primary and secondary alike, including ones of the two of them in their primary school uniforms, as well as solo ones, and then there were photos of Jesse and Rochella with the rest of their classes and teachers, and then there was a very old picture of Rochella in a baby blue dress with a tiny boy who I could just about tell was Alistair in a suit, also baby blue.

'That's Alistair and Rochella as a page boy and flower girl at Barry and Claire's wedding,' said Mum, before I carried on looking at the other photos. There were Jesse and Rochella's prom photos, which included solo ones of Jesse in his baby blue suit and Rochella in a bright red, strap dress, and then there was one of Rochella and a slim girl with dark hair, in a violet, high slit V-neck dress, who Mum said was Sarah, Jane's husband's sister's daughter. There was also a photo at Jesse's prom of him stood between Fred, who was in a blue suit with a white shirt and a blue waistcoat, and a girl with blonde curly hair, wearing a baby pink dress, matching gloves, and a silvery gold tiara.

'That's Jesse's girlfriend, Annie,' Mum said. 'Lovely girl. They've been together since year eleven and I get on well with her mother.'

'Who's the black haired boy in the black tuxedo, stood next to Fred?' I asked.

'His name is Matt Weller, and he was in Fred and Jesse's tutor group at Fleetview,' Mum said.

I felt more resentful yet. I turned away from the photos. Mum asked what was wrong.

'All this stuff I missed out on,' I said, 'cos I'd left with Christian.'

'Did you not get to go to your prom?' Mum asked.

'What Christian said about the trouble I was in meant I missed my prom,' I reminded her.

There wasn't anything Mum could say to make me feel better about it, other than, 'I am sorry. We will talk about everything, but first, you ought to make a start on unpacking your things. You can do whatever you want with your new room.'

I looked round my new room. It's slightly bigger than my old room back at Christian's, not that it matters, as I knew that now I was with my mum, brother and sister, who were going to be nicer to me, I wouldn't want to spend a lot of time shut up in my room.

My new room has a white, built-in wardrobe with sliding doors by the door, and a matching chest of drawers next to my bed. The bed was already made, with a plain red duvet cover.

I opened one of the bags of the clothes Christian made me wear. He'd always dressed me in clothes that looked like a fucking tent on me, or weren't clean and warm or cool enough. He never gave me any pocket money so I couldn't even go out and buy my own stuff to wear.

Mum came in at that point.

'Goodness me, are they the clothes your father bought you that you said were the wrong size?'

Mum picked up the first baggy t-shirt and tutted.

'I'll take you shopping tomorrow, for some clothes that actually *fit* you, *properly*, Jamie,' she said. 'I am not going to have you going around looking like a ten-year-old boy who's been going through his teenage brother's wardrobe, now you are living under my roof. Please at *least* tell me your father made sure your school uniform fitted you, otherwise whatever must your teachers have thought?'

She then started muttering how she could not believe she let me go with Christian.

My baggy uniform was just one reason why I was bullied at school.

'Obviously you'll have to keep those clothes for now, just so you actually have something to wear, but it'll all have to go when I've bought you some better clothes,' Mum said.

I nodded. Mum left me to carry on packing, telling me to shout for her if I needed a hand.

I opened the wardrobe. There were already hangers on the rail. I hung up all of my trousers, shorts and jackets, and then shoved my underwear, shirts, jumpers and sweaters in my chest of drawers. There was no desk in the room, so I had to put the three remaining boxes under the bed.

Afterwards, Mum must've remembered she hadn't shown me the rest of the house, so she showed me the garden, which is all on different levels, graduating downwards.

She then showed me the bedrooms, starting with her room, which is the master bedroom at the front of the house, and is all brown and cream, and then Rochella's is the large room at the back of the house, next to mine and behind Mum's. It's all pink and white. There's a canvas photo of some pink roses hung on the wall above Rochella's bed.

Jesse's room is all black and red, and the bed had a black, grey and white camouflage duvet set. There's black furniture and there are posters of artists such as Lost Prophets, My Chemical Romance, Foo Fighters, Devin Townsend, Alice Cooper, The Muse and lots more. I noticed a rack of C.Ds, and supposedly all of the bands in the posters.

The spare bedroom, which is between mine and Rochella's rooms, is all white, with pink cushions and a lamp on the bedside table.

After Mum finished showing me the bathroom, we went to have some soup for lunch.

Mum did have to tell me not to leave my bowl on the worktop, but she was patient about it, as she had probably stopped to think that that had been how Christian brought me up.

'Christian was being a hypocrite this morning, cos he left his plate in the lounge, right after telling me off,' I told Mum, who sighed and tutted.

Later on, around five, I heard a car driving down the road. I glanced out of the window and saw a Mini Cooper pull into the drive. I didn't know whose it was. I shouted for Mum.

'Someone's parking their car in our drive,' I said, before Mum came rushing in. She walked over to the window and peered out.

'Oh, that's Fred,' she said. 'He gives Jesse a lift to and from college everyday.'

I looked out the window. The front passenger door opened, and I saw Jesse get out, grab his rucksack, and fling it over his shoulder, before he shut the door, and then Fred's car backed out of the drive, and drove back up the road.

I went into the hall as Mum opened the door.

'Hello, love,' she'd said, as Jesse came in. 'How was college?'

'Same as usual,' he said, before he looked at me. He gave me a weak smile. I could tell he wanted to make me feel welcome, and was trying not to seem too awkward.

'Alright?' I managed.

'Hey,' said Jesse. 'Um, I've just gotta put my bag down. Er, when did you get here?'

'It was some time after nine o'clock,' Mum told him. Jesse dumped his bag down by the stairs, but Mum told him to stow it in the cupboard under the stairs, before she went to the kitchen.

Jesse came over, leant in and whispered, 'She's *well* anal about tidying, you've probably noticed.'

We both went to the kitchen and Jesse got out a can of Relentless.

'Aren't you going to offer Jamie one?' Mum prompted.

'Do you want one, Jamie?' Jesse offered, awkwardly.

'Please,' I said, so Jesse got out another one.

'Mum was showing me some photos,' I told Jesse.

'Just the ones on the dining room sideboard,' Mum added. I told Jesse about the photos I'd seen of him with Fred, Natalie and Lizzy, as well as his prom photo with Annie.

'I didn't get to go to my prom,' I said, starting to feel a bit glum again.

I saw Jesse look round at Mum, frowning, and then she gave Jesse a warning look.

'Why don't you tell Jamie about what good friends you are with Lizzy, Fred and Natalie?' she said.

'Me, Fred, Lizzy and Natalie have known each other since we were five and Natalie was seven,' Jesse told me as we went to the lounge, 'and me and Fred have been at both primary and secondary school together, and both been at Fleetview sixth form doing our A-levels.'

'Was Lizzy at Fleetview too?' I asked.

'No, she doesn't live in Chickerell, so she wouldn't have been in the catchment area for it,' said Jesse, but I didn't know what a catchment area was. Mum explained that it was when you had to live within a certain number of miles from a school in order to be able to get in. I had heard about parents having to pretend to be religious or using money as a bribe, passed off as a "donation," to get their children into a certain school.

'Is that why people try other ways of getting their children into a school?' I asked.

'They do try to lie and bribe their children into certain schools,' said Mum. 'Bit naughty, has to said, and it probably wouldn't work with Fleetview.'

'You're not saying Lizzy's parents tried that, to get her into Fleetview?'

'Oh, no, the Grahams would never do an unethical thing like that. Just some people can be very cheeky, and they do try that sort of thing. But no, Colvin and Jane had every intention of sending Lizzy to Carrie Mount, and that was where she went, as well as her brothers.'

'But she was still just as close to us because our mums were best mates,' Jesse said.

Rochella came home at twenty to six. I was in the kitchen when I saw her come in. I heard Mum tell her to go into the kitchen and say hello to her brother. She led Rochella into the kitchen.

'Hi,' she said.

'You okay?' I said, unsure of what else to say.

'Good, um, thanks for asking,' said Rochella, taking her bag off and over to the stairs to put it in the cupboard.

She asked what was for dinner when she came back in, so Mum said we were having pasta with salmon and peas, so Jesse said that he was fine with whatever.

'Sweet,' Rochella said, sitting down at the breakfast bar, next to me. 'You going to help us make it, Jamie?'

'Yeah, sure,' I said.

'Jamie's never done any proper cooking before,' Mum told Rochella. Sounding curious, Rochella asked what sort of things I ate at Christian's, so I told her how I'd lived on frozen food, like chicken nuggets, burgers and waffles, and food out of tins, like soup and beans.

Rochella looked shocked. So did Jesse.

'Did you even have any vegetables?' Rochella asked.

'Only broccoli, frozen peas and carrots and canned sweetcorn,' I told her.

Jesse grimaced. Rochella said they'd all show me what to do when we cooked. Mum said we should all start the cooking at six.

When we began, Mum provided everyone with an apron and reminded us to wash our hands before cooking, and then we began. Mum left me in charge of the pasta, instructing Rochella to assist me, as I'd never cooked pasta before.

Afterwards I couldn't help feeling that was easy, as long as I didn't splash boiling water everywhere when I tipped the casarecce into the saucepan, or let it boil over whilst everything was cooking.

I helped tidy up the kitchen, and then me and Jesse dried everything Mum washed, and Jesse showed me where everything went when I put it all away.

'I think you did quite well, there, Jamie,' Mum praised me, when the four of us were sat round the table at dinner. 'Especially considering you haven't cooked pasta before. Mind you, it can be quite easy as long as you know what you're doing.'

Rochella suggested I ought to be shown how to fry food, as she reckoned it would be the next step up from boiling.

I had to help clear the table and load the dishwasher, and then we all sat down to relax in the lounge, with cups of decaffeinated tea and coffee.

'What did you used to do when you were at Dad's?' Rochella asked. 'Did you hang out with friends?'

'I didn't have many friends, cos I lost contact with the only friend I did have after I...' I broke off, as I wasn't sure of whether or not Mum told Jesse and Rochella about my past. 'I did have one friend at school,' I went on. 'Dave. Dave Fox.'

For some strange reason, Jesse and Rochella raised their eyebrows at each other. They were probably just astonished I only had one friend.

'I wonder what he's doing now,' I said. 'It was his birthday a few months ago. He said he wanted to go into Photography. Maybe he's doing something like that at college?'

At this, I noticed Jesse and Rochella's mouths fall open, and they looked round at each other, eyes wide.

'What is it?' I asked them, frowning.

'Uh, nothing,' said Rochella, quickly. My head was swimming.

As I went to bed later, I thought about how different I discovered life would be. This was the first night of my new life with Mum. It would be stricter when it came to tidying, as Mum obviously isn't the type of person who likes things being left lying around. I wouldn't be stuck on food out of packets all the time. And Mum would be getting me some clothes that fitted me, so there would be no more baggy clothes.

And why were Jesse and Rochella acting so weird when I mentioned Dave? Did they know who he was?

Shit, yeah, they did! Because that was how I found Rochella's Facebook wall and knew she was my sister!

Christian hadn't told me shit about my mum or sister until I was seven. He explained that, two years after we left, he'd found out my sister suffered from a blood clot to the brain, and died. My mum had been so upset about it that she had overdosed herself and died on the way to the hospital.

It was just me and Christian. I had no one. No one to turn to, and no one to protect me from the way Christian treated me. No one to make him stop being an arsehole.

One day, not long before the Halloween just gone, when I was home alone, on Facebook on Christian's computer, I was looking at Dave's page. We never unfriended each other. I came across a 'People you may know,' list. One name caught my eye. Rochella Naerger. That was my sister's name! 'Dave Fox is a mutual friend,' it said below.

I clicked onto her page. There were a lot of recent posts on her wall. I noticed something familiar about her profile photo. I looked at her photos. There was an album named, 'The Brother I Never Knew,' which I found curious. I looked at the photos. There were photos of a blonde woman on a hospital bed, holding a baby, and perched on the edge of the bed, right next to the woman, with his arm round her was Christian! My eyes fell on the comments. People were asking, 'Is that Jamie, the brother who left with your dad when you were little?'

Then it had dawned on me that the baby in the photos was me!

Wait. That didn't make sense. That couldn't be my sister! She died two years after I left with Christian! I didn't get it. Rochella couldn't have uploaded any of these posts, but apparently she had. Rochella had to have been alive! But I asked myself why Christian would lie to me about such a thing. But that was a stupid question to ask anyone, including myself. But yes Christian did mistreat me, but I never thought he'd tell me a downright lie!

This meant my mum would be alive too!

Christian came home and saw me on Facebook. One look at Rochella's wall and I saw him freeze. I knew what that look meant. I asked Christian what was going on.

Christian told me he made everything up about my mum and Rochella dying, but I'd got up and left the room before Christian could go into any details. I didn't want to hear the rest. I couldn't see any reason why someone would want to fake the deaths of their family.

I had to talk to Jesse and Rochella about it. I really wanted to see Dave again. I never wanted drift away from him because of what happened.

Christian started it. If he hadn't taken me away from the house we'd lived in with my mum and sister Rochella, and then treated me like shit my whole life, I would never have been driven in the direction I'd gone in.

He started neglecting me when I was nine.

He never bathed or showered me regularly. I went to school reeking like shit. At break time one day, I sat on the bench next to two girls, and one of them went, 'Ew, he's *smelly*!' and then they both giggled and ran off.

'Tramp!' one boy nearby shouted.

'Bet he's got fleas,' one of his mates said.

I had to go without enough food. Whenever I was ill, Christian never gave me medicine, or took me to see the doctor.

Whenever Christian left the house, he never called anyone round to look after me. I was left alone, and allowed to play in dangerous places.

When I was twelve, he would scream at me and say mean things when I'd done nothing wrong. He talked down to me, shamed me and made fun of me. He also made threats.

'You're a worthless piece of shit, you know that?' he yelled at me, one night.

'I've done nothing wrong!' I protested, scared.

'"I've done nothing wrong! I've done nothing wrong!"' he mimicked. 'Are they the only words you know?'

I tried to answer, but he just told me to fuck off up to my room before he ripped my face off.

When I was fourteen, he would thump and punch me because he said it was the only way to make me stop misbehaving, but it also happened when Christian was pissed out of his mind.

'You're drunk!' I'd shout.

One time, he whacked me round the face with the back of his hand, bellowing at me to shut up. I begged him to stop but then he grabbed my arm, dragged me up the stairs and locked me in my room, shouting through the door that I wasn't going to school the next day. I pleaded with him to let me out. I spent the whole of the next day, looking miserably and hopelessly out of the window. I was a prisoner.

Because it was all I knew, being treated this way, I thought it was the normal way to treat people, especially because Christian told me that a good thumping was the only way to win your arguments with women and kids, and I believed him.

That didn't mean I was okay with him doing it to me, though. By the time I was fifteen, I'd had enough.

I stole some cigarettes and vodka and smoked and drank when Christian left me home alone. I stayed out late, spraying graffiti on walls.

At school, I stole from lockers, and smuggled vodka and cigarettes into school, which the teachers caught me doing.

'This is a serious matter,' the head had said. 'Jamie knows the rules against smoking and drinking on the premises, as well as stealing, and if this continues, I will have no choice but to suspend him.'

'You stupid boy,' Christian had sneered, with a disgusted look on his face.

The head said he couldn't take any action, other than to give me a weeks' detention, during which I was on litter duty.

I could hear the mates Dave hung around with talking about me.

Gareth 'Gaz' Long, Kris Olsen, and Lennie 'Len' Ross were all twats. They'd always had beef with me for no reason. I did nothing to them, but they'd get fucking grumpy whenever Dave wanted to hang out with me. And they teased me any time they had the opportunity.

'Professor Zitface really got himself in deep shit, there,' said Gaz, the leader of the trio.

Another reason I was bullied was for having terrible acne, which Christian neglected to take seriously, *unsurprisingly*.

'Serves him right, going through other people's lockers. What did he need money for? Top of the Range spot cream?' said Len.

I didn't want to be at school or home after the amount of trouble I got in. I bunked off and went to places like the park, or town, or bars, and not go home until eleven at night but that just got me in even more trouble.

Christian said he couldn't cope any more, and I went into care. I was so fucking angry! It was all Christian's fucking fault for the way I was feeling, and now he'd given up on me! My social worker knew he'd driven me to it as well, and she still bloody warned me to behave in the foster home I was in, like it was my fucking fault!

Things got worse after that.

Gaz, Kris and Len took the piss when I was still at school after going into care.

Gaz had come over to me and said, 'Oy, Jamie! Is it true, what Dave's saying, that your old man chucked you out?'

'You told them?' I said to Dave.

'I'm sorry, it just kinda slipped out.'

'Aw, you don't have to say you're sorry,' Gaz said, in a patronising tone. 'We won't judge him just because he's got anger issues and nobody wants him, not even his own daddy!'

That triggered me.

'Oh, fuck you!'

I punched Gaz in the nose, knocking him to the floor, before running up the corridor. I heard Dave calling after me, but I didn't stop.

I ran out of school and down Fleet Street, and then across the car park outside the Co-Op.

I got arrested for stealing alcohol *and* smacking Gaz down.

The fuzz looked me up and I got tagged, so I had a curfew to stick to. I also had to move schools as the foster mother I was living with then had said I'd have to go if there was any trouble, and the new foster parents that could take me didn't live locally to the school I was at with Dave. That was the last time I ever saw Dave.

A month after that, I started breaking my curfew. I was arrested again for vandalising a car and spraying graffiti on the garage door it was parked in front of.

I was removed from school altogether and was sentenced to an eight-month detention and training order that was made up of four and a half months in a young offenders' institution and then three and a half months of community service.

I fucking hated being behind bars, and having to reflect how I changed. I was never going to forgive Christian for being the reason I was so angry I snapped.

Whilst I was banged up, I thought about Dave and how I missed him. That was what made me regret what I did.

After finishing my sentence, I was still in care for another year before moving back in with Christian, who said he felt he would be able to cope with having me back.

The only thing was, Christian never owned up to the mistakes he made, even though he wasn't mistreating me quite so badly any more. He was still a dildo some of the time, but he wasn't too bad apart from that.

Even aside from Christian, my life wasn't the happiest, mainly because of those mates of Dave's.

I didn't go to college after my sentence, so I never made any other mates, even though I was held back two years at school, so I could redo my G.C.S.Es. My grades weren't too bad, though they could've been better.

I never had a girlfriend, because I never went out to meet any and I was never interested in dating anyway. My life on the whole had become a lot duller since moving back in with Christian.

I'd found out Christian had been lying about Mum and Rochella dying and then, one morning in December, out of the blue, Christian came up to my room.

'I've been on the phone to your mum,' he said. My mum? My mum who I hadn't seen for years? My mum who I was led to believe had topped herself by overdosing? Had I heard Christian right?

'Why would you call her after shutting her outta both our lives and telling me she'd died when she hadn't?'

'I regret everything I said and did, concerning your mum and sister.'

Yeah, sure he did!

'You have a right to meet your mother and your sister,' he went on. 'I told your mum that you wanted to meet her. She did question it, as we hadn't been in touch for years, and she wanted to know how I got her land number.'

'Yeah, how *did* you get her number?'

Christian said Mum was with B.T, so he was able to look up her number in the phonebook.

'Yeah, she *does* want to meet you, of course,' he said. 'She *is* your mother, after all. Your mum asked if you wanted to meet her in the Christmas holidays.'

'I'll need time to think about it,' I told him.

I didn't know how to feel about it. I'd only just found out my dad had been lying about the deaths of my mum and sister, who were actually alive, and now I was being asked if I wanted to meet her? I didn't know whether to feel pleased about it, or how to feel about the fact that she'd let Christian take me. Whose idea was it?

Two weeks later, I decided I did want to meet her, so Christian called Flora, my mum, and arranged for her to come round the day after Boxing Day, at half past eleven.

I was sat in my room that morning, stomach whirling, my palms sweating. This was going to be the very first time I'd see her after all those years.

The doorbell rang at half past eleven, on the dot. I heard Christian answer it.

'Flora,' he'd said, by way of acknowledgement as he let her in. I heard my mum ask where I was, and then I heard Christian's voice shouting my name and telling me to get downstairs.

I slowly got up off the bed, and left the room. I went over to the top of the stairs. Stood at the foot of the stairs was my mum. She looked up at me, like she had seen a ghost.

'Jamie?' she said, weakly.

'Mum,' I said.

I walked down the stairs. Mum looked at me, and said she couldn't believe it was me. There were tears in her eyes. She gave me a hug.

Christian left us alone to talk. Mum told me about my sister Rochella, and my brother Jesse, who she'd been pregnant with when me and Christian left.

I told Mum about my life. I was glad Christian was out of the room, because Mum asked what he'd been like, because she said that he hadn't made her very happy.

'He used to hit me and call me names,' I told her.

Mum looked horrified.

'Were you well looked after?' she asked.

'I was never given enough to eat and my clothes never fitted properly,' I had to tell her. 'And I was led to believe you and my sister were dead.'

Mum looked furious. She got up and left the room. I heard her saying to Christian, 'I should never have let Jamie go with you!'

I could hear Christian acting like he didn't know what she was talking about, the prick!

'I had no idea you were going to treat Jamie like dirt,' Mum then shouted. 'You were a good father to him and Rochella when we were together, even though you didn't make me happy. I should've known better than to think letting you have either of them was the right option. You used to hit me, and I was naïve to think you would never do that to Jamie or Rochella!'

Mum then told him what I told her about him never buying me clothes that were the right size and not giving me enough to eat.

'Is it my fault he's so bloody greedy he keeps mithering me for more food?' I heard Christian shout.

'Don't give me that!' I heard Mum bark back. 'I can see he's skin and bone and his clothes are way too big for him!'

'How is it my fault if he's still starving, every evening, after four whole goddamn chicken nuggets?' I heard Christian shout.

'Oh, you have got to be kidding me!' I then heard Mum groan, in that disbelieving way. 'Please tell me that you actually did give him more than just four measly chicken nuggets for dinner! No wonder he's still hungry! I'm not surprised he always asked for something else to eat after dinner! Did you even let him have any pudding? And I can't believe you made him think we were dead! Did you even care about Rochella?!'

'I do wanna meet her,' Christian insisted, not that I believed that. 'And I wanna meet your son, Jesse.'

'*Our* son, Christian,' Mum corrected him. But before I could hear any more, I heard the kitchen door shut, presumably to have a private conversation.

I waited for nearly an hour before they both came back into the lounge.

'Your father and I have been talking and we think it may be a good idea for you to meet your brother and sister one weekend,' said Mum. It took fifty-five minutes to discuss and decide that?

Christian said that he was going to meet Rochella and Jesse one weekend, that he'd get in touch with Mum to let her know when he could, and then I'd meet Jesse and Rochella after that.

After Mum left, Christian rounded on me, having a right go at me for telling my mum that he hadn't been looking after me properly.

'Well, she asked!' I argued. 'I couldn't just not tell her!'

Fuck me! I couldn't believe I'd stood up to Christian like that. I'd never done it before.

Christian shut right up after that.

'It made your mum insist that she wanted you going to live with her,' he said, calmly. 'I was against it cos she'd just met you. I wasn't going to let her take you off me just like that. She says it won't be immediate and she wants you to give it some thought.'

He left the room. I didn't know if Christian would think about it at all, but I definitely did. I kept turning everything over in my head, the bad choice Mum had made, her apology for it, and whether I'd be so desperate to get away from Christian I'd choose to live with the mum I'd known for only five minutes.

But then, after I had thought about it, and remembered how much I hated Christian for basically ruining my life, I realised I *was* that desperate, as I felt more like Christian's prisoner than his son, and I remembered Mum was so angry with him for the way he'd treated me, and she seemed like she really was sorry for letting him have me.

So I decided I did want to go and live with her, even though I had no idea what life at Mum's would be like, but I really did hope, I had to believe it would be somewhat better than life with Christian. I knew it would be really weird, though hopefully I wouldn't feel that way after some time had passed, especially once I'd met my brother and sister.

The day after New Year's Day, however, Christian had made firm arrangements to go round to Mum's house and meet Jesse and Rochella, but I wouldn't be going. Christian said it was because they wanted to take it one step at a time, so Jesse and Rochella would meet Christian first, and *then* me, just as I met only Mum first, then Jesse and Rochella, just so that it wouldn't feel like too much for us, all at once.

The theory was that Mum would bring Jesse and Rochella round the following week.

Christian left me home alone one Saturday, to meet his long lost daughter, and second son who he didn't know existed.

'So...' Christian began. 'Mum is fine with Saturday the twenty-second. As are your brother and sister.'

I nodded. I wondered what they were like. Mum said that Jesse in particular looked just like me, and that we both took after Christian, whereas Rochella took more after Mum, though me and Jesse had done, too, somewhat.

The next Saturday, I went downstairs to wait in the lounge. Mum, Rochella and Jesse were meant to be coming at eleven, but they were a few minutes early. Mum had led Rochella, who I recognised instantly from the Facebook photos, and Jesse into the house.

We went to my room to get to know each other while Mum spoke to Christian.

I started telling them about my school life, and how I had to be taken out of school, but didn't tell them that it was because I became a young offender, and then Jesse asked what Christian was like.

I knew I couldn't lie about Christian being a kind father, so I told them he 'wasn't very nice,' but that was all I said.

But before Jesse or Rochella could tell me anything about themselves, Mum came in, looking *well* hacked off, and told Jesse and Rochella it was time to go. I just knew Christian had said something.

After Mum, Jesse and Rochella left, I demanded to know what Christian said.

'We spoke some more about you going to live with her, Jesse and Rochella,' he said.

What had he said about it, though?

'Why would Mum get so angry about it?' I asked.

'All I said was that I'd changed my mind and felt it would be good for all five of us, and then your mum accused me of only thinking of meself!'

'You sure she was getting arsy over nothing?' I said. I knew what was going on. Christian wanted me gone, and this was his chance. Damn bloody right he was only thinking of himself!

'Do you wanna go?' Christian asked. 'I really do think you ought to, I know you wanna, and your mum's keen for you to come.'

'You haven't thought about what Jesse and Rochella would make of the idea,' I pointed out.

'Well, assuming they are keen on it, would you want to?'

I knew I did. Christian clearly didn't want me and had been making my life a living hell. However weird it was going to be, moving in with Mum, Jesse and Rochella, I was pretty sure they'd treat me a lot better than Christian did.

'I do,' I said. 'But only cos, as much as you were using it as an excuse, you are right about how it would help all of us, not just cos you want rid of me.'

'Since when did you get it in your head to start giving me your lip?' Christian lectured me, shocked.

'Since I became fed up of the way you treated me,' I snapped. 'No wonder Mum wanted me to come with her when she came round to meet me.'

;I didn't have to take you with me when we left Mum and Rochella!' Christian said, but I had a comeback for that too.

'You definitely didn't have to and you shouldn't have done!'

'Well, let's hope Jesse and Rochella are fine with it, or we're both screwed,' said Christian. 'I had to tell your mum about you doing time, and she fucking seems to be bloody well blaming me for it!'

I stormed up to my room. Christian never wanted me and he was the most selfish bastard I knew! He acted like it was in no way his fault I went so far off the rails. I couldn't wait to fucking well leave and live with Mum, whenever that would happen. As weird as it would be when it did happen, I was willing to make it work for the best. And I hoped that I'd find out, soon, when I'd be leaving Christian's.

I liked to think Mum would tell Jesse and Rochella about Christian treating me like fucking scum and that, even if they weren't sure about the idea at first, they would come round to it in time.

Since meeting Jesse and Rochella for the first time, I did see them a couple of times, just to get used to the idea.

When Christian had spoken to Mum about it, they agreed it wouldn't happen immediately after that discussion, but in a few months time. Well, a few months had passed, and now here I was, lying in my new bed, in my new room in my mum's house.

Mum said we'd talk about how I became a young offender, but I had no way of knowing when that would be. Probably when Jesse and Rochella weren't around, if she hadn't told them yet.

Mum came in to wake me at seven on my first morning with her, opened my curtains, and told me to come down for breakfast.

'What would you like for breakfast?' she asked, once I joined her in the kitchen. I asked if there were any beans, so I could have beans on toast, but she said she didn't but asked if I liked eggy bread, adding that Jesse and Rochella were having some, so the four of us had a breakfast of eggy bread.

Jesse and Rochella couldn't stay and chat because they had to get ready. But Rochella did have time to ask what I was up to, after she'd finished her breakfast.

'I'm taking Jamie into town,' Mum told her. 'He needs some more decent clothes. You've noticed how baggy the ones he was wearing yesterday were?'

'Ah, yeah,' Rochella agreed. 'Anyway, I've got to get on.' And then Rochella left the kitchen.

Mum gave Jesse a lift to college, on her way to taking me into town.

'I thought I'd take you into Burton,' she said. 'Get you some nice trendy clothes. Do you like the sound of that?'

I said I was happy to go with whatever.

We went through Dorothy Perkins and upstairs to Burton. I went to look at the sweatshirts. I came across one I liked. It was a navy one. Mum spotted it and asked if I liked it, which I said I did, so Mum asked what size I normally wore. I told her Christian bought me anything in a medium size or above, not caring if it was an extra large.

'I'd try on a medium,' she suggested. I found one that had an M label on it, and took it off the rack, then carried on looking at the clothes.

'Jamie?' I heard Mum call me. She came rushing over with a black wool coat. I looked at it and nodded. I started looking at the coats. I also came across a grey puffer jacket, so I searched for a medium sized one.

Next, Mum took me to look at the jeans. I liked a pair of skinny indigo jeans. Unfortunately, they didn't have any mediums, so I looked at some other pairs instead.

I found some black skinny jeans, indigo tapered leg jeans and some mid blue straight leg jeans.

I also found two jumpers I liked; one dark red and one dark grey, as well as one navy cardigan and one grey cardigan.

Mum also bought five shirts; a navy short sleeve shirt, a dark red long sleeved shirt, a checked long sleeve shirt, also dark red, a greyish green short sleeved shirt and a denim long sleeved shirt.

Mum also wanted to buy me some new shoes, too, as all I had was one pair of grubby trainers with fraying laces.

She bought me two pairs of shoes; dark brown leather and grey suede, plus four pairs of trainers; light brown suede, white leather, grey suede and black mesh.

Unsurprisingly, it cost a fortune in total, but Mum insisted it was worth it, plus she said she could afford a whole lot more than that because of how much she was paid an hour.

After we left the shop, we went for lunch in this place called the Criterion.

I remembered what I was thinking about in bed last night, and wondered if I ought to try to talk about Dave.

'You remember how I found out Rochella was alive?' he said.

'Yes, you saw her Facebook page,' she said, before asking how I came across it, which I was glad she did. I explained that I was looking at my friend Dave's Facebook updates, and then saw Rochella's name in his friends' list, thought it looked familiar, and started looking at it.

'I saw the way Jesse and Rochella looked at each other last night when I talked about him. It's obviously cos we both knew the same Dave Fox,' I said.

'Okay,' said Mum. 'What about him?'

I said that, after what happened, we grew apart, even though I didn't want us to, and was hoping that, if Jesse and Rochella were still in contact with him, they could get me a chance to catch up with Dave.

'Dave still hangs out with Jesse and his friends and he's very chummy with all of them,' Mum said.

'Do Jesse and Rochella know about... you know,' I asked hesitantly. Mum seemed to know what I was getting at, and said that she had told them, but had asked them not to ask me any questions as she sensed that it would be a touchy subject. She wasn't wrong there.

She seemed positive that a catch up with Dave would be a possibility if I spoke to Jesse about it, and she said she was sure Jesse would be able to arrange something and would be more than happy to.

In the car on the way home, I thought about the ups and downs of living with Mum, compared to living with Christian.

I was able to tell, very quickly, that Mum was strict about cleaning and tidying, but all the good points were worth adapting to that for. Mum treated me to lunch and some new clothes in the right size, and I was looking at multiple chances to try some interesting new foods, and hopefully learn how to cook them, and with any luck, I'd get to see my best mate again.

What else I faced whilst living with Mum, Jesse and Rochella was unclear, but I had to believe that, whatever it was, it would be a whole lot better than life with Christian. But the most important thing was, I was with a family that loved me and would never, ever neglect or abuse me.

Chapter 9:

Dave's Second

Monday 14th March 2011

Ever since I came back from my suspension after I crashed and burned in the worst way possible, I'd been unable to look Alyssa in the eye during classes until a few weeks back. I eventually managed to move on and felt a right bell end for hoping I could've dated my teacher.

Stuart had been talking me into giving the Spanish exchange student we met recently a chance. Her name was Rosa Suarez. I wondered why Stuart didn't seem keen on trying to win her over himself, as he did say she was fit.

I saw Tom near the shop. Tom caught my eye and came over.

'Hey,' he said, sitting down. He seemed unusually bubbly, considering what went on between him and Scarlet.

'You okay?' I asked.

'Yeah, I'm good,' said Tom. 'Chilled with Dan last night.'

'What did you get up to?' I asked.

Tom answered, 'We had a bit of a drive round in that Range Rover again.'

'What, you mean the one that you and Dan nicked?' I asked, horrified. I couldn't believe it.

'Yeah, I mean, Scarlet doesn't want anything to do with me anymore,' said Tom, 'so why should I still be caring what she'd say if she found out I was still going around in that old runner?'

I couldn't believe what I was hearing. Just because Scarlet pushed Tom away, he thought he might as well carry on doing what split them up in the first place?

'When I was upset that Scarlet still wouldn't take me back, Dan had my back. And then when I hesitated when he suggested going for another ride in it, he started acting like I was being ungrateful to him for being there for me! And what's more, he was right!' Tom added. I glared at him.

'Coward,' I said, angrily, 'you *fucking* coward!' He always was. Tom had never had a spine to say no to Dan!

'Sorry, but if you and Dan wanna stay mates with us lot, then this joyriding shit has to end,' I told him, before getting up and walking off. I was not, not, *not* going to be mates with Tom or Dan until they realised what they were doing was wrong.

I went to sit at another table, as I couldn't leave the student lounge until I'd met with Lizzy and the boys. I saw them enter the student lounge.

'Alright?' said Fred, sitting next to Jesse.

'Yeah, cheers. You alright?' I said. 'You seen much of Charlie, lately, Lizzy?'

'Yeah, a bit,' said Lizzy. 'Don't forget, we're still being careful around Fraser.'

Lizzy really needed to stop giving a flying fuck what Fraser thought. It had fuck all to do with him!

I then started talking about the new Spanish exchange student.

'Reckons I stand a chance with her, Stuart does. She is fit,' I admitted. I was keen to get to know her. She was so sexy. She had long, black hair, dark brown eyes and olive skin. She was also very cheerful and bubbly.

'What made him think you'd stand a chance with her, anyway?' Jesse asked.

'Stuart said that he'd noticed Rosa and her friends talking, about me, and looking at me, going bright red whenever she did it,' I told him, Fred and Lizzy.

'Whoo! She has got it bad!' said Fred. 'You are in there!'

'Oh also, Tom came over and spoke to me before you three came in,' I then told Jesse, Fred and Lizzy. 'He and Dan have gone driving around in the stolen Range Rover again, if you can believe that.'

Jesse screwed up his eyes in disbelief and said, 'Fuck sake!'

I then told him, Fred and Lizzy what a coward Tom had been, letting Dan talk him back into it again, and how I'd given Tom an ultimatum where either he and Dan stopped it, or we'd all cut ties with them, something Lizzy said she would second, as did Fred and Jesse.

I asked Jesse how Jamie had been settling in, bearing in mind he'd only been living with him, Rochella and Mrs Naerger for a week so far.

'He seems happy enough,' said Jesse.

Something about Jesse's long lost brother had been going through my mind over the last couple of months, ever since Jesse had said that he'd found out he had a long lost brother. A brother named Jamie. Jamie Naerger.

Jamie Naerger was my best mate at school, back when I lived in Beaminster, but I never saw or heard from him again after he had to be taken out of school during year eleven.

The way I knew for sure that it was the correct Jamie was because when we went to school together, Jamie talked about how he'd grown up living with his dad, who he left with when he was too young to remember. He'd mentioned his sister and his mum, but he said that they were dead, and he never mentioned any brothers.

When Jesse first said that he had a brother named Jamie, who'd left with their dad before anyone knew their mum had Jesse on the way, I knew it rang a bell.

Over the last week, Jesse had asked if I'd been mates with Jamie, because Jamie had claimed we were mates at school and had found out me and Jesse were mates and wanted to catch up.

'But Mum said to give Jamie more time to settle in,' Jesse had said. 'I just mentioned it because I said to Jamie I would.'

I understood. Jamie might've been desperate to see me again, but Jesse was right about Jamie needing more time.

As it came on to quarter to eleven, we went to class, agreeing we'd meet in the canteen at lunch.

Whilst working in the darkroom in class, Stuart started asking if I thought I'd go for it, as far as Rosa Suarez was concerned. I did want to, there was no doubt about that. And now I felt pretty sure, after what Stuart said, that she liked me, I was definitely up for it.

'I saw Priscilla earlier,' Stuart said. 'And she was asking me about Charlie and Lizzy.'

I looked round at Stuart. I remembered seeing her watching Charlie and Lizzy on Jesse's birthday.

I didn't need to ask Stuart what sort of questions Priscilla had asked, the way she'd looked at them. She clearly wanted to know exactly how serious Lizzy and Charlie's relationship was. She had it bad for Charlie and was gutted that he was with Lizzy. I said this to Stuart.

'Well, she's clearly had a change of heart, she never looked twice at him back at Carrie Mount,' Stuart said. 'Maybe it's one of those things, where you don't actually realise you fancy someone until they're not single any more.'

Even though I agreed, I still wasn't so sure why Stuart was bringing this up.

'Hey,' I said at lunch, sitting down next to Lizzy, who was also sat with her mate Isabel in the canteen. I wondered where Nikki was, so I asked.

'Not in the best mood,' said Isabel. 'Dan's being a reckless prick.'

'I know why,' Lizzy said. 'Tom and Scarlet broke up over the same thing.'

As expected, Isabel looked shocked and concerned.

'Nikki should give Dan an ultimatum; her or the car. But I know she won't,' she said. 'She likes him *way* too much!'

She sighed.

'Oh, did I tell you, I've got a new boyfriend!' she suddenly said, excitedly. Lizzy looked confused.

'I didn't even hear anything about you splitting up with your last boyfriend, Ellis,' she said. 'What happened with him?'

'I didn't really feel the same way about him anymore,' said Isabel. 'Now I'm dating your mate Fred.'

Hang on, had I heard her right? Did Isabel say that she was going out with *Fred*?

'Who?' I asked.

'You know, Fred, very admired by the girls,' said Isabel. 'I know he was dating Ruby-lynn, but he says they split up.'

Fred and Ruby-lynn had split up? Why hadn't Fred said anything about it?

But I didn't feel like getting worked up about that. During class, after lunch, I was in the classroom, arranging my photos, with Rosa at the back of my mind. The thought of going out on a date with her felt amazing.

But how was I going to ask her?

The answer to that came at afternoon break. Me and Stuart headed to the student lounge. I'd just got a drink from the vending machine, when Stuart had pointed Rosa and her friends out to me. They were sat at a nearby table. Rosa was smiling at me, bashfully, and she was blushing.

'Stick around. I think I might get a drink, actually,' said Stuart. I waited whilst Stuart put some coins into the vending machine. Out of the corner of my eye, I saw Rosa standing up and walking in my direction.

'Excuse me, are you queuing for the vending machine?' she asked, looking round at me with her dark mysterious eyes. I was speechless. I gazed at her, mouth hanging open.

'Oh, no, I-I've finished,' I stammered, coming back down to Earth. I stepped back to let Rosa queue up behind Stuart.

'What is your name again?' Rosa asked.

'D-D-Dave,' I answered, nervously. Rosa watched me, smiling. I didn't know what to do, so I just said, 'Whereabouts in Spain are you from?'

'Madrid,' she answered. Wanting to make more conversation with her, I asked if it was nice there, and she started telling me about all the places she liked to go in Madrid and all the things she enjoyed doing. I didn't find it easy to understand what she was saying because of her strong Spanish accent, but I tried to sound interested. I then asked if she'd been around town at all.

'There's a restaurant I would really like to go to, which I haven't been to before,' she said.

'Oh right?' I said, curiously. 'Which one's that?' I looked over at Stuart, who gave me the thumbs up, encouragingly.

'I think it's called Prezzos. I think it's an Italian restaurant,' said Rosa. Should I maybe take that chance, and ask her on a dinner date there? I'd only ever been there once, for Mum's birthday.

'I am actually Italian myself,' I told her.

'Oh really?' said Rosa, sounding interested.

'Well, actually, I'm English in the sense that I was born in England, but most of my family's Italian. It's only my granddad from my dad's side of the family and his lot that are English, hence the English surname. My name is actually Davide, but everyone calls me Dave for short.'

Rosa seemed very intrigued my background history as I enlightened her.

'I don't s'pose you'd be interested in going to Prezzos for dinner with me some time, would you?' I asked, wanting to move the conversation back to dinner.

Rosa gave me a great big grin, like she'd been waiting her whole life for me to ask her out.

'Yes!' she cried. 'I would *love* to!'

After we arranged to meet at Prezzos on Tuesday at six in the evening, me and Stuart went back to class.

'Told you she was digging you!' said Stuart, ecstatically.

The next class went by *very slowly*, mainly because I was thinking of Rosa, the hot girl I was going on a date with.

At the end of the lesson, I went to meet Fred and Jesse at the opening to the car park. We were going to the William Henry for drinks. Did Jesse know that Fred had split up with Ruby-lynn? Not that I was going to ask him. And I wasn't sure about asking Fred myself, either.

When we arrived, we went to get drinks, then, as per usual, talked about what we'd been up to, so I took great pleasure in telling Fred and Jesse about the fit Spanish girl I had a date with.

'*Sweet*!' said Fred and Jesse in unison. Jesse asked what we were doing for our date.

'We're going to Prezzos,' I said. 'She said she'd noticed it in town and wanted to try it out, so it gave me the perfect opportunity and excuse to ask her out!'

Fred and Jesse looked stunned at my luck.

Jesse got up to go to the men's room. I watched him disappear through the door, and then said to Fred, 'Isabel says she has a new boyfriend.'

Fred gave me a look of both shock and discomfort.

'Okay, fine, yes, I *am* two-timing Ruby-lynn and Isabel,' he admitted.

I could not believe this, I was in shock. Fred was two-timing Ruby-lynn! I knew he was never famous for being a keeper, but I thought his feelings for Ruby-lynn had changed that. Guess not. But what I was not prepared for was what Fred said in addition to confessing.

'Ruby-lynn and Isabel aren't the only two girls I'm dating, but there are girls at college, then there's a girl that works in Gamestation,' he confessed.

I wasn't expecting any of this! Finding out Fred had been two-timing Ruby-lynn and Isabel was shocking enough, but hearing that he was also dating loads of other girls at the same time was *beyond* deplorable. Why would Fred do that? How *could* he?

'Jesse knows too,' he said, 'and since you know about Isabel, it's pointless keeping it a secret, just, *please* don't tell the girls, *especially* not Scarlet or Ruby-lynn, obviously.'

'Well, Lizzy already suspects something,' I told him. Well, I might as well have told him.

'I admit that Natalie's suspected,' said Fred.

'So I guess it's just Scarlet and Ruby-lynn I'm keeping it from,' he said. I didn't know what to think.

'I won't tell Ruby-lynn or Scarlet,' I said. Fred smiled, gratefully, and thanked me.

Jesse came back from the toilets. We both tried to act natural. Luckily, he'd launched into conversation too soon after he'd sat down to notice either of us acting strangely, anyway.

'Don't forget Matt's house party next Saturday night,' he'd said, to which Fred said he was still able to come, but Ruby-lynn wanted him to say she couldn't.

On the way home, I was still stunned at what Fred told me. I wanted to try and understand why Fred was doing it, because I thought he really liked Ruby-lynn. I'd wondered if maybe Fred had even developed stronger feelings for her than any other girl he'd been out with, but now I wasn't sure, now I knew he was also dating other girls at the same time.

When I got home, I planned what I was going to wear. I still had the smart clothes I bought when I wanted to impress Alyssa.

I chose the grey, short sleeved shirt, the grey chinos and black shoes.

On my way into college Tuesday morning, I saw a familiar looking Range Rover drive past me and Stuart. I saw Dan poke his head out the window.

'Alright, losers!' he yelled at us. He laughed and drove the car into the car park. I looked round at Stuart, who was glowering as he watched.

'He's *actually* driving to college, now?' he said. As he and I walked closer to the college, we saw Tom get out of the front passenger seat.

'For fuck sake,' I said. 'After what I said, they're taking the piss. Are they ever gonna get it into their heads?'

'This is my brother and his mate who gives him too much power we're talking about,' said Stuart.

We entered the college grounds, just before Dan and Tom caught up with us.

'Hey, whassup?' Dan called after us. Me and Stuart grudgingly turned to look at him and Tom. Dan started talking about the rides to and from college we were missing out on.

'You'll have to come home at some point, Dan,' Stuart warned him, 'and when you do, you will be in deep shit.'

'Who's gonna make me?' said Dan, getting in Stuart's face.

'Don't, Dan,' I said, grimly. Why were he and Tom even talking to us, after how clear I made it we didn't want anything to do with them if they carried on driving around in the car they stole.

'I'm surprised you ain't been caught yet,' I added.

'Well, they clearly don't miss it very much,' said Dan, smugly.

'I can only assume the owners have been away for months if they haven't reported it missing.'

'They could be travelling down under for all we know,' said Tom.

'How did you even manage to steal it anyway? No one's stupid enough to leave a door key under the door mat any more.'

'Well don't forget the course I'm doing,' said Dan. 'Yeah, it's mainly based around motorbikes, but I did learn a thing or two about cars and how they work as well.'

'He had all he needed to know hotwiring,' said Tom, before asking me, 'What's all this about you going on a date with the Spanish slapper?'

I felt a rush of white-hot anger running through me. How dare he call Rosa a slapper!

'Don't call her a slapper, dickhead!' I hissed at Tom, who then gave me a confused look, as though he had no idea what he'd done wrong.

'What's wrong with slapper?' he asked.

'You're calling her a whore, which you'd better not do again!' I spat at him. I felt Stuart grab my shoulders and then he told me to come away with him.

I was fuming. Hearing Tom talking about Rosa that way is not on. Stuart said he and Dan were just jealous.

'Why should Dan be jealous? He has a girlfriend!' I pointed out.

'Well, not for much longer if he keeps this up,' said Stuart.

Me and Stuart met with Jesse and Fred in the student lounge at break and told them what we saw. They were just as annoyed about it.

'And they're jealous that *I* have bagged Rosa Suarez!' I told them.

'Haha! There's a kick in the teeth for them both!' Jesse chortled, triumphantly. Stuart told Fred and Jesse how rude Tom had been about her, but Fred told me not to let it get to me then asked if I was looking forward to my dinner date.

'I am excited,' I told him, truthfully.

'You'll ace it,' Jesse said, encouragingly.

After college, I arrived home at five, leaving me only half an hour to get ready before I had to go out again. I donned my outfit, squirted on the perfume that I bought from Avon originally to impress Alyssa, grabbed my coat, then left.

I only just made it on time. Rosa Suarez was waiting outside the entrance to Prezzos. She'd dolled herself up quite a bit, but not so much that it was over the top. She looked so pretty.

'Hey,' I said, still feeling slightly on edge.

'Hola,' said Rosa grinning. 'Shall we go in, then?'

'A table for two, please,' I requested to a waiter when we'd both come in. The waiter showed us to a table at the very back of the restaurant, next to one of the windows. Rosa took off her coat, to reveal a striking dress that was that pale pinky orange I think they call peach. I was mesmerised.

'Wow!' I said. 'Nice dress!'

Rosa grinned.

'Gracias,' she said.

'So do you like it here in England?' I asked, when we both sat down.

'I'm still getting used to it,' Rosa said.

'How long are you in England for?'

'I go back to Spain before the summer holidays,' Rosa answered.

A waiter came to take our orders for drinks, so I ordered a bottle of white wine. We began reading the menus. I couldn't remember what I had the last time, but I wanted to try something different this time.

'Do you want starters, also?' asked Rosa.

'Yeah, why not?' I said. I faintly remembered having the baked mushrooms for starters last time I went. This time, I thought I might try the mozzarella in breadcrumbs. Once I decided what I was having for main course, I closed my menu and put it down on the table. Rosa followed suit and then asked what I was doing at college, so I told her all about the Photography course I was doing, and how I'm hoping to get a career in that sector.

Rosa looked fascinated

'Wow! That sounds very exciting!' she said.

'Er, yeah!' I said, trying to sound enthusiastic, though still feeling a bit awkward. 'What sort of career would you like?'

'It's always been my dream to be a fashion designer. I'd most likely specialise in costumes for plays.'

'That sounds absolutely amazing,' I said, before a waiter came over to our table and asked if we were ready to order.

'You are ready to order?' Rosa asked.

'Yeah, sure, um, ladies first,' I only just had the courage to say. Rosa ordered the crab cakes for starters and the chicken Milanese for main course and I ordered the mozzarella in breadcrumbs, followed by the goat's cheese and red pepper pizza for main course.

I got up to go to the men's room after Rosa and I handed the waiter our menus. As I washed my hands when I finished, I couldn't help feeling pleased about the progress I was making so far. I was worried I'd make a tit of myself, or we'd have one of those awkward silences. I was too busy feeling happy about this to notice the long bit of loo roll hanging out the back of my trouser waist band, just like a tail, with which I'd been walking back to the table. People were staring and sniggering as I walked back to the table, which I noticed, just as I was pulling my chair out to sit down.

'Why's everyone laughing?' I said, sitting back down.

'Look at your trousers,' Rosa told me. I stood up, looked over my shoulder at the back of my trousers and saw the loo roll.

Oh, right,' I said, slightly embarrassed. I pulled the loo roll out of my trousers, stuffed it in my pocket, because I couldn't think where else to put it, then I sat back down and offered Rosa a glass of wine.

'Have you been to many other countries?' I asked, as I filled her glass. I had been wondering what other countries she'd been to, besides England.

'I've been to Brazil,' said Rosa, and she told me about the holiday she once had in Rio, before saying, 'I have been to Cameroon and Germany, also. What other countries have you been to? Have you ever been to Spain?'

'I've been on a few the trips to Denmark, Ecuador and Haiti. I've not been to Spain before, though,' I said. 'Though my friend Lizzy has, once. I've always wanted to go to Barcelona in Spain.'

'I do enjoy going there,' said Rosa, before our starters arrived, so we tucked in, whilst talking about the other countries we'd like to visit. After we finished, the talk turned back to college courses.

'Have you always been interested in Photography?' asked Rosa.

I'd opened my mouth to answer, but let out a very loud burp.

'Whoops! Sorry,' I said, feeling myself turn red. 'That's never happened before.'

'You have had a lot of that stuff,' said Rosa. She wasn't wrong about that. Wanting to move on from that, I started telling Rosa about how, before I became interested in doing a course in Photography, I'd been into I.C.T.

After we finished we main courses, we ordered our desserts. I ordered a milk chocolate fudge cake and Rosa ordered a honeycomb smash cheesecake, then Rosa told me about the family she was staying with, whilst she was in England, and about the girl who she'd been learning English from.

'Is she going to stay in Spain when you go back?' I asked.

'That is the plan,' Rosa said.

We had our desserts, and then I asked for the bill. After I paid, we left and decided to take a walk along the harbour, whilst we swapped hobbies and interests, hers of which included ballet dancing and horse riding, mine of which include swimming, gymnastics, tennis, badminton and playing on my Xbox.

As we continued our stroll, we talked and got to know each other more. We talked about what music we enjoyed listening to, what films and T.V shows we liked watching, what books we liked to read, and what we got up to with our friends. I even got her number!

Afterwards, I walked her to her bus stop, which was the Chickerell bus stop. Rosa was at the back of a long queue. The bus was approaching.

'I had a very nice evening,' said Rosa. 'Thank you for inviting me to dinner.'

'You're welcome,' I said, starting to feel nervous again. Next thing I knew, Rosa had leant in and kissed me on the lips. I felt like I was dreaming. I couldn't believe it happened so quickly.

'I shall see you tomorrow,' she said, after she broke away.

'Yeah,' I said, breathless with happiness. 'Bye, then.'

'Adios,' said Rosa, before I turned to leave. As I walked towards the back of Debenhams, I looked over my shoulder at her. She waved, and I waved back.

On the way home, I relived what had just happened in my head. Rosa is such a stunningly arousing girl. I couldn't believe she actually fancied me.

In the photography studio the next day, Stuart asked, straightaway, how it went, so I did not waste any time and I told him everything. Stuart looked dumbstruck.

'Fuck me, you lucky prick!' he said, astounded. He asked when I'd see her again, although I hadn't made any more arrangements with her, yet.

'It won't be hard though, now I've got her number!' I said, overjoyed. Stuart stared, his mouth open with the utmost amazement.

Rosa came over at break. I was in the canteen with Fred, Lizzy and Jesse. None of the others, apart from Stuart, had met her before, so it gave me the perfect chance to introduce them to her as she joined us.

But my happiness was made brief when I caught sight of Dan and Tom sat at the nearby table, giving me dirty looks, and out of the corner of my eye, I saw their expressions harden when Rosa leant in to kiss me.

I just shrugged it off. It was just like Stuart said. They were jealous. But I had no way of knowing they were in no rush to let it be.

I was sat at one of the benches outside the canteen with Rosa at lunch, when Dan and Tom came over.

'How's it going, Diavlo?' said Dan, casually, as though he was greeting a mate of his. Rosa looked up at him and Tom.

'Hola,' she said, and then she looked round at me. 'Are they friends of yours?'

Before I could say anything, let alone deny we were mates, Tom said, 'Yeah, that's right.'

I could feel rage building up inside me. I looked up at both Tom and Dan, evilly. Dan smirked.

'How very nice,' said Rosa, grinning.

'So,' said Dan, 'is she your girlfriend?'

I glared at Dan. What was he doing?

'We are seeing each other,' said Rosa.

'Sweet,' said Tom. 'See you around.' Then he and Dan walked off. I looked over my shoulder at them, and then looked down, uncertainly. I did not know what that was about, but I had a very bad feeling Dan and Tom were up to something, and I didn't like the sound of it, whatever it was.

'They seem friendly,' said Rosa, grinning. Great. Now there was a catch, as Rosa had now obviously bought that they were my mates.

I thought more about all this when I went back to class. If those losers were planning something against me, there was no way they could ruin things between me and Rosa. Was there?

I couldn't have been more wrong. Me and Rosa bumped into them at break the next day.

'Do you fancy hanging out after college?' Tom asked us. I was hoping Rosa would politely decline, but, annoyingly, she was up for it. I really didn't want to.

'No, I really don't think we should,' I said, but Rosa gave me a disappointed look.

'Why not?' she said.

'Yeah, why not, Diavlo?' asked Dan, still talking like we were mates. I felt trapped. Rosa pleaded with me to come, and said it would be fun.

'Aw, come and join us, or your girlfriend will be *so* upset,' said Tom, mockingly. I looked round at Rosa, who was looking at me with pleading eyes. It was hopeless. I had no choice but to go along with it. I unwillingly agreed.

Just before walking off with Dan, Tom pulled me aside and muttered into my ear, 'You are in way over your head, mate.'

We went to the canteen.

'Why don't you want to see them after college? They're your friends, and they are so kind,' said Rosa.

Dan and Tom were not kind at all. They were just trying to spoil everything between me and her. And now that she thought they were nice mates of mine, they had her where they wanted her, which made it easier for them to have me where they wanted me too, whether I liked it or not.

After college I grudgingly went with Rosa to meet the pricks. They were stood by the Range Rover.

'I still can't believe you're still driving around in that car, after what happened,' I said to them.

'Oh, c'mon, you lot really are making a big deal out of it, Diavlo,' said Tom. How could Tom say that, since that was what he and Scarlet broke up over? I supposed he was trying to make it easier for himself to not regret it, by letting Dan make him think like they weren't to blame and as if Scarlet was just overreacting and dumped him over nothing.

We all got into the car. I got into the back with Rosa.

'Where are we going?' she asked, excitedly.

'Thought we might chill out at Lakeside,' said Dan, carelessly. He started the car up and drove out of the car park. I looked out of the window, and saw Fred and Jesse as we drove past. I caught Jesse's eye and Jesse gave me a look of disbelief. I knew he must have been wondering what the hell I was playing at, hanging around with Dan and Tom, driving around in the stolen Range Rover again.

I sat nervously in the car as we drove along the seafront. I hoped Dan wasn't going to play up with his driving just as Tom had done, mainly because I didn't want Rosa getting hurt.

Thankfully, Dan drove smoothly, all the way to Lakeside.

We didn't do any bowling. We just sat and had drinks and played on the games there. Tom asked Rosa if she fancied a game of pool. She didn't sound very sure about it, though.

'I do not know how to play pool,' she had said.

'I'll teach you,' said Tom, winking at me, and smirking. Fuckhead.

I watched, doubtfully, as Tom and Rosa got to their feet and walked over to the pool table. Then I looked round at Dan.

'Why are you two doing this?' I asked him, anxiously. Dan looked round at me, like he was completely at sea.

'Doing what?' he asked.

'Are you and Tom trying to come between me and Rosa?'

'I have no idea what you're talking about.'

'Then why are you both acting like you're still mates with me, when neither of you have owned up to what you've done wrong?' I asked.

'Because me and Tom ain't done anything wrong,' Dan said.

'I'm not going to own up when I haven't done anything wrong,' I told Dan.

'Well, we both feel that you, Fred and Jesse were being a little unreasonable, making us choose between you three, and what we were just doing for fun,' said Dan. 'And now Rosa is keen to be friends with me and Tom, you can't refuse to hang out with us, as long as Rosa wants to. And I'm hoping that's gonna happen quite a lot. So, if you decide not to join us, you'll hardly get any time with her. Is that what you'd like?'

'No,' I said, shaking my head.

Dan leant closer and whispered, 'That's what I thought.'

Dan leant back, and watched Tom and Rosa playing pool. I felt sick with rage. Fucking twats! Who did those wankers think they were? Neither of them could bear that someone like Rosa wanted me and neither of them!

I sat and watched Tom and Rosa play. Rosa seemed to be enjoying herself. That was part of the problem. If she had been out of her mind with boredom, I would've had a good enough excuse for not meeting up with Tom and Dan.

Tom and Rosa came back over after they finished their game.

'Tom won,' said Rosa. 'He's very good at it, but he did try to go easy on me.'

I asked Rosa if she wanted to have a go at air hockey, which she said she was willing to give a try. I went easy on her, which earned me a lot of heckling from Tom and Dan afterwards, saying I was crap. I knew they knew I was just taking it easy on Rosa. They were just being arseholes.

When we left the bowling alley, I was hoping to make an excuse and say that me and Rosa had to go home, but Tom asked us if we fancied joining him and Dan another spin.

Knowing perfectly well what Tom meant by that, considering he'd used same words the last time, I said, 'Count me out. C'mon, Rosa, let's go home.'

But Tom was not giving in. And neither was Dan.

'Hey, how do you know Rosa don't feel like joining us?' asked Dan. 'C'mon Rosa. Just cos Diavlo ain't coming, doesn't mean you should have to miss out on all the fun.'

Dan opened the left back passenger door, inviting her to follow him in. I looked round at Rosa, hoping she would say no.

'Well, I've had quite a lot of fun,' she said. 'It would be a shame to call it a day so soon.'

'Damn right it would,' said Tom. 'This is only the beginning.'

I was furious. Rosa got into the back next to Dan! Tom walked round to the driver's seat, triumphantly.

'You are sure you won't join?' asked Rosa. I was enraged to see Dan put his arm round her, as though *she* was *his* girlfriend. What about Nikki?

'If Dave wants to be a pussy, that's his choice,' Tom told Rosa.

'See you tomorrow, then, pal,' said Dan, leaning over to pull the door shut, shooting me a malevolent smirk before the door slammed shut.

I watched, angrily, as the Range Rover pulled out of its parking space, and drove out of the car park. I had this feeling where I wanted to beat Tom and Dan to a pulp, but couldn't. They were both stealing Rosa off me. I was going to fucking kill them, they weren't going to get away with this!

I caught the bus home, alone. As soon as I walked in through the front door, I went straight to my room, and didn't come out for the rest of the evening. I didn't want to talk to anyone. I'd been dating a fit girl for just one day, but now those shit stains were driving a wedge between us.

I was still in a shitty mood when I went into college the next day. The first person I bumped into was Jesse, and he did not look impressed.

'So, you broke the pact, then?' he said. I suddenly remembered Jesse and Fred had seen me in the Range Rover. Great. How was I meant to explain that?

'I tried to say no, but Rosa was really keen to go and kept begging me to come,' I told Jesse. At first Jesse was puzzled as to why Rosa was involved, so I explained how Tom and Dan led her to believe we were still mates, which she fell for, and how they started encouraging me and Rosa to hang out with them, and because she thought they were really chummy, she wanted to.

'And then they invited her to go for a ride in the car,' I said. 'I tried to get her away before they could ask, but they just wouldn't take no for an answer.'

'Then they went off with her and left you?' asked Jesse in disgust.

'Yep,' I said. 'And Dan started acting like she was his girlfriend.'

Jesse started cursing about Tom and Dan under his breath.

'Doesn't Dan feel bad about Nikki?' he grumbled. I could tell he was angry on my behalf. 'I hope Rosa hasn't got hurt,' he added.

I already decided I was going to go after Tom and Dan if she had.

I was still feeling angry about what happened last night in class. I was barely paying attention to what Alyssa was saying.

I saw Rosa outside the canteen at break. Neither Tom nor Dan were around.

'Hey' I said when I reached her. I was glad she wasn't hurt. Well, I couldn't see any cuts or bruises on her anyway. But what I was not glad about was her talking, thrilled, about what she got up to with Tom and Dan after I left.

'It's such a shame you missed it,' she said. This obviously did not make me feel better, knowing she actually enjoyed the joyriding. Apart from anything, it just encouraged them. She then went on to say that she couldn't understand why I was so against joining them. That was when I cracked.

'They are *not* my friends, we fell out over that car you were driving around in, because they *stole* it, and neither of them will admit it's wrong!' I snapped. Rosa gave me a stunned, hurt look.

'Then, why were they acting like they are still your friends?' she asked. I didn't get how she could say that, since they certainly weren't exactly acting like my friends when they called me a pussy right in front of her. Anyway, how was I meant to explain to her that Tom and Dan were just putting it on to steal her off me, and expect her to believe it? What if she just thought I was being melodramatic? I was sure they would convince her of that if she told them what I said. It was no use. She didn't look like she was going to believe me.

I couldn't win. It was just like Dan said yesterday. It was either he and Tom got to hang out with both of us whenever they asked, which they'd make sure would be a lot, and Rosa would want to as well, or they'd hang out with Rosa without me, which would mean they'd get to spend heaps more time with her than I would, and if that happened, she'd forget all about me and want to be with either Dan or Tom. I had to hang out with them too, and endure any taunts from them.

They kept barging in whenever they saw me alone with Rosa, asking to join us, and subtly criticising me if I objected, and Rosa backed them up, saying there was no reason they couldn't join.

Even outside of college there was no escape. They asked Rosa what she was getting up to and, regardless of whether or not she had plans with me, they asked to meet up with her. If she did have plans with me, they asked to join her and me, and if she didn't, that meant they got some time with her *without* me.

Monday 21st March 2011

When I found out Tom and Dan met up with Rosa without me on Saturday, I was beside myself.

I tried to explain to Rosa what was going on, and how I didn't like Dan and Tom butting in every time I had some time alone with her, but she never took it seriously.

I talked to Fred about it. Fred agreed they were just trying to steal Rosa off me, by being so malicious, it would make me not want to hang out with them, so they would get Rosa to themselves, and also by showing me up in front of her, to make her see me as a boring bastard who couldn't take a joke.

'Although, she's kind of at fault too, if I'm honest,' he said. 'I mean, if she would just listen to you and take what you were trying to tell her seriously, it probably wouldn't be quite so easy for them.'

I had to admit Fred was right, there. Rosa should *want* to spend time with me *alone*, *without* Dan and Tom barging in.

'I know why they're doing it, too,' I told Fred. 'It's because you, me and Jesse won't be mates with them unless they stop what they're doing. But have they been interfering in either of your lives at all?'

Fred shook his head, but he looked worried. I could tell he was worried that, if either Dan or Tom found out Fred was dating more than one girl, they would expose it to everyone. But I felt pretty confident that, as long as it was just Fred's word against theirs, and they didn't have any proof, would anyone believe them over Fred?

But anyway, there was still nothing I could do. No one else, for that matter, could do anything either. Times of meeting up with the three of them were becoming unbearable. I didn't have any fun with Dan and Tom, and they were spoiling things between me and Rosa. They made snide comments, made to look like harmless jokes, about certain things I did, and Rosa found them more entertaining than nasty. They played spiteful pranks whenever I hung out with them, and Rosa just saw it as silly mucking around and she laughed.

Ordinarily, you could probably say I was so paranoid about them stealing her off me when she might only ever like them as mates, I was desperate enough to tag along too and put up with them being dicks.

We'd all been invited to Matt Weller's party, the coming Friday, as we were friends with him, and Dan and Tom had beaten me to inviting Rosa to come with them, which I discovered when she asked if I was coming with her, Dan and Tom. I was really angry when she also told me she made arrangements to meet with them so they'd make their way there together. She asked me if I wanted to catch the bus there with them. I resentfully accepted.

Friday 25th March 2011

Me, Dan and Tom went to meet Rosa at the house of the family she was staying with, the Enderbies, at half six. It was a small, terraced house on Franchise Street.

Polly, a podgy girl with a round, sweet looking face and light golden blonde hair, whom Rosa had been learning her English from, let us in, told us Rosa was just finishing getting ready, and invited us to sit and wait in the lounge.

Me, Dan and Tom went to sit in the lounge. Polly came in after she'd called Rosa to say we'd arrived.

'Have you learnt a lot of Spanish from Rosa?' Tom asked her.

'I've learnt numbers in Spanish,' she told him. 'And colours. And countries, too.'

She told us about the arrangements for her to go over to Spain in September, and how she was really excited, as she said she'd never ever been to Spain before, and was eager to learn about the Spanish lifestyle, as she knew nothing about it.

Rosa came in, wearing a sexy floral top with a plunging neckline, with a floaty light green, sequined skirt and brown, suede, high heel boots. Her hair was curled again. Tom flashed me an unpleasant smirk.

We walked down to ASDA, where we'd arranged to catch the bus to Matt's house in Chickerell. We got on and paid when the bus arrived eleven minutes later. I got on just after Rosa and followed her to two empty seats next to each other.

'You get back!' spat Tom, elbowing me out of the way. He barged straight past me and sat down next to Rosa, leering at me, cruelly. I really wanted to strangle Tom, but I knew that would, sure as eggs were eggs, turn Rosa against me.

I had no choice but to sit behind them, next to Dan. I looked over at Rosa, with the greatest bitterness I felt towards both the knobs.

The bus drove along Newstead Road. I caught Tom's eye. Tom shot me another vindictive smirk, then moved closer to Rosa and put his arm around her. I was dumbfounded how Rosa was actually comfortable with this. I gave Tom a livid, bitter look, which probably wasn't a very wise move, considering it would only give him the satisfaction.

The bus ride to Matt's house was a twenty-three minute journey, but when we were driving along Chickerell Road, reaching the turn to Glennie Way, Dan rang the bell, and we got off at the Glennie Way West bus stop, then walked until we got to Trenchard Way on our right, then turned left into Mohune Way, and eventually arrived at Matt's.

Matt answered the door five seconds after I rang the bell.

'Hey, mate!' he said, once he'd opened the door.

'Hey,' I said. 'This is Rosa.'

Rosa stepped forward to greet him.

'Ah, hola senorita!' said Matt, jokingly, as me, Rosa, Tom and Dan walked in.

'Hola,' she said. 'Very nice to meet you. I have met some of Tom's friends from college also, and they have been very welcoming.'

'Very nice to meet you too,' said Matt.

Me and Rosa went into the lounge, where Fred and Jesse were sat. I offered to get Rosa a drink, saying I'd leave her with Fred and Jesse, then went to the kitchen, where I found Charlie and Stuart with Lizzy and Scarlet, so I went to talk to them.

'Where's your new girlfriend?' asked Scarlet.

'In the lounge with Fred and Jesse,' I said, before beckoning Charlie and Stuart away to have a man talk. 'Rosa had made arrangements to get the bus to the party with Dan and Tom, meaning I had to as well, and Tom was all over Rosa on the bus, right in front of me, just to spite me!' I added.

'Don't let him or Dan know that it's getting to you, it's what they want,' Stuart warned me. 'But can I just ask, why are you worrying that them spending more time with Rosa than you do is going to make her want one of them more than you? You shouldn't be with someone you don't think likes you enough to not do that.'

This gave me a slight wake up call. I needed to take this up with Rosa, no one else. Especially not Dan or Tom, as it wouldn't make them stop.

I got Rosa a glass of vodka and Coke, whilst Charlie and Stuart went back to talk to Lizzy and Scarlet, then, as I turned to take it back to the lounge, I saw her coming into the kitchen with Dan.

'Gracias,' she said, as I gave her the can. As she went off to talk to Stuart, Charlie, Lizzy and Scarlet, Dan leant in to whisper to me.

'You've not been having words with any of your mates, have you?' he murmured.

I wasn't taking any more of this. I was well over the limit of what I was willing to put up with.

'I want you both to stop this. *Now*!' I hissed at Dan. 'She's *my* girlfriend, and me, Fred and Jesse were *not* being unreasonable about what we said was going to happen if you didn't face up to your mistakes. So keep your sleazy hands *off* her, *both* of you!'

But I was wasting my breath.

'Me and Tom ain't fucking going down, okay?' Dan spat. 'And none of you have any way of making us give it up, so I'm afraid you're gonna have to keep doing as we say, or you might just have to let your little sweetheart go and move on.'

I stared angrily at Dan, then turned, and walked out of the kitchen, through the lounge, and over to the door to the downstairs toilet. I tried to open it, but it was engaged. I stood thinking, heatedly, about what Dan had just said. I was powerless. As infuriating and despicable as what Dan and Tom were doing, I couldn't deny Dan was right. Nobody could make him or Tom stop, so if I wasn't willing to go along with it, I had to let Rosa go, unless I could get through to her, that was.

As soon as the toilet was free, I went in to use it. The first thing I saw when coming back out after I'd finished was Scarlet hurtling out of the lounge in tears. She flung the front door open and darted out, Ruby-lynn running after her. Then I saw Tom come out of the lounge, looking triumphant. He'd strolled over to the front door, which was still open, and stood framed in the doorway, no doubt watching Scarlet running away from the house. I just knew he had said or done something.

'What did you say to her?' I raged, grabbing Tom's shoulder, making him turn round to face me.

'I'll let you know,' said Tom, smiling, coolly, then he meandered back into the lounge. I stared after him. What was he on about?

I needed to find Rosa. I went to the kitchen, where I saw Rosa with Natalie, but I bumped into Lizzy on my way over to them, so I asked if she saw Scarlet crying.

'Tom was making her upset about how she dumped him over the joyriding,' she told me. 'And he was saying that he stood a pretty good chance with Rosa, and was going to show Scarlet what she was missing.'

'Not on my watch he doesn't,' I said, before walking over to Rosa.

'Can I talk to you?' I asked her.

'Of course,' she said, then I led her into the dining room.

'Do you really like me?' I asked.

'I do, of course,' she said. 'Why do you ask?'

'It's because of the amount of time you spend with Dan and Tom,' I explained. 'I hardly get any time alone with you. I'd have thought you'd want more quality time with me.'

'I like spending time with Dan and Tom,'

'They keep making a fool of me.'

'They are just having fun,' said Rosa. 'And I don't mind about time alone with you because I'm not that kind of person.'

I decided to leave it at that. I didn't know whether that conversation made me feel better or worse. She did say she liked she, and didn't start acting guilty and saying that she actually liked either Dan or Tom, but hearing that she wasn't fussed about quality time with me didn't help.

I watched as she walked off, then Fred came over.

'I tried to talk to her about the lack of time I get with her,' I told him. 'But she said she liked me, but she also said she wasn't the type of person who minded about quality time.'

'Ah, right, well,' Fred began, grimacing, 'you kinda need to think about whether you're okay with that. And, I'm not gonna lie to you, but you two were kind of rushing into things. I never said anything about that at first because you were really happy.'

I always knew, deep down, I hadn't exactly taken it slow with her. We went on a date when we barely knew each other, then right after that, we became a couple. I wasn't sure what I wanted to do.

I got myself a drink, and then went back into the lounge, but the sight that met my eyes made me feel like my stomach was shrivelling up. Tom was dancing with Rosa. She had her back to him, and he was running his hands over her thighs, her waist, her hips, her stomach... *and* her tits! Whilst kissing her neck! And Rosa wasn't showing any indication that she wasn't comfortable with it. On the contrary, she seemed to be enjoying it to the highest degree! She was running her hands over the backs of his, and his forearms, tipping her head back onto Tom's shoulder, her eyes shut with bliss.

I couldn't believe it. How could she do this to me? I stormed right over to her and Tom.

'What the fuck is this?!' I yelled. Everyone in the room went silent. Tom and Rosa stopped in their tracks, and then I was appalled at what Tom said next.

'Er, do you mind? We're kinda busy here,' he said.

'I *do* mind, remember that is *my* girlfriend you're touching up!'

'Well, Rosa should be allowed to decide that for herself,' said Tom, smugly.

'Rosa, why would you do this to me?' I demanded to know. 'I thought we had something!'

Rosa gave me an uncomfortable look.

'I'm sorry, I actually don't think this is going to work between us,' she said. People gave disbelieving laughs. I was full of mixed feelings. I was livid, first of all. She went off with someone else, and *then* broke it off with me when I caught her? I was distraught! She didn't want me any more!

'Oh, yeah, great, well, you sure picked the right moment to tell me!' I shouted, sarcastically.

'Aw, you ain't gonna cry, are you?' teased Tom, still holding Rosa round the waist. I stared angrily at him.

'I'm not going to cry one tear,' I said, grimly. 'Not in front of *you*!'

And with that, I stormed over to the front door, out of the house and over the driveway.

I heard Fred's voice shout, 'Dave, wait!' But I didn't stop. I yelled back to him to leave me alone because I wanted to be on my own, before carrying on down the road.

I didn't know what to think. I could not stand that Tom and Dan had won the battle. What they'd been doing was beyond wicked, and they'd been able to get away with it. All because of a fall out that wasn't even my fault. To say it was unfair would be an understatement. And I was furious and so fucking hurt at what Rosa did.

Had she maybe fancied Tom, and possibly Dan too, all along? Because that was what it was made me wonder now.

Chapter 10:

Fred's Second

Tuesday 29th March 2011

As soon as I came home, Dad asked if I was going to start getting ready to meet Ruby-lynn.

'Huh?' I replied, confused. Dad repeated the question, but I scowled and said that spending time with Ruby-lynn wasn't all I did.

'I'm not saying it was, it's just you said you had arrangements with her tonight,' Dad said. I was perplexed. I denied it, as I definitely didn't have arrangements with her. Dad looked mystified, and said he was sure I said I did, and then I remembered I *had* said that, to cover up the fact that it was actually Jodie I was meeting.

I met Jodie Binns in Tuatara Bar and exchanged numbers. She was a bit over-sensitive for my liking, and she was vaguely clingy, but I didn't let that put me off. I was going to her place on Chickerell Road, as I couldn't risk being seen out in public with her. We were going to have a romantic night in, with pizzas, popcorn and movies, as her parents were out and her fourteen-year-old brother was out with some friends. I told the other four girls I was seeing that I had to do my coursework. I hoped no one I knew, who lived in Chickerell, would see me on my way to Jodie's, especially Annie Bailey, as I'd beared in mind she also lived on Chickerell Road.

'Oh yeah, I *am* going to get ready to meet her, then,' I said, though not in the most convincing way. Dad asked what was going on and why I was acting so bizarrely about it, and then I snapped at him, saying I just forgot I was seeing her, then hurried upstairs.

This wasn't the first time I'd snapped at someone as I tried to keep track of all the lies and excuses I'd made. My dating had got out of control. Once I'd bagged a girl, I was on the look out for the next one.

Covering my tracks took so much effort and energy that it had begun to have a bearing on my moods and coursework. Scarlet and Mum and Dad and Max were the only ones, apart from all the girls I was dating, who didn't know what I was up to. I had no choice but to tell Lizzy, after she confronted me about me dating Isabel the same time I was dating Ruby-lynn, and I thought I might as well tell Natalie. They both swore they'd never tell, though I could tell they weren't happy about having to keep such a thing from Ruby-lynn.

After I showered, I put on something slightly less casual, put on some perfume, left the house and drove to Jodie's.

'Omigod, hi!' she squealed, sounding breathless with excitement, before throwing herself at me. She was wearing a *lot* of perfume. She then took me by the hand and pulled me inside.

'I thought, as it's Tuesday, we can do the Two for Tuesday deal at Dominoes!' she suggested.

'Er, yeah, maybe, I guess,' I said, as I followed her up to her purple room. She showed me all her Blu Rays, inviting me to choose some to watch. I noticed she had both the Night at the Museum films on Blu Ray. I got them out.

'Can we watch these two?' I asked, showing them to her.

'I'm happy with whatever you pick,' smiled Jodie. We went back downstairs to the kitchen, where Jodie offered me a drink, so I asked if she had any Sprite, and Jodie poured me a glass of Sprite and herself a glass of orange squash, and then, after she got out the Dominoes menu, we sat and read the menu in the lounge.

'Shall we put the film on then?' she asked, once she'd finished phoning through the orders, so we started watching the first Night at the Museum movie, but, throughout the film, we were distracted by each other a few times, when Jodie just wanted to climb onto my lap for more kissing.

I was starting to feel a minor twinge of guilt. I realised I didn't even really like her that much. I couldn't be with her any more if I didn't fancy her, but I didn't want to think how devastated she'd be if I told her I wanted to break up, and that wasn't even taking into account the fact that I was also seeing four other girls behind her back.

After breaking away after one kiss, Jodie said, 'I really do like being near you. When you're around me, you're all I can think of.'

Oh God. This was all too one-sided. But it was after what she said next, that the guilt had *really* kicked in.

'Here's the thing, Fred,' she had begun, 'I think I love you.'

The L word. And it wasn't just her it made me feel the guilt for, but the other girls as well. I really did like them, but I wasn't sure that that amounted to actual love for most of them. That was what had made me realise that, really, I'd been leading them all on. The power had gone to my head. I'd been so obsessed with the status I'd gained from dating so many girls, I never stopped to think about *them*, their *feelings*, the effect it would have on them if they knew I'd been deceiving them.

I didn't have much opportunity to think about whom I was going to stay with and who I'd send packing, or what I was going to do about ending it with the four I wouldn't choose to continue dating. And I still had the plans I'd made with Gabrielle tomorrow. Would I split up with her? Maybe it would be too soon to decide yet. I'd have to do some serious thinking.

I already knew Jodie was going to be one of the girls I'd end it with, as I didn't like her the same way she liked me, but apart from that, it wasn't going to be an easy decision to make.

I planned to think about what choices I was going to make when I arrived home, but I felt too drowsy, so I decided to head to bed.

I didn't have much chance to think about it on Wednesday at college, either. I was so busy in classes, and I wasn't alone during lunch. Jesse and Abi had come to meet me.

'Hey, fittie!' Abi beamed, giving me another one of her sweet smiles. I did love those smiles. But would I miss them a lot if I chose to let her go?

Whilst Abi went to queue for her cooked lunch, I spoke to Jesse.

'I'm ending it with some of them,' I whispered to him. Jesse didn't look as thrilled about this as I was hoping.

'*Oh*, just *some* of them?' he muttered.

'I'm going to decide to dump all but one of the girls I'm dating,' I explained. 'The only thing is, I don't know which one I want to keep, yet,' I added.

Jesse bit his lip, looked around, thoughtfully, then said, 'Well, only you can decide.'

I sighed.

'Decide what?' said a voice.

It was Fraser. He'd sat down opposite Jesse.

'Hi Fraser,' I said, awkwardly.

'Hey,' said Fraser, casually

He then asked me and Jesse if we'd seen Lizzy at all. Me and Jesse shook our heads.

'It's just I've noticed her spending rather a lot of time with Charlie,' Fraser explained. 'You wouldn't happen to know if they've got something going on, would you?'

Uh oh.

'I really don't know to be honest,' I told Fraser, hoping I didn't sound too much like I was desperately covering up for Lizzy. 'Why?'

'Well, I'd rather there wasn't, if I'm honest,' said Fraser. I looked round at Jesse. He looked as if he didn't get it any more than I did.

Jesse asked why.

'Oh, it's just, I'm not really that keen on the idea of Lizzy or Alistair dating my mates at the best of times, but especially as this is Charlie we're talking about,' said Fraser.

'Why are you so against Charlie going out with Lizzy?!' I asked, indignantly. 'You know what he means to her! Why are you having to be such a dick?'

Fraser gave me a hostile look, got to his feet and looked down on me.

'Because I know stuff about Charlie, that you lot don't and Lizzy won't even *try* to see!' he snapped, before storming off.

But I didn't understand it. What Fraser did know about Charlie, that we didn't? Me and Jesse exchanged uncomfortable looks.

Tom came strolling past, arm in arm with Rosa. Just as they were joined by Dan, both boys looked round and spotted me. They stared at me for a minute, before shooting me self-satisfied smiles, raising their eyebrows in a superior way. It was the sneering type of look someone would give you, by way of saying, 'I've got you now,' without words, and I didn't like it. What were Dan and Tom going to do?

They came over at that very moment. They were both smiling cruelly.

'We know your little secret,' Dan sneered at me. I needed to act cool.

'What secret?' I said, trying to sound like I couldn't care less.

'We knew it when Isabel told Nikki and Dan that you two were dating,' Tom said. Shit! They knew about my multiple coexisting relationships. Still, what could they do? Would anyone believe Dan or Tom if they tried to tell people what I'd been up to, or was it just their word against mine?

'So, what do you plan on doing?' said Jesse, using the same nonchalant tone I had. 'I hear you and Nikki are having more just a rough patch over what you and Tom are doing, Dan. And they know you're both at war with the rest of us. I wouldn't bank on her or Isabel believing you. They won't even feel the need to confront Fred about it, so he won't even need to lie to them.'

Tom didn't smile, but he raised his eyebrows slightly.

'Well, even if he did, it wouldn't be any different from the other lies he surely would've had to tell,' he said. 'Right, Fred?' he added, looking round at me. I sighed and told Jesse that Tom did have a point, before turning my head to look at Tom and Dan again.

'But if you are planning on using my secret against me, you'd better be quick in coming with a way to convince Isabel and Nikki one hundred percent,' I said to them both, complacently, 'because I will be ending it with all but one of the girls. I doubt you'll be able to come up with a believable story in such a short space of time. And if you can't do it before I'm back to seeing only one girl, it'll be too late, no matter which one I choose. Like I said, Isabel and Nikki will think you're making it up to get back at me, and the other girls will just think you're a pair of sad pricks who have such shitty lives they have to go and stir up trouble in other people's. So bring it on.'

Dan and Tom's faces changed, into angry, disappointed expressions.

'This isn't over,' said Dan, before he and Tom turned and marched off. I couldn't help feeling somewhat accomplished. Dan and Tom knew none of the girls I was dating would believe either of them if they only had their word for it. But Jesse took that moment as an opportunity to warn me to be cautious, in case they tried to dig deeper to be able to prove it.

Damn. I'd have to be very wary of them both. I was more anxious than ever, now, to make a decision before Dan and Tom could do anything.

Abi came back with a plate of shepherd's pie and sat down. She gave me a kiss on the cheek before tucking into her lunch, then stopped in her tracks and said, 'Are you wearing girls' perfume?'

Jesse looked up, petrified. The smell of Jodie's perfume from the night before must've stuck to me.

'It's my mum's,' I lied. 'It's probably stuck to me, I think.'

'Right. Okay,' said Abi, giving me a weird look. But it obviously made her suspicious. This was becoming a major mess.

I'd have to see how things with Gabrielle went that night. I was going up to Dorchester that night. We were going to the Plaza cinema together to see Everywhere and Nowhere. I felt lucky to be able to drive, because of the number of bus journeys I'd have to make otherwise.

I drove straight to Gabrielle's house from college, as the time of viewing we'd picked at the cinema meant I had no time to go home first. When Gabrielle answered the door, I was relieved to see she wasn't too dressed up either, though I still thought she looked beautiful. I still liked her, so I knew the decision to dump her wouldn't exactly be set in stone.

'Hey,' she greeted me. 'You looking forward to seeing the movie?'

'Yeah, should be good,' I replied, as me and Gabrielle walked back to the car. We got in, I started up the car, then began the journey up to Dorchester. We chatted as I drove, but I had another close call when I brought up a conversation, which I *thought* I'd had with Gabrielle before, something to do with what I was up to over Easter.

'What? I don't remember us talking about that,' Gabrielle said.

'I definitely remember talking about where I spent Easter weekend,' I said.

'We definitely didn't!'

God, I suddenly remembered it was actually Isabel I had that conversation with. I looked round at Gabrielle. She was giving me this look like she thought I was hiding something, which I obviously was, but I didn't want her knowing that!

'What? God, *I'm* sorry. I just thought I *did* tell you about that. Clearly *not!*' I snapped.

We spent the rest of the car journey in silence. I was really annoyed with myself. I wished I thought about whom I had that conversation with a bit more thoroughly, rather than just saying it. And now I'd made things awkward with Gabrielle too.

The sooner I made up my mind who I wanted to keep, the better. Hopefully things would calm down a bit, once I was only seeing one girl. It might probably be for the best if I broke it off with her and Abi, since I'd made them both suspicious. Then, with them two and Jodie out of the picture, I'd have only Ruby-lynn and Isabel to choose from. They were the two I liked the most. It was like chalk and cheese with them, though I didn't know who was the chalk and who was the cheese. I liked them equally for different reasons. I liked Isabel's laugh, her sense of humour, and her artistic side. It was a different story with Ruby-lynn. I couldn't quite put my finger on what it is that I liked about her, apart from her bright blue eyes and her daring sense of style. It was one of those unexplainable things.

As I parked by the Co-op near Trinity Street and stopped the engine, I knew I should apologise to Gabrielle for the way I spoke to her.

'I'm really sorry I snapped,' I said. 'I've just been really stressed.' That wasn't exactly a fib. I was stressed all right, though I wasn't going to tell her why, obviously.

'Okay,' she sighed. She looked like she chose to believe me, just because she didn't want to press it any further. We got out of the car and, after I went to pay for the parking, we walked along the pavement up to the cinema.

There was a very long queue in the cinema lobby. Me and Gabrielle finally got to the front, bought our tickets, two Pepsis, and a large bag of sweet popcorn to share, and went to screen two, where the film was showing.

'I thought it was great! What about you?' said Gabrielle, as we walked back to the car after the film had finished. I didn't have very many interests in common with Gabrielle. But was that a good enough reason to end it with her? Did I like her enough to not let it be a reason?

We drove back to Gabrielle's house.

'Thanks for tonight,' Gabrielle said, after I'd pulled up outside her house. She leaned in and kissed me.

'No problem,' I said, doubtfully. We said goodbye to each other, then Gabrielle got out. I watched as she walked over to her front door, and let herself in, and then drove home.

So maybe I wasn't not so sure if I wanted to stay with her, anyway. Part of me felt glad about that, as it meant I had another less girlfriend to choose from.

But none of this was going to be easy. It was hard enough trying to decide how to split up with one partner, which you're only supposed to have to do at a time, but having four to break it off with just made the word 'complicated' a massive understatement.

Jodie would be harder to break up with than Gabrielle, because of how she was. She was besotted. Her reaction to breaking up was unimaginable. I was focussing on breaking up with her first, and then hopefully, breaking up with the others wouldn't be quite so hard after that.

Over the last couple of days, I started thinking about what I was going to say. I asked the boys for advice on what to say. As I'd only ever been on casual dates before, I'd never had to go through this trouble before. Lizzy and Dave seemed relieved I was going to cut ties with all but one of the girlfriends I had. I explained why I wanted to do it. Keeping quiet couldn't have been easy for them, but I assured them that once I did what I had to do, they wouldn't have to for much longer.

But I still had to decide between Ruby-lynn, Isabel and Abi who I wanted to be with.

Friday 1st April 2011

I was hanging out with Jesse, Lizzy, Charlie, Isabel and Nikki in the canteen at lunchtime. My phone kept beeping. I guessed it was ringing with texts from the other four girlfriends. I ignored it. I'd read and answer the messages later.

'How's things progressing with you and Lizzy then?' I asked Charlie, whilst we waited for Lizzy, Nikki and Isabel to come back with their cooked lunches. I knew I ought to warn Charlie about what Fraser had said the other day. Charlie asked exactly what Fraser asked, so I told him Fraser wondered if I knew of anything happening between Lizzy and Charlie, because he'd clocked they'd been spending a lot of time together, and that Fraser said he didn't like the idea of them having a relationship.

'I really couldn't give a fuck what Fraser thinks!' said Charlie, sounding annoyed and slightly defensive. 'I do like her.'

I looked at him.

'Then that's all that matters.'

Charlie nodded.

Charlie stood up and said he was going to get a coffee.

Jesse spoke to me about Isabel, saying he'd noticed I didn't sound particularly fussed any more.

'She's not going to be the one you're keeping, is she?' Jesse murmured.

'It's not that. I still really like her, that's the problem,' I explained, keeping my voice low. 'Because she's not the only one.'

'Ruby-lynn?' Jesse asked. I nodded. I went on to tell him I also still liked Abi, but I already knew I wanted to dump Gabrielle and Jodie.

Lizzy, Isabel and Nikki came back to the table with their lunches.

After we finished our lunches, Isabel wanted us to talk outside, alone. I realised I'd left my phone on the canteen table with Jesse, Lizzy, Charlie and Nikki, but thought nothing of it.

'I was wondering, maybe in the summer, if you wanted to go away for a weekend?' Isabel asked. But I couldn't get excited about this, though I tried to look excited.

'Yeah, that would be great.'

Isabel went on to say that it didn't have to be abroad, just somewhere like Devon or Cornwall. I tried to sound enthusiastic.

'If you think it's too soon in our relationship to be talking about going on holiday together, just say, I won't be upset,' said Isabel.

I shrugged.

We stayed outside for another ten minutes, before Nikki came out and came storming over. My heart sank when I saw my phone in her hand.

'Are you going to tell Isabel who the fuck Abi and Gabrielle are, Fred?' she asked, glaring at me. 'Or am I going to have to do it for you?'

Desperate, I said, 'Maybe this isn't the right time.'

'No, I am not going to let you get away with your deceptive behaviour!' Nikki shouted. 'Look at his phone,' she added, chucking my phone to Isabel. 'He's been going out with other girls behind your back!'

Isabel looked at my phone. She looked absolutely crushed at what she saw. I couldn't bear how upset she was. She looked up at me, her eyes full of tears, her face screwed up like she was going to cry, and threw my phone at me. I looked at the messages and discovered some flirty texts from Gabrielle and Abi. By this time, Isabel had disappeared round the side of the London building.

'Isabel, please don't leave me! *Please*!' I begged, running after her.

'I can't even look you in the eye,' she sobbed, angrily. I stormed back over to the canteen, furiously. I'd never felt so angry. Normally it would take a lot to fire me up, but I was fuming, now.

'WHY THE FUCK DID YOU HAVE TO DO THAT?!' I bellowed at Nikki. But she was clearly not sorry for exposing me.

'Isabel is my best friend, Fred,' she growled. 'What if I went out with Jesse and I'd been unfaithful to him?'

'Your phone kept beeping with texts whilst you were outside with Isabel,' Jesse explained. 'I'd tried to shut off the ring tone because we were all finding it annoying, and Nikki saw the messages.'

I felt tears filling my eyes and running down my cheeks. I combed my fingers through my hair. I couldn't believe how stupid I'd been.

I wanted the day to be over because I wanted to get home as soon as possible. I couldn't believe what had happened. I'll never be able to forgive myself.

Not long after that, Gabrielle and Abi dumped me too. Isabel had tracked them down via my Facebook page and told them everything.

And yet, Lizzy, Natalie, Jesse and Dave were so supportive. They didn't abandon me and tell me that I'd brought it all upon myself. We agreed I should just stick to Ruby-lynn and date her properly.

She and Jodie were now the only two I had left, only one of which I still wanted, so it was a no-brainer. I was nervous about having to tell Jodie I didn't want to be with her any more, but I wanted to do it before Ruby-lynn discovers I'd been seeing someone else and I lost her too.

Monday 4th April 2011

I'd arranged to go round Jodie's house after college, so I could tell her.

'Wow, you are looking so gorgeous!' she said, when she let me in.

She was so smitten with me. I was definitely not looking forward to ending it with her, breaking her heart, ruining that happy mood she was in, reducing her to tears.

We sat on Jodie's bed together.

'I want to talk to you about something,' I told her.

'Oh my God,' she said, grinning, 'I know what you're going to say. It's those three little words, isn't it?'

Oh great. I knew it wasn't going to be easy, but I wasn't expecting this. This was going to be harder than I anticipated, by the looks of things.

'Okay, well, it's not easy to say,' I began, 'but I think we should stop seeing each other.'

This wiped the grin clean off of Jodie's face. You'd think I'd just told her she wasn't going to have a birthday this year.

'What? Why?' she asked, her voice shaking.

'I don't feel the same way about you anymore,' I said, truthfully.

'But we had something really good!' Jodie insisted.

'Well, no, we didn't,' I replied, 'because, to be honest, it was never really anything serious.'

At this, Jodie said, 'We could make it serious!'

I knew she was just saying whatever she could to get me to change my mind and not leave her. Poor girl.

'No, we can't.'

'Why not?' she asked.

'I'm just not as into the relationship as you are,' I told her. She tried to say something else, but I said, 'I'm sorry, but my mind's made up.'

'But... I really enjoyed it when you fingered me!' Jodie sobbed, dramatically. Jesus Christ, I was well glad I hadn't decided to break up with her in public, because of the attention her reaction would've attracted.

'I'm really sorry, but that the only thing worse than ending our relationship here and now would be leading you on even more, which could end with me hurting you even more' I told Jodie. She continued to sob dramatically. The bedroom door opened and Jodie's mum poked her head round the door.

'I thought I could hear someone crying,' she said, reprovingly.

'He broke up with me!' Jodie cried, looking over at her mum. She continued to sob. Mrs Binns came rushing over.

'What is your problem, young man?' she shouted at me, outraged.

'I'm sorry, but I've made up my mind, and Jodie has to move on and she'll find someone else, but she needs to get on with her life until then,' I tried to tell Mrs Binns, but she told me to leave her house and never come back.

On my way home, I didn't know whether to be relieved on or not. At least I'd done it, but she took it so badly and her mum got cross with me too. But that didn't matter though, not now I knew I wouldn't have to see them again.

Now I could be with Ruby-lynn and only Ruby-lynn, and knowing I could focus on just one girl was a weight off my mind. I was glad that she was the one I still had, because, oh my God, everything was coming clear! I'd liked her more than the others anyway, it had always been there, and made me regret seeing other girls as well.

On Tuesday at break, Lizzy was gob smacked when I told her how Jodie took the break-up, and how her mum got involved.

'Oh my God!' she'd laughed, flabbergastedly. 'Bet you're glad you're not seeing her any more!'

'Don't, I still feel terrible she was so gutted!' I groaned. 'But now that she, and the other three are clean out of the picture, things between me and Ruby-lynn can go back to the way they were *before* I started cheating.'

'Well, let's hope so. It may take a while for things to die down,' said Lizzy.

'We'll just have to take certain precautions until they do,' I told her.

We talked about what Natalie was doing for her birthday. It was Friday, the twenty-ninth of April. I told Lizzy that Natalie had previously said that V wanted to take her out and for us all to join her, which I wasn't too sure about.

'Sounds decent of him though, considering he's been taking up so much of her time and attention,' said Lizzy.

'Well, yeah, I guess the least he can do is include us in things they do together,' I agreed. But even over the stress of what I'd been up to, I was still concerned about what was going on between Natalie and V, mainly because of the bag of weed I found in Natalie's room. It worried me that V could get Natalie into the same scrapes he got into, or worse, he'd end up hurting Natalie if she did anything that crossed him.

'How haven't Natalie and V got bored of each other?' Lizzy asked, rhetorically.

'Your guess is as good as mine,' I said.

This had been worrying all of us, the amount of time Natalie had been spending with V. If I didn't know any better I'd say she was out helping V deal the cannabis she'd been keeping a hold of for him, as I went poking around in her room one time when she was out, and found it gone from her dressing table drawer.

Me and Lizzy went into town after college because I wanted to meet Ruby-lynn after work. We were quite early, as we'd arrived in town at twenty to five and Ruby-lynn didn't finish until half past five. We didn't know how to occupy ourselves. Normally, I would've had a browse around Gamestation, but obviously I couldn't now.

Me and Lizzy decided to look at the D.V.Ds, upstairs in WHSmith. It was just my luck to bump into Jodie and her friends.

'That's him,' I heard her mutter to the others as soon as me and Lizzy had reached the top of the stairs. They all gave me cold looks as we passed then turned their backs on me and went downstairs.

Lizzy noticed.

'Is that one of the girls?'

I nodded.

'The one who didn't take being dumped very well,' I said.

Me and Lizzy looked at the A to Z selection of movies on D.V.D.

I found two D.V.Ds I wanted to buy, Superbad, and Shaun of the Dead, and then went to pay.

After we left the shop we said goodbye to each other as Lizzy was going to catch her bus home now, and then I walked through St Thomas Street to Zellweger's.

I walked through the pharmacy towards the other end of the shop. I saw Ruby-lynn restocking shampoos.

'Hiya,' I said, walking over to her, grinning. Ruby-lynn looked up.

'Hi!' she beamed, sounding pleasantly surprised. 'I wasn't expecting to see you here.'

'I wanted to surprise you,' I told her, grinning.

126

'Well, it worked,' said Ruby-lynn, reciprocating the grin.

'Is this your boyfriend, then?' asked one of Ruby-lynn's colleagues, coming over, looking delighted.

'Yes, this is Fred, and Fred, this is Chloe.'

'Nice to meet you,' said Chloe, smiling.

'Likewise,' I said, before turning to Ruby-lynn and asking her, 'If you're not doing anything after work, do you fancy coming for a coffee when you get off?'

'Yeah, that would be great,' she said.

When Zellweger's shut at five thirty, me and Ruby-lynn said goodbye to Chloe, and then we went to Café Nero. We ordered some coffees and then sat at the table under the stairs.

Ruby-lynn asked if I knew if Natalie had any plans as to what she wanted to do for her birthday.

I told her about V saying he wanted to do something special for Natalie's birthday, to which the whole gang were invited. Ruby-lynn froze, before asking if I was actually going if V was organising it. I said I wanted to, if it was for my sister's birthday.

'Well, I want to be there for Natalie's birthday too,' Ruby-lynn admitted. 'But I'm scared. He's in the type of gang that carry knives and guns and stuff.'

'I understood I don't want to be around someone like that,' I said, 'but I felt that, as it is Natalie's birthday, we should just sit it out and not ruin everything for her by making a fuss as he is Natalie's boyfriend.'

'That maybe it will be okay,' Ruby-lynn said. 'V won't try to hurt me in front of Natalie.'

'If he wants to, he'll have me to answer to,' I told her, and I meant it. That was how much she meant to me.

I didn't care so much now that I'd been found out by Gabrielle, Abi and Isabel, and I made my own choice to break up with Jodie. I liked and cared about Ruby-lynn more than them, and I've never thought this highly of a girl before. I was definitely not going to let anyone hurt her, especially not V.

Ruby-lynn gave me a grateful smile.

'Thanks,' she said. She took hold of my hand. I felt my stomach do a somersault. I'd never felt this feeling before. What I had with Ruby-lynn was special. I never wanted to lose that.

After we finished in Café Nero, I offered her a lift home.

'That would be great,' she said. So we walked to the multi-storey car park.

'I do like your car,' said Ruby-lynn, when we reached the car. 'When did you get it?'

'It was a present for passing my driving test,' I told her, as we both got in.

'I bet you were well pleased with it,' she said.

'It definitely made passing my test one of the happiest days of my life,' I told her, starting the engine. I began to drive out of the car park and asked Ruby-lynn, 'Do you plan on learning to drive?'

'When I get the money together for it,' Ruby-lynn replied.

'What sort of car would you want if you could drive?' I asked.

'Ideally, I'd want a Nissan Murano.'

'Sweet,' I said, as we drove along Commercial Road. 'Any particular colour?'

'I'm not too fussed about car colours, though I would prefer a one in either dark blue or bronze,' said Ruby-lynn.

'Maybe if you tell your parents, then you might get one as a present if you pass,' I suggested.

'Glad I'm not taking lessons or about to sit a driving test right now,' then' said Ruby-lynn. 'My mum's been facing a *lot* of money problems, so my dad would be the one having to fork out.'

'Have the money problems been particularly bad?'

'Our lives have become about scraping money together, we've had to sell the T.V, and Dad has been trawling skips for old TVs, microwaves, and other appliances to fix up and sell on.'

Christ!

'Oh, God,' I said. 'How did it get so bad?'

'I have no idea how it happened.'

'If there is anything I can do to help, let me know,' I told Ruby-lynn.

'Well, I don't know if there is. But if some way you can help comes up, I'll tell you,' she said. I nodded at her, smiling.

'Do you want to come in?' Ruby-lynn asked when we arrived at her house. I really wanted to, but I had coursework to do.

'Perhaps some other time,' I said. Me and Ruby-lynn kissed goodbye, then I drove away after I watched Ruby-lynn go indoors.

I was so happy. I still wished I hadn't gone out with other girls behind Ruby-lynn's back, but now that all ties had been cut with them, I was determined to put my relationships with all four of them behind me, and just enjoy my one relationship with Ruby-lynn.

I joined Natalie in the lounge when I got back home. She was sat on the sofa in the bay window, watching Friends. I joined her.

'So,' said Natalie, 'back to seeing just Ruby-lynn, then?'

'Yep,' I said. 'And I couldn't be happier. Ruby-lynn's the one I like the most. Just wish I knew that earlier. I'm well glad she wasn't one of the ones that found out. I wouldn't be any where near this happy if it had been one of the other girls I'd been left with. I'd be badly missing Ruby-lynn, and be feeling that, even though I liked the girlfriend I did have left, it wouldn't alter the fact that she wasn't Ruby-lynn, and that would be a bad thing.'

Natalie looked round at me, bemused.

'Wow! You really like her, don't you?' she said. I nodded.

Natalie turned her head back to the T.V, her eyes wide with amazement.

'What does V want us all to do for your birthday?' I asked her. Natalie looked round.

'V's thinking of taking us all out for drinks and a slap up meal,' she said.

I was stunned and worried at the same time. V certainly was very generous, but the amount of money he'd spent did make me wonder if V had been spending money on those items he'd bought for Natalie to gain her trust.

'Who does he want to invite?'

'He wants to invite the gang, and Mum and Dad and Max,' Natalie said.

So, V wanted to invite the family too? Should I be relieved or concerned about this? I didn't know if it was because he was genuinely a nice guy deep down, or if he just wanted to gain, not only Natalie's confidence, but ours and Mum and Dad's as well. It all felt weird, and not in a good way. I didn't argue. Though I hoped he'd be nice on Natalie's birthday, and not try to hurt anybody.

'So, was there any place he has in mind?' I asked.

'V's suggested places like the Spy Glass,' said Natalie.

'Will we be able to get a reservation?' I asked.

Deep down I knew it was daft, not to mention fucking bonkers, going out for dinner with someone who was worse than trouble, but the fact that V wanted to do something really nice for my sister put, not just me, but the others in a moderately thorny position of not being able to decline.

'Yeah, V said it wouldn't be a problem,' Natalie said.

Even though it'll be all right on the night, this doesn't mean nothing dodgy is going on when it's just Natalie and V alone together.

Friday 29th April 2011

On days where which ever one whose birthday it is has college or work, my lot save unwrapping birthday presents for the evening, as we usually have to get ready, but, as we have a meal to go to on Natalie's twenty-first birthday, we saved it for afterwards, so Natalie would have something to look forward to later.

I picked Jesse and Ruby-lynn up, and brought them to the Spy Glass, where we met with Natalie, Mum, Dad and Max, who had come in Dad's car.

When I parked the car and we got out, I saw Natalie, Max, Mum and Dad with Lizzy who, thanks to their residence on Bowleaze Coveway, lives closest to the Spy Glass. They were walking over to whom I guessed was V.

'So, you're V, then?' I heard Dad say, shaking hands with V, as me, Jesse and Ruby-lynn walked over to them all. 'Natalie's told us nothing but good things about you.'

'Good, I should hope so,' said V, looking from him and Mum to Natalie, superiorly. I looked over at Ruby-lynn. She looked like she was bricking it. V looked over at her.

'I believe you and I have met before,' he said, walking over to her, me and Jesse with Natalie in tow. They'd met before? When? Where? How?

Ruby-lynn gave V a dirty look.

We all went inside. There was so sign of the others by the bar. I was quite surprised, as I thought Scarlet would've arrived before me.

Rather than getting seated and leaving her and Dave to look for us, we decided to go to get drinks from the bar. I listened as Mum and Dad had a conversation with V.

'So, what do you do?' asked Mum. V looked at her, blankly. Why was he giving her that look?

'Hmmm?' asked V. That was very bizarre. It was like V couldn't understand what Mum was saying.

'What sort of job do you have, she means,' said Dad.

'Um...' began V, sounding uncertain. I could tell that V knew he couldn't say he was a drug dealer, nor could he say he was unemployed, as Mum and Dad would hardly believe that, due to their knowledge of his ability to afford to spoil Natalie.

'V works as lawyer,' Natalie told them, quickly. Yeah right! Some one who went around dealing drugs, a lawyer? What was more, I was livid Mum and Dad had no idea they were letting their daughter go out with that kind of man. I knew I ought to tell them, but I remembered what Natalie said about asking Ruby-lynn why she and I had been watching the Matrix films together, when neither of us even liked the Matrix and, in actual fact, it had been Gabrielle I'd watched those movies with. And even though Natalie didn't need to ask, for the sake of knowing why, as she would have worked out that it was another girl I watched it with, it was still her way of keeping me quiet about the bag of weed, and if I didn't hold up my end of the deal, my happiness with Ruby-lynn would be history. There was no way out. I knew I was getting my priorities wrong in staying silent about illegal drugs so that Natalie wouldn't say anything to Ruby-lynn, but I couldn't help it.

Scarlet and Dave arrived five minutes later and she and Dad got into a conversation about how Kevin was as we were shown to our table. I sat down between Jesse and Ruby-lynn. I wanted to tell Ruby-lynn of my new suspicions, as well as to ask her what was wrong, because, according to V, they'd met before and she looked petrified the second she saw him. But I couldn't say anything about it to her at the table, as I didn't want to risk Natalie or V noticing.

We ordered our drinks, and then V had started having friendly conversations with some of the others. He was just trying to make us all like him!

The drinks came, and V stood up, raising his glass.

'I'd like to propose a toast,' he began, 'to the birthday girl, Natalie, my girlfriend.'

'Aw!' Mum beamed, happy for her daughter.

'Happy Birthday, Natalie,' said V. We all raised our glasses as we wished Natalie happy birthday. Natalie blushed, smiling, bashfully.

It wasn't until after we'd all had our starters and finished our main courses that I got a chance to talk to Ruby-lynn. We'd gone to the bar to get another drink.

I asked her what was wrong.

'I've seen him before, because he'd come into Zellweger's, back in October, gone behind the counter and started threatening my colleague, Gemma. He and his mates had guns and he'd said they'd shoot me if Gemma didn't empty the cash drawer and give him all the money in there, and Chloe, the one you met when you came into Zellweger's to see me, told me about V, because he led a gang who were rivals to a gang that her boyfriend used to be in, and that one of V's gang had stabbed him and left him to die and he had to stop going round with his gang after that.'

Ruby-lynn confirmed what I'd been worrying about, that if Natalie did anything to upset V or anyone in his gang, she could get seriously hurt! Dear God! Natalie is dating someone who robbed Ruby-lynn's workplace?! I didn't know what to do.

'That wasn't even how I knew he was lying about having a job as a lawyer,' I told Ruby-lynn. 'Just the fact that he was in the violent type of gang disproved that.'

'That still doesn't explain how V can have so much money if he's unemployed,' she said. 'What if he earns all that money, dealing drugs?'

It had to be that, and I half-hoped it was that and nothing worse.

'I still can't understand why Natalie is with V,' Ruby-lynn said, 'even after what he did to Gemma'.

'Maybe she doesn't know,' I suggested. 'Or maybe she won't believe it, maybe she doesn't even want to ask him.'

I looked over at the table. I saw V staring at me.

'We'd better go back,' I whispered to Ruby-lynn. 'He's looking at us. I bet he knows we're talking about him.'

Me and Ruby-lynn walked back to the table and sat down.

'You two having a bit of a heart to heart?' joked V.

'Yeah, that's right,' I said. Me and Ruby-lynn exchanged nervous looks.

The waiter asked if we were having any desserts, so we all placed our orders for desserts.

'It's so generous of you to pay for everything, but we wouldn't have minded,' Mum said to V.

'Oh, but I insist!' said V. Only Mum, Dad and Max were fooled by this, the rest of us knew exactly what he was trying to do.

As soon as the puddings arrived, I tucked into mine. Despite the host being a drug dealer who robbed shops, I couldn't deny that it had been a good night, all the same.

After the party, I gave Jesse and Ruby-lynn a lift home. When we arrived at Ruby-lynn's house, I walked Ruby-lynn to her door.

'Thanks, Fred,' she said. 'I guess I was right about V not hurting me. It was quite a good night.'

'I did enjoy it,' I agreed. 'I knew V wouldn't hurt you, because he wasn't doing it to hurt anyone. He just wanted us all to trust him. But it won't work with me.'

Ruby-lynn smiled, before she said, 'Good night.'

'Good night,' I said, before I kissed her, cupping the left side of her face. We broke apart after eight seconds, then Ruby-lynn went inside, and I walked back to the car to run Jesse home.

After I dropped Jesse off, I drove back home, thinking about what to do next about the possible new leads I'd found, regarding the situation with Natalie and her boyfriend.

Should I ask her how he really got so much money, and tell her I knew he didn't have a job because I saw how he reacted when Mum and Dad asked him what he did for work? But wouldn't she just snap and say it was none of my business?

More to the point, what about the fact that he came into Zellweger's, held Ruby-lynn at gunpoint and threatened one of her colleagues? How was I meant to break that one to her?

But I was also thinking about Ruby-lynn, and how I'd promised myself I would not follow through if any other attractive looking girls showed an interest in me. I was determined to be good to Ruby-lynn, fully, this time.

Monday 23rd May 2011

For another three weeks, I was so happy with Ruby-lynn. But three more weeks was all it was.

After college, she came to meet me, and she looked distraught.

'IS IT TRUE?!' she screamed at me, beside herself. 'Have you been seeing other girls behind my back?'

I heard gasps of other students nearby in the grounds.

I was shaken. How did she find out? Had someone blabbed?

'W-what? But... how, how did you -,' I stammered, speechless.

'Scarlet spoke to me!' Ruby-lynn raged, her eyes glistening with tears. 'Scarlet bumped into Lizzy and Isabel, and asked how they were, and Isabel said that she was still upset that you two broke up because you'd gone behind her back and had been dating other people! She was shocked when Isabel said that, and asked when it happened,' Ruby-lynn told me. 'Isabel said it was a month or two ago and that Scarlet told her I'd been with you since before Christmas, and that Isabel had said, "Oh, so he was lying about breaking up with Ruby-lynn and was still seeing her as *well* as me and the other two girls Nikki and I found out about?"'

I was devastated.

'Ruby-lynn, I can explain,' I just about managed to say, all choked up.

'It's a little late to explain anything!' Ruby-lynn cried. 'You are dumped!'

She stormed off, leaving me overcome with sorrow. I did not know what to think. I looked at all the people who'd seen and heard everything. They were all staring, their eyes like lasers burning into me.

I sat in the car, emotionally numb with the shock of what happened. I couldn't even cry. I felt like I couldn't do anything.

When I eventually started the car, I drove home, reliving what had just happened. Ruby-lynn broke up with me!

I wished I could've had a chance to explain why I did it, and how I stopped it because I wanted to be with her and only her but she was so mad at me.

'If I knew we were likely to see Scarlet, I would've suggested going somewhere else,' Lizzy said, apologetically at college the next day. 'I was praying neither of them would say a thing. It wasn't until Scarlet asked how Isabel was that either of them mentioned you. It probably would've been okay if it weren't for that. And I'm really sorry.'

But I knew, deep down, I couldn't blame anyone but myself.

'It's okay, Lizzy,' I said. 'There was no way you could've known. What are you apologising for? Not being psychic? And if it's anyone's fault, it's mine.'

And that went without saying. Nikki was still angry with me for betraying her best friend, and things weren't much better at college. Rumours had spread about my cheating, and nobody wanted to go out with me, because I now had a rep for being a player.

Why wasn't I happy with what I had with Ruby-lynn in the first place? It was only now that I'd lost her that I could truly appreciate how lucky I was.

And that was exactly what Scarlet thought.

Wednesday 1st June 2011

I'd come home after college and Scarlet was in the lounge with Natalie and, naturally, she gave me the cold shoulder.

'Look, I am really sorry I cheated on Ruby-lynn,' I said to her, but Scarlet didn't want to know.

She blanked me completely.

'I'd tried to explain that I'd stopped it and why, but she was too upset and angry with me to listen!'

'Not exactly a big shocker, is it?' Scarlet snapped. 'I always knew what a conceited, self-righteous player you were! Ruby-lynn never even meant anything to you, *did* she? She was just another girl for you to add to the number of girlfriends you could say you'd been out with!'

I suddenly felt a flow of red-hot anger. Yes, I *was* dishonest towards Ruby-lynn! But to say I didn't give a shit about her was taking it too far!

'Don't question how I felt about Ruby-lynn,' I growled at Scarlet. But Scarlet didn't look like she was going to back down.

'If you thought as much of her as you're making out, why did you start being so damn unfaithful to her?' she questioned me.

'Because I didn't appreciate what I had with her when I first starting dating her,' I told her, truthfully. 'I miss Ruby-lynn every single day and now I'd do anything to make it right. Far from hurting no one, I've hurt the one girl I truly care about.'

These words had been on my mind, ever since we broke up, but this was the first time I'd ever said them out loud. The good part of it was that I'd finally let it out and got it off my chest.

Scarlet shut up after I said that. She seemed to have understood, but I knew that wasn't going to eliminate how angry she was on Ruby-lynn's behalf.

Meeting up as groups was awkward too, now. Scarlet and Ruby-lynn wouldn't talk to me at all, so the gang decided not to have get togethers where I'd have to be around them.

I'd begged Ruby-lynn to give me a second chance, but she told me she couldn't be with a boy she couldn't trust.

I opened up to Lizzy about it. We were on a bench on the seafront together, after college on Thursday.

'Maybe just give her some space,' Lizzy suggested. 'She might come to forgive you, she might not. But constantly asking her for another chance will do the exact opposite of what you're trying to do.'

I didn't hold out much hope that that would work, but Lizzy was right about not pestering Ruby-lynn.

'I miss her so much,' I said. 'I hope one day, she'll be able to forgive me and see how sorry I am.' I felt Lizzy put her arm round my shoulders, before she said it might be a good idea if I tried to move on, and if Ruby-lynn did forgive me, I could think about whether I still wanted her back, and if she didn't forgive me, I'd find someone else.

But the idea that I'd have to move on from someone who meant the world to me was none other than prize torture. But if I did meet someone else, then hopefully I wouldn't mind if she didn't want me back. I had to do it.

'Thanks, Lizzy.'

After having a chat, we stood up and went to meet with Jesse and Natalie, who had met for a drink in the William Henry.

It suddenly occurred to me that Lizzy was friends with Isabel. She knew of our friendship. Had it occurred to Isabel that Lizzy had known something about what I'd been up to whilst I'd been cheating? If Isabel did think that, then she'd be so mad at Lizzy for not telling her, as they were meant to be friends.

'Listen, Lizzy,' I started. 'I know that you're quite chummy with Isabel, and that she knows we're mates, so she may or may not wonder if you knew what I'd been doing behind her back, so she's probably gonna get upset with you for not telling her if she does, and I really don't want you losing a mate over my mistake, so, if she asks, you knew nothing. Yeah?'

Lizzy nodded. She looked baffled, but she seemed to have taken on board what I said. Lizzy wouldn't thank me if Isabel was upset at her for not telling her. But Lizzy wasn't going to grass me up because of how long we'd known each other.

Natalie got up and said she was going to powder her nose.

'I'm amazed she's even been able to find the time to see us today,' said Jesse.

This gave me an opportunity to tell him and Lizzy what I suspected about V lying about being a lawyer.

'Damn straight he was lying!' said Lizzy. 'What kind of lawyer goes around robbing shops? He's hiding something.'

'You don't say,' I said, sarcastically.

I also told them that, when we went out for Natalie's birthday, Ruby-lynn said she recognised him as the man that came into Zellweger's and committed armed robbery. They were just as shocked.

'But if he's having to rob shops for money, how is he able to afford to spoil Natalie all the time?' asked Jesse, curiously, once he'd got over the shock of what I just said. 'You don't get that much money from stealing from shops.'

None of us understood it.

'It doesn't give us any clues as to why Natalie keeps disappearing to go and see V,' Jesse went on to say.

'Our discussion on the matter will have to be cut short now, because Natalie's coming back from the toilet,' Lizzy warned him.

Natalie sat back down and asked if anyone was up for another drink, saying she had time for one more before she went to see V again.

I sighed.

'When will we get to meet Jamie, Jesse?' asked Lizzy.

'Patience,' Jesse teased. 'When he feels ready, my mum's gonna arrange something. Because we can't chuck it all on him at once.

'Oh, yeah, course,' said Lizzy.

'Jamie seems to be really happy with me, Rochella and Mum,' Jesse went on to say.

'I can't blame him, if his dad's been a lousy father to him,' I said.

'Mum took him into town the day after he'd moved in, because his dad never made sure Jamie had clothes that fitted him properly,' Jesse said. 'She bought him loadsa stuff.'

'Lucky him,' I said.

'So, whilst you were at college, your brother got to bond with your mum over a mother and son shopping spree,' said Natalie.

'That's right. All right for some, ain't it?' Jesse groaned.

We had another drink, before Natalie went off to meet V, and the other three of us headed home.

On the drive home, I'd cheered up a bit after me and Ruby-lynn broke up, but she definitely isn't someone who'd be easy to get over after a break-up. I've never met anyone like her before. And who knows if I ever will again?

Chapter 11:

Lizzy's Second

Thursday 2nd June 2011

I was just passing this white townhouse, with black doors and window frames and a red Mercedes parked in the drive, when I saw the front door open out of the corner of my eye, and caught sight of a familiar looking dark man with a number one haircut. It was V. Another man, a tall, fair haired man with a goatee, followed him out, and handed V a very large wad of money in notes. I was curious, but I thought nothing of it and carried on home.

I went straight up to my room as soon as I got home. I bumped into my mum on my way upstairs.

'Hi, darling,' she said. 'Had a good time with your friends?'

'Yeah, Fred and I met Natalie and Jesse in Wetherspoon's for a drink,' I told her. Mum asked how Fred was, as she knew Fred and Ruby-lynn split up, and I said he was still upset.

'Of course, he will be,' said Mum. 'What went wrong between them?'

'Er... long story,' I said, uneasily. Mum didn't need to know Fred had been dating other girls the same time as Ruby-lynn.

I said I was going to get on with my coursework. I wasn't that fussed about it any more. I was more interested in the Design side of Art and Design, but the course was more focused on the Art side of it. I was thinking of what else I might want to do at college.

But still, I couldn't not do my coursework, even though it wouldn't matter if I didn't get a good mark. I brought all of my Art stuff downstairs to the dining room. I cleared myself some space on the dining room table as usual, and then spread all my coursework out. I was coming close to the end of the course, and I was on the final project.

Dad coming in from the kitchen and offered to make me a cup of tea or coffee whilst I was working hard, so I said I'd love a mocha.

I called it a night with my coursework when Mum told me she needed to lay the table ready for dinner, so I cleared all my college things away and took it upstairs. We were having chicken crown with parmentier potatoes, carrot and swede mash and a white wine and tarragon sauce.

I was nearly finished with my coursework, but I was too tired to do any more work on it that night. As it would be Friday tomorrow, and I like taking Friday evenings off from homework and coursework, I decided I'd leave it until Sunday and would finish it off then.

Me and Dave talked about courses the next day in the college canteen at lunch. Dave said he was planning to do the next course up from his. He asked what I was doing, and I said I didn't know. I looked round at Dave, hoping he'd give me some advice, but he shrugged. Maybe I'd look on the Internet after college, to see what other courses I'd like to do.

'Hang on,' Dave suddenly said, 'why's Charlie talking to Priscilla?'

I looked round. Charlie was by the door to the stairs up to the student lounge. He was talking to a familiar looking, curvy, busty, slightly chubby girl with long, curly, red hair.

God, it was Priscilla Atkinson, who was in Fraser's year at Carrie Mount. She was the school bully, not that she dared to go near me with Fraser around, and she's the biggest slapper I know! I'd been relieved she'd never got in with Charlie back then. I didn't know whether or not I could feel relieved right now, though.

I watched as Charlie looked right, caught sight of me, and by the look of it, he'd said goodbye to Priscilla and starting walking over to me and Dave.

'All right, honey?' he said, when he reached us. He sat down and kissed me.

'Who was that you were talking to?' I asked him. I wanted to ask, 'Why were you talking to Priscilla Atkinson?' But I thought it would sound jealous and possessive, so I thought it was better to act like I didn't know who she was and like I was merely expressing curiosity.

'Priscilla's a mate I knew from school,' he said. 'Are you still up for meeting for coffee at Costa tomorrow?'

'Of course,' I confirmed.

'Awesome,' said Charlie. 'You know I'd stay and chat, but I've gotta be somewhere.'

Where? Where did he have to be? It wasn't even the end of break yet! I saw Dave frowning after him as he exited the canteen.

He then looked round at me and said, 'You still meeting us at Wetherspoons after college on Monday?'

Scarlet had invited a small group of us to have drinks with her at the William Henry.

'Yeah, course,' I said. 'Who's coming, again?'

'Well, Fred's not invited, "*naturally*, for what he did to Ruby-lynn," as Scarlet put it,' Dave began, 'Natalie can't come because she's seeing V, as usual. And Jesse can't come because he's with family that night, so it's just you, me, Scarlet, Ruby-lynn and some mates Scarlet said she was bringing.'

'Cool,' I said, casually.

At my two o'clock, I saw Tom with Rosa Suarez. I'm still livid that Tom's hateful plan to steal Rosa off of Dave as personal revenge against him worked, and that Rosa went along with it. And Tom was also trying to hurt Scarlet for dumping him.

They were stood by the vending machines and they were meant to be kissing, but it looked more like they gnawing at each other's faces like they hadn't eaten for days. Tom kept grabbing and squeezing her tits, understandably making people passing by glare and stare with revolted looks on their faces.

'God, why don't they get a room?' I said, watching in disbelief. 'She may not care that much about quality time with her boyfriend, but she certainly loves P.D.As to the point where she doesn't care about getting stared at whilst getting felt up.'

Dave got up and walked off.

I went to class. It was when I thought that Tom had moved on from Scarlet pretty quickly, that it had occurred to me that neither him nor Dan even fancied Rosa. Yeah, they might have thought she was fit, but I was prepared to bet every penny that that was it, and they were just using Rosa to screw both Dave and Scarlet over, especially when I remembered Tom upset Scarlet at the same party he'd stolen Rosa off of Dave.

I spoke to Fred about this at lunch, and he agreed.

'Do you wanna know what I reckon as well?' said Fred. 'Dan's manipulated Tom. Maybe not intentionally though.'

Intentional or not, I wouldn't put it past him. Tom had never in his life said no to Dan. Ever! Not even when he convinced Tom it would be funny to spike Mr Spalding's coffee with viagra when we were in year nine. It gave him a *massive* boner in front of the whole History class and it wouldn't go down for hours!

We all knew Tom was gutted that Scarlet dumped him over it, and that Dan was the only one who was there for him, and made him believe he didn't need any of us, including Scarlet, and that we were making a scene out of them "having a bit of fun". And if Tom had been so upset about Scarlet, and only Dan stuck by him, he would've been so grateful he wouldn't have been able to find it in his heart to go against him.

It wasn't until I saw Tom in the student lounge during afternoon break that I thought I ought to at least try to reason with him. Little did I know what a mistake *and* a waste of time this turned out to be.

I saw him in the small shop in the corner, looking at the ice creams, and walked over to him.

'Hey,' I said when I reached Tom and stood on his left, directly facing him. He looked up, acknowledged my presence, and then went back to looking at the ice creams. I watched as Tom slid open the glass lid, took out a Twister, and slid it shut again.

'Things going well, then?' I asked. 'You know, with your girlfriend who you stole off one of your mates, just to get your own back on him? At least you were with Scarlet for all the right reasons.'

Tom glared at me as he joined the queue.

'She dumped me, remember?' he retorted. 'But I'm over her, and not everything I do is to try to hurt her, okay? So just leave it out!'

'Oh, you're over her?' I said, sarcastically. 'And, whatever you did to upset her at Matt's party was proof of that, was it? Neither of you love or fancy Rosa, do you? You were both just trying to hurt Dave, and now that you have, Scarlet's next, *isn't* she?'

'Leave me alone,' Tom mumbled, before walking away. But I wasn't finished.

I followed him and said, 'Everyone knows how upset you were about Scarlet, and nobody gets over something like that *that* quickly! It's obvious you were truly sorry about the joyriding!'

'Then it was Scarlet's fault for refusing to give me another chance, then, wasn't it?' Tom replied, continuing to walk away from me, not looking at me.

'Is that why you're letting Dan manipulate you into backtracking your apology?' I asked. 'Because he was there for you when Scarlet wouldn't take you back, and was acting like she was wrong to turn you away. You were so upset that she wanted nothing more to do with you, I bet it was just so easy for Dan to get you exactly where he wanted you. You didn't dare refuse him, you never have.'

Tom stopped abruptly, and then turned on the spot to face me. Had I got him to see the light at least just a tiny bit?

Nope, I was wrong.

'You are *wrong*, Lizzy,' he growled. 'You *all* are. Dan was there for me when you lot weren't. And he said it was because you twats were focussing on all the bad parts of what happened that day, and being negative about it, and ignoring the good bit about it.'

I was outraged. Tom called us all twats. Including me. *To my face*! Dan accused me and the others of being the kind of people to look on the downside of everything, just because we called him out on all the lives he'd put in danger?! I knew he was arrogant, self-righteous and stuck up but he had really outdone himself this time.

'Oh God!' I sighed, tipping my head back in disbelief. I then faced Tom again, and said, 'Dan has always been *so* -,'

'What's that?'

I looked round and caught sight of Dan himself walking over to me and Tom from my nine o'clock. He had stepped up beside Tom, facing me, arms folded, and said, irritably, 'I've always. Been. So. *What*?'

I froze. Shit!

'If you have a problem with me, be brave and say it to my face, rather than slagging me off to my mates. Bit pathetic, if I'm honest,' said Dan.

I stared straight back at him. All right. If he wanted to hear it, he'd have it straight.

'Okay, I have several problems with you, Dan, we all do,' I said. 'You've always been so full of yourself. Nothing you ever do is bad, is it? You never accept responsibility for what you do. You don't think of it as that bad that you endangered the lives of people who were meant to be your friends, as well as a field full of sheep, you only seem to care how fun you thought it was, and that was why we all ditched you.'

When I finished, I looked at him, waiting for him to answer. Dan peered at me, as if he was examining me, then looked down, pursing his lips, and then, looking at me again, he said, 'Well, that's all very interesting, but I actually have better things to do than listen to you claiming that Tom and I are the villains.'

I scoffed, before I turned on my heel and marched off. Seriously, Dan was incurable! How could he still act so innocent, even after I told him how little he cared about the danger he put everyone in? I gave up trying to get through to him and Tom. But I still wasn't going to let them get away with hurting Dave and Scarlet.

I was still fuming about Dan's failure and refusal to get it all into his stupid little head on the bus home, and when I'd got off the bus to call in at the newsagents and walked the rest of the way from there. I didn't even fancy having my Crunchie Bar on the walk home.

But all of this was driven out of my mind by something else. I was passing V's house again, when I saw another man waiting outside the front door for someone to answer. I stopped and crouched behind the wall, and peeped over the top. I watched as the front door opened, and listened, hard.

'Where's this girlfriend of yours, then?' I heard the man ask. I narrowed my eyes. Why was this man asking about Natalie?

'She's upstairs, all ready for you,' said V.

My heart stopped. V was letting other men have sex with Natalie! But why? I suddenly remembered the previous man I saw the day before, giving V cash, then the horrifying, sickening truth hit me. Natalie was being primed for prostitution!

I carried on walking home. It explained everything. V had more than enough money for his house, his car and to spoil Natalie because of the money he must've made in the past, out of other so-called girlfriends he'd turned into prostitutes, and he'd treated her to numerous gifts to make her think she could trust him, and she'd gone missing to keep up with his demands. Though I didn't know how he was able to afford to spoil and impress the first girlfriend as he wouldn't have had that much money back then. Probably cheap gifts with the proceeds from dealing drugs. The only question left was, why had Natalie agreed to it? All I could do at the moment was to tell Fred at the first opportunity. I needed to arrange when we could meet again and discuss it outside of college.

I went to prepare my outfit and make-up for tomorrow.

I went to my room, and searched my wardrobe. I came across my white lace, long sleeved skater dress with the scoop neck and chose to wear that tomorrow. Next, I looked at my shoes to decide which ones would go best with my chosen dress. I picked out my silver pumps. They were a bit scuffed at the toes. Not a problem, as I reckoned I should have a silver pen somewhere that I could cover it up with. I went to my dressing table and laid out my foundation, a beige eye shadow, and my matt nude lipstick, with some matching lip-gloss, my mascara, and my liquid eyeliner.

After dinner, me and my dad had a look on the course finder on the Euro Capital House College website. Dad suggested looking at courses in Dance and Performing Arts, reminding me how impressed my dance teacher at school had been. So I typed 'Performing Arts' into the search bar. I came across eight courses I thought I should go for. Luckily, I spotted a Routes into Dance and Drama. It was a level one course, with no entry requirements. Perfect! I applied for it right away.

I went to bed in a very good mood.

The next morning, I got up and whipped the curtains open. It was a sunny day with blue sky. I put on my make-up and got dressed, before I had some toast and strawberry jam for breakfast, with a glass of strawberry and banana smoothie to drink.

Me and Mum left the house at twenty to ten, and drove to town in Mum's Mars red Kia Motor. We parked into the multi-storey car park and walked through Bond Street together as far as St Thomas Street, said goodbye, and then Mum walked up St Thomas Street to Andrew Care, whilst I continued up Bond Street towards St Mary Street, and then walked up St Mary Street to Costa Coffee.

It was five to ten when I arrived. Charlie showed up fifteen minutes later. He was ten minutes late, but I didn't let that bother me. We kissed hello, and then went inside. We grabbed a table by the window.

'So... what would you like?' said Charlie. I decided I'd have my usual hot chocolate with cream and marshmallows and a caramel shortcake. Charlie got up and went to the counter to order.

I sat and gazed at him. I hoped I could get to the bottom of what was going on with him, as he'd been acting weird lately, wanting to go to places he didn't even like, contradicting what he said about not worrying what Fraser thought and all that, but I couldn't help worrying, just a tiny bit, whether it might make things awkward between us if I touched on the subject of him not being warm with me when we were alone, and if I might put him on the spot in any way.

'What do you hope to do next year, as it was looming?' Charlie asked when he came back and sat back down. 'Do you planned on doing the next Art and Design course from the one you're doing?'

'No, actually, I'm not as fussed as I thought I was,' I told him. Charlie sounded both interested and taken aback.

'Do you plan on staying at college and doing another course, or do you think you might go to uni or into employment?'

I told him about the Dance and Drama course I applied for the night before.

'Ah, sweet!' Charlie said. 'It is that just a level one, you know, start you off with?'

'Yes, it is.'

I picked up my hot chocolate and began drinking it as soon as our orders came. Charlie asked me if I'd ever tried espresso and if I'd like to try some of his, which I said I would, so Charlie passed me his espresso and I took a sip of it. Urgh! Horrible! Charlie sniggered at the face I must've pulled.

'You don't like it, do you?' he laughed.

'It is a bit strong,' I admitted. Understatement of the year! I gave Charlie back his coffee.

'Yeah, espresso's not everyone's cup of tea, I admit,' said Charlie. I drank some more of my own hot chocolate, and then put down the tall glass mug it was served in. I forgot about the cream and was left with a cream moustache, which Charlie politely picked me up on.

'Oh shit!' I said, grabbing a serviette. This was starting off to be rather embarrassing. I wiped off the cream. Charlie watched, smiling.

'Sorry, I'm crap at this,' I added.

'No you're not,' said Charlie, smirking. I was taken aback, and asked him if he really thought that. Charlie said that getting a cream moustache was nothing compared to what happened on his first date. I was stunned.

'Right,' I said. 'So, what happened on this disastrous date, then?'

'I sat at the wrong table, went to the loo with the door unlocked and my date burst in on me, I farted when she let me have some of her coffee, as I did with you and then spilt it all over her.'

'Wow, that did seem pretty bad,' I admitted.

'It was,' Charlie agreed.

Maybe things were sort okay between us, then?

The door opened and I caught sight of Priscilla and a couple of her friends coming in. She did a double take when she spotted me and Charlie. She had a resentful, desirous look on her face and then quickly looked away. It was obvious that Charlie wasn't just another man Priscilla was hoping to get into bed with. I almost felt sorry for her. I knew how much it hurt to see someone you fancied with someone else. I've always found it hurtful enough watching my celebrity crushes snogging actresses in films, and that's only acting!

Charlie suddenly leaned in and kissed me.

'I can't believe I never asked you out before,' Charlie said, quite loudly, as he broke away again.

'It's okay, because you have now,' I told him.

'Why haven't you been snapped up by someone else before?' Charlie asked. 'I'm sure other guys have asked you out.'

'They weren't ones I fancied back,' was my answer. I had been asked out by some boys at Carrie Mount, but either I didn't fancy them, like I told Charlie, or it was when I just didn't feel emotionally ready for a boyfriend.

Out of the corner of my eye, I could still see Priscilla watching us, bitterly. Poor cow.

'I've wasted too much time caring what Fraser thinks,' said Charlie. 'It's stupid that so many people have a problem with their mates dating their brothers and sisters.'

I'd always agreed. If any of my mates wanted to date Alistair or Fraser, I wouldn't have a problem with it. Except Alistair's spoken for so if anything, they'd have to take it up with Sophie.

Charlie leant in and kissed me again.

'Let me come back to yours,' he said.

We finished our food and drinks, and then left the restaurant, hand in hand. We caught the bus home to together.

Fraser had been out with Adam and Dustin, but he'd come home earlier than expected and walked in on me and Charlie on the sofa. He didn't say anything. He just stood there, gawping at us, mouth hanging open, his eyes narrowed in disbelief.

'Seriously, Charlie. Really?' he said at last.

Charlie stood up.

'What is your problem?'

'I've just walked in on one of my mates with my sister, what do you think my problem is?' Fraser spat.

'What do you really have against me and Lizzy having a relationship?' Charlie asked

'You know exactly why!' was and Fraser's answer.

'Fraser, this is ridiculous! You might have a problem with me dating your mates, but that does not make me out of limits to any of them!' I shouted.

What just happened there? I'd never argued with him about me being off bounds to his mates, I'd always gone along with it.

Before Fraser could answer back, I carried on, saying, 'I go out with whoever I like! I don't have to ask you!'

Fraser didn't say anything. He looked down, sighed, looked back up at me and said calmly, 'No. You're right. It's not really up to me.'

I couldn't believe it. I'd actually made him see sense!

Fraser looked from me to Charlie.

'You, though, Charlie, you knew what I'd think if you in particular went out with my sister,' he said. 'I'm not having another row about it.'

And then Fraser went storming out of the room and up the stairs. I was confused. So there was another reason why Fraser didn't want me and Charlie going out?

'What's he talking about, Charlie?' I asked him. 'Have you argued about this before?'

Charlie sighed and rolled his eyes.

'Charlie, *speak* to me!' I demanded.

'Look, Fraser's just being stupid and unreasonable about the whole thing,' Charlie said. 'But we're together and he has to accept that.'

But I couldn't just let it be. It was clearly nothing to do with Fraser's issues with me dating his friends. No, he'd talk to me now!

'Does it have anything to do with the fact that you'd insist on going to places you don't even like,' I asked. 'That time when I saw you -'

Oh my God.

'Do you like someone else?' I went on. 'I need to know, and would it be Priscilla if I'm right?'

Charlie was giving me a very guilty and fearful look. He looked down and then nodded.

'So you were just using me because you wanted Priscilla? Be honest, I'm right, aren't I?'

'Yeah.'

I shut my eyes tight, trying not to cry. I did *not* want to cry in front of Charlie. I couldn't take it in. I didn't know what to feel. I was too shocked, even to feel angry.

'Please say something,' Charlie whispered.

My eyes snapped open. Okay. If Charlie wanted me to say something, I'd let him have all I had left.

'Fine,' I said, close to tears. 'I will say a few things. One, don't *ever* use girls like that, because it's wrong, and you are *not* innocent! Two, don't you dare use me like this again and not be honest. I should've known there was something, it was that bullying tart, Priscilla! Three, never make out that my brother is in the wrong when he kicks up a fuss about the things you do, you knew what you were doing, and so did he, and finally, four, leave my house and never talk to me ever again! GET OUT!!!'

But to my outrage, Charlie didn't go. He stayed and started apologising profusely, and said, 'What I've done is a mistake.'

But I cut across him, shouting, 'No, you're *not* sorry! You'll do it to the next girl you meet, and the next, just until you get what you want, and damn right it was a mistake! To be honest, you're a using bastard!'

Charlie looked at me. He seemed to want to say something else, but had run out of words, luckily.

'Right. You, out!' said Fraser angrily, storming back in.

I could tell Charlie was not going to argue with Fraser, now he knew he'd been found out. He gave Fraser an annoyed look and then stormed out.

I sat back down on the sofa and broke down in tears. How could I have been so stupid? Deep down, I knew it was too good to be true, but I'd wanted to ignore it and believe I'd finally bagged the man I'd been after for so long, but he never liked me that way.

'I'm such an idiot!' I wept. 'And I never listened to you. I just thought you were being stupid about how you felt about your mates getting involved with your brothers and sisters!'

'It's not your fault,' Fraser said, gruffly. 'I only told you my mates were off limits to you. I never said why else I didn't want you dating Charlie, to anyone, not even Adam or Dustin. They all thought it was just because I'm not keen on you or Alistair dating my mates, which I'm still not. Even Stuart thought that was all it was; don't think I never noticed him constantly warning Charlie to be careful about me catching you two together, and Charlie not giving a shit. It was really because I knew you'd fancied the pants off him for years and he didn't feel the same way because he had it bad for Priscilla and would stop at nothing to win her over, and she'd never looked twice at him until she got jealous seeing you two together. I'm just sorry you had to find out this way.'

I nodded. I knew I wasn't to know, but I still wished I hadn't been so ignorant. It all made sense. Charlie didn't want Fraser catching us together because he knew Fraser would only go on about him using me to make Priscilla jealous. And it must've been so easy for Charlie to make out that he was only keeping it secret because he knew Fraser didn't want his mates dating me or Alistair and to make it look like that was the only reason Fraser didn't want anything happening between us.

I spent most of that evening in my room. I texted Fred, partly to tell him that me and Charlie had split up, but mainly to ask him about our arrangements the next day. We were going round Jesse's, and I was planning on telling them both exactly what I saw on passing V's house.

'We were thinking of going for a drink at the Marquis Granby and maybe have something to eat?' said Jesse.

'Me or Jesse will pay for your food as a consolation treat,' Fred said.

'Yeah, sounds great,' I said. 'I've got something I need to tell you both, especially you, Fred,' I said on the way, before Fred agreed the three of us could talk about it when we got to the pub. I didn't mind Jesse being there, as I needed to tell him too.

When we arrived, we went to get drinks from the bar and then found a table. I sat opposite Fred and Jesse and whilst we had our drinks, we talked about the gig Fraser's band, Rebel Tourbus, were having on Saturday the eleventh of June, at Finn's.

'What time does it start, Lizzy?' said Fred.

'Seven,' I said. The boys decided they would try to arrive there earlier, so they could have a drink beforehand. Jesse said that Auntie Flora could give him and Fred a lift there, and that they could pick him up at ten past six, which Fred said he was fine with, so they could be there for half six. Fred then talked about how much he was looking forward to hearing some of Rebel Tourbus's music.

'Who else is coming?' Jesse asked.

'Isabel's coming, and so is Nikki,' I said. 'And Scarlet and Ruby-lynn will be there too.' Uh oh. Scarlet, Ruby-lynn, Isabel and Nikki were still not on good terms with Fred.

'I guess I'll just have to keep my distance from them, then,' said Fred, and then he asked what I wanted to tell him and Jesse.

'You know I said V lived near me?' I said. Both boys nodded. I explained how I'd pass V's house on my way home from the bus stop.

'Right?' said Jesse, frowning. 'So?'

I swallowed.

'The point is, one time, when I passed his place on my way home, I saw a man giving V money,' I went on. Fred and Jesse exchanged puzzled looks. They clearly didn't know where I was going with that, so I continued.

'And then, another time, I saw V letting another man into his house, and the man asked, "Where's this girlfriend of yours?" obviously meaning Natalie,' I said. Fred and Jesse listened, frowning, as I told them that, in answer to the man's question, V had said that Natalie was 'upstairs, all ready for him.'

Fred and Jesse jumped back in their seats as their expressions changed from baffled to horrified.

'Are you getting at what I think you're getting at?' said Fred in disgust. I nodded, uncomfortably.

'Lover boys, they're called,' Jesse said. 'They normally go for girls aged around fourteen to fifteen. They lurk around schools and cinemas, waiting to pick up girls. They pretend they just want a girlfriend, when they're just looking for girls to turn into prostitutes.'

'I *knew* V was no good when, one, Ruby-lynn told me what he'd done right in front of her, and two, when I found the cannabis in Natalie's room!' Fred said.

'Why would V go for someone of Natalie's age, if lover boys usually go for under sixteen-year-olds?' I asked.

'Maybe it's because she has that kind of look,' Jesse suggested. Judging by the outraged look Fred gave him, he'd clearly taken what Jesse said the wrong way.

'Are you saying my sister looks like a slut?' he asked, indignantly. I face palmed, shutting my eyes tight.

'Um, no,' Jesse said, uncomfortably. 'I'm just saying... she's... sexy, which V knew would sell.'

Both me and Fred glared at him, in disbelief. I understood what Jesse was getting at, but the way it was coming out really wasn't doing him any favours.

'Anyway, what are we going to do about it?' I said. 'Shouldn't we go to the police?'

'But we can't, as we don't have any proof,' Fred said.

'None of us even see her any more. What are we gonna do?' said Jesse.

I felt helpless. I didn't know how we could get proof, or what we could do besides going to the police if we couldn't prove what was going on.

Dad came to pick me up at ten to ten. I sat in the car in silence, wondering what to do, whether to tell anyone else. I didn't know if Fred was going to tell Auntie Claire or Uncle Barry, or how they were likely to react that their daughter had been sleeping with random men under her boyfriend's roof.

'Are you okay, sweetheart?' asked Dad, as he drove along the esplanade. 'You've not said anything all journey.'

Should I tell Dad what I'd found out? Since I knew he and Mum were friends with Claire and Barry, after all, and me, Fred and Jesse couldn't take this all on ourselves. But I couldn't see what good telling Dad would do.

I went to bed as soon as me and Dad arrived home. But I couldn't sleep. I was worried about what to do, as well as still missing Charlie so much! I had liked him for ages, so naturally I felt the happiest I'd ever been, which made the discovery that he never really wanted me so much more upsetting.

I carried on thinking about V and what to do. All I knew was that I definitely didn't want to do just nothing. I stayed awake, turning it all over in my head, until one in the morning.

I probably might've dwelled on this all day at college, if it hadn't been for the day's events.

Dan and Tom were still causing trouble. They'd both been all over Rosa, right in front of Dave, in the student lounge at lunch.

'Look, Dave, isn't she just *so pretty*!' they had taunted. Me, Fred and Jesse told him just to ignore them, but it was clear that Dave couldn't stand it any longer and went storming over to the three of them.

'YOU SHITTING WANKER!' he bellowed, grabbing Tom by the front of the shirt, pulling him up from his seat and then throwing him onto the floor. 'ALL OF THIS IS YOUR FAULT!'

'Hey, hey, hey, hey!' Fred shouted, as he, Jesse and I went running over to Dave, Tom, Dan and Rosa as Dave pinned Tom to the floor.

'Are you a fucking lunatic or something?' Dan shouted, pulling Dave off of Tom. Tom got to his feet.

'Fuck you, Dave!' Tom yelled. 'You're so jealous of me and Rosa, you're so pathetic!'

Dave went storming out. Me, Jesse and Fred ran through the door Dave left through, and walked through the upstairs corridor of the London building. We were betting he wasn't going to be in any of the classrooms. Jesse went to see if Dave was in the boys' toilets.

'He's not in there,' he said, when he came back out. He, Fred and I went downstairs. When we reached the bottom of the stairs, which was right by the entrance, I looked through the glass in the automatic doors and there was Dave, leant backwards against one of the brick pillars, sulking.

'You okay?' asked Jesse, cautiously approaching Dave.

'Do I *look* okay?!' Dave shouted. 'I mean, Jesus Christ, they're such a pair of turds!'

I didn't know what to say to make him feel better. How can you make someone feel better about their ex, who had been stolen off of them by their enemies, apart from telling them they'd find someone else?

'I know you're angry,' I'd tried. 'What they did was unforgivable, *and* unreasonable, given they're doing it as revenge on your decision not to be mates with them, over something that was their fault to begin with. They never should've done any of this.'

But that didn't work.

'Why are they getting away with it if they're in the wrong?'

'The reason you never had a way out of Dan and Tom's plan to steal Rosa off you was because Rosa wasn't right for you,' Jesse pointed out.

'I tried to tell Rosa I didn't want them barging in, every time we hung out,' Dave explained, 'and that it would be nice for the two of us to spend some quality time together, but she just said she wasn't the kinda girl that was bothered about quality time with her boyfriend, and that she liked Dan and Tom joining with us.'

'Okay, I rest my case,' said Jesse.

'Yeah,' I agreed. 'Did you really think you'd have been able to keep on seeing each other any way, and make it work long distance? It's not like Rosa and her family have actually moved to here. Rosa's only on an exchange programme and she's due to go back soon. So, on the bright side, it means Tom will have to break up with her.'

'Well, yeah,' said Dave. He sighed.

'Are you still up for meeting Scarlet and Ruby-lynn later?'

'Yeah,' said Dave. 'We're meeting at five, so we'll just catch the bus there straight from college. Meet me outside the Photography Studio if I'm not already outside the classroom you're in.'

I nodded.

Dave said he was going to go to the Learning Gateway for bit, to get some work done. He walked off.

After college, Dave and I caught the bus into town and grabbed seats near the back. Ruby-lynn texted to ask if me and Dave were on our way and to say that she was already there. I texted back to say we were on the bus and it probably wouldn't be long before we'd be there.

The bus made a U-turn round the King's Statue and pulled over to the number ten bus stop. Me and Dave got off and walked to the William Henry.

Ruby-lynn was waiting just inside the door.

'Scarlet's just texted, she said to grab a table and she'd text when she's come in,' she told us.

'Cool,' said Dave, 'so... up the steps?'

'Sure,' me and Ruby-lynn said together. We chose a long table that had dark red leather booth seating on one side of the table. Me and Ruby-lynn sat down on the booth seating as Dave sat on the chair opposite Ruby-lynn.

'Shall we get drinks?' Dave suggested.

'Nah, let's wait for Scarlet and her mates to get here first,' I said, wanting to be polite and not start without them.

I heard a phone beep. Ruby-lynn pulled hers out. I saw her look at the screen, before she said, 'They're just coming in,' and then frantically typing, most likely telling her where we were sat.

I looked over at the stairs and saw Scarlet walking up them. She didn't say who the friends were that she was supposed to be bringing along, but I could only see one person following her over to our table. Oh my God, it was *Will*!

'Hi,' she said, when she and Will reached us.

'Alright?' said Dave. 'Where are the others? I thought you said you were bringing "friends" as in "plural".'

'Oh yeah, Becky reckoned she and Jonah wouldn't be able to make it back from Yeovil in time so she said they'd have to give it a miss,' Scarlet said, sounding slightly disappointed that they weren't coming. 'She sends her apologies. So anyway, this is Will, and Will, this is Dave, Ruby-lynn and Lizzy.'

As soon as Will saw me, his eyes lit up.

'Hi,' he said, sounding amazed.

'Um, hello,' I said, managing an awkward grin. I saw Scarlet look from me to Will, with a bemused expression on her face. Only Fred, Jesse and Natalie knew about my history with Will. I'd never told anyone else, so naturally she was going to wonder why me and Will were acting the way we were.

'Um, okay, now that we all know each other, why don't we get drinks and sit down?' asked Scarlet, wanting to break the awkwardness.

Scarlet didn't ask me anything about Will when I went with her and Ruby-lynn to get drinks for ourselves as well as the boys, though she did say, 'You can be the one to get Will's drink for him.'

I ordered Will a Bacardi and Coke and myself my usual orange and passionfruit J2O

Will had seated himself opposite me, next to Dave when we'd come back to the table.

'So, Will, why don't you tell everyone what you're doing for work?' Scarlet asked. Courses and jobs. Yes, I know I said Scarlet was all about careers and stuff, but why does she have to always start off a conversation by asking people about what they're doing at college, or what they're doing at work?

Although, to be fair, I obviously didn't know what sort of career interests Will had ever had, so I listened as, at Scarlet's request, Will told us all about the part time job he had at Swag Surf.

'I wanted to go into employment for a bit, just to get a bit of money coming in while I decide what I want to study after finishing my A levels, which were Film Studies, Media Studies and Computer Science at the Casterbridge School,' he told us. Though I noticed he looked like he was talking to me more than the others, most of the time, because of the amount of time he'd looked at me, whilst only glancing at the other three a few times. Even though it was Ruby-lynn who had then asked him where he planned to go from there, he was looking at me more than her.

'What are you doing at college? Or for work or whatever,' he said, still looking at me and sounding slightly awkward, like he was trying to talk directly to me whilst trying to keep the conversation flowing naturally.

I told Will about the Art courses I'd done, before I had decided to venture into Performing Arts after realising Art and Design wasn't for me. I found that I, too, was finding it hard not to make it look like I was only talking to Will and, like Will, could only manage a few glances at the others. Will was looking at me with undivided attention as he listened. And the music that was playing on the sound system at the time was already beginning to add to the mood of a moment to come, the song "Jai Ho" by Nicole Scherzinger. Some sort of moment me and Will would end up sharing at some point in the afternoon.

'We're going to leave you two to tell Will about your jobs and courses,' Scarlet said, looking from Ruby-lynn to Dave. 'Me and Lizzy are going to powder our noses, aren't we, Lizzy?' she added, looking round at me with wide eyes and sounding rather insistent.

I thought I'd better do as Scarlet said. We both went over to the ladies' toilets. I went in with Scarlet in tow.

She pushed the door shut, turned round to face me and said, 'What was going on there?'

Where was I meant to begin?

'Okay,' I began. 'Me and Will actually have met before.'

Scarlet's mouth fell open.

'What? When? Was it more than once?'

'Today's the sixth time,' I told her, and I explained about the five previous times we'd met, including the kiss three years ago, and the kiss that nearly happened in the sea. All the while, Scarlet had her eyes wide and mouth open in astonishment.

'Jesus, you never told me any of this?' she said when I'd finally finished.

'Um...' I said, uneasily, 'well, no.'

Scarlet didn't ask why. I think she was just so overcome with bewilderment.

We went to rejoin Ruby-lynn, Dave and Will.

I went to the bar to get another drink a bit later on. I glanced back at the table and saw Will getting up. I watched as he came towards me.

'Alright?' he said, smiling.

'Yeah,' I said, nervously.

'How do you know Scarlet, then?'

'Well, as well as meeting her through her stepbrother-in-waiting from her dad's new family, I also know her and Dave through some mutual family friends,' I told him. 'What about you?'

'Jonah and Becky are cousins,' Will said. 'I was at Casterbridge with Jonah and I'm sure Scarlet's told you how she knows Becky.'

'Yeah,' I nodded, remembering Scarlet telling me about Becky before, without me having actually met her.

I glanced round to see if there was a bartender free to serve us.

I then looked up at Will, and looked into his eyes. I remembered what I felt the previous times we'd caught each other's eyes. A feeling like my stomach was doing somersaults. The emotion that almost scared me, because it felt so intense. It was coming back to me.

'Listen... I'm sorry about last time,' he said.

I gazed up at Will, dumbstruck, before I said, 'It's okay.'

Will looked at me, like he wanted to say more, but he didn't, so I went on to say, 'I'm not going to ask why you said it wasn't right, but I'm sure you had a good reason.'

Will nodded.

'What can I get you?' came the voice of a bartender.

'I'll buy you a drink,' Will offered.

He ordered an apple and mango J2O for me, and a Coke for himself, before we went back to join the others.

The five of us stayed and chatted for another hour and a half, before we all left and walked towards the seafront.

We said goodbye to Ruby-lynn before she entered the number one bus shelter and stopped at the number ten bus stop, which was presumably where Will was getting his bus. Dave and Scarlet said their goodbyes before Dave began his walk home and Scarlet rushed off to catch the number two bus, leaving me and Will alone together.

We faced each other.

'I want to ask you something,' I said. 'I just need to know.'

'That's fine,' said Will. 'Just ask.'

I took a deep breath.

'After today, will I ever hear from you again?'

'Well, I don't see why not,' he said, smiling. 'Now I know you're a mate of Scarlet's. Not gonna be as hard, hopefully.'

'Okay, good,' I said, nodding.

Will looked into my eyes, I looked into his, and the next thing I knew, Will was leaning in, cupping my face and kissing me. His lips were as soft and sweet as they had been the last time.

Will broke away, slowly.

'Come with me,' he whispered, and then took me by the hand. I felt a weird, swirly feeling in my stomach as Will led me towards the beach, down onto the sand, along the beach and over to a row of beach huts. I followed him over to one that had a canvas screen hooked up over the front of it.

Will unhooked it, gave me a smile and led me in by the hand. I helped him hook the canvas back up so we were completely hidden.

Then we looked at each other. My heart was beating fast. Me and Will kissed again, Will running his fingers through my hair. All the recent ill-fated events and the grief and worry they'd caused had been wiped away. I was intoxicated.

We broke apart again, before Will undid the zip on his trousers.

'Are you comfortable with this?' he whispered.

I nodded.

'One hundred percent?'

'Yes,' I whispered, before following suit. Will leaned in and kissed me again, and I felt the warmth of his body as he pressed me against the wooden slatted wall of the beach hut. I felt him inside me, sending a pleasurable thrill through me as he moved his body against mine, kissing my neck and shoulders, making it hard for me to keep quiet as I was sent into a helpless frenzy.

Afterwards, we broke apart again, breathing heavily. Then we sat down, side by side on the pebbles, looking down, and both silent for a few seconds.

I looked round at Will. He looked at me.

'You all right?'

I nodded. I didn't know what would happen next. I didn't want it to lead to the same post kiss confusion as before, when I was fifteen.

I stared straight ahead.

'You thought it would be awkward if you got in touch with me after that kiss,' I said. 'But you know, it doesn't have to be, as long as we don't make it awkward.'

'I know.'

I looked round at him.

'I've just come out of a relationship.'

Will looked at me.

'And you need time to move on?'

I nodded, looking down.

'That's okay,' he said, 'and like I said, we can see each other again more easily, now.'

I looked round at Will. He gave me a smile.

We left the beach hut and walked back up to the esplanade. We said goodbye at the five zero three bus stop.

'I'll be in touch,' said Will, '... somehow.'

I gave Will a feeble smile.

'Bye then.'

'See you,' said Will. He turned and walked off. I was just watching as he began to walk up the pavement along the shops, when he slowly turned on his heel and then came back over.

'What's your surname by the way?'

I was surprised and mystified, but I answered the question.

'Graham.'

'Graham,' Will repeated, smiling. 'Cool. Thanks. See you around.'

I smiled at Will, before he turned away.

I sat on the bench in the bus shelter and started to think. All the uncertainty of my emotions had come back. The emotion of not knowing want I wanted. Ever since Charlie had asked me out, Will had been instantly forgotten. And now I wasn't with Charlie any more. And I'd seen Will again, in fact had done more with him than just seen him, and now I was back to where I was before me and Charlie started dating. And now it was worse and more perplexing than before, because I was still hurting over Charlie, and my anger towards him for heartlessly using me had just added to that feeling.

But I knew I couldn't spend my time moping over Charlie the same way Scarlet had been over Tom. Charlie wasn't worth it, after all. Though neither was Tom, to be fair, but at least Tom had actually dated Scarlet because he actually liked her, unlike Charlie. He was wrong to string me along. All I was, was his ticket into Priscilla's pants, and I knew constantly thinking about him was not going to change that and I just had to move on and accept that, though I knew it was not going to be easy.

Will was on my mind over the next few days. He had been my first. My first kiss and more.

We're on the beach. We're laying on our towels, side by side, me in my sky blue tankini from Amazon, Will in navy blue Fat Face swimming shorts.

We're looking up at the clear blue sky, listening to the chatter of the masses of people on the beach, enjoying the warmth of the sun.

I feel Will move up closer to me so that our heads and shoulders touch. We both turn our heads to look at each other, gazing deep into each other's eyes.

'When will I see you again?' asks Will. I look down, biting my lip, and say 'Soon... I hope.'

Me and Will smile at each other and then continue to look up at the sky. I close my eyes again. I move my arm closer, so that my forearm touches Will's. I feel the touch of Will's hand as he reaches out to hold mine. I don't open my eyes. I can hear my heart beating fast, and I'm sure that Will can hear it too.

'Let's go into the sea,' he says. I open my eyes and look round at Will, who's looking round at me, smiling. God, he has the cutest smile!

I grin and sit up and we both stand up, still holding hands, and we both run over the sand and into the water. I scream as Will splashes me. Laughing, I splash him back in retaliation. We both fall about laughing. Will then comes over to me.

'You're so gorgeous,' he says, looking deep into my eyes. I look into his eyes. Those gorgeous brown eyes. Will leans in for a kiss, and then...

When I woke up it took me a while to realise it had been a dream. I didn't know whether this was making me more or less puzzled about my feelings.

Saturday 11th June 2011

I didn't have much time to dwell on the dreams. I had to help Fraser with the concert.

As we had to be at Finn's early, I started getting ready at two thirty. I'd had a shower, and then put on my make-up. I'd already chosen my outfit: a lilac short sleeve top that showed my navel, with my white skinny jeans. I picked out a grey lilac eye shadow trio from Borjois Paris to tone with it.

Then I blow-dried my hair with my Tresemme hair dryer, then brushed back my t-section, back combed the back of it, secured it at the back of my head with a diamante barrette, and straightened all the remaining hair. Last of all, I sprayed it to keep it all in place.

Finally, I dressed, ten minutes before me and Fraser had to go.

I helped load up the car, and then four of us drove into town and parked in the Melcombe Regis car park. Me, Fraser and Dad unloaded all the equipment the four of us could carry between us whilst Mum went to pay, and carried it to Finn's.

Adam and Dustin were already there, setting up the equipment they'd brought on the stage. Alistair and Sophie were there too, helping to plug everything in.

Everything was more or less ready by half past six, which was when some of the gang were starting to arrive. Nikki and Isabel had arrived first, with Stuart in tow. There was no sign of Charlie, to my relief.

Fred, Jesse and Annie had arrived not long afterwards, so I went with them all to get drinks.

Seven minutes later, Scarlet arrived with Ruby-lynn and joined the others for a drink. I was a bit nervous as to how Fred and Ruby-lynn would react around each other. Ruby-lynn just said, 'Hi,' to Fred, who nodded at her, awkwardly.

I went to chat with Ruby-lynn and Scarlet. Neither of them asked me what happened with Will after we met up on Monday, though Scarlet wouldn't, because she's not one to pry in other people's love lives. She says it's their decision if or when they enlighten her.

On the dot of seven o'clock, Fraser, Adam and Dustin got up onto the stage.

'Hey everyone!' called Dustin, and everyone quietened down. Me, Ruby-lynn and Scarlet made our way to the front of the crowd. 'Cheers to you all for coming to Finn's to enjoy the debut of REBEL TOUR BUS!'

Everyone cheered and clapped.

'I am Dustin, and it is a pleasure to be playing here in Weymouth, my hometown with my two best mates, Fraser,' and he waved his left hand to his left as everyone cheered again, in Fraser's direction, 'and Adam!' He waved his hand backwards in Adam's direction and the audience gave another cheer.

'To start off with, we are going to play a song made famous by Darren Styles,' Dustin went on, 'and it's called FLASHLIGHT!' And the whole audience cheered and screamed again, then the band started on their own guitar cover of Flashlight, and Dustin sang. It sounded amazing. I love the hardcore remix of it I have on my MP3 player, but the band's cover was terrific. My brother's an excellent bass guitarist and it's really cool that he's in a band.

I joined in with the crowd, dancing and jumping with my hands in the air. I was already having such a good time, and I was so glad that my mates had come as well. It was just a shame that Natalie couldn't come. I knew she'd be gutted to miss it.

The crowd gave a cheer when the song finished.

'WHOOHOOOOOOOOOOOOO!' I screamed. It was such a good song, and I was thrilled that other people like the music just as much. Dustin thanked the crowd.

Halfway through the concert Dustin announced he was going to play another one of Darren's Styles' songs, "Outta My Head." I was ecstatic. I love this song too.

I hadn't enjoyed it for long, however, because I spotted someone I recognised, someone who was not welcome. V. And I was outraged at what I saw him doing. He was selling drugs! That was it! First he subjected my best friend to prostitution, and now he was dealing at my brother's gig! I began walking through the crowd towards him. I reached V, who then looked round and saw me.

'Hello again!' he said cheerfully.

I looked at him, grimly.

'Stop selling my best friend for sex!' I hissed, but V just smiled.

'What's the matter?' he said. 'Are you jealous that your friend is getting more cock than you?'

But V was not getting round me.

'I'm not jealous that she's being forced into something she doesn't want any part of!' I shouted, furiously. 'You fucking stop it right now, or you'll be sorry!'

And I kicked him in the groin, making him drop the bag of cannabis he had as he made a grunt of pain and clutched his groin. I snatched it up off the floor.

'You give that back!' he snarled. But I was not going to do anything he said.

'*Make* me, cock face!' I said, and then started rushing through the crowd in the direction of the toilets so I could flush the weed away.

When I reached the toilets, I looked back and saw that some of the security men had seen what was going on, came over and started trying to wrestle V out of Finn's. Fred and Jesse were watching. I went into the girls' toilets, went into the nearest cubicle, undid the bag, decanted it down the toilet, and flushed it away. I hoped it wouldn't block.

When I came out of the toilets, Fred came over to me.

'What was that about?' he asked, obviously referring to what he and Jesse had seen.

I told Fred about how I'd caught V dealing, so I'd taken it off him and flushed it away, and that he'd got angry with me.

Fred gave a heavy sigh, his mouth very thin. He didn't say anything but I knew what that look meant. He was too angry to talk.

'Come on, let's carry on watching the gig!' I said, trying to sound enthusiastic, desperate for Fred to not let his anger ruin his enjoyment of the night.

Me and Fred went back into the crowd. By this time, Rebel Tourbus were playing a song called "Doesn't Matter." Me and Fred joined Jesse and Annie as we danced to the music.

Five songs later, I suddenly heard an alarm sound. The sprinklers suddenly went off. Boys shouted and swore. Girls squealed. People were panicking. I heard fizzing noises as sparks flew from the speakers, amplifiers and other electronic items on the stage, and the manager bellowing, 'OUTSIDE EVERYONE! DO NOT PANIC! MOVE OUTSIDE USING THE NEAREST EXIT IN A CALM FASHION!'

I walked out of Finn's with Fred and Jesse. I was fuming. It went without saying that I knew who it was.

'First he makes my sister into a prozzy, then he ruins your brother's gig,' said Fred, annoyed. I looked round at him, feeling awkward.

'Is this my fault, because I confiscated his weed and flushed it down the toilet?'

'No, of course it isn't!' said Fred, sounding shocked that I was blaming myself. 'He was trying to sell illegal drugs at your brother's gig, and you wanted to stop him. We'd all thought we'd got rid of him after he was kicked out. You didn't know he'd sneak back in and find a way to set off a fire.'

The fire engine had arrived, but the strangest thing was, as the fireman had discovered, there was no fire. That was when I realised V must've held a cigarette lighter up to the sprinklers to set them off.

Annoyingly, we couldn't go back in to continue the gig, because most of the equipment was damaged when it got wet, so we all had to call it a night.

People were groaning about how annoying it was that such an epic gig was ruined. Once they knew there was actually no fire in the building, they were moaning about the low life prick that had obviously triggered the alarm for a prank, and talking about what an absolute loser he was.

I was *so* going to take V down! I couldn't believe Natalie was going through with what he was making her do. But regardless of why she agreed to do it, I was going to put a stop to it, one way or another!

Fraser wouldn't talk to anyone when he, I, Mum and Dad arrived home. He'd gone straight up to his room in a sulk. I felt really bad for him. That was the band's first gig and it had been fucked.

I checked my phone as I was getting ready for bed a bit later on. I saw a friend request. My heart leapt when I saw whom it was from.

Chapter 12:

Natalie's Second

Sunday 12th June 2011

The man who I'd been in V's bed with had just left. I was fucking annoyed at V that I'd had to miss Rebel Tour Bus's gig the night before, just to keep up with his demands. I had no way of knowing when or if this was going to finish but, truth be told, I didn't want to carry on with it, but I had no choice.

V came in, looking pissed off. He came over and sat on the bed.

'I hope you've not been talking to your mates about what I do for money,' he said. I glared at him. Why did he think I'd been telling people what I'd done?

'I don't know what you're talking about,' I said.

'You don't?' said V, pretending to sound astonished. 'Then how does your little blonde girly friend know what I've been up to, hmmm?'

'I don't know how Lizzy found out,' I said.

'You tell this Lizzy, next time you see her, that if she dares to stick her nose in where it doesn't belong, she will only end up wishing she hasn't, or I'll release the video,' he ordered. 'Do you want to know what she did last night? She confiscated my weed, that I was going to sell, and I got kicked out. Stupid girl. She had a lot of nerve, the way she spoke to me. I just don't think she has any idea with whom she is dealing. So I thought I'd stir up trouble at that little concert she was at. By setting off the sprinklers.'

I felt anger flooding me. How dare he talk about Lizzy in that way! She has never been stupid. He was just angry that she'd figured out what he'd been up to, because she's, in fact, the exact opposite of stupid, and she'd had the guts to stand up to him. And what he said he'd done at the gig was just appalling. That was Lizzy's brother's gig!

'Why can't you just find yourself another girl?' I said.

'Because girls like you are hard to come by, and you've made me the most money yet,' he said.

'Well, I don't want to spend the rest of my life sleeping with men, just so you can make money,' I told him, defiantly.

'Of course it won't be like this forever,' said V, 'though, for the time being, I need some way of getting money. And don't forget the video.'

I was powerless. I didn't want the video of me being gang raped being released to the public. What if Miriam, my boss saw it? And worst of all, I couldn't bear to think of Mum and Dad's reactions. There was no way out.

Still, knowing Lizzy had somehow found out gave me a bit of hope. Lizzy wasn't the type of person to stay out of something like this. She would've told Fred by now, though what if she'd maybe stopped to think how Fred, my brother, would react? What if Lizzy had let that stop her telling him? Would she?

'I'm going to a party tonight at my mate's house, and one of my other mates, who's my next customer will be there,' V said, as naturally as if he was telling me he'd need me to go out and pick up his dry-cleaning.

I unwillingly agreed to meet him in town at seven so he could pick me up and we would drive to V's friend's house.

I went back home that afternoon. I went straight upstairs to have a shower, and then changed, and went back downstairs and into the lounge, where Fred was sat, texting. He looked up when I sat down.

'Been sleeping with another stranger, then?' he said. So Lizzy _had_ told him.

'I haven't been sleeping with strangers' I lied, obeying V's orders. But Fred didn't believe me.

'What else V could possibly have meant by, "She's upstairs, all ready for you"?'

Great, now what?

Before I could say anything to cover that up, however, Fred said Lizzy had also seen a man giving V some money.

'What does that prove?' I said, standing up and walking over to where Fred was sitting, towering over him. 'Lizzy's just over analysing again. Like she always does.'

Fred stared ahead, frowning, his mouth hanging open, and then stood up and faced me.

'Right, don't even make this about Lizzy okay?' he snapped. 'Just give it up, we know what's going on.'

'Well, tell Lizzy from both me and V that if she meddles in any of this, V's gonna make her regret it!'

'Except he won't find out if she does until it's too late and the police get involved, unless you tell him, which you won't, because you're meant to be on our side!' Fred shouted back. 'What's more, let me tell you a couple of things about him that I heard from Ruby-lynn. He came into Zellweger's, when she was working, and threatened one of her colleagues, who then had to empty out the till drawer and give him everything that was in it. And, one of his gang had once stabbed a guy from a rival gang, someone who was dating another one of Ruby-lynn's colleagues, and he had to quit gangs after that.'

'Yeah, right!' I snapped. I didn't know whether to be shocked or not. I mean, I was shocked that I never knew he'd actually made Ruby-lynn, her colleagues and her workplace a victim of armed robbery, but given what he'd told me before about getting done for armed robbery *and* the way he was exploiting me and not giving a fuck that I didn't like it, I wasn't shocked to find out he was still capable of that. I didn't think Fred was making it up, but just for the sake of V not following through on the threat he kept making, I had to make out that I didn't believe Fred or Ruby-lynn one bit.

Fred looked outraged.

'Oh, so you're calling me and Ruby-lynn liars, now?' he said.

I looked at him, refusing to say another word to him, and then stormed out of the lounge.

I went to sit in the garden. I wanted to be alone. But oh my God, Fred was right. V would only know about anything Lizzy did if I tipped him off and if I did that, I'd be turning my back on my best friend. If V grilled me about it, I'd have to lie through my teeth.

Fuck, what would V do to me or Lizzy if the police got involved? This was getting harder and harder, and more frightening!

I got ready at five o'clock and then caught the bus into town. V picked me up from the back of Debenhams.

'Looking as sexy as ever,' he said, clapping his left hand onto my right thigh as we drove along Radipole Lake.

V's friend lived at Spa Road. V pulled into the space next to where his friend's car was parked in his drive, then he and I got out. I could hear dubstep music playing inside.

'C'mon, then,' said V, putting his arm round my shoulders. He rang the doorbell. A tall, gangly man with blonde hair slicked back into a ponytail answered.

'V! How are you, mate?' he boomed, then he looked round at me. 'I see you've brought your missus!'

'Yep, I indeed, I have!' said V, as he and I went inside. 'This is M.'

'Hi,' I said.

M led us to the kitchen for a drink. He poured us both a glass of vodka.

'You go into the lounge, I'll be there in a minute,' said V. I went into the lounge. There was nowhere to sit. The sofas were taken up by couples so I stood by the doorway, not really wanting to talk to anyone.

A group of girls caught my attention when I noticed they looked like they were whispering. They kept looking at me.

'Hey, check her out,' one of them had said, pointing. They giggled. Then they stood up and walked over to me.

'What's up, darling?' said a second one, patronisingly.

I was not in the mood to start being hassled by anyone at a party I didn't even want to be at.

Trying to get past, I just said to them, 'Whatever!' but a third girl had stepped out in front of me and said, 'Hey, we ain't finished yet!'

A fourth girl joined in and asked, 'Where are your mates?'

But I wasn't having it. I turned away and said, 'Just back right off.'

But it was no use. The fifth girl stepped out in front of me and said, 'What's up with you?'

I looked around me. All five girls had circled around me. I was surrounded.

'No need to be so touchy!' said the third girl.

'Join us for a spliff!'

'No.'

'What was that? Did you just say no to Meygan?' the third girl asked.

'She totally did.'

'Fuck off!'

'What, you think you're too good for us or something?'

'I'm being serious! Fuck off!'

V came back into the lounge and the girls backed right off when they saw him come over to us. I couldn't help feeling grateful, despite everything.

'Thanks,' I said to him.

One of V's friends, who I remembered as T, came into the lounge and walked over to me and V.

'Nat, you remember me mate, T, don't you?' said V. 'Why don't you two go upstairs, have some alone time, yeah?'

I did as I was told and went upstairs with T. We went into the spare room. T checked it was empty before leading me in and shutting the door.

I let him do what he wanted. He told me to lie down on my front on the bed. I felt T lift the back of my skirt away from my arse, and then he slowly eased down my tights and knickers. Then I saw his shadow cast on the bed as he lay down on top of me, and then I felt him inside me. He gripped me round the shoulders, the right side of his head touching the left side of mine.

After five minutes, I felt T let go of me. He rolled off of my body, next to me on the bed. I hoped he was finished and that I could get up, now, but he lay back on top of me and went for it again.

After he stopped, he got up and said, 'The others will be up in a minute.' I sat up, frowning at him.

'The others?' I said. 'I thought it was going to be just us two.'

'To begin with,' said T. I looked down, uncomfortably. Both me and T then heard a knock on the door.

'That'll be them, now,' said T. He walked over to the door and let V, S, another one of the men I met on my way to meeting V, M, and F. I looked over at them, frozen with fear and shock.

'Ah, yeah, she's all ready for us,' said M, grinning, as he and the others came over to me.

I was terrified. But I knew there was nobody about who could help. I had to let them all do what they wanted. They didn't care if I wanted it or not. It was horrific.

I was still in shock, afterwards. As I went downstairs with them all, I couldn't believe it had really happened. Being expected to have sex with one man at a time was bad enough, but being forced into a gangbang made me feel like I wanted to projectile vomit. I followed the men into the kitchen. Some more of V's mates were sat around the kitchen table.

'Have a look at this, baby!' said V, ecstatically. S opened a bag and poured white powder onto the table.

'Is that - ?' I began.

'White magic!' shouted S, excitedly. He divided it up, picked up a straw and snorted a sample through it. Some of the men in the kitchen, who were watching, cheered. I was horrified. It was like something out of a soap opera.

S asked if anyone else wanted some. T said that he was definitely having some, so S handed him the straw, and T snorted some of the mephedrone. The men cheered and clapped.

'Fuck me! I definitely have to take summa of this!' said V, eagerly. He looked round at me. 'What about you, babe?'

But I said I wasn't sure, but V gave me a threatening look. Shitting myself he'd release the video, I caved in and me and V snorted some of the mephedrone, as some of the girls at the party came in. They started taking some, too.

Later, that evening, most of the people at the party, me included, were in the lounge, dancing around, completely high. I was walking, swaying, around the room, my eyes shut, smiling, feeling euphoric. I forgot about the misery I'd been through from being forced to sleep with random men.

'I feel so *good*!' I said, opening my eyes, grinning.

'This is the best night of my life!' V said when he'd come over. I laughed. V put a roll up of meph in my mouth and lit it for me then I smoked it, and then gave it to him to smoke, then we kissed and danced together. M came over.

'Ah, that is awesome shit!' he shouted. He and V laughed. I looked up at the ceiling, grinning excitedly, twirling dizzily on the spot.

After five seconds, I looked down and fell onto the floor. What happened there? I got up, staggered over to the sofa, and fell onto it. V came and flopped onto the sofa next to me.

'You alright?' he shouted. I didn't answer. I started breathing heavily. I was starting to feel really sick. I told V this, but he didn't seem very concerned.

'The room's spinning!' I gasped. 'My heart's beating really fast! I'm going to have a heart attack! V, get me out of here, now!'

But V laughed and said, 'Stop being stupid!'

But I wasn't being stupid. I really did feel like I was going to have a heart attack! I needed to get out and fast.

I tried to get to my feet.

'Oy, where you going?!' I heard V shout, as I staggered through the crowd, but I didn't stop, I carried on over to the front door, snuck out of the house, and went hurtling down the drive towards the pavement. I walked slowly down the pavement. I didn't know where to go, or what to do. Everything was hazy.

After eight more minutes I couldn't walk any further. I felt too dizzy. I collapsed on the pavement. I couldn't move. And there was no one around to help me.

As I lay on the pavement, I could just about make out a shadow of a person. Then I heard a familiar voice. This person looked like they were on the phone.

A moment later, I saw a flash of blue lights and heard the sound of a siren. Was it an ambulance, or a police car?

My memories were still hazy. The next thing I could remember was being inside the ambulance, sirens blaring, the ambulance racing along the road. Amongst all this, I felt relieved. I had escaped. I looked over at the person who had found me. I could see them more clearly now. It was Dave. He was looking over at me with a worried expression on his face.

The next thing I remembered was waking up on a hospital bed. Dave was one side of me and Fred and Mum were on the other side. Mum looked like she'd been crying. How long had I been in the hospital? I kept drifting in and out of consciousness. Dave, Fred and Mum were talking. I couldn't hear most of what was being said, but I knew Dave was telling Fred and Mum how he'd found me lying on the pavement. I tried to keep my eyes open.

I heard the sound of a door opening and saw a doctor come in.

'How is she?' I heard Mum say.

'The mephedrone has over-stimulated her heart,' the doctor explained, 'but we have reason to believe that she will make it.'

I heard Fred, Dave and Mum give huge sighs of relief, before the doctor added, 'Although she's lucky nothing worse happened.'

Mum thanked him. Just as I was beginning to come to a bit more, I heard Fred start to tell Mum that he, Jesse and Lizzy had found out that V was just pretending to be my boyfriend and made me have sex with strangers.

Mum wouldn't believe it, but Fred had told her what Lizzy said she'd seen.

'Oh my goodness, what is she even doing, going along with something like that?' Mum asked, horrified.

'I still don't know why she'd want to do that,' said Fred, before Dave pointed out that V had obviously threatened me, somehow.

Oh my God, the video! What was I going to do now? I'd run off from V, and I didn't want to go back to what V was making me do, but what if he uploaded the video of me getting gang raped? I was between a rock and a hard place. But Fred and Mum would want to know why I'd been keeping to V's demands, and that was why. But if they got involved, that would make V angry, and what would he do then?

'He's also in a gang,' Fred continued. 'He went into Zellweger's, where Ruby-lynn works, and threatened one of her colleagues before we went out.'

'Well, she's going to get a serious talking to from both me and Barry when she gets discharged,' said Mum, crossly. 'Firstly, about keeping secrets from us, secondly, for taking drugs, and thirdly, for going around with gangs.'

I knew I'd have to be prepared for that. But what was I going to say? There was no way I'd be able to carry on obeying V's demands, so he'd release the video. Everything had turned into a complete mess. If I'd listened to Fred earlier, I wouldn't have found myself blackmailed into prostitution. I wouldn't have ended up at a party where I was given drugs. I wouldn't have been lying, half dead in a hospital bed. And when I realised I wasn't feeling right, who was it that got me out of there? Dave, not V, because V didn't care about me and Dave does. I trusted V but he *never* gave a flying fuck about me. All those lovely things he did for me was only to gain my confidence. He'd been grooming me.

Monday 20th June 2011

Mum hadn't spoken to me about V whilst I was still in hospital, but the day after I'd been discharged, both Mum and Dad sat me down.

'Your mother and I have a few things we want to discuss with you,' Dad told me, sternly. I said nothing. I just nodded.

'Firstly about the fact you'd been under the influence of drugs,' Dad went on. 'Would you care to explain how you ended up in that situation?'

I took a deep breath and said, 'I went to a party with V, and he'd pressured me into it, then he wouldn't take me seriously when I told him how the drugs had affected me.'

'Which brings us onto the subject of V himself,' said Mum. 'Did you know he was in a gang when you started going out with him?'

I looked down, and nodded, guiltily.

'Was Fred telling the truth when he said that V had been making you sleep with other men?' Mum then asked.

'Yes,' I whispered. I couldn't hold it in. I burst into tears.

'Oh darling,' said Dad, giving me a hug.

'I never wanted to do it,' I sobbed.

'Why did you agree to it if you never wanted to?' Mum asked after me and Dad broke apart again.

'When I went to meet up with him one night, when I still trusted him, some of his mates came to meet me instead,' I explained. 'They said V didn't want me going out in the dark on my own, and then...' I couldn't bring myself to say it, but I knew I had to. 'They... gang raped me.'

Mum and Dad stared at each other, outraged.

'That's not all, though,' I went on. 'The next day, he told me he had a video of it, and threatened to release it if I didn't do what he wanted. So I went along with it, because I couldn't bear the idea of anyone seeing it. What if Miriam had seen it?'

'It's okay darling,' said Mum. 'We will speak to her and explain what happened. Is this why you've been skipping work?'

'Yes,' I said. 'I tried to tell him I had work, but he didn't care. He just told me to call in sick or something.'

Mum gave me a hug and told me that now she and Dad knew what had been going on, they could deal with it.

'You can't tell the police!' I cried. Mum and Dad frowned.

'Natalie, this is a very serious matter and it needs to be dealt with!' Mum told me. But even if V got arrested, his gang could still come after me in retaliation, and I told Mum and Dad this, but Dad shook his head and said there was no way they could get at me as long as they took extra precautions to keep me safe.

But I still worried. V knew where I lived. He or his gang would come round. What if they hurt Fred or Mum or Dad, or worse, my little brother Max to try to get at me? I couldn't bear it. But I knew I couldn't live in fear. I knew I couldn't let V and his gang win this. But my knowledge of what they were capable of made me feel helpless.

Mum handed me my phone, saying I could have it back.

I sat in silence as I listened to Dad phoning the police. What would happen? Would they come round? Would they want to speak to me? What was I supposed to do if they did?

I looked at my phone. I'd had twenty-eight missed calls from V, as well as stacks of text messages from him. I was dreading reading them, but I had to know what he'd said.

The first one was dated Monday the thirteenth of June, the day after I'd been sent to hospital. It said, 'You had a lotta nerve running off from me last night! i'll giv you 1 last chance. be round mine @ 10 tonight and I'll delete the video and never release it.'

My stomach swirled. I read the next text, which was dated the fourteenth of June, and said, 'I've released the video so now you're just asking to make things worse for yourself if you don't do as I say. Be round mine at 1.'

So now the video was out there. I'd have to be prepared for people whispering, pointing and giggling when I went out. I knew rising above it wouldn't be easy, as I have a quick temper and I'm easy to wind up. I hoped not many people at my work would see it.

And should I show the texts to the police? Was there much of a threat in that message, apart from, "you're only making things worse"? No. Maybe not. How was I making things worse? He didn't exactly specify what he was going to do. The next message said, 'Ur trying my patience. il go after ur mates if you don't do wot i want.'

It was this text that really panicked me. V was getting really angry now. And he'd threatened to go after the others. I didn't know whose safety to fear for the most out of Lizzy's, who I knew lived near him, or Ruby-lynn's, because I knew Ruby-lynn worked at Zellweger's, which he had the audacity to rob.

I scrolled through the rest of the texts. Message by message, they were getting more and more threatening and aggressive.

Mum had entered the lounge with a handful of coasters.

'All right, darling?' she said, walking into the dining room. She pulled open the left hand drawer of the mahogany cabinet in the dining room and slid the coasters into it.

'V's been texting me,' I told Mum. Mum slid the drawer shut and then looked up at me.

'Show me,' she said. I picked up my phone, which still had my much one-sided text conversation with V open on the screen. Mum took the phone and looked at the messages.

'It'll be okay. You will need to tell the police about this,' she told me. But this attempt to reassure me and put my mind at ease did the exact opposite.

'But Mum, we can't! You've seen the texts, he's angry enough as it is!'

'Once we get the police involved, he won't push his luck!' Mum debated. But I was the one pushing *my* luck, involving the police, even after he said he'd get either Scarlet, Ruby-lynn or Lizzy.

Dad hung up after he'd finished and came into the lounge, where I was sat.

'The police are going to come round this afternoon,' he told me. 'They want to speak to you, so I said you'd be available.'

I froze. This afternoon?

'It's okay,' Dad reassured me. 'Just tell them everything that happened.'

That was easy for him to say. What would the police ask me? And what was I going to say? And what would happen after the police spoke to me? I knew I couldn't give them a different story to what I'd told my Mum and Dad. I was stuck.

'She's also had a text from V, threatening to go after one of the other girls if she didn't go along with what he wanted,' Mum told him before I even knew she was going to say anything.

'You're to show the police the texts,' Dad told me. Now I *really* wished I hadn't said anything to Mum about the texts!

I was shaking like a leaf as I spoke to the officers who had come round; P.C Norris, a tall, beefy man with a stern looking face, and P.C Hopes, who was a short, plump woman with dark brown hair tied back in a French plait.

'When did this start, Natalie?' asked Norris.

'January,' I said.

'What happened before that?'

'We started going out, back in September,' I said, slowly. 'Then, in January, I was s'posed to be meeting him for a drink at the Marquis of Granby, so I walked there. And then two of his mates showed up. They said V didn't want me going out in the dark alone, and I felt protected, but then some more of his friends showed up, and they surrounded me. One of them tried to make me give them oral sex, but I ran away from them but they caught me and raped me.'

'Okay,' said P.C Norris, taking notes. 'And then what happened?'

I went onto explain how V had called me the next morning, accusing me of cheating and he said he had a video of what happened and said he'd release it if I didn't do what he told me. Norris told me that if a video had been made, it could be used as evidence against the men who had raped me.

'And he gave me drugs at a party, last Sunday,' I told the constable. Norris asked if I knew what drugs they were.

'I think I remember one of the guys referring to it as white magic,' I said, hoping the police would know what it would've been, as white magic would only have been a slang name for it, but then remembered, despite drifting in and out of consciousness on the hospital bed, I'd been able to hear the doctor mention mephedrone, which I told the constable.

'Do you know what V's full name is?'

'I only really know him as V. I know where he lives, but I don't know his exact address.'

'Do you have a photo of V?' Norris then asked. I did have some on my phone, but I didn't want to show them to the police, as I knew I'd most definitely be for it if V found out, and he was bound to. I'd got V into enough trouble with the police and therefore myself into enough trouble with V as it was. I didn't want to make it any worse.

'Don't you still have some photos of him on your phone, Natalie?' said Mum, holding up my phone. I looked up at Mum, wide eyed.

'Can we see these photos?' asked Norris, his eyebrows raised.

'I deleted them!' I said, quickly.

'Well, clearly not all of them,' said Mum, scrolling through my phone, 'you still have about two or three of the two of you together.'

She handed the police constable my phone.

'Miss Curtis, I understand that you're afraid of saying anything against this V as you're worried it will make things worse, but as long as you give us all the correct information you can, we can make sure that won't happen,' said Hopes, as Norris looked at the photos.

'Oh, yes,' he said. 'He's been in prison before. Victor Stark.'

Great. V was really going to get me now.

'One of my friends lives near him,' I told them after I'd shown them the texts, which I'd had no choice other than to do.

'And you said that another one of your friends works at a shop where he'd stolen money from?' said Norris. I nodded. Hopes muttered to Norris that she and one of the other police officers had to make a visit to Zellweger's, months back, because of a robbery that had happened. The robbery that Ruby-lynn had witnessed!

'That was the same robbery,' I blurted out. 'My mate, Ruby-lynn, works at Zellweger's, and V threatened one of her colleagues!'

'Ah, yes, that was what we were told,' said Hopes, casually.

After the interview, the police thanked me and Mum, said they'd be in touch, and left the house. I didn't know whether to feel more or less nervous. I was glad to have got the interview out of the way, but I didn't know what would happen next, but I was still terrified that I'd be in for it, now that the police were involved.

I went to the kitchen, where Fred was rummaging around in the cupboards. I hadn't spoken to him very much, since what happened.

'Hi,' I said.

'Hey,' said Fred, not looking up at me. I wanted to say I was sorry, as Fred was still blatantly in a bit of a mood with me for not listening to him.

'Listen, Fred, I know you're angry at me for not believing you about V,' I said. Fred stood up with a can of Coca Cola in his hand and looked at me.

'I'm just glad you're okay,' he said, sounding like he hadn't forgiven me.

'But I should've listened to you, but I threw it back in your face, and look where it got me. And I'm sorry,' I said.

'It's fine,' said Fred, walking straight past me, without even looking at me. What could I do? I'd apologised, and admitted I was wrong, but it was quite clear that Fred didn't want to know. Maybe I ought to give him some space and he'd come round eventually.

I knew I also had to apologise to the girls for throwing their warnings back in their faces, especially Ruby-lynn, after what she'd said she'd seen him do.

The next day, I decided to go to Lizzy's house. Dad gave me a lift, as I didn't feel safe walking past V's house on my own.

Dad stayed and waited in the car until I was indoors. I approached the Grahams' front door, rang the doorbell and waited. Uncle Colvin answered.

'Hi Colvin,' I said. 'Is Lizzy here?'

'Yeah, sure. Come on in,' said Uncle Colvin, standing back to let me in. I heard the noise of Dad's car revving up and driving off, now that he knew I was safe indoors.

Colvin called Lizzy to tell her I was here.

'Okay, I'll be right there,' came Lizzy's voice from the kitchen. A few seconds later, she came out of the kitchen and greeted me with her usual hug.

'I need to talk to you in private,' I said, so me and Lizzy went up to Lizzy's room. We sat on Lizzy's white day bed.

'I heard about what happened,' Lizzy whispered. 'Are you all right now?' she added.

'Yeah,' I said. 'It was because I was at a party with V, who I want nothing to do with any more. All of you were right. You, Fred, Scarlet... *Ruby-lynn*... Did you really know V had made me become a prostitute?'

153

Lizzy nodded, and told me she'd seen men going to V's house, giving him money and going upstairs to have sex with me. She also told me she'd walked past V's place on her way home from the bus stop, and saw him getting arrested.

V had been *arrested*?! I could hear my heart starting to beat very fast. I looked down, biting my bottom lip, frantically.

'What's wrong?' asked Lizzy, frowning. 'Knowing he's been arrested should be a relief, shouldn't it?'

Sweet, simple Lizzy. She doesn't seem to get it. She always thinks that ratting someone out for messing with you will put a stop to it in a jiffy.

I let her in on my worries that V would send his gang after me, but Lizzy just said that, as long as we all took the right actions, V and his gang couldn't win.

'Why would you subject yourself to prostitution, just because he asked?' she asked, so I told Lizzy exactly what I told Mum and Dad.

Lizzy said she guessed I was still worried he'd release it, except he had now, but now that Mum and Dad knew, they said they'd speak to my boss.

'Oh God, yeah, what if he or she sees it?' said Lizzy, though agreeing that Miriam would see that it wasn't my fault.

'And the way I see it, if he does release it, we can find it and show it to the police, then V's fucked!' said Lizzy, with a superior smile. It was just like the police had said. And I couldn't help smiling too. Lizzy can be quite brainy and she knows it.

'I hope that crap chud gets put away for life,' she said. 'What happened at the party?'

'I don't want to talk about it any more,' I said.

'Have you been okay?' I asked Lizzy. 'Fred said you split up with Charlie.'

'Yeah,' said Lizzy, looking down. 'He was leading me on the whole time!'

I was shocked. I had heard from Fred that Lizzy and Charlie weren't together anymore, and I knew something was up because they hardly got up to anything together, but I was enraged. That arsehole!

'Bastard!' I said.

'I should've seen it coming, because he always insisted on taking me to places I knew he didn't like, because Priscilla would be there,' Lizzy said, and he'd backtracked what he'd said about us not feeling the need to go out of our way to hide our relationship from Fraser because he'd expose his true intentions in front of me.'

'Had all that been going on right from the start of your relationship?'

'Almost.'

'And it was worrying you the whole time? Why didn't you say anything about it to any of us?' I asked, shocked that she'd kept it all to herself.

Lizzy sighed.

'I wanted to,' she said. 'But you lot all had your own problems. I didn't want to burden any of you with mine. Plus I hoped I was over-analysing so I guess I'd been burying my head in the sand.'

'So you had to keep it all quiet, even though you didn't want to,' I said, and then I sighed and gave Lizzy a hug.

'Of all the people he could've gone after, *her*?! Seriously?!' I said, in disbelief.

'It's alright, though, because I am managing to move on okay,' Lizzy reassured me, breaking away. Lizzy did seem to have bounced back quickly from the break-up. Was this normal for her, since Charlie was her first boyfriend?

'There's something else I need to tell you,' Lizzy said. 'You know I told you about Will?'

So now she and Charlie had broken up, she was back on Will.

'Yeah, what about him?'

'Well, when I met Dave, Ruby-lynn and Scarlet for drinks, I knew Scarlet was meant to be bringing some mates, and one of them was Will!'

Oh my God! Scarlet knew Will? How did none of us know that before?

'How come you never knew that sooner?'

'Well, it might've had something to do with the fact that Scarlet never knew I'd met Will, until now.'

I was shocked.

'You never told her?'

'What's the big deal?' Lizzy said. 'She's not the only one I never told. You, Fred and Jesse are the only ones I ever did tell.'

Whoa! Literally only me, Fred and Jesse knew about all this?

'So what happened?' I asked. 'Will met you all for drinks, and then...?'

'After we all left Wetherspoons', we said goodbye to the other three and then Will kissed me again, and we went and...' Lizzy pulled a face like she wasn't sure how to word what she was going to say, 'did it in a beach hut.'

Did Lizzy just say she and Will did it in a beach hut?

'No fucking way! You're not a virgin any more?'

'Nope.'

'Congrats!' I said. 'This is so awesome! Are you two an item? When you gonna see him again?'

'We're not an item. I said I still needed time to move on from Charlie. All this has been really confusing. I need to make sure I am completely over him before I can start seeing anyone again.'

What was wrong with her? I could see her point, yeah, but this was Will we were talking about. But I knew Lizzy needed to do what was best for her and she obviously couldn't help how she was feeling.

Me and Lizzy sat, chatted and watched movies before I said it was time I was heading home.

'Are you going to be okay?' asked Lizzy, as I was about to leave with Auntie Jane. I reassured her that Mum and Dad had everything under control. Me and Lizzy shared a goodbye hug then me and Auntie Jane got into the Kia Motor.

As we drove to Chickerell, I asked if there was anyone that could give Lizzy a lift to and from college, as V's house wasn't far from where they lived. Auntie Jane looked round at me and frowned.

'Does she have to walk past there, every time she walks to the bus stop?' she asked. I said she did, and that I wasn't sure how long V would be in custody for and was worried that he'd go after Lizzy.

'Hmmm,' said Auntie Jane, sounding uncertain. 'Right, okay. I see your point. I'll make sure there is someone free to give her a lift, or just make sure she and Fraser walk to the bus stop together.'

But would V stay away from Lizzy, just because Fraser was there? Oh well, at least Lizzy wouldn't be on her own.

My escape and V's residence near the Grahams' house would put Lizzy in danger and she needed to be protected, especially since Lizzy is more vulnerable than me. But if V wanted to get at Lizzy, he'd have to answer to me.

When I got home, I went to the kitchen to make myself a cup of coffee. As I filled the kettle, I was joined by Mum.

'Are you okay?' she asked.

'Yeah,' I said, before offering Mum a coffee. I got two mugs out and put a teaspoon of coffee in each.

'Your father and I have spoken to your boss, and she has said you should have this week off,' said Mum.

I looked round at her. That was all Miriam had said about the fact I'd been turned into a prozzy?

'We've explained what happened. Obviously she was shocked that you'd been blackmailed into something like that, and she understands that it wasn't your fault,' she said.

I felt more relaxed at this. But it would still be fucking humiliating if anyone else saw the video, but now I'd pick that over the prostitution any day. And I remembered what Lizzy had said about being able to use it as evidence against V and his gang. But it didn't erase my worry at what would happen, now that V had been arrested.

But that was driven out of my mind by something really nice that happened an hour later.

I heard the doorbell ring, so I went to answer it.

It was Dave. I hadn't forgotten he was the one who'd found me. I was quite surprised to see him there.

'Hi,' I said to him. 'I wasn't expecting you to come round.'

'I wanted to see how you were,' said Dave.

'I haven't been too bad,' I said.

Dave asked if he could come in, so I invited him into the lounge, where Fred was on his laptop. He looked up when me and Dave and his expression lightened when he saw Dave, obviously grateful to him for finding his sister.

'Hey Dave,' he said.

'All right?' said Dave. 'I just came round to see if Natalie had been okay.'

'Cool,' said Fred, before going back to his coursework.

'When did you come home from hospital?' Dave asked as he and I sat down on the sofa in the bay window.

'Sunday,' I answered. 'The police came round yesterday.'

'About the drugs?'

'There's more to it than that, but I don't want to go into any detail about it,' I said.

Out of the corner of my eye, I noticed Fred looking up from his laptop.

I then asked Dave if there was anything he wanted to do. Dave said that, whilst he'd initially only come round to check up on how I was, he wouldn't mind listening to some music.

I took him up to my room, where I keep my iPod docking station. My iPod, which is the third generation of iPod touch, was on my bedside table. I picked it up, plugged it into the docking station, and then let Dave scroll through my music and choose a song.

He eventually picked one and pressed 'Play.' Within seconds, the Black Eyed Peas' "Rock Your Body," was sounding from the docking station.

'So you're a fan of the Black Eyed Peas?' I asked Dave, astonished. He'd never struck me as a Black Eyed Peas fan.

'I wouldn't say I'm a fan, but their music's all right,' said Dave. 'I'm more into Take That. And Oasis.'

I told Dave about some of my favourite artists being Example, Britney Spears, N-Dubz, Black Eyed Peas, Swedish House Mafia and David Guetta.

I enjoyed having a conversation with Dave about music. He told me about the gigs he'd been to in the past, as he was also into bands like Snow Patrol, Pink Floyd, Plan B and Kings Of Leon.

'What other songs do you like, by the Black Eyed Peas?' he asked.

'I don't have very many of their songs on my iPod' I told him. 'Do you like Taio Cruz? Because I have some of his music on my iPod too.'

'I'm not into many of his songs but I do like "Shine A Light," which I think is also by McFly,' Dave said.

'I have that song on my iPod so we could listen to that one next,' I said, but Dave said he was happy just to let the music play, then he could see what other songs I had that he liked.

'I heard what happened with that Spanish girl you were seeing,' I said. 'I'm sorry. What Dan and Tom did wasn't fair.'

'No,' Dave agreed, looking down.

I had a good time with Dave, and I was so grateful to him for, not just getting me to hospital, but coming round to make sure I was okay.

'Thanks for letting me stay round for a bit,' said Dave as he and I said goodbye.

'Any time,' I responded. 'And thanks for... well... caring.'

Dave smiled and started walking off along the pavement. I shut the door, feeling very happy. I went into the lounge where Max and Dad were sat on the sofa nearest the door and sat on the armchair.

'Was that another boyfriend?' asked Dad.

'No Dad,' I tutted. 'That was Dave, as in your mate Gary's son, who found me and was in the ambulance with me on the way to hospital. He came round because he wanted to see how I was.'

At that moment, Mum came in and sat next to Dad on the sofa.

'He's such a nice boy, Barry. Caring enough to come and see our Natalie,' she said to him.

Fred came in and sat down on a sofa by the bay window. Mum suggested having a takeaway, saying she felt the family could do with a treat, given the recent events.

We had a Chinese takeaway and I ordered sweet and sour spare ribs, mixed vegetable chow mein and Singapore fried rice. As we ate our food, we watched a couple of Walt Disney films.

I had a brilliant evening, and the texts I'd had from V hadn't worried me very much. In fact, I'd forgotten all about it during the evening. Me and Fred didn't speak very much, but when I went up to bed, Fred said goodnight and gave me a weak smile, which I reciprocated.

On Wednesday, I was constantly on my guard, waiting for an angry text from V after his arrest, but I hadn't heard from him all day. He must still have been in custody. I didn't know how long he'd be in custody, for what he did, or if the police would let him go at all.

I had my chow mein leftover from the night before, as I couldn't quite fit it in with my rice and spare ribs, so I had that for lunch, though I felt too nervous to be hungry. I decanted the contents of the round foil container onto a plate, and micro waved it for four minutes.

As I walked over to the cutlery drawer to get a fork, my phone beeped.

My heart started thudding, madly, as I rushed back to the dining room with the fork in my hand and picked my phone up to look at the text. Oh thank fuck, it was from Ruby-lynn.

I sat down and tucked into my lunch, deciding I'd read the text and answer it after I'd finished eating.

As I tensely ate, I wondered what Ruby-lynn had written. Most likely wanting to ask if I was okay.

Things hadn't been easy between us, as Ruby-lynn knew I knew Fred had been doing the dirty on her, and I hadn't told her.

When I finished my chow mein, I picked up my phone to read the text. Ruby-lynn had asked me to ring her, so I did, curiously.

'Hello?' came Ruby-lynn's voice, after five rings.

'Hey, it's Natalie.'

Ruby-lynn said hi back and, sure enough, asked how I'd been. I told her I'd been okay, since coming out of hospital.

'I've had a load of texts from V,' I told her.

'What's been going on between you and V since you've been in hospital?' Ruby-lynn asked.

'It's over.'

'Came to your senses, then?' Ruby-lynn responded.

'I'm sorry for not believing you,' I said. 'Fred only recently told me what V did at Zellweger's.

I then explained how I'd been blackmailed into becoming a prostitute, and about V pretending to be the perfect boyfriend, just to gain my trust.

'How did you manage to get the drugs that landed you in hospital?' Ruby-lynn asked.

'I was at a party with V, then we all took meph,' I spelled out. 'And then I began to notice something didn't feel right. And I tried to tell V this, but he wouldn't listen to me. So I legged it. Lizzy said she'd seen him getting arrested as she went past his house. She lives near him, you see.'

'Yeah, I've also heard V's been arrested, as the police had suspicions about him, and knew he'd been the one to rob Zellweger's.'

'He's probably still in custody.'

'Of *course* he's still in *custody*!' Ruby-lynn said. 'After getting arrested for both what he did to you, *and* armed robbery.'

I told Ruby-lynn what I remembered V telling me before, about the fact that he had been in jail before, for armed robbery. Ruby-lynn asked me how I felt about telling my parents all about it.

'I do feel relieved to got it off my chest,' I admitted, 'but even now I still feel terrible at the idea of them knowing their baby girl had been raped by sick, dirty bastards.'

'But at least you've escaped now,' Ruby-lynn assured me. 'You won't have to go back round and sleep with anyone he asks you to, ever again.'

'Yeah,' I agreed. I told Ruby-lynn about the talking to I got from Mum and Dad, and my worry that V's gang would be out to get me, but Ruby-lynn said, 'Once they know V has been arrested, they'll have to watch it.'

I still wasn't sure.

'They can just threaten to get me if I get the police onto,' them I told Ruby-lynn.

'You'll just have to be careful where you go,' Ruby-lynn advised me, adding that I should at least go out with my hood up, or wear a hat, so none of V's gang would recognise me.

I knew it wasn't the best idea, but I supposed it would help a bit.

I stayed on the phone to Ruby-lynn for a little while longer.

'How have you been since... you know, your split from Fred?' I hesitantly asked. 'I'm so sorry for keeping what he was doing from you.

'It's okay,' Ruby-lynn said, though she still sounded a bit iffy that I never told her.

'Have you spoken to him at all?' I asked. I hadn't heard much about Ruby-lynn from Fred.

'We talked very briefly at Rebel Tour Bus's gig, but I haven't completely forgiven him yet.'

Well, of course she hadn't! It was going to be a *very* long time before Ruby-lynn felt she'd be able to trust Fred again, if she did at all, that was.

Over the rest of the week, I'd begun to feel a little braver about leaving the house more, as each day went by. I still hadn't heard from V, but, like Ruby-lynn said, it was unlikely he was going to be let out, after what he'd been arrested for.

Saturday 25th June 2011

Dave invited me out at midday, so the two of us met for a coffee in Costa.

'So...' Dave began, hesitantly, 'you said you didn't want to go into detail about how you ended up in the state I found you in.'

I confirmed I had. I knew Dave knew that V was just pretending he was my boyfriend the whole time, just so he could force me to be a prostitute for him, but I was aware Dave probably understood it was something dodgy I didn't want to talk about, meaning he wouldn't let on that he knew.

'I was at a party with V,' I told him. 'He gave me the drugs, and wouldn't listen to me when I tried to tell him what was happening because of the drugs.'

I said nothing more than that.

'I get you,' Dave said.

As we drank our cups of coffee, we talked about what Ruby-lynn told me about V getting arrested. Dave agreed that there was only a very small chance that V would make bail.

'After committing two serious crimes, both of which you all had proof of, especially if he's been in prison before, it's definitely not looking too good for him, I'd say.'

'Fred seemed a bit awkward with me,' I told him.

'Give him time,' Dave told me. 'He'll come round. '

I smiled at Dave. He was right, I knew that.

At twenty to five, me and Dave decided to leave. We began walking down St Mary Street, then through Bond Street, until we reached the number eight bus stop, and said goodbye, before I caught the bus home.

Tuesday 28th June 2011

The staff kitchen was empty when I returned to work. No Martin doing his usual man looking whilst searching for the milk in the fridge.

I decided to make myself a coffee. I filled the kettle, boiled it, put a teaspoon full of coffee in a yellow mug that had a few chips on the handle, and then opened the fridge to get the milk. I picked up the pint that was on the shelf in the door. It felt very light. I held it up to see how much was left. Enough left for only one person. Martin can't stand black tea or coffee, so it would have to be black coffee for me instead, but I didn't mind.

As I was pouring my water into my mug, I heard the door open. I looked up, just as Martin entered.

'You feeling better then?' he asked.

'Yeah.'

Martin asked me to make him a cup of tea whilst I was at it, reminding me not to add any sugar, so when I made him his tea, I emptied the almost empty pint of milk into his mug.

'That's the last of the milk,' I said, chucking the pint into the bin. 'One of us will need to pop out and get some more. I deliberately didn't use what was left, 'cause I knew you'd want white tea or coffee.'

I brought both mugs over to the table, where Martin was sat, placed both drinks on the table, and sat down opposite him.

'So, what was wrong?' Martin asked, sounding mystified. 'You've been off of work a *lot*! I tried to ask Miriam, but she wouldn't tell me. Have you been all right?'

I sighed.

'It was something pretty serious,' I said.

Martin gave me an alarmed look.

'But it's over now,' I reassured him. 'And I really don't want to talk about it. I just want to forget it ever happened, now that it no longer is.'

Martin nodded and said, 'Okay.'

At nine o'clock, me and Martin went to our desks.

I had a satisfyingly quite morning. During my coffee break, I'd had a text from Jesse, inviting me to come for a drink with him and Fred in the William Henry after work. Fred had been slightly friendlier towards me over the last couple of days, so I liked to think he was slowly starting to forgive me. I accepted Jesse's invite.

The rest of the day dragged by, it was so quiet, but at long last, I was packing up, ready to leave at closing time. I met Jesse and Fred upstairs, sat opposite each other at the very back in the William Henry.

'All right?' said Jesse, once I'd reached their table. 'Get yourself a drink, and then sit with us, yeah?'

'Cool,' I said. I walked over to the bar and ordered a Magna's, and then went back to join Fred and Jesse and sat next to Jesse.

'How was college, you two?' I asked.

'Yeah it was alright,' said Fred. I knew Fred had still been on the receiving end of a load of vile insults from girls at college, after his simultaneous dating.

'Why couldn't Lizzy come?' I asked.

'Said she was busy,' Fred answered. 'She's been acting really weird since the gig. Have you noticed?'

I didn't tell Fred, as desperate as I was, that when I asked Lizzy how she'd been after she and Charlie broke up she said she'd met Will again, through Scarlet and that stuff happened. That was for her to tell if she wanted to. I just said she seemed surprisingly chirpy and didn't even get snappy at me and tell me to stop asking, as I knew I would if I was in her shoes and people kept asking me if I was okay.

'Then that's good, isn't it?' asked Jesse, frowning. 'It means she's over Charlie.'

'That fast?' Fred said, cynically.

'What it is to us?' Jesse asked. 'As long as it means she's moved on.'

'Jesse's right. It's just a bit weird, that's all,' Fred admitted, before I warned them not to be fooled and telling them that Lizzy had been worrying something might've been up, almost the whole time she was with Charlie and never had the courage to let any of us in on it, before Jesse changed the subject and said, 'Fred told me what happened with V. We already knew he'd made you, er,' Jesse lowered his voice to a whisper, 'sleep with blokes for cash.'

'Lizzy told you, presumably?' I asked. Both boys nodded. I told them he'd been arrested for, not only that, but for what happened at Zellweger's.

'Ah, so they were already onto him, then?' asked Fred. I told him that Ruby-lynn had called me and said that it was very unlikely he'd be released from custody because of it.

'V's gang are still out there, and they could get you if you're not careful,' Jesse pointed out, just in case I wasn't already aware of it! 'I know how you were forced into it.

'Send me the link if you ever come across the video online, so I can show the police,' said Fred. 'Then we've got his gang, too.'

This partly made me feel glad that V had released the video, as it meant I could easily get hold of it if I found it somewhere on the internet. I hoped someone did find it soon, as I was worried that one of V's gang would go after the others if they couldn't get me.

I asked if we could talk about something else instead. We started talking about Jesse's birthday, which was on the twenty-forth of July. Jesse told us that Matt Weller had surprised him with tickets to You Me At Six's gig as an early birthday present. He said we could all do something in the day time for his birthday, and that he'd look at the Cineworld website, to see what movies would be on, on his birthday, and what times they were showing, and then text everyone, which Fred and I both said we were happy with.

Out of the corner of my eye, I caught sight of a short, dark, round faced girl with black ringlets. I'd seen her a few times. She's Annie's best friend, Sherri. You know, Annie, Jesse's girlfriend.

She was with a tall, thickset lad with dark brown, curly hair. I caught her eye. She smiled and then I saw her lead the guy in our direction. Jesse noticed her too.

'Hey Sherri, how's it going?' he said, when she and the boy came over. 'Is this your bloke? Annie said you had a new boyfriend, it's Will, isn't it?'

'Well, it's William, but I prefer to be known as Billy, actually,' said the boy.

'Ah, fair enough,' said Jesse. 'And Annie says you're from Northern Ireland, is that right?'

'Oh, I think Annie might've got her Irelands mixed up, Billy's actually from the Republic of Ireland.'

'Yeah, that's right, I'm from Dublin, originally,' said Billy.

'So... you're Billy from the Republic of Ireland?' Jesse said, slowly, his eyebrows raised, sounding like he was making sure he'd heard Sherri right.

'Yes, that's right,' said Sherri.

'Well, it's good to meet you, we'll have to go on a double date at some point,' Jesse. And then, after some small talk, Sherri and Billy said goodbye and left.

I looked from Jesse to Fred, who was smirking at Jesse.

'You thought that was Lizzy's Will when Annie first told you about him, didn't you?' he said.

'Yeah I did,' Jesse admitted. I was bursting to tell him and Fred that Lizzy had seen Will again and they got it on, but best friends don't go blabbing to people about each other's love and sex lives.

At six thirty, we decided to head home. Fred drove us home in his Mini Cooper. He played the music on his iPod as we drove home.

After Fred dropped Jesse off, he turned round in his seat to look at me.

'I'm sorry I didn't forgive you before,' he said. 'I was just getting frustrated you still wanted to be with him, even though you knew what he was capable of.'

'No, don't be sorry,' I told him. 'I was being stupid and stubborn, and I keep going for the bad ones, no matter what you say, so it wasn't unusual for you to behave in the way you did.'

'Okay, well, I felt, after what you'd been through, I should've supported you,' said Fred.

I smiled at him.

'It's okay, because you're supporting me now, at least.'

Fred smiled back, before inviting me to come and sit in the front, and then we drove home.

I thought about everything Lizzy, Fred and Jesse had said about what would happen if we found the video of me being raped, and shown it to the police. I can't help wishing I'd thought of that, myself, when V first threatened to release it. It would've been a lose-lose situation for him if I'd refused in the first place. He wouldn't get what he was asking for, then he would've released the video, making it easier for me to report them, as V was the only one who had access to the video before then.

But it didn't matter now, not now that V had been arrested, and I knew the video was out there somewhere, and that the humiliation of people seeing it was just a small price to pay for having a chance to get hold of it.

Chapter 13:

Ruby-lynn's Second

Tuesday 28th June 2011

'I'm sorry, Ruby-lynn, but I need to borrow some more money.'

I was furious, but I couldn't say no. Mum was desperate. She had been over the past ten months.

I half-heartedly logged onto my online bank account on my phone, and transferred one hundred and fifty pounds over to Mum's account. I didn't know why Mum had been so desperate for money, lately. I didn't exactly take it very well when I found out Mum had sold the television, and I'd decided my own stuff wasn't going any where, no fucking way!

I didn't want to be selfish, but the mysterious money problems Mum was facing had already taken away enough as it was. We weren't even allowed to turn on the heating, so I was glad now that it was finally getting hotter.

My life had turned into an absolute mess, and Mum being broke wasn't the only reason why. Whilst me and Fred did sort of chat at Fraser's gig, I wasn't halfway close to forgiving him for breaking my heart. I still really liked him and I knew he was sorry, but I just didn't feel I could trust him properly any more, and I knew he had a reputation for being a ladies' man. I really thought Fred saw me as something extra special, and he seemed to care about me a lot, and that just made the betrayal even more hurtful. I'd been left wondering how long I'd be finding it hard to trust boys for.

The money I transferred didn't leave me a lot of money for the next day. I was supposed to be going shopping after work the next day with the girls.

We'd been going on these frequent shopping trips because we felt all four of us needed some retail therapy, since Charlie had been using Lizzy the whole time, V had been a gang boy who posed as Natalie's boyfriend to use her as a prostitute the whole time, Fred had been cheating on me, *nearly* the whole time, I don't know, and Scarlet had not been allowed to move on from Tom because of his and Dan's refusal to leave her be.

I was glad Natalie was able to spend more time with us again. Now that I knew Natalie had been forced into something, whether she liked it or not, it was easier for me to understand why she'd kept disappearing.

I was so annoyed about the money I was left with. Only fifty pounds! How much could I buy with that? I'd have to make do with charity shops. I'd hit a real low point.

'I've transferred over a hundred and fifty,' I called to Mum. She'd better be grateful it wasn't less. She'd bled me dry enough already. But Mum just thanked me.

I logged out, and then went to sit with Dad in the lounge. He was reading the paper. I looked over at him, wondering if I should say anything about the fact that Mum had to keep borrowing money.

'Dad?'

Dad looked over at me.

'What's up, love?'

'Why is Mum always so low on money?' I asked, in a hesitant voice. Dad sighed.

'I really don't know, and I know it's annoying that you're having to lend her money all the time, because so am I,' he said. 'But try to be understanding. There is obviously something wrong, or she wouldn't be asking.'

'But I'm supposed to be going shopping tomorrow, and I haven't got much money left, after what I'd just had to transfer over!' I argued.

'There isn't a lot anybody can do, Dad said. 'Mum's short tempered enough, after I've tried to get her to tell me what's going on.'

I might as well have given up if I couldn't even get my dad to try to do something about it.

I caught the bus to work Wednesday morning, not looking forward to shopping with the girls as much as before Mum asked me for money.

I had a very dull day. My shift had drifted by, very slowly. When I finished at one, I began walking down to Debenhams, where I was meeting the girls.

They were already there. I gave them all hugs and kisses on the cheeks when I reached them.

'You been okay?' asked Scarlet.

'Yeah,' I said. 'So, where to first?'

Scarlet suggested Debenhams first, as we were stood right outside, after all. We all entered Debenhams. I looked at the shoes whilst Scarlet scuttled off to look at the handbags, and Lizzy and Natalie looked at perfumes.

None of the shoes in stock were my style, so I went to have a look in Jane Norman, where I was joined by Scarlet, ten minutes later.

'Look what I've just found,' she said. She held up a soft pale denim blue whipstitch tote bag from Mantaray. She told me it was thirty-nine pounds. I nodded and said that it was very nice.

We went to join Lizzy, who was now looking at the Benefit range. She was looking at their lipsticks. I watched as Scarlet started admiring the array of skincare products. She looked at some tinted lip balms. I began looking at the eye shadow palettes. I was drawn in by a particular eye shadow trio. It included a base colour in pink, a cocoa contouring colour, and a liner in a rich, chocolate brown. My heart sank when I saw the price; twenty-six pounds and fifty pence! That would leave me with less than half the money I had after buying just one item. What was I to do?

I don't know what made me do it, but the next thing I knew, I'd picked it up and stashed it in my bag. Oh my God, what had I just done?

'Are you all right?' Lizzy asked, as we left the shop. But I didn't want to tell anyone I'd just shoplifted. I hadn't put the eye shadow back. As stunned as I was, I wanted it so badly, whatever was going on with Mum, I wasn't going to let it stop me from getting what I wanted.

Next, we went to Peacocks. I watched, enviously, as Lizzy picked up some silver gem drop earrings. They were gorgeous, not that they've ever been the sort of thing that I would wear. I spotted a pair of gold pineapple stud earrings. They were only two pound forty. I could pay for them, easy-peasy. But hang on a minute. I'd need money for my cinema ticket. One more time couldn't hurt, could it? I looked around to make sure no one was watching, grabbed the earrings, and slipped them into my bag.

I still couldn't believe what I was doing, but shopping with the girls hadn't been a lot of fun, recently. It was hard not to feel jealous of the other three over all the new clothes, shoes, accessories and make-up they'd bought when I had to make do with items from charity shops, which I was definitely *never* going to steal from. It was bad enough that I was shoplifting anywhere but I knew just how low it would be to shoplift in shops where all the profits go towards fighting heart disease and cancer and helping children and elders.

I hadn't spotted very many clothes I was interested in buying, but I knew I couldn't risk stealing any clothes because of the security tags, anyway.

In T.K Maxx, I saw a few t-shirts I liked the look of, that weren't too expensive. I grabbed a basket and, in it, I put a white t-shirt with a red and indigo Rolling Stones logo, a black t-shirt with pictures of female villains from four Disney films, another white t-shirt with pop art pictures of the Notorious B.I.G, a grey melange t-shirt with Kiss written on the bust in black and a grey New York t-shirt.

It came to thirty-seven pounds and ninety-five pence when I paid, leaving me with just twelve pounds and five pence. I was really pleased I got to buy some clothes I actually wanted.

After a few more shops, we went to have a late lunch in McDonalds. I'd had to pay for my food, so I didn't have a lot of money left, after that.

As we ate, we talked about the movie the eight of us were going to see on Jesse's birthday, on the twenty-fourth of July; Green Lantern. It was Jesse's decision, of course. No thanks to the amount of money I'd had to lend to my mum, I'd been able to afford to buy Jesse a birthday present. I bought him a set of two Guinness glasses from Debenhams.

Luckily, we'd decided to call it a day after we'd eaten anyway, as Lizzy in particular was laden and said she didn't think she'd be able to carry much more, and Scarlet and Natalie didn't have any hands free with all the bags they were carrying, but agreed to meet to go shopping again on Saturday.

We'd said goodbye to Natalie when we reached Bond Street, and then carried on up St Mary Street towards the sea front.

'Do you want to come back to mine?' Scarlet invited me, after we'd said goodbye to Lizzy.

'Sure,' I said.

So we both joined the long queue at the number two bus stop. I was relieved I hadn't been able to buy much, as it looked like it was going to be crowded and we were going to have enough trouble with all Scarlet's shopping.

The bus pulled over to the stop. Everyone piled on, including Scarlet with some difficulty. She over balanced as she stepped on.

'Whoa!' she screamed, falling backwards. I tried to catch her, but ended up having to unbury her from underneath her shopping, which had all fallen on top of her, and then I had to hold Scarlet's shopping for her whilst she searched for her bus pass. We were able to find seats near the back of the bus.

'I'll show you my shopping when we get back home,' said Scarlet. It hadn't been easy for us to show each other the mass of our exciting purchases whilst sat at the table in McDonalds.

I couldn't wait to show Scarlet my new t-shirts. But I decided I'd better not show Scarlet the stolen earrings and eye shadow. She knew I hadn't bought anything from Debenhams or Peacocks and she'd go ballistic if she knew I'd been shoplifting.

'Are you okay about coming to the cinema with all of us?' Scarlet asked me. I stared at her. Why wouldn't I be?

'Of course I am. Why do you ask?'

'Well, Fred's obviously going to be there, as he and Jesse are best friends.'

I could see where Scarlet was coming from.

'I don't have to sit next to him or anything, but I'm, not going to let what happened to make us break up ruin my enjoyment,' I said to Scarlet. 'I am quite looking forward to it,' I added, and I told Scarlet about the present I'd bought for Jesse, which Scarlet said she reckoned he'd like, before telling me about the My Chemical Romance t-shirt she'd bought off BlueBanana.com for him, as she knew Jesse liked band t-shirts.

As soon as we departed the bus on Littlemoor, the walk to the Harts' house in the Finches was made to take longer than usual by all the heavy shopping bags.

Scarlet rang the doorbell as soon as she and I arrived at the Harts' house, as she said it would be easier than having to search her handbag for her keys when she had a lot to carry. Stuart answered the door.

'Hey. Have fun shopping, then?'

'Good thanks,' said Scarlet, as I followed her in. Both of us went up to Scarlet's room and were finally able to put down all our shopping. Scarlet showed me the ribbed vests she'd bought in Peacocks, in mustard, purple and dark green, all for just four pounds each, plus a red and blue water colour patterned, three quarter length sleeved blouse at twelve ninety-nine, a black and yellow ditsy floral print long sleeved blouse at sixteen ninety-nine and a mustard floral three quarter length sleeved bardot top at twelve ninety-nine. The other clothes she'd bought had come from T.K Maxx, Debenhams, New Look, Dorothy Perkins and Top Shop.

'Let's see what you've bought, then,' she said, when she'd eventually finished, so I gladly showed her the t-shirts I'd bought from T.K Maxx.

'I couldn't buy as much as you three,' I told Scarlet, 'because my mum's had to stop my pocket money and she's always having to borrow some of my earnings.'

'I would've lent you some money,' Scarlet said.

'That's kind of you to offer, but I really shouldn't be troubling other people with it.'

'So, why is your mum so low on money, then?' Scarlet asked, curiously.

'I really have no idea what's going on,' I said, 'and I really hate that we've had to sell the T.V.'

Scarlet patted my shoulder and suggested going downstairs to the lounge to join Stuart. We entered the lounge to find Stuart on the sofa with his new girlfriend, Portia cuddled up to him. They were watching 50 First Dates. They both looked up and saw me and Scarlet.

'Alright?' said Stuart.

'Don't mind if we join you, do you?' asked Scarlet, as she and I walked over to the sofa that Stuart and Portia weren't cuddled up on, and sat down.

'No, not at all,' said Stuart. The four of us continued watching the film, before Mrs Hart came in and asked if me and Portia wanted to stay for dinner. She said she was cooking roasted Mediterranean vegetable lasagne, so we both accepted.

I'd only ever tried lasagne with bolognaise sauce, so I was intrigued to try what Mrs Hart was cooking, to see what it would taste like.

'So, what have you two been up to, today?' asked Mrs Hart, when we were all at the dinner table. I listened as Scarlet told Mrs Hart all about our shopping trip with Lizzy and Natalie. Mrs Hart turned to me and asked if I'd bought many things.

'Just a few t-shirts from T.K Maxx,' I told her.

'Ruby-lynn's not had a lot of money, lately,' Scarlet explained.

'Are you still working at Zellweger's?' Mr Doherty asked.

' Yeah I am, but it's because my mum has been so low on money that, not only did she have to stop my pocket money, but borrow some more out of my wages.'

Mrs Hart raised her eyebrows

'How frustrating,' she said.

'How's Natalie been?' asked Mr Doherty. 'I've heard Barry and Claire are disgusted about how she ended up in that situation, but I don't know the full story. I understand they don't want to tell people.'

'All I can tell you about it is that the guy who was to blame for it was the same guy that came in and robbed Zellweger's a while back,' I told him, cautiously. Scarlet looked round at me. Mr Doherty gave me a shocked look.

'Zellweger's was *robbed*? You must've been so scared!'

'I was fuming afterwards,' I said. 'He's been arrested for that *and* what he did to Natalie.'

Mr Doherty and Mrs Hart exchanged concerned looks.

I was glad that Natalie had finally seen sense, but I was still slightly irritated that she took so long. But I knew even though V was in custody, his gang were still free to come after Natalie, especially as they were probably now angry at her for getting V arrested.

I caught two buses home; the number two, and then the number one.

It was when I was walking back to my house and approaching the front garden that I noticed something strange. There was a man, who looked at least fifty, stood at the front door, talking to my mum. I didn't catch any of what had been said, but I did see Mum give him something. As I tried to look closer, I could make out a wad of twenty-pound notes. Mum was giving him money! But why? And had she been giving him cash before? Had that been why Mum had very little money? I had to know. I was not going to take no for an answer. I'd seen her giving him money and I'd been skint long enough, so if it did have something to do with that, I was going to get to the bottom of this, one way or another.

The man thanked my mum and then left. I quickly hid, so that the man wouldn't see me and know I'd been spying. I waited and watched as the man walked away, and then when I thought it was safe, I walked to the front door, trying to look innocent, in case the man glanced back at me, and let myself in. I went to my room first, to dump my shopping on my bed, and then went to the kitchen. Mum was sat at the table, drinking a cup of white coffee, resting her head in her left palm, looking stressed. This did make me feel guilty for getting so angry. Mum couldn't help it and it was understandable that she was getting very erasable. I just wished she'd told us what was wrong. She looked up and smiled when she saw me.

'Hi, darling,' she said. 'Have a good time in town?'

'Yeah,' I said. I sat down opposite Mum. I couldn't start by sounding demanding.

'I saw a man at the front door,' I said. Mum looked up at me, her eyes wide. I carried on. 'I saw you giving him money. Was this the first time?'

Mum looked down. I could tell that she knew she'd been caught out. She shook her head.

'Why have you been giving him money, and is this why you're always broke?' I asked. Mum sighed and explained that she was in debt.

'I borrowed five thousand, two hundred and fifty pounds from Patrick Legg, you know, my friend from work, and his neighbour, Mr Rittman, the man who had come round, would collect the repayments and take it to him.'

It sort of made sense. I knew who Patrick was and had actually met him once. But I was astonished at the amount of money. Five thousand, two hundred and fifty pounds?

'What on earth did you need so much money for?' I asked.

'It was your T.V, darling!'

Oh no. All of this trouble had been on the account of my damn T.V? I felt *so* guilty! But I had no way of knowing my mum would have to borrow some money.

'But why did you borrow money? Couldn't you and Dad have gone halves on it?' I asked, seriously hoping Mum was not going to say, 'Oh, I didn't think of that.'

'You remember, sweetie, he was in hospital, having his operation,' Mum reminded me.

I remembered now, when I'd been given the T.V, whilst my dad was in hospital, because he'd had to have his appendix removed. I understood that it would've been unfair of Mum to ask him for money when he hadn't been well. She explained that she'd been unable to make the repayments, so Rittman made a deal with her, that they would go halves on fortnightly instalments of seven hundred and fifty pounds, and she would then pay him back fortnightly instalments of three hundred and seventy-five pounds afterwards.

'The only thing is, I'd have thought it had all been paid back by now,' she said.

So now I knew. Mum told me all about Mr Rittman, how he was on Jobseekers Allowance and lived down Goldcroft Road, the same as Mr Legg. I asked her how he'd got involved.

'He knew I couldn't make the repayments, so he'd offered to help,' Mum explained. 'Patrick trusts him, so I trusted him. He was as friendly about it as he could be, but warned me that even though me and Patrick were friends, he knew Patrick wasn't the type of person you messed with.'

This made me feel a bit uncomfortable, but Mum reassured me that it was okay, as long as she kept repaying the debts. But I couldn't help wondering if what Mr Rittman had said about Mr Legg not being someone to be trifled with was just his way bribing her into letting him get involved.

She'd kept it from both me and Dad. He'd come in to the kitchen at that point.

'Have fun shopping with the girls?' he asked, walking over to the kettle to re-boil it.

'I did,' I said, feeling pleased with my new t-shirts again. 'I bought some stuff I liked.'

'You can show me and your father,' said Mum.

Mum had perked up when I showed her and Dad my new tops, and she said she was happy that I had a good day. I felt no shame in showing them the earrings and eye shadow, as they needed never know I'd actually nicked them, and I definitely wasn't going to let them know that.

Saturday 2nd July 2011

I did it again the next time I went shopping with the girls. Luckily I'd brought a bigger bag with me when I met with them. I hadn't intended on going shoplifting again, but I'd taken a fancy to more items than I could afford. We didn't go into a lot of shops that had clothes or jewellery I was interested in, until we reached Claire's Accessories. They had exactly the sort of accessories I could wear with my new t-shirts! I found some pairs of doughnut studs, unicorn drops, metallic rainbow hoops, silver cross studs, silver diamante skull studs, silver 3D pyramid studs, neon star confetti shaker drop earrings, heart shaped USA flag studs, gold plated cubic zirconium and star cluster studs, glittery ice cream cone drops and silver heart shaped hoops.

Sadly I had nowhere near enough money to buy all of them. I couldn't possibly pick between them. I looked around, nervously. There was another customer looking at the hair accessories, nearby. I couldn't risk trying anything in front of that lady, in case she looked round and saw and ratted me out. I pretended to be looking at the earrings, glancing at the lady, every now and then, to see what she was doing. I saw her move slightly further away, so I took my chance. After double-checking no one else was nearby, I grabbed all the earrings I wanted, and plunged them into my handbag.

'Ruby-lynn, come and look at these chokers,' Natalie called me. 'I reckon they'd be your thing.'

I walked over to where Natalie was looking at the variety of chokers. A cord choker with interchangeable pendants caught my eye. I picked it up and looked at it. I reckoned it would go brilliantly with the Kiss t-shirt I'd just bought.

I walked away to look somewhere else, so Natalie wouldn't see me slip it into my bag, then I looked at the pendants. I spotted a rainbow heart pendant, which I'd grabbed and put in my bag.

I then moved onto the bracelets. I looked at the bangles and cuffs, but I couldn't find any I liked. I began looking at the stretch bracelets, and found a pink and black spiked and round bead bracelet, so into my bag it went. I also found the same one in black and white, so grabbed that one, too. In went a purple cord bracelet with a star charm, set of six gold nose studs with a rhinestone of a different colour each, a pair of black and neon stripe legwarmers, some long hot pink, fishnet arm warmers and a trio of gold rings, one with the letters, 'OMG,' one with a portion of fast food fries, and one with the same heart as the heart pendant I'd just swiped. All the while, I was on my guard, waiting to hear the sound of someone sternly clearing their throat from behind me, and then I would turn to see one of the shop assistants stood there, arms folded, wearing a reproving facial expression. But it didn't happen.

I left the shop with Lizzy, Natalie and Scarlet, surprised I got away with it again.

We stopped for lunch at Subway. Scarlet and Natalie were before me in the queue, so I looked at the board to decide what I wanted. I saw Lizzy sidle up to me out of the corner of my eye.

'You okay?' she asked. I looked round at Lizzy, nodded, and then carried on looking at the board.

'I know how things have been since you and Fred broke up, and that it's not just because of that,' Lizzy said.

'I've been really frustrated, because of Mum having to borrow most of my money,' I told her.

'Come round mine after we've finished here,' said Lizzy. 'I noticed you haven't bought anything today. I could guess that you must've been feeling envious of us because of the stuff we'd bought and that. I've got some clothes that I don't want, and they would defo be your thing. If you come round mine and look at them to see if you want any of them, you can have anything you want out of that stuff.'

I felt horribly guilty that Lizzy thought I hadn't bought anything, which I hadn't, strictly speaking, but also, she didn't know I had anything, whether I'd paid for it or not. I knew it was dishonest of me to play up to this and take Lizzy up on her offer, but I couldn't help it. It was a very generous offer, and I didn't have any plans, so I accepted at once. What sort of clothes was Lizzy chucking out? I hoped she'd be right in saying they were *my* style. Mine and Lizzy's styles could only be more different from each other's if I was a Goth and she was a chav. For a start, Lizzy's style is slightly girlier than mine and I go for bright, vibrant colours, whereas Lizzy prefers pastels and neutral colours. I'd be surprised if even the clothes Lizzy was getting rid of would be something I'd wear.

When it was my turn, I ordered a six-inch tuna sub with mayonnaise, cucumber, tomatoes, red onions, lettuce, and green peppers with a packet of tangy cheese flavoured Doritos and a cup of Pepsi Max. I waited for Lizzy to buy her order, and then we both sat opposite Scarlet and Natalie at the table they had bagged. The two of them were already showing each other their new clothes, jewellery, accessories and make-up.

'Oh, nice of you both to wait for us!' Lizzy had said, sarcastically, when she and I had sat down.

'Why don't we wait until after we've eaten?' I asked. Scarlet agreed, since she said she was starving. We tucked into our sub sandwiches. I savoured the heavenly taste of mine. Scrumptious! I got really messy with it though.

'Enjoy your lunch, Ruby-lynn?' Scarlet joked, as I tried to wipe mayonnaise out of the tips of my hair.

After we finished our lunches, Lizzy, Natalie and Scarlet began showing each other their clothes. Natalie picked up on the fact that I hadn't bought anything.

'I said she could come round mine so she could have a look at the stuff I'm throwing out,' Lizzy told her and Scarlet.

'Oh, yeah, that stuff that used to be your thing but now you've ditched it for more girly stuff,' said Scarlet.

'So how much stuff are you getting rid of?' I wanted to know.

'Loads of it,' said Lizzy. 'If you don't want any of it, I can always sell it.'

I looked forward to seeing what Lizzy had to offer. It was very generous of her to offer to give me some of her old clothes.

After we left, me and Lizzy caught the bus back to Lizzy's place. This was only the third time I'd been round hers since becoming her friend.

When we arrived, Mrs Graham made us both a drink of orange and passion fruit J2Os mixed with white grape and elderflower Schloers. I'd tried J2Os and Schloers, but never heard of mixing the two together.

'Other people find it bizarre,' Lizzy told me. 'I really don't get how it's weird. They taste really nice together and it's a really good idea I came up with.'

I took a sip of my drink. It tasted absolutely divine.

'Yeah, it is so nice, and definitely not weird,' I said. 'Anyone who thinks it's weird is not only weird themselves but fucking stupid.'

Lizzy smiled.

Me and Lizzy took our drinks upstairs, but instead of going to Lizzy's room, we went to Alistair's old room, where there were almost a dozen big bags. And it was mine for the taking? I was stunned.

'These are all the clothes you're getting rid of?' I said.

'Uh huh,' said Lizzy, opening the nearest bag. 'I think this is the bag with the ones I reckon you'll be interested in.'

She stuck her hand in the bag and pulled out a pair of sky blue jeans. A pair of jeans to go with my t-shirts. Perfect!

'Obviously you'll have to try on everything you want, to make sure it fits,' said Lizzy. I said I'd put everything I liked the look of on a pile for me to try on. Lizzy let me rummage through the bag for more clothes I wanted. I found a yellow vest with armholes that came down to the waist, and black writing saying, 'LOVE ME FOREVER (AND A DAY).' This one was going on the pile.

The next item of clothing was another vest top, white with a lilac and white picture of a girl wearing a strappy checker top and large sunglasses, but this one wasn't my cup of tea. I put it aside, and then carried on looking. I found a pair of shamrock green trousers. I was definitely having these. I put them with the top and the other jeans. I also looked at another top with waist-low armholes. It was white with a triangle of bright colours and the words, 'BERMUDA TRIANGLE,' but I wasn't fussed about this one either, so it was another no-go. I chose some more pairs of jeans; yellow, deep pink, lime green. I couldn't find any more tops I wanted, but that didn't matter, I was more interested in finding trousers, shorts and skirts to wear with the masses of tops I had.

I tried on all my chosen clothes and fitted every one of them.

Lizzy rummaged in another bag, and then pulled out three bandeaus; one red, one black and one grey, and handed them to me.

'These are to wear under the yellow top,' she said. 'Don't want to be showing off the side of your bra underneath it, do you?' she added with a smirk. I smiled back.

'Thanks Lizzy,' I said, and I gave her a hug.

Lizzy got a plastic bag out of the hall cupboard for me to put all of the clothes in.

We went back downstairs to have another drink, afterwards.

'All those clothes are so different to what you wear now,' I said. 'I find it so hard to believe you were ever into that stuff.'

'Ah, well, people's styles change from time to time,' said Lizzy.

'I used to go for the trendy style, with more monochrome clothes thrown in,' I admitted. ' I used to specialise in spots and stripes. And that was before I dyed my hair pink. My hair was light brown then, my natural colour.'

Lizzy looked up for five seconds, tilting her head, and then said, 'I'm trying to imagine you with light brown hair and black and white stripy clothes.'

We both laughed.

After we finished our drinks, I caught the number five zero three bus back to town afterwards and, because it was a warm, sunny day, I wanted to make the most of it, rather than getting the bus so I walked the rest of the way back home. I was walking up Rodwell Road, passing the turn to Longfield Road, and approaching the turning to Elwell Manor Gardens, when a man with a Mohican stepped out in front of me.

'Alright, good looking?' he drawled, smirking. Immediately, I felt uneasy. I knew he was going to try something on with me.

'Leave me alone,' I mumbled, trying to dodge past him, but he dodged too.

'I've heard a lot about you,' he went on, 'and your sexy friend, Natalie. Such a naughty girl she was, running off from her boyfriend, getting the filth onto him.'

I scowled at him. Natalie was escaping from sexual exploitation. V wasn't her boyfriend. He just made her think that so she'd trust him.

'Just stay away from all of us!' I growled, trying to push past the man, but he told me I wasn't going anywhere. What was I going to do? I'd have no choice but to turn around and run back. I began running back down Rodwell Road, but a bald man came out at me from Longfield Drive. I had no way but to turn down Longfield Road. I ran down the road, but to my despair, I came up to a brick wall, a dead end! I was cornered. There was no escape. Terrified, I turned around and faced the two men. What were they going to do to me? As they came closer, the man with the Mohican pulled out a gun, and I started sobbing.

'WHAT THE FUCK DO YOU WANT?!' I screamed.

The bald man held out his hand.

'Gimme' your phone.'

I shook my head.

'You fucking give him your phone or I will blast you in the head,' snarled the man with the Mohican. I opened my bag, took out my phone, and then handed it to the bald man, who then searched my contact list.

'At least you have Natalie's number,' he said.

'What are you going to do? I asked, still weeping.

'I am going to ring her, and when she answers, I will pass it over to you and you will say exactly what I want,' sneered the bald man, 'and nothing but that, unless you want to die here and now.'

I nodded. The bald man rang Natalie's number and then put it on loudspeaker. I looked up at him, my face tear-streaked and screwed up in anger, as the man with the Mohican held the tip of the gun to the side of my head. Within seconds, I heard Natalie's voice. As the bald man mouthed to me, I began to speak, sobbing as I did so.

'Natalie, you need to come to Longfield Drive at Rodwell Road immediately. If you don't do this, V's mates have said that they are going to bang my brains out, literally and then metaphorically.'

I heard Natalie's voice sound panicky, a split second before the bald man hung up.

'You should count yourself lucky she picked up straight away,' said the man with the Mohican.

'Don't you get it?' I snivelled. 'V's been arrested, and he's never going to get let out! It's over!'

The man with the Mohican smiled.

'Well, we'll just see about that,' he said, silkily.

I felt sick. If Natalie came, would the men make her tell the police to let V go, so that he could have her back?

'What are you hoping is gonna happen when she gets here?' I sobbed. 'Are you gonna rape her here, right in front of me? Are you gonna take us both to V, and he'll sell us both for sex? Or are you gonna take her and let me go, knowing I'll be able to run off to the police -'

'You won't say a word to the police!' the man with the Mohican spat, angrily.

'Tell me what you're going to do, because I'd really like to know,' I cried. The man raised the gun and pointed it at me, narrowing his eyes, and telling me he could just kill me then if I wanted.

'Okay,' I whispered. The man lowered the gun. Seven seconds later, I saw five police officers emerge, pointing guns. One shouted, 'Drop your guns and get onto the ground!'

The man with the Mohican looked over his shoulder, and then grabbed me by the arm, dragged me forward, pointing the gun at my head and said, 'You lot put your guns down, or Miss Bubblegum Hair gets it!'

BANG!

I staggered back as the man yelled out, dropped his gun and fell to his knees, clutching his left leg. I looked down at him and saw a bullet wound in his thigh. I seized my moment. I grabbed the gun and took it up off the ground, before the bald man had a chance to pick it up, and ran to hide behind the police. Just then, I heard a siren, coming from my left. I turned my head and saw a police car driving up the sloped road. It pulled over to the kerb, all four of the doors had opened and out got two more police officers... and Fred and Natalie!

'Ruby-lynn!' they both shrieked, together, running over to me. They both gave me a hug.

'Are you okay?' Fred asked.

'I'm fine,' I said.

'We decided to call the police, the minute I had that call from you,' Natalie said as the police arrested the men.

'Yeah, and the police said they were already on it, because a resident of one of the houses down Longfield Drive had seen everything out of her window and rang the police,' Fred told me.

A short and skinny lady of about seventy, with short, untidy curls in a creased, sky blue fine knit cardigan with a grey and butter yellow paisley dress and pale grey penny loafers that were slightly scuffed at the bottoms came out of a nearby house. Her large, round, translucent rimmed glasses were hanging lop-sided on her face, like she'd fallen asleep in front of the television.

'I heard a shout so I looked out of my window to see what was the matter, and this poor young lady was being threatened by those two horrible men,' she said.

I smiled at the lady, gratefully.

The police car with the two men in it drove off, and the other car, which was parked at a distance from the scene, drove Fred, me and Natalie to our houses. Fred caught my eye. I looked round at him.

'I'm glad you're okay,' he said to me.

I nodded.

'Thanks.'

We didn't say much during the car journey. I didn't know what to do. Just the sight of Fred hurt so much. I was so angry with him for what he did, and yet I still had strong feelings for him, but he'd completely betrayed my trust in him. I sighed.

As soon as I walked in through the front door, I was approached by Mum and Dad.

'Where on Earth have you been? I would've thought you'd be home ages ago!' Mum grilled me in alarm.

I was still shocked about what had happened.

'You probably won't believe me if I told you, but some guys came over and threatened me at gunpoint,' I told her and Dad.

Both Mum and Dad looked at me, frowning.

'What men?' Dad asked. I told him and Mum that they'd been friends with the guy who'd been exploiting Natalie. Mum and Dad were horrified. Mum clapped both her hands to her mouth in horror.

'It's okay, they've been arrested,' I reassured them. They ushered me to the kitchen. Mum made me a cup of hot chocolate and Dad sat down with me at the table and asked what was going to happen next, but I didn't know. Something else then just occurred to me.

'There are more of them out there,' I said, 'but I like to think that now they know that V and two of the gang have been arrested, they'll know to watch their backs, because the police are hot on their tail.'

Dad sighed and told me to be careful.

I looked down, and drank my hot chocolate. I hoped I was right. If they knew that threatening one of Natalie's friends had only got another two of them done by the police, that would hopefully discourage the rest of them from trying the same thing again. But what if they came up with something smarter, in a way that they won't get into trouble, and would be able to worm V and the two men out of custody? Although, deep down, I knew that didn't seem likely.

Saturday 9th July 2011

I heard more about it when I went shopping with the girls again. We'd started the day with a coffee in Costa, and Natalie said that the men who were still free had been arrested, because it turned out Lizzy had been searching the internet for the video, found it and shown it to Fred, the very last time she'd come round, and they'd reported it to the police, who had recognised the men in the video, after their previous histories.

'Told you, didn't I?' Lizzy said, superiorly. 'The victim always wins in the end, whenever they take the right actions.'

'Me and Fred had got into a row about the call that V's mates made you make, because I thought that Fred was just going to hand me over, Natalie said, 'but Fred told me that he wasn't planning on doing that, but he wasn't going to let the men do such sick things to you, either.'

'Those two guys threatened me down a road that had a row of houses with residents on either side of them!' I said. 'Did they not stop to think that someone might have seen and heard everything and told the police? Which actually did happen! They probably thought they'd be able to hold any residents that got involved at gun point.'

'I just wish I never got myself into that position in the first place,' said Natalie. 'I'm so sorry I didn't listen to you girls before.'

'We can't blame you for being blinded by love,' Scarlet told Natalie. 'At least it's over, now.'

'How's your mum been?' Lizzy asked, so I began telling her I'd found out why Mum was so low on money.

'That does sound a bit dodgy, if your mum still hasn't paid back all the money, even though she should've by now,' Lizzy agreed

'At least I sort of know what's going on now,' I said.

When we finished our drinks, we began our shopping in St Mary Street. I hadn't bought anything so far, nor had I stolen anything.

It was when we were in T.K Maxx that I'd found something I actually fancied. I was looking at the shoes and come across a pair I was keen on - white with black stars - when I seized hold of them and rammed them into my shopping bag.

But what I didn't know was there had been a security guard standing nearby, and I hadn't seen him until I'd caught his eye as I put the shoes in the bag. I froze for a split second, and then ran. I ran towards the door. I heard Scarlet shout my name, sounding confused, as I legged it out of the shop, setting off the alarms as I went because I hadn't stopped to think there was probably a tag attached to the shoes.

I ran up New Bond Street, not daring to stop. I looked over my shoulder as I continued running, and saw the security guard chasing after me, speaking into his walkie-talkie.

I ran up towards the seafront, and then stopped, looked around in a panic, deciding which way to go next, and then turned right and ran past the New Vic and towards the Alexandra Gardens. The guard was still running after me. I ran past the Alexandra Gardens, and then reached Custom House Quay, where I turned right and ran along the harbour, which was crowded. I knocked into people and almost collided with a small child I could easily have fallen right over. His irritable mother shouted after me, but I couldn't stop. I ran towards the town bridge. I got nearer and nearer to the bridge, I caught sight of another security guard, hurtling down the steps. There was no way out. It was too late to turn off anywhere and I couldn't go back because of the guard who was chasing me.

Wait a minute, my one hope was running under the bridge, before the other guard made it to the bottom of the stairs.

No such luck. I was caught.

'Slow down there, young madam,' said the guard who had come down the steps and headed me off. 'How about we go back to T.K Maxx, eh?'

And I was marched down St Thomas Street. People were staring, pointing and muttering in disgusted voices about what a disgrace it was. I couldn't believe it was really happening to me, people talking about me with such outrage.

I was brought back into T.K Maxx. Lizzy, Natalie and Scarlet were still there, stood watching, with puzzled and concerned expressions on their faces.

Lizzy had stepped forward and said, 'Ruby-lynn? What's going on?'

But one of the guards raised his arm, motioning Lizzy to back away, and said, 'Stand back please, ma'am.'

I was brought to a back room, where I was asked to hand over anything I'd taken. Trembling, I slowly took the trainers out of my bag and handed them to the security guard. The next few events went by in a blur. The police were called, and I was arrested and taken to the station. Mum was called and was told that I was going to be cautioned.

I sat in the car in silence as Mum drove me home. She didn't say anything either. I was dreading the arrival home. I knew Mum would have kittens - no, *lion cubs* - over the whole thing.

'I cannot believe that you would do such a *stupid thing*!' she'd said, furiously, the second we came in through the front door. 'What the hell was going through your mind? Bloody shoplifting!'

I looked at Mum, guiltily.

'I'm sorry, Mum,' I mumbled.

'Well, so you should be!' Mum spat. 'I am so ashamed of you. I know it's because of all the money I've been borrowing off of you, but honestly! Bloody shoplifting, you stupid girl!'

But Dad came in and told her not to call me stupid. Mum marched up the stairs, muttering about how this was the last thing she needed.

'I know your mother was a bit sharp, pet, but do you have any idea how shocked we were when we received a phone call from the police, saying you'd been arrested for shoplifting?' said Dad.

I sighed.

'I know I shouldn't have done it,' I told Dad, 'but I am so fed up of being left with hardly any money!'

I really wanted to tell Dad why Mum was constantly skint, now I knew, but I didn't know if it was my place.

It was probably best to avoid Mum until she'd calmed down. I went to my room. I had a text from Scarlet, asking me to call her. I remembered she, Natalie and Lizzy had seen what happened and were worried.

I called Scarlet. It rang for nine seconds before she answered.

'Ruby-lynn! What the hell happened?' she cried.

I didn't want to, but I had to tell her I'd been shoplifting every time we went shopping, because I'd felt so jealous of them. I thought Scarlet would be horrified and angry but it wasn't what I expected. She'd said, 'Oh my God, Ruby-lynn!' in a tone that sounded slightly sympathetic, but still shocked at the same time.

'I know,' I agreed. 'I feel really guilty for Lizzy as well. She invited me round her house, last Saturday, specifically to have a look at the clothes she was getting rid of, to see if I wanted any, under the impression that I hadn't bought anything, when I'd been stealing stuff out of Claire's Accessories!'

Scarlet sighed.

'Even though you've been dishonest to let Lizzy think you didn't get anything that day, Lizzy will probably understand why you did it. But you need to get to the bottom of what's going on with the debt your mum is in, as that's naturally the reason you've been stealing, and something definitely isn't right.'

No need for her to tell me that.

A development reared its head the very next day. Mum had calmed down after the shoplifting incident, though she was still a bit huffy with me. She'd got me to drop off Rittman's repayments that day. Mum had given me the address, so I went round to Rittman's house. It was a large, semi-detached house. There was a navy blue Jaguar X-Type parked in the driveway.

I crossed the drive to the front door and rang the bell. Mr Rittman answered the door. I had trouble fighting back my laughter when I saw him. He had a bushy black handlebar moustache, and his hair was backcombed and gelled back. He looked like such a twonk!

He looked puzzled to see me at the door. He wasn't to know I was the daughter of the woman he'd been supposedly helping to repay a debt.

'Can I help you?' he asked.

'My name is Ruby-lynn West,' I said.

'Ah, yes, Rubianne's daughter,' he said, letting me in, 'come in, come in.'

He led me through to the dining room. As I walked past the lounge, I caught a glimpse of the fifty-five inch screen T.V, and then as I glanced through another door, I saw a black treadmill, and a Panasonic Hi-fi system. I recognised it at once, because Scarlet's mum and stepdad have the exact same one, and when I admired it the first time I saw it, Mr Sparks said that it had cost one hundred and seventy-nine pounds and ninety-seven pence.

I followed Mr Rittman through the orange dining room with its dark wood and black marble fireplace and white gold Acer Chromebook on the glass desk in the alcove to the left of the fireplace. In the other alcove was a large black music system with a speaker either side.

I went into the kitchen after Mr Rittman.

'I guess you've seen my new car in the drive, ' he said, 'cost me a flipping fortune, it did, but not bad for a second hand car. I believe you have come with the money to be repaid?'

I nodded and handed him the envelope that I'd brought the money in. As Rittman took the envelope from me, I noticed he was wearing a gold Armani watch.

Rittman took the money over to the breakfast bar, sat down, and took it out of the envelope.

As he counted it, I looked around the kitchen. There was a thirty-two inch screen T.V mounted on the wall above the breakfast bar. I saw a shiny black iPhone on the worktop, next to an iPad.

Rittman finished counting, thanked me, told me to tell my mum he'd give her a call to arrange when the next instalment needed paying, because he was taking a week's holiday in Rhodes in Greece and staying in the Elakati Luxury Boutique Hotel for seven nights, and then he showed me out.

So he had a new Jaguar, an Armani watch, two expensive stereos, two expensive TVs, a gold Acer laptop, a treadmill, an iPhone, an iPad and was going on a seven night Greek holiday in what sounded like a very expensive hotel, all of that despite him being on the dole? How did he have enough money for all of that? If I didn't know any better, I'd have said he'd been profiting from the loan.

I told Mum this, but Mum wouldn't believe it, though she was easily confused.

'But Mum, how can someone on the dole afford such luxuries?' I argued. 'After all, you were the one who was mystified as to how you still could not have paid back all the money you'd owed!'

'What money?'

I turned round. Dad stood, framed, in the door way to the lounge. Mum froze. Dad gave her a piercing look.

'Rubianne, *what money*?' he repeated, impatiently. I looked down at Mum. Mum looked down at her lap and sighed. I knew what that meant.

'I borrowed some money, and there's a bloke that's been helping me pay it back,' she said.

'What bloke?!' shouted Dad. I thought it probably best to leave the room at that point, as I scented a row coming on.

I'd gone to my room and shut the door, but I could still hear Dad's angry voice, and Mum's scared, upset, apologetic voice. Dad was enraged that his wife had secretly borrowed money from someone, and trusted a stranger to help her.

I was scared too. What if Dad then got angry with me for not telling him? What was I going to do?

However, it came to a head when me and Scarlet were at the Sparks' house on Monday. Mrs Sparks had been cleaning out the freezer and had offered me the food. To say that I was touched would've been the understatement of the decade.

I brought home the food, and when Mum saw it, she was just as touched, and then she sighed and said, 'This can't go on.'

'What are you going to do?' I asked. Mum asked to clarify what I'd suspected, and I repeated that there was no way Rittman could afford to live such a swanky lifestyle if he was on J.S.A.

'He was wearing an Armani wristwatch!' I told Mum. But it was when I told her about the holiday in Greece that really threw her.

'There is no way somebody on the dole could afford a holiday like *that*!' she agreed, before she called the police.

When the two police constables arrived, Mum explained that she'd wanted to buy me a new T.V, but it had cost five thousand, two hundred and fifty pounds, so she'd borrowed it from a man she knew. She was then unable to make the repayments, so she went halves on instalments with one of the man's neighbours, with the agreement that she would then pay him back in instalments after the man she'd borrowed from had all the money back that he'd lent to her.

'How much were these instalments, may I ask?' asked one of the constables, P.C McGuinness. Mum told them it was fortnightly instalments of seven hundred and fifty pounds, split into three hundred and seventy five pounds, and then P.C McGuinness asked her how long she'd been paying back the instalments.

'Since the start of September,' Mum said.

'Hmmm,' muttered the other constable, Bennett, suspiciously, 'that would've been twenty-two payments. Hang on a second.'

P.C Bennett did some scribbling in his notebook. I wasn't sure what he was writing, but after a couple of minutes he looked up at me, Mum and P.C McGuinness, and said, 'Five thousand, two hundred and fifty divided by seven hundred and fifty is seven so...' P.C Bennett began counting something, using his fingertips, looking up, thoughtfully, narrowing his eyes, and then said, 'so all the money should've been paid back around December, so unless you're now just paying him back, and he just hasn't told you, then I would say he's definitely profiting from the loan.'

'That's what I thought,' I said. 'He's on J.S.A but drives a Jaguar and wears a gold Armani wristwatch. And those are just two of the things he said he had, that you shouldn't be spending your money on, when you're on J.S.A. He said he was going to stay in a Boutique hotel in Greece.'

P.C McGuinness asked Mum if she had Rittman's address, so P.C Bennett wrote it down in his notebook as Mum said it. P.C McGuinness then asked Mum if she knew the name and address of the man who she'd borrowed the money from, so she gave him those details.

'Thank you for your time, ma'am,' he said, as he and P.C Bennett prepared to leave. 'I will be in touch.'

Mum closed the front door behind the two constables after they exited, and then turned to face me.

'So, what happens now?' I asked.

'Well, obviously, they needed the names and addresses so they could go round and speak to Patrick and Mr Rittman, especially if Mr Rittman's planning to leave the country,' said Mum.

'Do you think the guy who lent you the money knows he's been profiting?' I asked,

'I doubt it,' Mum said. 'I'm sorry I got so ratty with you about the shoplifting. I know how fed up you must've been, not that that excused what you did, but I was just stressed about all of this, and then you get arrested. I'm just so glad you were only given a caution. And from now on, I'm only going to borrow the money from a reliable source.'

I gave my mum a hug. Mum gave me a kiss, and then went back to the lounge.

On Tuesday, we'd received the news that Rittman had been arrested. It turned out that Mr Legg had been led to believe that he was getting his money back in fortnightly instalments of one hundred and eighty-seven pounds and fifty pence, and had no idea that Mum had been tricked into going halves on instalments of seven hundred and fifty pounds. Mr Rittman had also hoped that when Mr Legg had all his money back, Mum would start paying the agreed fortnightly three hundred and seventy-five pounds she supposedly owed him, not knowing that Rittman had, not only taken back the three hundred and seventy-five pounds he'd put towards the seven hundred and fifty pound repayments, but half of the three hundred and seventy-five pounds Mum had put towards the repayments, giving him a fortnightly profit of one hundred and eighty-seven pounds and fifty pence, the same as what Mr Legg had been getting each time. Over almost a year, Rittman had stolen four thousand, one hundred and twenty-five pounds.

Rittman was found guilty of harassment, later in the week, sentenced to fifty-one weeks in jail, and banned indefinitely from contacting us. Mum was given back four thousand pounds.

Patrick Legg said he was sorry for letting Mr Rittman get involved, that he couldn't believe he trusted him and he never should've listened to him. Mum said that she couldn't believe she listened to Mr Rittman, admitting she'd been gullible and naïve.

'I am sorry I have had to borrow so much of your money, darling,' she said to me, when Dad drove us back home.

'It's okay, it can't be helped,' I said.

'And I'm sorry to both of you for never telling you about all of this, I should've realised that you were just concerned and only wanted to help,' said Mum.

'It doesn't matter. It's over now, love' said Dad, and he was right. It *was* over. And I was more than relieved over it. Mum said she planned to pay me back every penny of the money she'd borrowed, by temporarily increasing my pocket money, which she was able to start again.

Though fifty-one weeks isn't long enough for Rittman to be in prison. He hadn't just stolen my mum's money; he'd stolen our lives too. We had to sell so much stuff, just to scrape money together, and we had hardly any money for food. And Mum had to borrow most of my earnings, leaving me with hardly any for when I wanted to go out with my friends. I will never forgive Rittman for the hardships he caused on my family.

Chapter 14:

Scarlet's Second

Saturday 16th July 2011

I'd had a difficult time of things, over the last couple of months. Tom had been dangling that Spanish girl in front of me ever since he'd stolen her off Dave. He reduced me to tears at Matt Weller's party, when he started talking about Rosa, and how sorry I would be when I saw them all over each other, having tons of fun, doing the things I had walked away from, and I had left the party, crying my eyes out. Seeing Tom and Rosa together stung like lemon juice in a paper cut. I still hadn't moved on from him. Maybe I would've done, if the bastard had just left me be. But Tom was doing this on purpose, just to punish me, make me jealous, make me miss him, make me regret ending it with him.

I'd arranged to meet the girls for coffee in Cafe Nero at eleven o'clock. Ruby-lynn in particular would have a lot to talk about.

When I entered Café Nero, I saw Lizzy sat at a table near the bay window, reading a Shout magazine.

'Hey!' I said, walking over to the table. Lizzy looked up from her magazine and saw me.

'Hiya!' she beamed, standing up and giving me a hug, before we both sat down opposite each other.

'How have things been after your split with Charlie?' I asked Lizzy.

'I'm... just fine,' she said, and she sounded rather happy.

Not what I expected. I'd have thought she'd say something like, 'Oh, it's been hard, but I'm getting there.'

Lizzy had never told me what happened after we all left the William Henry, and neither did Will, though whatever it was, I did wonder if that might have had something to do with why she was so happy?

'I wish I could say the same for me,' I sighed.

'Tom is a dick,' Lizzy said. I knew she thought I should just forget about him, but that was easier said than done.

'If he would just let me alone, I'd have moved on, but he won't stop,' I said. Lizzy rolled her eyes. I knew that Lizzy had been trying and failing to get through to Dan, Tom and Rosa, but they were impossible.

I heard the door open. I looked over at the door and saw Ruby-lynn and Natalie come in and come over to the table.

'Hi!' said Natalie, when Lizzy and I stood up to give her and Ruby-lynn a hug.

'How are you two?' said Ruby-lynn, after we'd exchanged hugs and kisses on the cheeks and she and Natalie had both seated themselves either side of Lizzy and I.

Ruby-lynn told us about the money her mum had got back after she'd been robbed. I'd been shocked when Ruby-lynn told me that her mum had suffered at the hands of a loan shark.

'All of that, just to fund his own luxurious lifestyle!' agreed Lizzy. 'Seriously, who can afford an Armani watch on J.S.A?'

'Well, you can afford it,' said Natalie. 'You just shouldn't be buying that sort of stuff if you're out of work, because you ought to be saving it for more important things, like food and bills.'

I'd been feeling awful that that was what drove Ruby-lynn to start shoplifting. I asked her how she was doing for money, and Ruby-lynn said her mum had begun to reinstate her pocket money.

Ruby-lynn then said she was going to get herself a frappucino and asked the rest of us if we wanted one too. We all accepted, so Ruby-lynn stood up to get a white chocolate and raspberry frappucino for Lizzy, a tiramisu frappe cream for Natalie, a coconut and chocolate frappucino for me and a toffee and banana one for herself.

I asked the girls what they wanted to do after we left Café Nero, and Natalie suggested going to the Alexandra Gardens.

'We could go on the carousel, there!' Lizzy squealed.

Ruby-lynn, Natalie and I looked at her, our eyebrows raised.

'What?' asked Lizzy, frowning.

I smirked, before Ruby-lynn said, 'No, actually, it might be a laugh.'

I wasn't sure about the rides in the Alexandra Gardens. They're really designed for just small children, especially the roundabout with all the cars, but then I did realise that the carousel was for all ages, but Natalie said she was thinking more about the games indoors, which I was up for, so after we finished our drinks, we left Café Nero, and started walking up New Bond Street, and along the sea front, towards the Alexandra Gardens. We saw the carousel and decided it would be a laugh to go on it, so we all bought tokens and queued up for the next ride.

'Always loved the carousel,' said Lizzy, nostalgically. 'It was my favourite ride when I was little.'

I smiled. Lizzy's a sucker for fairground rides. She enjoys days out at fairgrounds and theme parks more than nights out in clubs and bars, bless her.

Luckily we'd joined the queue shortly before the ride had begun to slow down to let everybody off, and we weren't that far from the front of the queue, either. We followed the rest of the queue onto the ride and ran round, finding ourselves each a horse.

I sat behind Natalie on the two-seater horse between Lizzy and Ruby-lynn's horses, so that all four of us were in the same row.

The ride started. As soon as it got going, it gave me an excited sort of thrill. It was fantastic!

When we got off, we went inside to have a go on some of the games. I teamed up with Ruby-lynn against Natalie and Lizzy on a game of Air Hockey, and we won.

After that, we had a go on some of the car racing games, dance games, shooting games, and other arcade games.

I was just approaching a claw crane grabber machine when I saw Dan out of the corner of my eye. No sign of Tom, but he was sure to be about. Not Rosa, though. Lizzy said she'd gone back to Spain at the end of June.

Great. Way to spoil my fun. I avoided eye contact with him, and then started searching my bag for my purse, but I could see him getting nearer and nearer.

'Hey, Scarlet!' he said, in a tone of blatantly fake surprise. 'Fancy seeing you here!'

'Yeah,' I said, not looking up at Dan, and pulling some coins out of my purse. Dan knocked into me. I dropped the coins.

'Whoops. Clumsy me,' he said, mockingly. I crouched down to pick up the coins, glaring at Dan.

'Tom's around,' he said, once I'd straightened up, 'He's hoping to go to Spain over the summer to visit his lovely, fun-loving girlfriend who's not a killjoy. Wish my one were like that. S'pose I could dump her like Tom did to you but, oh no wait, *you* dumped *him* and now he's made you regret it! See you around!'

And Dan strode off. He and Tom had already begun to get to me. Wherever I was, they would always crop up. They were both in desperate need of a hobby. At least they'd stopped making Dave's life a misery, with Rosa no longer around.

And I didn't see how or where Tom was planning to get the money to go to Spain, or where he'd stay.

I left with the other girls, before I'd had a chance to bump into him.

Lizzy said she had to take Penny for a walk on the beach tomorrow and asked if any of us fancied keeping her company. I accepted, but Ruby-lynn and Natalie had their own plans and things to do.

We all said our goodbyes and I caught the number ten bus back home to the Sparks' house. I was at my mum's place over this week, and I was to spend the next week with her, too. My dad had been away for a fortnight. He'd spent two weeks in Bradford on Avon, hosting a job search group that had been organised by Choices and Opportunities, the training charity that he works for, on a programme named Career Progress Group, as an employment advisor.

My sister, Crimson, was home from uni for the summer, having completed her second year. Her third and final year will start in September.

I went to the kitchen to make myself a cup of red bush tea with no milk. Crimson was already filling the kettle.

'Perfect, is that for making drinks?' I asked my sister. Crimson looked round and said that it was, and asked if I was having tea or coffee, and made sure there was enough water.

'Would you help me with dinner, later?' asked Crimson. 'Mum says we're having smoky Mexican chicken, tonight.'

'Sure,' I said, getting out a mug and a red bush tea bag. When the kettle had boiled, I made my cup of red bush, a cup of white coffee for Norman and three cups of tea for Crimson, Mum and Hudson, before Crimson and I brought the drinks into the lounge where Norman, Mum and Hudson were sat. I gave Norman his coffee before sitting down next to him, and then Mum asked me what I'd been up to with the girls, so I told her about my fun in the Alexandra Gardens, and going on the carousel.

'My goodness, it's been years since you've been on that carousel!' said Mum, astonished.

'Lizzy talked me into going on it,' I said.

'Well, I'm glad you had a good time,' said Crimson. I smiled.

At five o'clock, I began helping my sister with dinner. The food preparation took ten minutes. My eyes were streaming from peeling red onions, so my mum had to take over and cut them into wedges, and I greased the roasting tray and prepared some of the other ingredients.

When everything was together in the tray, Crimson heaved it into the oven and set the timer for forty minutes. Then, I helped Crimson wash up and dry up.

Mum came in and said that the food smelt very nice and that she was very pleased with her daughters, giving us both a hug and a kiss.

I went up to my room to fetch my phone charger, as my mobile battery was down to twelve percent. It beeped on my way upstairs. I looked at the screen and saw that it was Lizzy, asking if I was okay to meet at ten the next morning, so I texted back to agree on that time, went to my room, grabbed my charger, brought it back downstairs, and plugged my phone in down by the television in the lounge.

Dinner was ready at ten to six. We sat round the kitchen table and I seated myself next to Megan as Mum brought over the hot tray and placed it on the table, then filled each plate with a portion of the meal, and we helped ourselves to sour cream, salsa and guacamole.

I tucked in and enjoyed every bit of it. Whilst I'd been waiting for it to cook, my tummy had been rumbling up a storm and the smell of the food cooking had made my mouth water like mad. And it was worth all the work that had resulted in the mass of cleaning and tidying to be done after the cooking.

On Sunday, I didn't bother wearing any make-up when I went to meet Lizzy on the beach. I pulled on my plaid blouse hoodie and left the house. I caught the bus at nine and arrived at the beach quite early, so I sat on one of the blue and white wooden sheltered benches and waited for Lizzy.

Though I ended up wishing I hadn't been so early. I saw the very last two people I wanted to see approaching; Dan and Tom. I looked away again, as I'd done so in the arcade yesterday, praying they wouldn't recognise me. I pulled up my hood, in case they had at least recognised me by my hair.

But it was too late. They'd already seen.

'Oy!' I heard Dan shout. I didn't look at them, hoping I could pretend to be a stranger they'd mistaken for me, but it didn't work. Both of them had come over and stood in front of me, so that they could see my face rather clearly, though I was looking down.

'Dan said he saw you in the Ally G yesterday,' said Tom. 'Enjoying yourself... having the time of your life...'

I sighed.

'What is it, you're much happier without me, yeah?' said Tom. I gritted my teeth and looked up at him.

'Yes, I am,' I said, grimly. Dan walked closer to me so that he was stood right in front of me.

'That's not what it looks like, most of the time,' he said.

'Leave me alone,' I told the two of them.

'We're not finished with you yet,' Dan sneered. 'You can't run from this, you know. Not you... not Lizzy... not Fred, nor Jesse, or that twat Dave.'

I looked down at my lap. Why were they doing this?

Dan began to walk off, warning me not to forget, but then Tom hung back and told Dan to go on and he would catch up. He then sat next to me, moving right up close to me.

'You know, we could've avoided this,' he sneered. 'You dumped me, and then didn't want to know when I tried to apologise, and now you have to see me being the happiest I have ever been with Rosa.'

I felt tears welling up in my eyes. I knew I mustn't cry in front of Tom, but he was being utterly vile to me.

'What's that? Do I see your eyes going all wet and shiny?' Tom taunted.

I didn't know what to do. I hated Tom and Dan so much. And I didn't even know that it was possible for someone to be this stubborn.

'What are you doing?' said an angry voice. I looked up. It was Lizzy, stood with Penny at her side.

Tom stood and straightened up, and then said, 'I'm just reminding her what's what.'

But Lizzy gave an annoyed groan and said, 'Look, Tom, you've told her, now please give it a rest!'

Tom marched over to Lizzy, faced her defiantly, and said, '*I* should give it a rest?'

'Yes. You should,' said Lizzy.

Tom looked over his shoulder at Dan, who was stood watching, and shouted, 'Oy, do you hear that, Dan? She thinks we should give it a rest!'

He and Dan laughed. Lizzy gave Tom an evil look, her mouth very thin.

'Tom, please don't start on her, I get it,' I said.

'You heard her,' said Lizzy. 'Just fucking go, you're not wanted here.'

'The beach is public property, and I have the same right to be there as you, Scarlet and your dog.'

Lizzy glared at Tom, her mouth thinner yet.

'I think you both have forgotten, *I'm* the victim here!' Tom growled. 'I *was* actually sorry, and then she broke my heart, when she could've forgiven me.'

I stood up and marched over to him.

'You do know that you can't keep it going with Rosa,' I said. 'You'll have to split with her, and then what will you do? Where do you plan on getting the money to visit her, hmmm? Where in Madrid will you stay?'

Tom tried to smack me, but thankfully, I was too quick for him, and grabbed his wrist to stop his palm striking against my cheek. I then slapped him round the face, as a punishment for trying to hit a girl when he was a boy.

Tom grabbed me by the scruff of my neck.

'I'm gonna make you pay for that!' he shouted, dragging me down onto the beach and over to the water.

'GET OFF!' I shrieked, angrily. I could see Lizzy running down to us to pull Tom off. Penny was barking and growling at Tom. Dan came over and grabbed Lizzy by the shoulders of her top to stop her. I was screaming at Tom to get off.

'Shut that dog up!' Dan shouted.

'Get off me, Dan!' Lizzy yelled. 'Tom, get off of Scarlet, right now!'

'Not 'til I've taught her some manners!' Tom shouted. 'It's rude to hit people!'

I did the only thing to make Tom release me, and stamped hard on his foot. I felt Tom let go of my hair, just as he was about to dunk my head in the sea, and hopped backwards, yelling, clutching his right foot. I then grabbed the back of his hoodie, and shoved him into the water.

'OY!' Dan roared, throwing Lizzy down onto the sand and running at me. I reacted fast and crouched down, making him trip and go flying over me, into the water.

Lizzy stood up, walked over to the boys, and faced them both, defiantly. They both stood up and walked over to her.

'I'm going to say this loud and clear, and I will *not* say it again, so you'd better listen good and proper' she said to them. 'You and Scarlet are not together any more and never will be, whether you like it or not, so both of you stay away from me, her, Fred, Jesse and Dave, and let him and Scarlet move on from you and Rosa, because if you don't, believe me when I tell you, there will be hell to pay.'

'Oh yeah?' Tom said. 'Well, what are you gonna do?'

'I'll be having words with, not just Alistair and Fraser, but Scarlet's stepbrother, Norman, from her mum's new family, and they'll be after you and Dan,' Lizzy warned him. 'And you two could combine your strengths and it wouldn't be a match for just one of them, so imagine what all three them could do if they had each other to help, and none of them are cowards or pacifists, so you wanna think very carefully next time you think of torturing Scarlet and Dave about how you stole Rosa off of Dave and how it's somehow Scarlet's fault that Rosa's having fun times with you when she isn't.'

Tom looked from me to Lizzy. I could tell he knew that what Lizzy said about setting Alistair, Fraser and Norman on him was more than just a threat. It was a solemn promise.

He stalked off. Lizzy had won that argument. But I couldn't hold it in any longer, and broke down into fresh tears.

'You can't let them drag you down,' said Lizzy.

'The boys are everywhere I go and they won't give it up,' I snivelled.

'Well, now they know they could get beaten up by my brothers and your stepbrother if they don't stay away, they'll have no choice but to back down and forfeit the war, either that or something very bad will happen, and they will end up wishing they hadn't been so stupid,' Lizzy promised.

'I guess I should just start trying to act like I don't care,' I said, wiping my tears, realising that Dan and Tom could see it was getting to me, which was why they kept doing it.

'Dave could've done with following the same advice,' Lizzy pointed out, 'but hopefully Dan and Tom will get their comeuppance.'

I did like to think that would happen, as they both deserved it.

'They don't even fancy Rosa,' said Lizzy, pulling a small plastic bag out of her pocket. 'They're just trying to get back at you and Dave.'

Well, it was working. But I heard that Rosa hadn't handled it brilliantly.

'OH MY FUCKING GOD!' Lizzy suddenly shrieked. She stood up and came running over to me, the fingers of her right hand covered in dog poo. Blurgh! It turned out that the bag that Lizzy had used had a big hole in it, and she'd got poo all over her hand.

'Oh *gross!*' I screamed. Lizzy ran to the nearest bin to chuck away the bag, and then over to the sea to frantically rinse the poo off.

'Omigod, omigod, omigod, it's so gross!' she cried, gagging. 'And it fucking stinks!'

I said Lizzy needed to get to the nearest toilet immediately, to properly wash her hands.

I waited outside the ladies' toilets at Bond Street for Lizzy, taking charge of Penny's lead, whilst Lizzy spent about fifteen minutes trying to completely wash her hands.

'I'll check all the bags I bring with me every time I take Penny out, from now on,' she said, grumpily, when she finally emerged from the toilets, sauntering down the steps. Penny looked up at her, with her big puppy dog eyes.

'Sorry if I offended you, Penelope,' Lizzy said.

'Do you have any more bags in your pocket?' I asked. Lizzy said she had one more, so we went back down to the beach, over by the pavilion, to carry on walking Penny. Lizzy had brought a ball thrower with her, so she and I took turns throwing the ball for Penny to fetch.

I enjoyed watching Penny splashing around in the sea. I love dogs. I'm actually hoping to get one myself at some point, preferably a Yorkshire terrier.

'I never asked, have you been okay since your split with Charlie?'

Lizzy took a deep breath and said, 'Well, I thought it would be hard and that I'd never get over him, given how much I liked him and how long I'd felt that way for, but I'm surprised at how little I miss him now. I mean, I still haven't completely moved on, but I don't know I if miss him quite so much, now. Though I don't want to start dating anyone else just yet.'

Normally I wouldn't have asked something like this, since it wasn't really any of my business, but for the sake of Lizzy's best interests, I thought I should say, 'So nothing happened between you and Will after he met with us?'

'Well, actually, yeah, it did,' said Lizzy, bashfully. 'But afterwards, I did tell him I'd just come out of a relationship and he was really understanding that I needed to get over that, first.'

'Oh yeah, definitely,' I agreed. 'And I know having a boyfriend might seem like a top priority, but it really isn't. I know that may not be a fair comment, coming from me because I know I've always been all about the career. But there's no hurry to find a boyfriend. Just enjoy being single. You never needed Charlie, no matter how much you wanted him, and I especially don't need Tom. I'd probably enjoy being single if he would just get off my case.'

Lizzy nodded.

'Thanks, Scarlet,' she said, gratefully.

We spent a good few hours on the beach, before I went back home.

There weren't a lot of people at home. Crimson, Norman and Katie were out with friends and Hudson was out playing tennis, so it was just Mum, Megan, who was playing on the trampoline out in the garden, and baby George, who was sat on Mum's lap on one of the patio chairs. Mum asked if I had fun with Lizzy.

'Yeah. After I saw Tom,' I said. I briefly said that he'd been going on about his new girlfriend, but said nothing more than that.

'You'll find someone else,' said Mum. 'Get yourself a nice cool drink and come out and join us.'

I went to the kitchen to get myself a glass of 7Up. I probably would've been able to find someone else, if Tom would just let me move on from him and like somebody else I met. Perhaps I just needed to not think about Tom, if I ever did meet someone, and just ignore Tom whenever he showed up with Rosa, and then that would show him!

And besides, I knew didn't need to be with someone who was stupid enough to let Dan brainwash him. If there's one thing I did learn it's that you don't need a partner or even a friend who can be easily poisoned against you by a bullying tosser, because if you choose to side with a moron like that, you're just as much a villain as they are.

I sat with Mum in the garden. What else could I do to take my mind off of Tom? I knew Becky Perry was home from uni for the summer, maybe I'd have a catch up with her?

Mum asked me about Jesse's birthday, so I told her about the film we were seeing at the cinema, and that we would be going for something to eat, afterwards, and how Jesse was going to a You Me At Six concert up in Bournemouth with Matt Weller, a mate from Fleetview.

I bought Jesse his t-shirt in advance, as I wasn't sure how long it would take to arrive, and I wanted to make sure I got it in plenty of time. I still needed to wrap it up, however. I still hadn't bought him a card. Damn, why didn't I think to buy one in town either yesterday or today? Oh well.

Crimson and I had a sisterly chat before bedtime, asking how I'd been since I'd split up with Tom, so I told her how angry I was at Dan, but had decided I was done with giving them the satisfaction.

'Good on you,' said Crimson. 'They're not worth it.'

When I went to my room, I was just about to get into bed, before my phone rang. It was Fred. What did Fred need to talk to me about, that was so important that he had to disturb me, right when I was heading to bed? I picked up my phone, and answered it.

'Hello?' I said.

'Sorry, Scarlet, did I wake you?' said Fred.

'What do you want? It's late,' I sighed.

'Dan and Tom have been for another ride around in the Range Rover, he said, his voice wavering over the phone. Great. So he called me at my bedtime for that?

'Oh, big deal,' I yawned. 'So what?'

But Fred wasn't finished. I felt as though my stomach had vanished. I realised he was going to tell me that something really bad had happened.

'The-the thing is... Scarlet... well,' Fred stammered, 'they crashed and... well, Tom... he's... Tom's dead.'

My heart began thudding fast. Did I hear Fred right?

'What did you say?' I said.

'Our lot and Dave's were out with Stuart and Leslie,' Fred told me, 'and Leslie had a call from Dan, saying he and Tom crashed, and Tom was knocked unconscious because he'd hit his head badly, so Dad had called the ambulance, but when they arrived, Tom was pronounced dead.'

I couldn't believe it! I was so shocked and upset, I couldn't even think or cry. I heard Fred's voice over the phone, asking me if I was still there, and begging me to say something. But I could not say anything. I didn't know what to do. I dropped my phone onto the carpet. I started breathing heavily.

'Scarlet!' Fred shouted. But I broke down into tears. The bedroom door opened, the light clicked on, and Crimson stood in the doorway.

'Scarlet, what's wrong?' she said, rushing over.

She'd obviously seen the call screen of my phone on the floor, because she picked it up and said, 'Who are you on the phone to?'

She held the phone up to her ear. 'Hello, who is this?'

'It's Fred,' came Fred's voice.

'Fred, what the fuck -'

'I need to talk to you -

'Why is Scarlet crying her eyes out?'

I watched as Crimson listened. I then saw Crimson's eyes widen and mouth open in horror. Then Crimson asked, 'Is Stuart there? I need to talk to him!'

I watched Crimson wait, and then I waited too, whilst Crimson spoke to Stuart, asking what was going on, before she handed the phone back to me, telling me Stuart wanted to speak to me.

'Scarlet, are you okay?' he asked.

'Stuart, what's going on?' I blubbed. 'Is Tom really dead?'

'I'm afraid so,' Stuart said. 'Barry did tell Fred he should've left it to me to tell you.'

I could not believe it. I didn't want to believe it. Tom was dead. He was gone. He was never coming back. And it was all because of *Dan*!

Over the week, I went back to my same depressed self I was when Tom and I broke up, and I heard more and more about it.

On Monday, I called Lizzy so that I had someone to talk to.

'I am so sorry Scarlet,' Lizzy said. 'I know that things have been just horrible for you, and now this.'

'I really hate Dan,' I wept. 'What's happened to him?'

'Dan came out of the accident with minor injuries,' Lizzy said. God I wished it was the other way round!

'I wish Dan had been the one who'd been killed! He caused all of this!' I cried, angrily.

'You're not the only one who wishes that,' said Lizzy. 'Me, Fred, Jesse and Dave feel that Dan deserved to be the one that died, and none of us are talking to him.'

'I don't blame any of you. It's his fault.'

'And he's been grounded until the end of the summer and banned from the funeral,' Lizzy added. 'Are you coming? It's on Friday the twenty-second.'

But I didn't want to go, as I was too upset.

Friday 22nd July 2011

I stayed shut up in my room. I didn't want to see anyone. I didn't even know if I wanted to go to Jesse's party, until I remembered what Ruby-lynn told me when I felt this way about Lizzy's birthday party, about it cheering me up, but at least Tom had still been alive. But this time, Tom was gone, forever.

But I knew that I didn't want to let Jesse down, just like I didn't want to let Lizzy down the last time I was this depressed.

Mum had bought a card for me to give to Jesse when she had popped out to Tesco the next day, and I wrapped up the present and wrote in the card.

When I got up on the morning of Jesse's birthday, I decided to put on a bit of make-up, to see if that would perk me up.

I wore my red and blue watercolour patterned, three quarter length sleeved blouse with some navy blue cropped jeans, and my black sandals. I looked at myself in my standing, beech wood framed floor-length mirror, and I felt a bit better already, but that was all that could be expected.

After a breakfast of toast and marmite, I grabbed the already wrapped present and card, put them in one of my shopping bags, as they were way too big to fit into my clutch bag, and then left the house and began walking to the bus stop to catch the number ten bus into town. The film would start at eleven o'clock and I was meeting the gang in the cinema at twenty to eleven, to make time to buy the tickets and any drinks or snacks we all wanted for the film.

I arrived in Cineworld at half past ten. Dave, Fred and Natalie were already there, waiting by the Pick 'n' Mix shop.

'Hi,' I said, walking over to them.

'Hey,' said Fred, giving me a hug. I did feel a bit funny about letting Fred hug me, as I hadn't forgotten the way he'd betrayed Ruby-lynn, but he was trying to be sympathetic, so, as angry as I had been on Ruby-lynn's behalf, I couldn't find it in my heart to rebuff Fred's attempts.

The four of us started talking about what we'd bought Jesse for his birthday, until naturally our conversation had to be cut short when Jesse arrived with Ruby-lynn and Annie, not long before Lizzy arrived.

'Happy Birthday, Jesse!' Lizzy had squealed, giving him a hug.

'Yeah, Happy Birthday,' said Dave. We wanted to give him our presents there and then, but Jesse thought it best to wait until after the film, when we'd be going to the William Henry for lunch.

We all bought our tickets and I bought a large Fanta, and then we went to screen number three. I sat between Ruby-lynn and Natalie when we'd all found our seats.

The movie was two hours and three minutes. After we'd come out of the cinema at the end of the film, we walked to the William Henry.

As soon as we were seated at a long table near the bar, I went with Ruby-lynn to get a drink.

'What did you think of the movie?' I asked her.

'It wasn't too bad,' said Ruby-lynn. 'What did you think of it?'

'I kind of liked it,' I said. 'Not usually my kind of thing, to be completely honest, but it was good.'

A bartender came and asked Ruby-lynn and I what we wanted, so I ordered an Appletiser.

'Have you been okay?' Ruby-lynn asked, after she'd ordered her drink.

'I am so angry with Dan,' I said.

'We all are,' said Ruby-lynn.

'I don't want to believe that Tom has really died,' I said. 'It should've been Dan.'

'Dan's lost virtually everything,' Ruby-lynn said.

I was not arguing against that, as his best friend had died, all his other friends hated him, and his girlfriend had dumped him.

'I keep thinking that it could've been me in that accident,' I said, 'if I hadn't broken it off with Tom. And I do feel lucky that we never crashed when I was in the car.'

'You did the right thing,' Ruby-lynn reminded me.

'Though I feel that, at the same time, if I hadn't cut all ties with him, maybe Dan wouldn't have had a chance to manipulate him. He did it when Tom was upset and heartbroken, and saw him as the only friend who would stand by him,' I told Ruby-lynn.

'Scarlet, this is *not your fault.*'

I wished I could believe that as easily. I didn't say anything.

I looked over at Ruby-lynn, and saw her looking over at Fred.

'You okay?'

Ruby-lynn looked round at me. I looked over at Fred, then at Ruby-lynn again.

'You still like him, don't you?'

Ruby-lynn nodded, looking like she was only just managing not to cry.

'And there's no chance you can take him back?' I asked. That was a slightly hypocritical question, considering.

'No.'

Ruby-lynn looked over at Fred again, longingly.

'It's shit,' she said. 'He really hurt me and I don't know if I'm ever going to be able to trust him again. And what's a relationship without trust?'

'That's why I dumped Tom,' I said. 'I wasn't sure if I could trust him not to take that risk again. And look what's happened. But we'll both get through it.'

'But just the sight of him still hurts,' said Ruby-lynn. She and I hugged, and then went back to the table to join the others.

'Been waiting for you two, so I can open my presents,' said Jesse.

Jesse opened Fred's present first. It was Linkin Park's new album, "A Thousand Suns."

'Cheers, mate,' said Jesse, patting Fred on the back, and then moved onto the next present Fred had given him, which was the Uncharted game on Playstation three. I watched as Jesse unwrapped the second Paranormal Activity D.V.D and a Fall Out Boy hoodie from Natalie, the third Crysis game on P.C and a Foo Fighter's beanie hat from Lizzy, a Star Wars poster from Dave, the Guinness glasses that Ruby-lynn told me she'd bought, a Paco Rabanne perfume gift set from Annie, and finally the My Chemical Romance shirt. He seemed very over the moon about all of his presents.

I ordered a cheeseburger with bacon and chips. I was way too full up afterwards for dessert.

We said goodbye to each other and told Jesse to have a good time at the You Me At Six concert, and then I caught the number ten bus back home. Crimson and I were due to go back to our dad's that evening so, when I arrived home, I went upstairs and began to pack everything I needed to bring.

I was dreading going back there, as I knew Dan had to come home.

When Crimson and I arrived at the Harts' house and brought all our bags up to our room, we went down to the lounge and were greeted by Stuart.

'Hey,' I said. 'Where's Dan?'

'Up in his room,' said Stuart. 'He won't come down.'

I wasn't surprised.

'So, Jesse's seeing You Me At Six tonight, then?' asked Stuart, as Crimson and I sat down.

'Yep, that's right. At the old fire station in Bournemouth,' I said. I remembered that Lizzy had been to a gig there, so I told Stuart and Crimson how Lizzy had seen a boy band I can't quite remember the name of, and she had V.I.P tickets, meaning she got to meet the band before the gig.

'She even bragged how she got a hug from the bass guitarist,' I said. 'Natalie was like, "Oh, you lucky bitch!"

I heard Leslie shout up to Dan to come down for dinner.

'How long has he been like that for?' I whispered to Stuart.

'Since it happened,' Stuart whispered back.

For dinner, we all had Florentine pizza, which had a topping of tomatoes, spinach, mozzarella and Parma ham with an egg cracked over the middle, followed by apple crumble for dessert.

Wow! How I'd managed to fit it all in after the big lunch I'd had is beyond me!

I was very tired afterwards. I fell asleep almost instantly.

Tom and I are walking through a graveyard at dusk. It's cloudy and misty. We're holding hands. When we stop walking, we turn to face each other, and then Tom begins fading, until I'm completely alone.

I woke up in a cold sweat. It took me a while to realise what had just happened. I couldn't bear it. It had been a nightmare. But Tom dying in the car accident hadn't been a dream. It was real. But how was I to accept that Tom was gone forever?

It happened more over the week. I didn't want to tell anyone. Mum, Dad and Crimson were already worrying about me enough over it. I didn't want to add to it.

Wednesday 27th July 2011

I'd been so withdrawn from everything that Dad had sat me down at the kitchen table, so he could talk to me.

'I know it's been incredibly upsetting for you, pet,' he said. 'And you mustn't bottle up all your emotions.'

'I didn't want you, Mum and Crimson worrying about me anymore than you were,' I told him. Dad held my hand and said that whilst he wasn't going to pretend that he, Mum and Crimson, as well as everyone else, weren't worried, they wanted to help me.

I told him about the dreams I'd been having about Tom.

'Listen,' my dad began. 'I think maybe it would be a good idea if we were to talk to your doctor about this.'

I blinked at him.

'I'm not ill, Dad,' I said.

'I know you're not,' said Dad. 'But she'll be able to point you in the right direction for the help that you need to get through this. I know that your mother will agree that we should sort this out together as a family.'

On Thursday, Dad said that he would call my doctor at Crescent Street surgery to book me an appointment, if I went out with some of my friends.

I met with Becky in town. I went to Mario's, near the Royal Hotel with her, which perked me up a bit.

'What was he like when you were still dating?' Becky asked.

'Well, hanging out with him was never a bore,' I told her. 'He was very spontaneous. I suppose that was part of the problem. Plus he never liked to disagree with Dan.'

'Doesn't sound like a good combination, if it was going to lead to something like that.'

'I know. They were both being so reckless and Dan wouldn't see that what he was doing was wrong!'

'Sounds like his mate really poisoned him,' she said when I told her how Tom had backtracked his apology. 'But he wasn't worth it if he was going to let that happen so easily.'

I went on to tell Becky how Dan had been crashing at Tom's ever since the first ride in it because of the argument he'd had with Stuart about the trouble he'd been in with Leslie.

'I suppose he would've had to come back home now,' said Becky. 'I reckon Tom's parents obviously aren't going to want the person responsible for their son's death taking refuge under their roof.'

'They'd banned him from the funeral, as well,' I told Becky.

'I would've come to the funeral with you, to support you,' Becky said.

'I couldn't bring myself to go because I'd been so upset.'

'How are you feeling, now?'

'I have been feeling a bit better over the last couple of days, though I'd been having nightmares about him,' I said. 'But before then, I was feeling worse than I had been after I'd first broken up with him. My dad's going to call my doctor and arrange an appointment for me, so that we can discuss what to do to get the help that I need.'

'You may be referred for counselling,' Becky reckoned, 'and you may even be put on anti-depressants, if you've been depressed.'

I asked Becky what she'd been up to since coming home from uni.

'Not a lot, to be honest. Been hanging out with my cousin. We went to the Haynes Motor Museum with my sister and both our parents, that day we were meant to be meeting you, Will and your friends,' she told me, and she showed me some photos of her with her cousin Jonah, her younger sister Lauren and her parents, auntie and uncle.

'Oh yeah, how did it go when Will met some of your mates? I'm sorry again that me and Jonah couldn't make it back in time,' she said. 'I honestly thought we would. But now I'm home for the summer, I'll have plenty of time to see you, and maybe Ruby-lynn as well? Maybe the three of us could meet up and go shopping?'

I did like that, very much.

I suggested Becky should meet Lizzy and Natalie at some point, telling her I'd introduced Ruby-lynn to them, back in Autumn, and that they got on brilliantly and how I was sure Becky would too. She seemed eager to meet them some time.

'Dave, Ruby-lynn and Lizzy did get on with Will?' Becky asked.

'Yes, all three of them got on just fine with him,' I told her, my mood brightening ever so slightly.

'The last time we were round Jonah's place, Will said he enjoyed meeting them, ' Becky said. 'He said there was one girl in particular who he hit it off with.'

'Oh yes,' I said, remembering what had gone on between him and Lizzy. 'What did Will actually say?'

'He just said he'd met a girl he liked, mentioning that she was someone he'd met before and they really hit it off,' she told me.

So Will didn't tell anyone anything happened, then? Well, that proved he was definitely a gentleman. He didn't hide that he liked Lizzy, but he didn't go blabbing about whatever they got up to after we left Wetherspoon's.

I cheered up as I talked to Becky. When I went home that afternoon, and went into the lounge, I was surprised to see Dan in there.

'So you've finally emerged from your hiding place?' I said to him.

'Yeah,' he said.

'Well, I've got nothing to say to you, you're the reason Tom died!' I snapped.

'You have to hear me out!'

At first, I refused, thinking Dan was going to beg for my forgiveness, which I was adamant he was not getting, but it wasn't what I expected.

I agreed to listen to him, eventually, and then I sat down.

'Okay,' said Dan, calmly. 'I am going to go to the police.'

I frowned at him. Go to the police and tell them what? I told Dan to go on.

'I'm seeing them tomorrow, and I am going to tell them how I got the car,' he carried on. 'And I will be completely honest.'

I stared at him. Did he just say he was going to give himself up to the police?

'Dan...' I began.

'It's all my fault, and all I can do now is own up to it, accept responsibility, and face the consequences,' he told me.

I couldn't believe this. Yes, he deserved to go down for it, but I never expected him to change his tune. I wouldn't have been surprised if he'd lied to get out of it, and denied having any involvement in it.

'I know you're surprised,' said Dan. 'But Tom's my friend, and I will never forgive myself for getting him into this. And you were all right. I poisoned him against you all. I regret every bit of it and I want to do the right thing, even if it means getting sent to jail. And none of you have to forgive me, because I know I don't deserve it. I'm just here to tell you what I'm going to do.'

I nodded, and then said, 'Okay.'

Dan walked out of the lounge. I stayed sitting, and thought about all of this.

Dan was right. I did not have to forgive him, because what he did was unforgivable. I knew that if I would be able to find it in my heart to forgive him at all, it wouldn't be for a very long time, yet.

Even though I knew he was going to accept the punishment he deserved, I also knew it could never put a stop to the nightmares I'd been having. But I hoped that whatever my doctor recommended for me would help with that.

I suddenly remembered that my dad said he was going to book me an appointment with my G.P. I looked in the kitchen to see if he was in there, and then I looked in the utility room. I caught sight of him through the door out onto the patio area. He was sat at the table, reading the paper. I went outside.

He must've heard the door creak open and someone coming out, because he looked up to see who it was.

'Hi, love,' he said.

'Hi,' I said, walking over to Dad and sitting down opposite him.

Dad put down his paper, and said, 'I've rung the surgery about booking an appointment. Is tomorrow at half past three okay?'

'That time is fine.'

'Dan hasn't been giving you any hassle, has he?' asked Dad.

'It's fine,' I said. 'He just said sorry, and that I didn't have to forgive him.'

I wasn't going to tell Dad that Dan had told me that he was owning up to the joyriding.

I attended my appointment the next day. On the way there, my mind was someplace else. Dan was going to the police, to own up to what he'd done. What was going to happen to him? Would he be in custody? Would Leslie get a call from the police about it?

I dwelled on it in the waiting room at the surgery.

My G.P is Doctor Goldberg. She came out of her office wearing a mauve v-neck, short sleeve t-shirt with a grey denim pencil skirt and a pair of cream sandals.

'Scarlet Doherty?' she called. I stood up and followed Dr Goldberg to her office, as she asked me how I was.

She shut the door, invited me to take a seat and said, 'Now, your father says you've been having a rather unhappy time, recently. Is that correct?'

I nodded.

'So, what can I do for you?' Dr Goldberg asked me.

'I've been having trouble dealing with the death of my ex, and I want to know what would be the right sort of help for me,' I told her as she watched me, intently. 'I've been having nightmares about it. I'm with him, and he suddenly vanishes, and I'm on my own.'

I went on to say that Tom had died in a car accident, and I did have to tell my doctor the truth, as part of my grief was also anger at Dan for stealing the car, so I said it was because he had stolen a Range Rover, and manipulated Tom into coming joyriding with him, and neither of them would listen to anyone who tried to warn them, resulting in Tom's death.

'I see,' said Dr Goldberg, with an understanding tone. 'So, obviously the death of your former partner has been very upsetting, and it's understandable that you will feel angry at his friend, because he shouldn't have done what he did, and right now, you'll feel like nothing is going to make you forgive him.'

I nodded.

Dr Goldberg recommended a counselling company that I could get in touch with, and arrange an appointment with them.

She wrote down a phone number on a piece of paper, and handed it to me, advising me to ring the number to arrange an appointment. I said that I would.

I rang the number when I arrived home and, after giving a few details about what I needed to talk to a counsellor about, was able to arrange an appointment for Monday the fifteenth of August, at quarter past eleven.

I felt glad I hadn't gone through all of this alone. I was glad I went to see my G.P. I was glad I booked an appointment with a counsellor. I didn't know how I was going to get through it if no one helped me.

I sent a text, asking Ruby-lynn to call me back, saying I had some stuff I wanted to talk about, and then went back downstairs to make myself a cup of herbal tea.

Whilst I waited for the kettle to boil, my phone rang. It was Ruby-lynn, so I picked it up and answered.

'Hey,' Scarlet, you been alright?' she asked.

'Not too bad, thanks,' I said.

'What did want to talk about?' Ruby-lynn asked.

'Dan's said he's going to the police to confess to stealing the car.'

'Shit, *really*?' Ruby-lynn squealed. I still couldn't believe it, either. But I knew Dan had been just as upset about it, and that was why he decided to own up.

'Do you feel you're able to forgive him?'

'I don't know if I can,' I said. 'No matter what becomes of him, it will never put a stop to all the depression I've been suffering and the nightmares I've been having.'

'What are you going to do to handle it better?' Ruby-lynn asked me.

'I've been to see my doctor, and she gave me a number to call, to book an appointment with a counsellor.'

'That's a really good idea,' said Ruby-lynn. 'It may not look like it now, but they really will help you put things into perspective. But nobody's saying this is going to be easy, or that you're going to move on from it overnight.'

'I agree,' I said. 'Thank you for being there for me.'

'You're welcome.'

We then said goodbye, and ended the call.

I heard the front door open, footsteps coming in, and then the door slammed shut. I looked over at the door.

It was Dan. The police hadn't locked him up anywhere? I stared at him. What was going on? How could he still be free?

'What are you doing back here?' I asked. 'I thought you were supposed to be going to the police.'

'I did,' he insisted.

'Right. And did you tell them the truth?'

'Er, yeah, course I did.'

But I was still confused, so I asked, 'What happened after that?'

'Well, the truth is...' Dan said, '...I got off.'

What?

'What ever do you mean, "You got off"?' I demanded to know.

'The police were lenient with me.'

Lenient with Dan for joyriding and resulting in the death of his friend? This didn't make sense.

'I can't believe that!' I said. 'After what you did?'

'What's going on?' I asked him, but Dan seemed to be holding something back. Why would the police let him off punishment for stealing a car, driving around recklessly, and letting his friend die?

'Dan, *why* did they let you off?'

'Well, I don't know, do I?' said Dan, starting to sound defensive.

'Dan!'

He was hiding something, though I didn't have a clue what it was, I knew something was going down that he wouldn't tell me if it saved his own neck.

He walked out of the room. I stood up and followed Dan out of the room.

'Dan, if you told the police the truth, how can they let you off, just like that?' I demanded to know.

'I already told you I didn't know, didn't I?' Dan snapped, indignantly.

What was wrong with him? I followed him up the stairs.

'Are you hiding something?' I shouted. Dan stopped.

'Course I'm not fucking hiding anything!'

'Then stop walking away from me every time I try to talk to you about it!'

'Stop *trying* to talk about it when I tell you I don't *know* why they let me off!' Dan shouted, turning round to face me.

He then turned back round, and carried on up the stairs. I followed him, calling after him. Dan went into his room and slammed the door in my face. But I was not giving up. I shook my head, eyes raised to the heavens and my mouth very thin, then I opened the door and barged straight in.

'What the fuck? You've just come barging into my room!' Dan shouted

'I had no choice, you're hiding something, and I demand to know what you said to the police!'

Dan sighed. He then said, 'I told them the car was stolen, only...'

What was he going to say?

'I told them it was Tom's idea to steal the car, and that I tried to warn him and he wouldn't listen to me,' Dan gabbled desperately.

I couldn't believe this. Dan had really outdone himself this time. I couldn't believe that even now, he couldn't own up.

'You unbelievable lying faggot!' I spat. 'You never were planning to come clean, were you?'

'I'm so sorry,' Dan said, 'I just got there, and I went to talk to them and... I just couldn't bring myself to say it was really me.'

'But you could bring yourself to blame everything you did on your best mate, who is dead because of *you*?!' I shouted, outraged. Dan was so impossibly, unimaginably selfish. No one wants to go to jail, but it still happens to those that deserve it. And Dan was such a self-centered coward; he was willing to do the only thing he could do now, to scoop himself out of the quicksand.

I stormed out, not wanting to hear another word. I never thought Dan would stoop that low.

Chapter 15:

Jesse's Second

Saturday 30th July 2011

Since Jamie had moved in, me and Rochella had been spending time bonding with him. It was kind of awkward for the three of us, as the brother that me and Rochella never knew had just moved in with us. We had talked to him on his first evening there.

During Jamie's first weekend here, Mum came into the kitchen when we were finishing up after breakfast, rummaging in her purse, and then pulled out a wad of ten-pound notes.

'Ten pounds each,' she'd said, handing them to me, Rochella, and Jamie. 'Go out into town. Have some fun together on me, really get to know each other, okay?'

The three of us vowed we would, and then left and walked to the nearest bus stop the two zero six bus stopped at, which was outside the chemists'.

There had been a bus approaching as me, Jamie and Rochella reached it. We'd managed to arrive and flag it down in time, before we got on, and sat at the back.

'What do you fancy doing?' I asked Jamie.

'Well, I fancy grabbing a coffee,' said Jamie, so when we got off at the back of Debenhams, we walked to Café Nero. We'd been sat at a table in the back corner of the café, with an Americano each.

'You two at college, then?' Jamie asked.

'I'm doing an apprenticeship at college,' said Rochella, 'in Business and Admin. It's an advanced qualification.'

I told Jamie about the level two Diploma I'd just completed in Travel and Tourism, and the two-year Diploma I planned to do next year.

'So, that's the kinda career you wanna job in?' asked Jamie, interested.

'That's right,' I said. 'What do you want to do?'

'I'm not that sure, as what I've had going on didn't leave me a lot of chances to think about it.,' said Jamie.

'What was it like, meeting Mum?' Rochella had asked Jamie.

'Well... it's quite hard to put it into words, but I always felt like a part of me was missing, despite what Christian had told me, and meeting you two and Mum feels like the missing part,' Jamie described.

Rochella looked touched.

'I feel the same.'

I didn't say anything. I didn't know about Jamie when he was living with Christian, and he didn't know about me, so I couldn't really say I understood how they both felt.

After a couple of hours in Café Nero, we'd walked to the beach. It was beginning to cloud over. We went and sat on the beach for another hour and talked, getting to know each other, until it began to rain. It was about time we were making our way back home.

We ran down New Bond Street to the back of Debenhams to catch the bus home. We sheltered in the bus stop, and the bus arrived eight minutes later.

The rain had eased off when the bus reached our stop.

Jamie rang the bell when he, me and Rochella got to the front door. Mum let us in, made us all a cup of coffee, and then asked if we'd had a nice time.

We'd also done things as a family, to which Michael had been invited. Whilst Mum had told Jamie she was seeing someone named Michael, she hadn't told him about hers and Michael's intentions regarding their relationship, because she said he needed time to settle in before knowing that Michael would also be moving in, as well as his two daughters, in good time.

I knew Jamie was counting on me to arrange for Dave to come round, because Jamie was keen to catch up with him, but even that had to wait a while, because Mum said it wouldn't be a good idea to thrust so much upon Jamie so soon. But I hoped I could soon, for Jamie's sake.

I got up and went downstairs. I was meeting Annie in town that day. It was nine in the morning. Mum didn't really like anyone sleeping in later than half eight. I didn't know if Jamie would be up yet.

When I came downstairs, I could hear meowing coming from the kitchen. I went into the kitchen, where Rochella was filling the cats' food bowls whilst they were all prowling around her, looking up at her, meowing hungrily and impatiently, standing up on their hind legs, like they were reaching up for their breakfast. God, it was noisy!

Lucy, our grey tabby, jumped up onto the worktop.

'Lucy! Get down!' said Rochella, crossly. I went over, picked Lucy up as carefully as I could so she couldn't bite or scratch me, as she really doesn't like being picked up, and put her back down on the floor. She'd been flailing her paws with her claws out, and craning her head around with her mouth wide open like she was trying to bite me when I'd picked her up, so I had to be quick about putting her back down.

'She's such a naughty girl! She *knows* she's not allowed up there!' said Rochella.

Toby, our calico who had no tail, came over, stood up on his hind legs and put his front paws to my knees, looking up at me with big, pleading eyes as though hoping I was going to feed him.

'Don't look at me. I haven't got any food for you,' I said to him.

Rochella put the food bowls down and the cats piped down and tucked in at once.

Me and Rochella sat opposite each other at the breakfast bar and had a bowl of Rice Crispies each.

'You seeing any of your mates today?' asked Rochella.

'I'm meeting Annie in town,' I said. I didn't know exactly what we'd be getting up to, whether we were going for something to eat, grabbing a drink, watching a film in the cinema, or just having a stroll.

Jamie came in five minutes later.

'Alright?' he'd said, heading for the cereal cupboard. Rochella said that the box of Rice Crispies was still out if he wanted any, so Jamie grabbed himself a bowl and helped himself to some Rice Crispies.

Me and Rochella finished our breakfast. We knew we had to put our bowls and spoons in the dishwasher straight away, as Mum would only bang on at us.

Mum came in and asked Rochella if the cats had been fed, and then asked us what we were getting up to. I told her I was meeting up with Annie.

'It's about time Jane and Claire brought their families round,' said Mum. I turned to look round at Jamie, who'd quickly looked up from his breakfast at her. Mum reassured him they were all very friendly, but I'd already figured out, as I'd got to know Jamie, that he was relatively shy.

At ten o'clock, I caught the bus into town. There were some thirteen to fourteen-year-olds near the back of the bus, and they were being really fucking loud and immature. It reminded me of how irritating Lizzy found those sorts of kids. She'd always say, 'God, *why* are they not still at *Primary* school?'

I got off the bus, walked through town, and met Annie in New Bond Street.

'Hi, honey!' she squealed, holding out her arms, grinning. Me and my girlfriend hugged, and I lifted her off her feet as we kissed. We broke away as I put her back down again, before we walked down the street, hand in hand.

'Fancy a trip to the cinema?' she asked.

'Why don't we have a look at see what's on in there?' I suggested, and Annie agreed.

Annie took a fancy to No Strings Attached, but I knew it wouldn't be my sort of thing. We agreed on The Dilemma.

After the film, we went for something to eat, over at Yates. After a few drinks as well, we decided to head home.

'Do you fancy coming back to mine?' Annie asked. After the fantastic day out, I definitely didn't fancy ending it there and then.

'Yeah, that would be great,' I said, so we caught the bus back to Annie's house. We had to wait ten minutes for the bus. When we got on, we got seats near the back, where Annie always prefers to sit.

We got off the bus and walked to Annie's house. As soon as we arrived in doors, we were greeted by Annie's mum. Pandora's a lot like Annie; fair, blonde, girly and can be just as gooey as Annie.

'*Hiya*, Jesse!' she beamed, just the way Annie always does when she sees me. 'How's your mother, darling? Would you like a nice cup of tea?'

Me and Annie both accepted.

'I'll make one for daddy, too, Annie, as he'll be home, soon,' said Pandora, bustling into the kitchen. 'And I'll get you some choccie bickies as well.'

Me and Annie sat down at the table in the kitchen diner.

'Here we go!' said Pandora, bringing over two cups of tea and a plate of chocolate hobnobs, grinning kindly. 'How's your lovely friend, Freddie?'

'He's all right,' I said.

'How is Jamie was settling in?' Pandora then asked. 'And when will Annie, Anthony and I get to meet him? As I know your mum is hoping for us to some time.'

'Mum said it was about time,' I told her, even though she was referring to Lizzy, Fred and Natalie's lots, but I reckoned it wouldn't be too long.

Pandora said, 'Drink your tea, darlings, and help yourself to biscuits.'

Me and Annie had some biscuits and then took our tea up to our rooms. We put our mugs down on top of Annie's chest of drawers and Annie shut the door. Then she turned to look at me. I looked into her eyes, those beautiful, silvery eyes. She gave me a smile. She then walked over to me, cupped my face, and kissed me on the lips.

We began ripping each other's clothes off then Annie pushed me backwards onto her pink and white polka dot duvet, and took me inside her.

'You're so sexy,' I said to her. I slipped my hand inside her top and moved it up her warm body, towards her tits. I ran my hand over them. My other hand, meanwhile, moved its way, slowly, down her thigh. All the while, I was kissing her all over her neck, shoulders and collarbone.

It was six o'clock when I finally started making my way home. I really fucking love Annie. I can see an amazing future with her. I really want to go travelling with her at some point, maybe go to somewhere like Brazil. I don't normally go for girly girlies, but we sort of get each other.

I wasn't surprised when Mum started giving me shit for being back late for tea and not letting her know. I went to the lounge, where Rochella was sat on the armchair, reading the latest Cosmopolitan magazine.

I flung myself onto the sofa, still reliving my moments with Annie in my head. I grabbed the remote, which had been lying on the armrest of the sofa nearest to the chair Rochella was sat on, turned on the T.V and flicked through the channels.

'Mum says we're going to West Bay in Bridport tomorrow, and Michael's coming too,' said Rochella, looking up from her magazine.

Our family always used to go to West Bay with the Grahams and the Curtises whenever the whole group of us went out somewhere near Bridport when we were kids. We would stop there on our way back from wherever we'd been that day and we'd have a stroll around, as long as nobody was too tired out, and then go to the kiosks to buy chips and sit on benches to eat them whilst looking at the view.

I liked that Michael was coming too. Me and Rochella have always got along with him like a house on fire. I didn't know exactly when Mum was planning on telling Jamie about her and Michael's plans, and I'd been careful not to blurt it out, as it wasn't my place to say anything.

I'd have to be up early the next morning, so I didn't go to bed too late.

I got up at half seven to join the others for breakfast.

'We're going in Michael's car and he's coming for the four of us at half nine, so I need all three of you to be ready by that time,' Mum told us, bossily.

After I finished my toast and marmite, I went upstairs to put on my favourite Sleeping with Sirens t-shirt and grey cargo shorts.

It was really cramped in the back of Michael's paradise blue metallic Suzuki Alto, where I had to sit squashed between Jamie and Rochella.

When we arrived and Michael parked the car, we had a very long stroll along the harbour, and then the seaside.

'Mum said she reckoned I could meet summa the family friends,' Jamie told me, as though I hadn't been there when she'd said it. Was he getting at something?

'Yeah,' I said. 'What about it?'

'Can Dave come round?'

'Mum's really the person to ask,' I said, 'as she'd been the one who insisted she wanted to wait before you met anyone. Though if you're still friends with Dave on Facebook, and had been able to look at his wall, why did you never message him?'

'I've been worried about getting in touch with Dave after what I went through, and we've been going in different directions for so long,' Jamie explained. 'But if you still hang out with him, I actually stand a chance,' he added, sounding hopeful.

I was hoping that, once Jamie had met Fred, Lizzy and Natalie and got to know them, he could then meet Scarlet, Ruby-lynn and Dave, and hopefully join in all the things we did.

'You definitely can join with all of us, including Dave,' I told Jamie.

Jamie looked at me, gratefully.

When the five of us came back to the kiosks, we bought lunch from the kiosks, so I had a fish cake with chips, and we sat on a nearby low wall to eat.

'What's that you've got there, Rochella?' I asked, looking at the little pot Rochella had bought for lunch.

'Cockles,' she said. 'Want to try one?'

'Sure,' I said, and me and Jamie tried one, because neither of us had cockles before. Eurgh! They tasted fucking *well* icky!

When we finished, we went and put all our rubbish in the bin, went back to the car and drove to Charmouth.

It wasn't a very long car journey there. Charmouth isn't that far from Bridport. It had a pebbly beach with clay cliffs. Lizzy had told me about how she'd been to Charmouth with her lot and they'd used jagged pebbles to break apart large blocks of clay to see if they would find small fossils concealed inside.

I was definitely up for giving it a go. I persuaded Jamie and Rochella to join in, though Rochella did fuss about breaking a nail.

We both had an awesome time, and I had found loads of ammonite fossils of various sizes. Jamie seemed to have enjoyed himself. Nobody else had joined in so, as we'd been the only ones, it had been a good opportunity to have fun with my brother.

'Do you know the name of the course you're doing?' I asked Jamie. I knew Mum had helped Jamie apply for a foundation course.

'I know it's something to do with life skills and personal progression, but I can't remember the exact name.'

'What do you hope to do after that? Is there was anything you're interested in, in particular?' I asked him

'I dunno,' said Jamie. 'I s'pose I've always been interested in learning about electricity.'

'You could think about whether you'd like to take your interest in electricity further?' I suggested. Jamie agreed he could.

Mum seemed well chuffed we were getting on, especially when she'd seen us fossil hunting on the beach and chatting about courses.

When we got back in the car afterwards, we showed Rochella, Mum and Michael what we found and they were incredibly fascinated by it.

Michael stayed for dinner when we arrived home. We had lamb chops with carrot puree.

'Jamie's starting at college in September, aren't you Jamie?' Mum was telling Michael.

'Oh yeah? Tell me about what you'll be doing,' Michael said.

'I can't remember the name, exactly,' Jamie said, before Mum told Michael that it was a life skills award and certificate in personal progression.

'Ah, I see,' said Michael, sounding intrigued. 'And where do you plan on going from there?'

Jamie swallowed the mouthful of food he'd had and said, 'I thought of looking into learning about electricity.'

'Oh yes, because you were suggesting Jamie should consider it, if he's interested, weren't you, Jesse?' said Mum, looking round at me.

'Um, yeah, it was just an idea, you know... in case,' I said.

I started trying to tell people about the next level I was doing in Travel and Tourism, but they were more interested in talking to Jamie about what else he'd like to do. I had noticed that Jamie had been getting more attention than me and Rochella.

Michael asked Jamie if there were any other interests he might like a career in, and asked if he'd be interested in doing an apprenticeship, to which Rochella pointed out that they had some going at Euro Capital House College.

'You could maybe do an apprenticeship in Business and Admin, or Customer Service,' she hinted.

'Oh yes, Customer Service would be a good idea!' said Mum, eagerly.

Jamie probably didn't really know what he wanted to do, and didn't have any career goals, as he seemed unsure every time somebody asked.

After dinner, Mum let Jamie go into the lounge with Michael whilst me and Rochella had to help her with the washing up!

'Why doesn't Jamie have to help?' I murmured to Mum, as I dried the baking tray she'd just washed.

'I wasn't going to make Michael sit in the lounge on his tod, was I?' she said, quietly.

'Why couldn't me and Rochella have gone and sat with him too?' I asked, but Mum just said, indignantly, 'So I'm just supposed to do all the work without any help?'

But this wasn't fair! Whenever Mum needed something doing, that got somebody out of helping with the tidying, like keeping a guest company, Jamie would always get the pleasure of carrying out the task, so me and Rochella would have to help with the tidying.

'Why can't one of us keep Michael company for a change? Jamie never has to help,' I moaned, before Mum silenced me and whispered that Jamie would hear.

'They're perfect opportunities for Jamie to get to know him,' said Mum. 'It'll make it easier for Jamie to come round to the idea much sooner.'

'The idea of what?'

'You know,' said Mum. Why wouldn't she say it out loud to my face? It wasn't me she'd had to keep it from until she was going to discuss it with Jamie. And I was getting tired of having to keep my mouth shut about it. How much time did Jamie need? Yes, he'd spent his whole life not knowing us, who he'd now only lived with for about four months, but I wished Mum would just get her act together and do it.

I went up to my room after I finished helping. I'd left my phone at home all day whilst the five of us were out, and it had been on my desk.

I had one text. It was from Dave. It said 'Can i cum round urs tomorrow??'

I didn't have anything on tomorrow, so it was fine as far as I was concerned.

I took it down to the lounge where the others were sat.

'Jesse, are you going to come in and join us?' Mum asked.

'Yeah, sorry, I just went up to check my phone cos I'd left it in my room all day,' I said. 'Is it all right if Dave comes round tomorrow?'

I immediately noticed Jamie look up at me, his eyebrows raised.

'Well...' said Mum, 'if you'd like him to, I don't see any reason why he can't.'

She smiled at Jamie after she said it.

I texted Dave, asking what time he wanted to come round and instantly had a text back, asking if I was okay with twelve o'clock, which I said I was.

Later on, after Michael had left the house, Jamie collared me on the stairs.

'So Dave's coming round tomorrow, then?' he asked.

I nodded.

'Thanks.'

'*Dave* asked *me* if he could come round,' I told him. 'I only did all this in answer to his question.'

Jamie nodded. He then asked, 'Do you know what Mum's gonna tell me about Michael?'

'I do,' I said, 'but I can't tell you because I was forbidden to. It'll come out better, coming from Mum, anyway.'

'Okay,' said Jamie.

I passed him and carried on walking down the stairs.

'D'you feel threatened by me?'

I stopped. I looked over my shoulder and up at Jamie. He was looking down at me. I frowned.

'I heard you asking why I never have to help clean up the kitchen,' Jamie said. Great. He fucking heard everything.

'I'm sorry,' I said. 'It's not your fault. Mum had a good reason for wanting you to be the one to keep Michael company.'

'I get it,' said Jamie. 'No one likes housework and you're never the one who gets to not do it when Mum wants someone being kept company.'

I nodded.

'Next time some one comes round, you can do the honour and I'll muck in,' Jamie told me. I couldn't help feeling grateful, though guilty that Jamie had heard what I said.

'He seems to make Mum happy,' Jamie said.

'Mum had told me Christian made her a lot of things and happy wasn't one of them,' I said.

I continued down the stairs, went to the kitchen and helped myself to a can of Relentless. Mum came in and gave me a minor lecture about drinking energy drinks before bed time

'You thought Jamie was ready, then?' I asked her.

'Of course,' she said. 'I stand by how I felt about giving him time to get used to living here before he met Jane, Claire and their families, but I don't know why I thought it would be the same story with his best friend who he'd lost contact with. I suppose I just wanted to be safe instead of sorry.'

'Yeah,' I agreed. It always struck me as peculiar that she felt Jamie would need to be allowed to adjust to living with her before catching up with Dave, which had been why I was so reluctant to go along with it. But I completely understood why Mum wasn't keen on Jamie meeting Lizzy, Fred and Natalie immediately after he'd moved in.

'Alright mate?' I said, shutting the door behind Dave when I let him in the next day. 'Want a drink?'

'Nah, I'm good, ta,' said Dave, following me into the lounge, before we sat down on the sofa, either side of Tommy, the chubby brown tabby cat, who was lying on his side, asleep in the sunlight that was shining through the window. Dave smiled down at Tommy.

'Podgy little fucker,' I said, smirking down at Tommy as well. I heard the bathroom door open, footsteps coming down the stairs and then Jamie came in, slowly. He looked at Dave. Dave looked at him.

'Hey,' he said.

'Hi,' said Jamie. 'Been a long time.'

'Yeah,' said Dave, nodding.

Jamie said he was going to get a drink and asked if Dave wanted one, but Dave said he'd already declined an offer for a drink.

I stood up and walked over to the door.

'I'll leave you two alone, yeah?' I said, but Jamie said I could stay, so I sat back down.

Dave asked Jamie how he'd been after what happened.

'It's been shit,' Jamie said. 'It was really hard without you there.'

'I wish I'd stayed in touch to see how you were,' Dave said, 'but I didn't know if I should at the time, but I guess I could've been brave.'

'I should've got in touch if I needed you,' Jamie said, 'but I was worried you'd be awkward with me.'

'I wouldn't have been awkward,' Dave reassured him. 'So what have you been up to since moving here?

'I've been out to places with the family.'

'I hope he can chill with the others,' I said.

'When you made friends with Jesse, did you know he was my brother?' Jamie asked.

'To be honest, no, because Jesse knew nothing about you then, and when I was at school with you, you said nothing about a brother.'

'But you must've suspected something, since you were also mates with Rochella, who I did know about and had known about me,' Jamie pointed out.

Dave looked down, raised his eyebrows and said, 'Shit, yeah! And I did wonder, when Jesse mentioned he'd found he had a brother, if it was you, because everything he and Rochella said about what their dad said about Rochella and your mum to you was the same as everything you said your dad said about your mum and sister.'

Jamie asked Dave what he'd been up to, and Dave told him about the level three course he'd just completed in Photography.

'Is there another level up you plan on doing next year?' Jamie asked.

'Yeah, I plan on doing the Foundation degree,' said Dave.

'Are you with anyone?' Jamie asked.

'I did have a girlfriend, who was from Spain, but I don't wanna talk about how and why we broke up.'

It was still getting to Dave that Tom had got away with stealing Rosa off of him.

'I made a tool of myself, trying to win over the previous girl I liked,' Dave said. I stared at him, surprised he actually wanted to talk about the time when he crashed and burned with his teacher, but pleased he was no longer as embarrassed about it as he had been.

'Why, what did you do?' Jamie asked.

'Well, it was someone I knew I wasn't allowed to be with,' said Dave. 'She would've been sacked and arrested if anything happened between us and someone found out and... let's just leave it at that.'

I saw Jamie look down, raising his eyebrows.

Dave seemed to not need to ask Jamie if he had a girlfriend. He obviously knew Jamie well enough to know perfectly well that Jamie wasn't interested in having a girlfriend, as he'd told me when we'd got to know each other. Jamie's not gay; he's just not interested in being in a relationship.

I heard the front door open and Rochella and Mum's voices in the hall. Mum came into the lounge, holding a large shopping bag.

'Hello Dave,' she said, grinning.

'Hi, Mrs Naerger,' said Dave. Mum left the lounge, before I heard someone's stomach rumble.

'Sorry. That was me,' said Jamie. 'Do you wanna stay for lunch?'

'Well, I wouldn't say no to something to eat,' said Dave, as we stood up and went to the kitchen.

'Are you boys coming in for some lunch?' Mum asked. 'I bought two quiches, a bag of salad and some garlic bread for us to have for lunch.'

'Cool,' said Jamie. Mum asked him to get out five plates and tumblers, before asking Dave what he'd like to drink, and then asking me to get the Sprite from the fridge.

Rochella got out the two boxes containing the quiche Mum had bought, whilst Mum unwrapped the garlic bread and put it in the oven. There was a cheese and ham quiche, and a tomato and olive quiche. I had a slice of both quiches, as they both looked delicious and helped myself to some salad, and a couple of slices of garlic bread when it was ready, before the five of us ate our lunch at the breakfast bar

'Did you three boys have a nice chat?' asked Mum.

'Yeah, we did, ta,' said Jamie, and he told her how he and Dave had been catching up on what they'd been up to. She seemed very pleased that it appeared to have gone well. I could tell she was really looking forward to introducing Jamie to the others.

After lunch, Mum asked Dave if he'd stay for dinner too, which he said he would, and then we went up to Jamie's room, as Dave hadn't seen it yet.

'It's smaller than my room back at Christian's,' he said to Dave, 'but I ain't felt the need to spend so much time up here, so I'm not that bothered. And I've never really had so much stuff I'd need a bigger room, even though some of it's had to stay in the boxes under the bed.'

'Cool,' said Dave. 'So... is this permanent then, or are you just staying here for a few months?'

Jamie looked at Dave like he was on cocaine.

'You've gotta be joking! There is no way I'm going back to that shit hole!'

'Mum never let any of us forget that she was dead against Jamie living with Christian for another second,' I told Dave.

We stayed and talked in Jamie's room until Mum called us down for dinner, after which Dave went home.

'Thanks,' Jamie said to me.

'No worries,' I said, following Jamie into the lounge.

I was glad Dave came round. I wished Jamie could come out with us tomorrow night. We were going clubbing. Claire would be picking me up at eight, followed by Annie and giving us, Fred and Natalie a lift into town.

'Your mum told me we'd be able to meet Jamie soon,' Claire said, when she'd picked Annie up. 'Do you have any idea when it will be? It can't be between Friday and the next because we're going on holiday.'

'Where is it you're going?' I asked.

'Switzerland,' Fred said, and he told me about the week the family were planning to spend in Zurich and visit places like Lake Zurich, the Kunsthaus Zurich Gallery, the Swiss National Museum, hike the mountains at Uetliburg, and go shopping at Bahnhofstrasse.

'Dave came round to meet Jamie yesterday, as they were best friends at school,' I told Fred and Natalie. 'Did I ever mention that?'

'You didn't, but Dave definitely did,' Natalie said.

'Shame he couldn't have come out with us tonight,' said Annie. 'But I know your mum wouldn't have allowed it.'

'Yeah,' I agreed.

Claire dropped the four of us off outside the Royal Mail collection point, and we began to walk to Dolce Vita. Me and Annie let Fred and Natalie go on ahead whilst we talked.

'Mum's said your mum has invited her, Dad and me round to meet Jamie,' Annie whispered excitedly.

'Oh, okay,' I said. 'Mum never said anything to me about that. When are you coming?'

'On Saturday.'

'Awesome,' I said.

When we arrived at Dolce Vita, we entered to find Dave, Scarlet, Ruby-lynn and Lizzy dancing amongst the crowd. Stuart, Fraser, Adam and Dustin were there too. We went to join them on the dance floor.

'Hey,' I said.

'Hey, how you doing?' said Fraser. 'Come and have shots with me and the lads.'

Me, Fred and Dave went with Stuart, Fraser, Adam and Dustin to get shots.

As Fraser, Adam, Dustin and Stuart rejoined the crowd, Dave asked Fred how long he would be in Switzerland for. Fred told him he'd be there from the coming Friday to the next.

'By the time I'm back at college, everyone will have forgotten what I had going with five girls at the same time.'

After Dolce Vita, we went into the Lazy Lizard. When we arrived, Fred and I went to get jagerbombs, and then joined the others, who had sat down.

'Cheers!' we all cheered, as we clinked the glasses together, and then downed them, before me, Fred and Lizzy went for a dance, after which it was my turn to pay for the drinks, so everyone had one. I bought myself a vodka and Coke and sat with Lizzy, giving her a W.K.D Blue, and we watched as the others danced.

Lizzy took a *very* big gulp of her drink. Fuck me! Lizzy's usually the slowest when it comes to drinking alcohol, though for her own good it's probably just as well, as she's such a lightweight.

She was such a piss head that night. When the gang had gone up to dance, she was really going for it, and I was alarmed to notice she was barely keeping her eyes open and was very giggly.

Natalie and us lads were beginning to get a bit tipsy as well, though Fred seemed like he wasn't having too much trouble acting sober. Ruby-lynn and Scarlet didn't seem very drunk, either.

I decided to sober up a bit, and lay off the vodka. Me, Fred, Dave, Natalie, Lizzy, Ruby-lynn and Scarlet talked.

'I've been for an assessment with a counsellor, where we've agreed I should have therapy,' Scarlet told us. 'I'm waiting to hear back from them about when my next appointment is.'

'Did that help at all?' Natalie asked.

'It did help get a few things off my chest,' said Scarlet. 'Though I really don't feel like justice was served, considering Dan got off by actually *not* telling them the truth, even though he said he would.'

I was just as enraged as everyone else was. Dan didn't know when to quit. He and Tom had been unbearable dipshits. They'd marked Fred down as the next person they would go after, after what they did to me. Though what they did to me was pretty fucking pathetic in comparison to stealing Dave's girlfriend off of him and making his and Scarlet's lives a misery ever since.

We visited a few more clubs, before calling it a night. Me, Fred, Natalie and Annie went into Subway before getting a taxi home, and I grabbed myself a teriyaki chicken sub with sweet corn and peppers to eat as soon as I got home.

I let myself in, wolfed down my Subway sandwich, and then went up to bed.

I overslept, Wednesday morning. Mum didn't have a go for it when I went down for breakfast, though, to be fair, she knew I would've slept in if I'd been on a night out.

'Good night out?' she asked, as I poured myself a bowl of Cookie Crisp.

'Yeah, it was,' I said. 'Annie told me that she, Pandora and Anthony have been invited to come round to meet Jamie.'

'Yes, that's right,' Mum confirmed. 'I thought I mentioned it to you before?'

I shook my head. Mum said Pandora and Anthony would be coming round with Annie for lunch and to meet Jamie.

'When are Lizzy and Fred's families coming?' I asked. 'Or have you not decided that, yet?'

Mum told me that all she did know was that the Curtises couldn't come the next week because they'd be in Switzerland, but obviously I already knew that, but I also knew the Grahams were free that week, so they could come then.

I hoped to see Fred before he and Natalie went away. I texted Fred to see if he fancied meeting up the tomorrow.

I didn't hear anything back from Fred until three in the afternoon. He said he'd be up for it, saying he had something he needed to talk to me about anyway.

What, though?

Much later that afternoon, Mum suggested having an Indian takeaway that night, so I had lamb Balti, Aloo Chana and mixed vegetable rice. My eyes turned out to be bigger than my belly, because I was too full up to finish all of it in one night.

The next day, Fred came by to pick me up at eleven.

'Do you wanna go for a drink in the Marquis Granby?' I asked.

'Yeah, I'm cool with whatever,' said Fred.

I asked Fred what he wanted to talk about, but Fred said he was saving it for when we got into the pub.

'What were you going to say? I asked, once we'd sat down.

'Okay, um, here's the thing,' Fred said. 'Dan's been back to the police, and told them the truth. He's going to court.'

I wasn't sure if I heard Fred right.

'Dan knows he's been selfish, and shouldn't have chickened out at the last minute, because he was responsible for the death of his friend, so he should've at least done the right thing, and faced up to it. Dave was there,' he said. 'Also, he said he was sorry for talking Tom into stealing Rosa off of him. Though Dave says he can't really be with someone who doesn't see quality time with their other half as a high priority in a relationship.'

I could tell Dan was upset that he'd caused Tom to die, by talking him into stealing a car and driving it around, recklessly. I sort of understood he did have every intention of owning up to what he'd done, but just couldn't get it out and ended up saying that it had been Tom's idea to steal the car, but that still didn't make it right. At least Dan was doing what was right now.

'What they did to me was fucking sad,' I said. 'If spiking my drink so that I was too drunk to notice them drawing tiny little cocks all over my face and posting a photo of it on Facebook where everyone saw it was the best they had, they were out of their depth.'

'They did give me a bit of a hard time about how I'd been seeing other girls behind Ruby-lynn's back,' Fred said.

'I wouldn't have been surprised if they felt that seeing how miserable you were about it would be revenge enough, and just wanted to add to the guilt of it,' I told Fred, to which Fred agreed they did.

'I don't have clue if any of us are ever gonna be able to forgive Dan at all, but if I do, I'll probably be a pensioner by then,' I said. 'We all tried to warn him and Tom but they wouldn't listen to any of us.'

Fred agreed, before saying he couldn't stay out too long, since he needed as much time as he could get to spend packing for Switzerland.

He asked what I'd be getting up to in Weymouth whilst he was away, so I told him about Annie coming round with her parents to meet Jamie, though, I wasn't entirely sure what I wanted to do over the rest of the week, in all honesty.

Fred and I finished our drinks, and then Fred gave me a lift home. We said goodbye, I wished Fred and his family a great holiday in Switzerland, and then I got out of the car and let myself in.

'Is that you, Jesse?' Mum called from upstairs. 'You're back early. Is everything all right?'

'Yeah, Fred couldn't be out too long, he still had to pack,' I called up to Mum.

Six seconds later, Mum came down the stairs.

'I wish we all could've gone on holiday this year,' she said, 'but I couldn't find the time for it because I've been so busy making arrangements for Jamie. I hope we can arrange something for next year. When everything gets sorted.'

'Sure,' I said.

I went into the lounge, turned on the T.V, and switched the channel to Kerrang, and then sat down, got out my phone and checked my Facebook.

What could I get up to whilst Fred and Natalie were away, I wondered? The obvious answer would be to hang out with Dave or Lizzy or both.

I went out with Mum to buy some biscuits and ingredients for lunch with the Baileys yesterday, as well as dinner for the evening. Mum had decided on organic sesame chicken stir-fry, followed by nectarine and raspberry Pavlova for dessert. We bought some bourbons, garibaldis, custard creams and Jammy Dodgers to eat with our tea and coffee.

Me, Rochella and Jamie helped prepare the Pavlova for tomorrow. We'd spent an hour and fifty minutes preparing and cooking it in total.

Mum sounded excited about Annie and Pandora and Anthony coming round. She then enlisted everyone's help in making this Middle Eastern style lamb thing for dinner.

We tidied the house the next morning. It was a bright sunny day, so it was perfect weather to eat outside. Mum asked me to lay the table with her favourite slate heart shaped placemats and coasters and her best cutlery.

When the doorbell rang, I went to answer the door.

'Hiya!' said Annie, giving her boyfriend, yours truly here, a kiss hello, before coming in with her parents in tow.

'Hello there, Jesse,' said Anthony. 'You all right?'

'Yeah, course,' I said.

'And you must be Jamie,' said Pandora, looking past me. I looked over my shoulder to see Jamie coming out of the kitchen.

'Yes, this is indeed Jamie,' said Mum.

'It's a pleasure,' Anthony said, shaking Jamie's hand.

'The resemblance between you two is uncanny,' Pandora said, looking from Jamie to me.

'I'll still always be the better looking one though, right Annie?' I joked.

'Dream on, mate,' Jamie teased.

Mum asked if anyone would like tea or coffee, as Rochella led everybody into the lounge, carrying a large dinner plate with the biscuits arranged neatly. Me and Annie sat together on the armchair by the window.

'How do you like living with your mum so far, Jamie?' Pandora asked.

'I'm happier here than I was at my dad's,' he said.

'Of course you are!' said Pandora. 'Your mum said that your father wasn't very nice to you when you were with him.'

Jamie nodded. Mum came into the lounge, bearing a tray with seven mugs with the Paris skyline all the way round.

'Here we are,' she said, placing the tray on the coffee table. 'One black tea, two white coffees, three white teas and one chai tea.'

'Thanks, Flora,' said Annie, picking up her chai tea. She's a massive fan of ginger, which she says is one of the key ingredients in chai tea. Lizzy's also a huge fan of chai latte; she can't get enough of it.

'Jamie was just telling us how much happier he is here than back at Christian's,' Pandora said, as we had a swig of our drinks and helped ourselves to biscuits, so Mum told her, Anthony and Annie about how she'd discovered the neglect and abuse that Jamie had to endure throughout his life, therefore she'd insisted he came to live with her immediately, but Christian wouldn't hear of it, and it wasn't until he saw what was in it for him that he'd changed his mind.

'That's very selfish of him,' said Anthony, frowning.

'Very,' Mum agreed, before saying she and Rochella were going to get lunch ready, before they got up to leave the room.

'Will you be going to college or go into employment?' Anthony asked Jamie, so Jamie told him about the foundation course he had his name down for at Euro Capital House College in September.

'Very good,' said Anthony. 'And then, after that, are you going to decide where to go from there?'

'Yeah, that's right,' said Jamie. 'I'm not honestly sure what I wanna do next year, though I am interested in doing an apprenticeship or doing another full time course.'

'It all sounds very positive,' Pandora said and then turned to me and asked what I'd be doing next year.

'Yeah, I'm gonna stay on and do the next level in my Travel and Tourism course,' I said.

'Brilliant,' said Anthony.

'My friend Natalie has a job at Flyaway Paradise,' I told him and Pandora.

'Yeah, that's right, she does,' Annie agreed.

Pandora asked if I was hoping for a job in a similar place. I don't actually know exactly what I want to be. All I know is that I've always wanted to work in Travel and Tourism.

Fifteen minutes later, Mum and Rochella came back in, and Mum said that lunch would be ready in fifteen minutes, as she and Rochella sat back down.

Mum asked Annie how she was and if she was still at college, and she spoke of the level three Diploma she'd just completed in Beauty Therapy, and was now hoping to get a job in a beauty salon, now that she'd received the qualifications she needed.

'All of my mates come to me whenever they need their eyebrows plucking,' she said.

'And she's absolutely superb at giving massages to her poor mother,' said Pandora, taking Annie's hand.

'Ooh, how very useful!' said Mum, grinning.

Rochella asked Annie if she'd ever done electrolysis, which Annie said she'd done loads of times.

I never really got electrolysis. I know what it is, but why would anyone need to remove hair permanently, so it never grows back? Us blokes don't mind shaving. Rochella always whinges about this fucking rank hair removal cream she uses on her upper lip not removing *all* the hairs. What hairs? I once said to her to just shave it if it was so important but she was like, 'Oh no, it'll grow back all dark and prickly!' It wasn't dark *or* prickly when she tried using that stinking cream on it! No one could see it! That's not to say I think Annie has a pointless career goal, just because I don't get why girls want to remove imaginary hair with cream and wax and shit.

At one o'clock, lunch was ready. Mum asked Jamie to help serve up, whilst she sent me and Rochella out to take a seat at the table with the Baileys. Me and Annie sat side by side.

'You two look *so* alike!' said Annie, looking from Jamie to me, grinning. 'I'm starving. I'm looking forward to trying some of this sesame chicken, and I love stir fry!'

Jamie came out into the garden, bearing two plates, which he'd placed in front of Pandora and Anthony. Next, Mum came out with another two plates, which she'd placed in front of me and Annie. I poured myself a glass of orange juice and lemonade, and then poured some for Annie.

'Thanks, babby,' said Annie. Jamie came out with his and Rochella's plates, with Mum, who had her own plate. Mum invited us all to dig in, once she'd sat down.

I'm not really a huge fan of stir-fry. This one was okay, though I wasn't desperately fussed about having it again, no offence to the chefs!

When we had finished our main courses, Mum cleared away our plates, enlisting my help. We both put all the dirty plates and cutlery in the dishwasher. Mum then asked me to get out seven bowls and seven spoons and bring them out to the garden, and she would bring out the Pavlova.

'Mmmm! That looks simply delectable, Flora!' said Pandora.

'Thank you, Pandora,' said Mum, as she started serving up the Pavlova.

When I tucked in, I was struggling just a bit, because of how full up I was after the stir-fry, but I ate as much as I could.

The party finished off with a second cup of tea or coffee, before the Baileys said their goodbyes and told Jamie what a great honour it was to have met him, and that they were pleased he was happy living with his mum.

Later on, we had a board of all kinds of savoury biscuits, and wedges of Wensleydale and cranberries, double Gloucester, Stilton and red Leicester for dinner, as we'd had such a large lunch.

'What do you think of the Baileys?' Mum asked Jamie.

'They were friendly,' he said.

'Yes, they're lovely,' said Mum, happily. 'And Jesse's a very lucky boy, to have such a wonderful girlfriend. Next week, you'll be able to meet the Grahams, and the week after next, you can meet the Curtises. They're such amazing people. You'll really like them.'

Jamie smiled.

'Any idea what day they're coming, yet, Mum?' I asked.

'The Grahams are coming on Monday evening, and that Claire says she reckons she can have us round for lunch on the Tuesday after next,' Mum said.

At least everything went well when Jamie met the Baileys, especially since Annie's my girlfriend. I was a bit worried Jamie would be somewhat awkward with them, for some reason, so I was glad that didn't happen. I was looking forward to Jamie meeting Lizzy, Fred and Natalie next.

Chapter 16:

Jamie's Second

Saturday 6th August 2011

I hit it off with Michael, I liked the Baileys, and I looked forward to seeing what the Grahams were like when they come round for dinner. Was it them or the Curtises that had the two sons named Alistair and Fraser?

'So, Fred's away this week, then?' I said, as me and Jesse walked home from having a brotherly chinwag and a drink over at the Marquis of Granby.

'Yep.'

'You said he's your best mate?'

'I did say that,' said Jesse. He told me how they'd been best friends since they were five and had never let anything come between them.

I could've said that about me and Dave, were it not for the fact that Dave's other twatty mates bullied me, and Dave was torn between us. People could say that Dave was a bad friend for not ditching them when they turned on me, but I knew that despite everything, they were very good friends to Dave and always had his back. Neither I nor Dave knew why they had a problem with me.

Me and Dave had made plans for meeting up again, though we hadn't finalised a day, time or place, yet.

'What about Alistair and Fraser?' I asked Jesse.

'Them and Lizzy are the ones we're meeting on Monday,' Jesse told me.

'So they're the Grahams?'

'Yeah, that's right.'

'Do you hang out with them much?' I asked Jesse.

'Me, Fred, Lizzy and Natalie always hang out as a gang with Dave and two other girls we're friends with. Once you've met Lizzy, Fred and Natalie, you can start coming out with us, Dave, Ruby-lynn and Scarlet,' Jesse told me.

'And who are Ruby-lynn and Scarlet again?' I asked. I remembered Jesse mentioning them about once or twice before, but couldn't remember if Jesse ever told me how he knew them.

'Me and Lizzy became friends with Scarlet when we met her through Fred and Natalie, whose dad is mates with Scarlet and Dave's dads,' Jesse said.

'And that was how you knew Dave too?'

Jesse nodded.

'We all met Ruby-lynn back in October when she'd caught up with Scarlet, who she'd known at Our Lady of Wyke, and Scarlet had introduced us to Ruby-lynn when she came bowling with us and came out clubbing with us for Halloween.'

'Mum will want us to pitch in with preparing dinner again I take it?' I said. Since living with Mum, I'd worked out that preparing a delicious lunch or dinner for something as important as meeting somebody was a specialty of hers.

'I wonder what we'll be making for the Grahams, especially as Lizzy is *well* picky about food,' said Jesse. 'She won't eat anything she thinks tastes weird.'

What did Jesse mean by that? It sounded a bit strange.

'I did have to choose carefully,' said Mum, when I asked on Sunday, what we were cooking for the Grahams tomorrow. 'But I reckon they'll like pasta puttanesca. Everyone else is sure to as well.'

Mum then told us about the chocolate and orange trifle she'd also bought ingredients for.

'You can't go wrong with chocolate and orange, I reckon,' she said, as she and I unpacked. 'When are you seeing Dave again?'

'We haven't made any firm plans for the coming week,' I said.

'It's so nice that you were able to catch up with your best friend from secondary school,' said Mum. 'I knew Jesse and his friends were very chummy with him, but I had no way of knowing you were too.'

'He was my only mate,' I said.

'Could you not have made friends with his other friends?'

'They weren't keen on me, I dunno why.'

Mum frowned in a concerned way. I shrugged it off. I didn't want to talk about it.

Monday 8th August 2011

The Grahams were due to come at six. The puttanesca was on the go by the time they'd arrived and it was left up to me to boil the spaghetti, ten minutes before the sauce was ready.

Mum and Mrs Graham gave each other a kiss on the cheek when they greeted each other.

'Thank you so much for inviting us,' said Mrs Graham, as she, Mr Graham, Alistair, Fraser and Lizzy came in.

'My pleasure,' said Mum.

'Mmmm, something smells nice!' said Mr Graham. He asked what Mum was cooking, so she told him how she thought she'd go Italian this time, before she introduced me.

'Jamie, I have heard a lot about you,' said Mrs Graham. 'I'm Jane, and this is my husband, Colvin.'

'Hey there, Jamie. Great to finally meet you,' said Colvin, shaking my hand.

'Thanks,' I said.

'These are our sons, Alistair and Fraser, our daughter Lizzy and Alistair's girlfriend, Sophie,' said Jane

'Hi,' I said.

Mum asked Jesse to help her sort out drinks for everyone, before telling Lizzy we'd bought her some orange and passion fruit J2Os, her favourite.

Me and Rochella took the Grahams to the lounge whilst Jesse and Mum went to the kitchen to make drinks.

When we'd all sat down, we basically had more or less the same sort of conversations I had with the Baileys, such as them asking if I liked living with my mum, and what I planned to do at college and all that. The same thing would happen when I went round to see the Curtises, but at least they just wanted me to feel welcome, but it did feel like things were on replay with meeting everyone.

'Here we go,' said Mum, as she and Jesse came into the lounge with the drinks.

'Cheers, Flora,' said Colvin. 'I'm glad we decided to get a taxi here tonight, so we're not drinking and driving.'

'Definitely,' said Mum. She then looked round at Alistair and Sophie, and started asking how there were and if things were going well between them.

'Yeah, they are, thanks,' said Alistair, who then explained to me that he and Sophie had a house together.

'Are you two married?' I asked.

'No, no, we're just living together,' Sophie said. 'About three or four years it's been, now, isn't that right, Al?'

'Yeah, four years.'

'Is that how long you two have been together?'

'It was how long we were living together,' said Alistair. 'We started seeing each other six years ago.'

Mum then turned to Fraser.

'Fraser, tell me how your band is developing.'

'Oh, yes, I'm sure Jamie would be interested to hear about the band you and your friends have formed!' said Jane.

Fraser was in a band? This I had to hear more about!

'What position do you play in the band?' I asked.

'I'm the bass guitarist,' Fraser said. 'My mate Dustin is the lead guitarist and singer, and my other mate, Adam is the drummer.'

'What's the band called? And when did you first start?'

'It had been in the air for months but it hadn't been until September that we'd actually started making progress with it,' he'd said.

'What sort of music do you play?' I asked Fraser, and he told me about the covers the band was doing of songs by certain club and hardcore artists, and the gig they had in Finn's, a few months back.

'Oh, awesome!' I said.

'Yeah, it went really well, until some idiot ruined it by setting off the sprinklers in the bar!' said Fraser.

'Jesus, who'd do something like that?' I asked, shocked. What bad luck.

'Well that, and the reason why they did it is another story entirely,' he said, and I noticed him glance at Lizzy, who was looking down, with a slightly angry look on her face. Must've been someone she'd had a run in with who'd done it.

Dinner was ready at six twenty, so Mum led us to the dining room, where the table was laid with Mum's best cutlery and crockery. She invited the Grahams to take a seat whilst she, me, Jesse and Rochella went to serve up.

As soon as we were seated and served another drink, we tucked in.

I didn't like the capers, so I ate around them. Lizzy seemed to have really enjoyed hers! She was the first to finish.

'Finished already!' Mum said in astonishment. 'My, you must've been hungry! I do hope you'll have room for the chocolate and orange trifle.'

'Oh, I'll definitely have room,' said Lizzy, superiorly.

When we finished, me, Jesse, Rochella and Mum took all the empty plates out. Mum whispered, 'For someone who's so fussy about her food, Lizzy didn't half hoover up the lot!'

Either Lizzy was really hungry, or she was crazy for spaghetti sauces!

I brought Lizzy and Fraser's desserts in, and then sat down in my seat opposite Lizzy.

'So, you really like spaghetti then?' I asked her, as we tucked into our desserts.

'The tomatoey sauces on them, yeah,' said Lizzy. 'I don't like spaghetti carbonara, which is the creamy sauce made of eggs, and I don't like eggs in anyway other than baked in cakes and Yorkshire puddings. Do you like spaghetti carbonara?'

'Never tried it,' I shrugged.

'We ought to make it sometime, Jamie, the four us, so you can try it,' Mum recommended. 'The three of us like it, and I think you may too.'

Lizzy began telling me how she used to really like spaghetti bolognaise, and had made her own tomato and red pesto sauce, which she would eat with spaghetti and meatballs.

'I don't like to boast, but Lizzy is a *very* good cook,' said Jane, something Rochella and Jesse agreed with.

'What was it you said again, Jane? She makes a *mean* spag bol!' said Jesse.

'Well, it always turns out very well,' said Lizzy, beginning to look and sound modest. I had the feeling Lizzy was starting to feel bashful about everyone going on about what an excellent cook they thought she was. She probably didn't want to come across as big headed.

I helped Jesse, Rochella and Mum clear the table after we finished, whilst the Grahams went to the lounge.

'Why don't you three go and sit with the Grahams in the lounge and ask them if they'd like anything else to drink?' Mum suggested.

Colvin and Jane asked for another glass of white wine, each, but Lizzy, Fraser, Alistair and Sophie didn't want another drink, so Rochella told me and Jesse to sit down whilst she got another two glasses of wine for Jane and Colvin.

As Mum had had a glass of wine, she couldn't drive the Graham's home later, so she offered to pay for a taxi for them, something that Jane wouldn't hear of at first.

I'd become slightly tipsy myself, so I decided to head straight to bed.

I really hit it off with Lizzy. I was worried that Fraser would be ambivalent towards me, until we started talking about his band, which I loved hearing about.

Hopefully I'll get to go to another one of their performances, as I reckon I'll like the kind of music they do. Jesse's got me into My Chemical Romance, You Me At Six and the Foo Fighters, and I'm allowed to borrow his C.Ds any time I want.

Friday 12th August 2011

I didn't know what to do for the rest of the week, apart from hang out with Jesse. We'd gone into town.

'Fancy going into Gamestation?' Jesse asked. 'I'll need a new wingman, now Fred won't set foot in there anymore.'

What? Why did Fred not want to go into Gamestation?

'Why won't he go in there?' I asked.

'Well, I really shouldn't be going on about this, so you have to swear you won't tell anyone.'

'Okay. I swear I won't.'

'Fred went out with a girl who works in Gamestation but it ended badly. I'm not saying any more than that,' Jesse said. I didn't pry, as I knew it had bugger all to do with me, really. I was just curious to know why Fred would be so desperate to avoid going in there. What ever fucked up between Fred and this staff member doesn't mean Fred ought to be barred from the actual shop.

So was now Jesse's game-shopping buddy. When we walked in, I did indeed see a girl do a double take when she saw Jesse, and then look slightly awkward. I figured that was her.

Me and Jesse looked at some of the XBox games. I wasn't that fussed about looking at the games, I just came in because I said I'd keep Jesse company.

Jesse had picked out quite a few games, and then went to pay. He was served by the girl who looked at him awkwardly, and I noticed she sounded rather huffy when she asked Jesse if he wanted a bag and told him how much his purchases were in total. There wasn't any real need for that, just because he was best friends with the guy that broke her heart.

We left the shop afterwards, and I waited until we were a good distance away from the shop, before saying to Jesse, 'You've done nothing wrong, and she was still iffy with you.'

'Yeah, I know, I don't know what her problem is,' said Jesse. 'She used to be *well* matey with us, not to mention helpful when we were looking at games and shit, but since she and Fred broke up, the only interaction we've had is when she'd have to be the one serving me whenever I'd want to buy anything, and she'd never even say, "Have a nice day," like she used to.'

That was a bit off, fucking hell.

We were both getting a bit hungry, so we went off to Subway. I got a cheese steak melt with lettuce, before we caught the bus home, where we sat and ate our Subway sandwiches out in the garden.

'I'm well glad we're going round Fred's on Tuesday, rather than them coming round here,' said Jesse, 'you know, after the number of times we've had to cook for everyone.'

'Yeah. Nice to get a break from it,' I agreed. 'Did you say they came back today?'

'Oh, God, yeah, they do!' said Jesse. 'I'll probably hear from Fred tonight.'

Tuesday 16th August 2011

The next few days dragged by. We were due to be at the Curtises' house at twelve. I remembered Mum telling me Fred and Natalie were two of Claire and Barry's three children, and I asked who the third one was.

'Max is their youngest son,' Mum said, as we drove to the Curtises' house. 'He's about eight. Very good, sweet little boy, he is.'

Oh great. A kid. I've never really been very fond of kids. I was always the object of all their fun and games whenever me and Dave hung out somewhere there would be children. Dave would always tell me that it was just a bit of fun; I found it annoying and humiliating.

There was a time when I was at the park with Dave, and the shirt I was wearing was way too big for me, and there were a group of six to seven-year-olds running around, and one boy saw me, pointed and shouted, 'Hey, that big boy's wearing a dress!' The other children had laughed, and even Dave was trying not to fucking laugh!

And then there was a time when me and Dave were chilling at a beach, can't remember where, exactly. Dave's folks had asked Dave if he wanted to invite me. I accidentally knocked over a little girl's sandcastle. She'd burst into tears, and her mum had come running over and started giving me shit, like I'd done it on purpose! It had attracted another child's attention, a little boy who'd come over and kicked me hard in the shins, and stamped on my foot. Neither of those things would've hurt nearly as much if the boy hadn't been wearing his bright red jelly sandals. He didn't even get told off for it, even though both his parents saw everything! I'd been put off kids ever since, they're irritating little shits! I seriously hoped Max would be as good and sweet as Mum said he was.

'Hey, Mr and Mrs Curtis,' I said, to them both when we arrived.

'Oh, you don't need to use titles, you can call us Barry and Claire,' said Mr Curtis.

'This is our daughter, Natalie,' said Claire, 'and our sons, Fred and Max.'

Natalie and Fred were looking uneasy, but Claire told them, 'Well, be polite and say hello!'

Jesse, however, had also noticed the way they were acting.

'They're usually friendlier than this,' he'd whispered, as we all went into the lounge. Claire said she had Coke, Fanta, Ribena, ginger beer and sparkling water, so I asked for a glass of Coke, and then we sat out in the garden to talk.

'So, when did Jane come round?' Claire asked.

'Last Monday,' said Mum. 'Jamie got on very well with them all, didn't you, Jamie?'

'Yeah,' I said, but out of the corner of my eye, I couldn't help noticing Natalie whispering in Fred's ear, looking at me.

'Your mother and I were friends at school,' Claire said. 'We still stayed friends when I got married to Barry. We'd lived up in Yeovil for a while, and that was where Fred and Natalie were born, and then Flora and Jane brought their families up to Yeovil when Natalie was seven and Fred was five. '

'I knew that Lizzy and Jesse had been friends with Fred and Natalie since they were five and Natalie was seven,' I said, remembering immediately.

'That's right,' Claire confirmed. 'That was where, when and how they all became friends and the four of them became just as indivisible as me, Flora and Jane were.'

Claire suddenly looked over at Fred, who was just leading Jesse back into the conservatory. 'Fred where are you off to?'

'I just need to talk to Jesse about something,' said Fred, sounding shifty.

Claire sighed.

'Okay then.'

I was starting to feel slightly anxious. I was sure Fred was going to say something about me to Jesse. Why, though? He and Natalie had never met me and already they were being funny about me!

Claire said she was going into the kitchen to check on the food.

'Barry, you're friends with Gary Fox. His son, Dave, went to school with Jamie, isn't that right?' said Mum. Barry looked round at me, his eyebrows raised.

'Oh, you were friends with Dave Fox?' he said.

'Yeah, I was at school with him, and I've recently caught up with him about a month ago,' I told him.

'Me and Dave's dad, Gary, were friends when we used to work together,' he said. He spoke of how he'd met Mr Fox when he'd first started in two thousand and seven, after moving to Weymouth from Beaminster in two thousand and six.

Claire came out and invited us all to take a seat at the table on the patio and she'd bring everybody's meals out.

Mum began talking to Max, asking him how school was, and Max began talking about a play his class had performed about the Vikings. I felt too shy to try and have any conversations myself with Max.

Fred and Jesse had come out and sat down next to each other. Seven minutes after that, Claire had come back out and began serving everyone a plate of what turned out to be rotisserie chicken with this stuff made of cabbage and leek.

'What is this cabbage and leek stuff?' I asked Claire.

'It's a cabbage and leek bouillon,' Claire said.

'We've been trying to get Jamie into doing proper cooking,' Mum started explaining. 'All the stuff he had at Christian's was just tinned or frozen foods. He hadn't done any proper cooking from fresh when he was living in Beaminster so he doesn't know about much of this stuff.'

Barry looked bewildered, and said I should start a cooking course, then I could learn more about it, before Mum told him and Claire how I was going to start with foundation learning at college and that I was interested in looking at studying stuff to do with electricity. To be fair, though, Barry had given me another course option to think about.

Just as Mum was telling Barry and Claire how Max had been telling her about the Viking play he was in, I caught Fred's eye whilst we ate. He suddenly looked down at his food, clearly clocking I'd seen him looking at me.

Max began to tell Mum, Rochella, me and Jesse what other topics his class had covered, so he told us about his school projects about the Romans, Celts and Anglo Saxons, and about the Viking armour Claire helped him make out of foil and papier-mâché to wear on some Viking day they had.

I remembered when I'd worked on a project about the Anglo Saxons. It hadn't been very good because Christian had neglected to help me, obviously.

After main course, we had date and apple strudel for pudding, and then we had another drink and another chat before we said our goodbyes.

On the car journey home, I couldn't help feeling the tiniest bit disappointed about how it went. Barry and Claire seemed to like me as much as the Grahams and the Baileys did, and Max wasn't too bad, like I worried he'd be, but I couldn't understand Fred and Natalie's attitudes towards me. They didn't talk to me, and they seemed to be unsure about me. I didn't know why.

'Jesse?' I said, later on in Jesse's room, because I knew Jesse had noticed too.

'Yeah?'

'You know Fred and Natalie were a bit weird with me? You dunno why that was, do you? Only I did see you and Fred go off and talk.'

'Ah, er, yeah,' Jesse had begun, sounding uncomfortable. 'I don't really know how to say this, but... they know about your past.'

I was knocked for six! How could they know?

'How though?' I asked.

'Well, you know their dad is mates with Dave's dad?' Jesse said.

'Yeah?'

'Well, because they were good mates with Dave, through their dads' friendship, Dave had told them he was best mates with a boy named Jamie when he was at school, and how this friend of his was brought up by just his dad, because his mum overdosed herself to death after his sister had died of a blood clot to the brain, and then he had ended up getting in so much trouble with the law, he was taken out of school and sent to a young offenders' institution, and then when I told Fred and Natalie that you were my long lost brother and that Christian had been lying to you about Rochella's blood clot and Mum's overdose, they made the connection.'

But this did not make me feel any better. They still didn't try to get to know me. How did they know that I hadn't come to my senses and learnt my lesson after doing my time?

'They are bigger than this, so I can't believe they didn't give you a chance to prove you'd changed,' said Jesse.

I was really fucking pissed off. Ever since I completed my sentence, I had to put up with people that knew about it judging me, and now two of my brother's closest friends were doing the exact same thing!

'Well, next time you see them, do me a favour and remind them that they're better than that!' I snapped, before storming out of Jesse's room and into my own, slamming the door.

Through the door, I heard footsteps rushing up the stairs, and then Mum's voice say to Jesse, 'What was all that about?'

I listened. I could hear Jesse's voice, but couldn't make out what he was saying.

I was still smarting from it the next day. Neither of them had met me before, they knew about my past and assumed I was still a troublemaker, just because of it, how *dare* they!

Mum tried to talk to me about it at breakfast.

'I am a bit shocked,' she said, 'especially because Fred's usually a very understanding person.'

My arse!

Shit, I'd actually said that out loud!

'Language!' Mum had scolded me, though there's nothing wrong with the word "arse."

She asked me if I wanted her to phone Claire and ask her to have a word about it with both Fred and Natalie.

'Oh my God, don't do that! It'll just be embarrassing!' I said. I couldn't grass them up. That would make them hate me even more! That's what I learnt about bullies. That's why I never snitched on Dave's dickhead mates, because I knew I'd make them bully me more.

But it didn't matter because it was their choice and their problem, not mine, and I wasn't going to make them like me if they didn't want to.

But Jesse had other ideas.

'I still want us to meet as a gang at some point, and then they can get to know you better, and see you're not who you used to be.'

But I didn't hold out much hope of that going well, either.

I perked up a bit when I had a text from Dave, asking if I fancied hanging out in town on Thursday.

I caught the bus into town, and met Dave on the stretch of grass on the traffic island by the King's Statue, before we had a stroll around town.

'What you been up to?' Dave asked.

'I met the Curtises the day before yesterday,' I told him.

'How did you get on with them?'

'I got on with Barry and Claire,' I told him. 'Can't say the same for Fred and Natalie, though.'

As expected, Dave asked why, sounding worried and uncomfortable, so I said it was because they knew about my past because Dave had told them.

'Oh, shit, yeah,' said Dave, tipping his head back, grimacing, his eyes screwed up like he was in pain. 'I did say that I was mates with you, they must've realised both me and Jesse were talking about the same Jamie when Jesse told them all about you. I'm really sorry.'

'You're not to blame,' I said, 'I'm pissed off with Fred and Natalie for not giving me the benefit of the doubt.'

'I wouldn't have put it past Natalie to be slightly judgemental,' Dave admitted, 'but I'm surprised at Fred.

'Ever since my sentence ended, I've had no one to turn to,' I told Dave, 'and people didn't trust me if they knew how badly I'd gone off the rails.'

'Yeah, Gaz, Kris and Len kept on making jokes about it after you were taken out of school,' Dave said.

'Have you heard from any of them at all?'

'Not since moving here from Beaminster.'

'So, where are you living now?' I asked him.

'Near the train station. Very handy, actually, if I fancy a meal in the Pie and Ale house,' he said, triumphantly.

'Or a K.F.C or MaccyD's, since I noticed those near the train station,' I said added.

'Oh, yeah, definitely!' Dave agreed.

We carried on walking through town, before deciding to buy some lunch from this chip shop called Fish 'N' Fritz, and agreeing to catch the bus as far as ASDA, and walk the rest of the way to Sandsfoot Castle.

I bought some chips and a battered sausage, before we walked to the town bridge bus stop, which is outside this place called Rendezvous.

We caught the number three bus to ASDA, before getting off and walking up a road called Marsh Road and along this footpath called the Rodwell Trail to Sansfoot Castle.

The walk was approximately half an hour. It was peaceful, walking up the footpath, which was shaded by trees. We had to leap out of the way of passing cyclists a few times, but it was a very pleasant journey.

We sat in the garden at Sandsfoot Castle, which is surrounded by flowers and had a square pond in the middle and a fountain, and we ate our lunch on the grass in the shade. It was a very hot day, because it was August.

'Wish I hadn't worn trousers,' said Dave. 'At least I'm not wearing skinny jeans.'

'Oh God, yeah,' I said. I'd put on some very light shorts and a t-shirt with sandals, as I knew it would be hot out.

Me and Dave finished our lunches and walked across a bridge to have a look around the castle.

After spending some time admiring the view across the water, out towards Portland, from the back of the castle, we left and lay down on the grassy slope. I shut my eyes, feeling blissful, like I never had before. I felt so happy, here with my oldest mate, just the two of us, like it had been, the rare times them twat balls left us alone.

We stayed for forty minutes, before we got to our feet and began walking back to ASDA.

'What do you fancy doing now?' Dave asked.

'Wanna hang at mine?' I asked. Dave accepted the invite, so, when we reached ASDA, we waited at the bus stop for the number eight bus.

Out of the corner of my eye, I saw Fred and Jesse appear round the corner, and they started walking over to me and Dave.

'Alright?' said Jesse. Fred said hello to me and Dave, still sounding a bit awkward, but thankfully not as standoffish as he and Natalie had been, previously.

'Hey,' I said. 'You two getting the bus home?'

'Yeah, Fred's coming home with me,' said Jesse.

'Why have you not got your car with you, Fred?' Dave asked, frowning.

'There's a problem with the gearbox, so it's being seen to,' said Fred. 'I dunno when I'll have it back. Pain in the bollocks, I know.'

Dave talked about how he was getting his uncle's old Volkswagen van in three days time.

We talked about what we'd been up to. Jesse said that he and Fred had been chilling out with Matt Weller and Spencer Grantham-Stone, who Jesse told me were two friends he and Fred had known at Fleetview.

The bus arrived eight minutes later. It was a double decker, so we bagged the four front seats upstairs.

'*Sweet*!' said Dave, thrilled, as we sat down. '*Love* sitting at the front when I'm upstairs on the double deckers!'

I looked over and saw Fred and Jesse with one earphone each in one of their ears, listening to Fred's iPod.

'What you guys listening to?' I asked, wanting to strike up a conversation with Fred, to try and break the ice.

'Darren Styles,' Fred said. 'I love his stuff!'

'Isn't Darren Styles one of the artists whose stuff Fraser said he and his band were doing covers of?' I asked, remembering the conversation I had with him about Rebel Tour Bus.

'Yeah, that's right,' said Fred. 'Hard to say whether I prefer their covers or Darren Styles' to be honest.'

Me and Dave carried on talking. I'd dared to hope Fred wasn't so iffy with me now. He seemed to have lightened up a bit with me, though not as much as I would've liked.

It was when we were nearing the turning left to a road called Dennis Road, that I'd heard a loud bang, just before I felt the bus make a sudden, violent swerve to the right.

'Jesus, what was that?!' I shouted.

'I don't know,' said Dave, sounding panicky.

Next thing I knew, I felt like I was being tipped sideways to my right. This wasn't good. The bus was going to fall on its side!

'OMIGOD!!!!' Fred and Jesse were shouting. People were screaming themselves hoarse. There was another crash as the bus knocked against the bus shelter across the road from the turning left to Dennis Road, and had leant there. Oh my fucking God, Dave had been knocked unconscious! The stairwell was blocked, we were trapped!

'Dave! Dave, wake up!' I shouted, frantically slapping Dave's face, which was covered in cuts and bruises, trying to wake him up.

A girl was screeching, 'OMIGOD! HOW ARE WE GONNA GET OUT?!'

Everybody was panicking. People were banging on the windows, screaming for help, whilst others were shouting and sobbing hysterically.

'LIZZY! NATALIE!' Fred suddenly bellowed, hammering on the front window. I carefully scuttled over to the window and saw Lizzy and Natalie standing on the pavement, their hands over their mouths in shock. I saw Natalie look up and see Fred and I, and the second she had, she flipped out and she and Lizzy began running over to the door, but two policemen outside held them back, as Natalie screamed, 'THAT'S MY BROTHER UP THERE! MY BROTHER IS ON THAT BUS!'

I looked out of the windows. I could see the top of a lorry that been emerging from the turning to Dennis Road, and had knocked into the side of the bus, sending it sideways into the bus stop.

'How're we s'posed to get down?!' Jesse shouted in terror.

The passengers who'd been sat at the back of the bus had the answer to that. They were able to open the emergency hatch, but Jesse said there was no way he was jumping down from the upper windows of the bus.

'We *have* to, Jesse! It's the only way!' Fred shouted to him, firmly.

I scurried over to the window. There was a vast crowd down on the road. Cars had stopped and people had gone out to see if they could help. I saw people I recognised. The Baileys were down there, and so was Mum.

'Oh my goodness! My baby boy is up there!' she started crying, hysterically, as soon as she saw me. Another policeman had to come running over to stop her going any closer to the bus.

'JESSE!' Annie had screamed, the second she'd seen him come over to the window too.

I could see people climbing through the emergency hatch downstairs. Ambulances were outside.

'We have to get Dave over to the window and pass him down to someone!' I said to Fred and Jesse.

'Okay, c'mon,' said Fred, as he and Jesse rushed over to lift Dave up.

Anthony, along with two other men, were helping to encourage the passengers who'd been upstairs on the bus, down from the window.

'It's okay! We've got you, we'll catch you,' they were saying.

'Dave's up here! He's unconscious!' I shouted down to them.

Anthony shouted up to me to pass Dave down to him and he and the other men would grab him.

Fred and Jesse carried Dave over to the window, carefully raised him, eased him out, and let him down gently. Anthony caught him when they let him go.

Me, Jesse and Fred helped to try and cajole a group of girls who were sobbing and too frightened to move to go over to the window so they could jump out.

'It's all right!' Anthony was shouting up to them, when they'd come over to the window. 'It's okay, we'll catch you!'

As Fred let one of them down gently, she was begging him not to let go whilst he constantly reassured her.

'Go on, Jesse,' I wheedled to my brother, when his turn had come. I watched as Jesse stepped up onto the seat, and lifted his legs over and out of the window of the bus. I could hear Annie screaming his name down on the road outside.

The crowd gave a scream of fright as the weight of his body brought him down, and he was hanging onto the edge of the window.

'You can let go, Jesse, I've got you!' Anthony shouted. He grabbed Jesse as soon as he let go, and I saw Jesse run over to Mum, Pandora and Annie. Both Annie and Mum were in floods of tears.

Next was Fred's turn. I looked out the window and saw Lizzy and Natalie rush through the crowd, over to Jesse, Mum and the Baileys.

As soon as Fred had jumped down, he had joined them. I saw Lizzy and Natalie giving him hugs.

I went next. I let myself down the same way Jesse did, though more gently. I, too, ran over to the others. Mum was hugging Jesse.

'Jamie! My babies!' she sobbed, pulling me into the same suffocating hug she had Jesse in. As I looked round at the bus, I saw a car wedged underneath the bus, between that and the bus shelter. The driver was unconscious, his head leant on the steering wheel. Three more people were trying to get him out.

'Christ! How are they going to get him out?' I said.

'Fuck, it's Matt's dad!' said Fred in horror.

It took a whole mass of people to lift the bus and tip it upright again, so that they had a better chance of getting the unconscious man out of his car.

Those who'd come out of accidents with major injuries were taken away in the ambulances, as well as the majority of people who needed treating for shock, which included Natalie, Annie and Mum who, despite not being on the bus, were traumatized to have seen their loved ones on that bus.

Me, Jesse, Fred, Lizzy and Pandora and Anthony waited in the waiting room. Barry and Claire arrived with Max shortly afterwards, as they had been called and informed of what had happened.

'Oh thank God, Fred!' said Claire, breathlessly, throwing her arms round him. Barry followed suit, before asking where Natalie was.

'She's being treated for shock,' Lizzy told him.

A boy of about Fred and Jesse's age and his mum came rushing in. They turned out to be the wife and son of the man who'd been wedged in his car between the bus and the bus stop. Both their faces were tear streaked and their eyes red from crying.

Pandora had given Annie a hug when she'd come out, followed by Natalie and Mum.

'Come here, sweetheart,' Barry said, giving Natalie a hug.

Unfortunately, the staff wouldn't let us go in and see Dave, as they said they were only letting immediate family see those who had been seriously injured in the crash, and that Dave's parents were on their way.

When we all left the hospital, we had to get a lift home.

I went straight up to my room, shut the door, and then the reality of what happened had hit me, full on. I couldn't believe it. I'd really been in a bus crash. Worst of all, I was worried about what would happen to Dave. My best friend, my *only* friend! He'd been knocked unconscious! What if he'd suffered a serious brain injury? What if he died? Just a few weeks at the most after rekindling our friendship as well!

I began running my fingers through my hair, breathing heavily.

Wednesday 24th August 2011

To my relief, I found out that both Dave and the man were fine. Mum was still shaky for a few days, but she'd calmed down now.

It was midday, Rochella was out with her best mate, Jesse was round at Annie's, so it was just me and Mum.

She made us both a cup of coffee, and told me to sit down in the lounge.

She joined me, and said, 'There is something I need to talk to you about, and now that you have been living here for long enough, I think the time is right for us to discuss it.'

What she was going to say?

'What's it about?'

'Michael.'

'Have you two split up?' I asked, concerned, but Mum reassured me that they hadn't.

'He's going to move in with me in Autumn,' she told me.

I looked down, not sure of how to feel. I did like Michael. But Mum had more to say.

'I don't know if Michael ever told you about his children,' she'd said. She talked about Michael's daughters, Amy and Emma.

'Are they moving in, too?' I asked.

'Eventually, yes,' she said. 'Amy's the eldest. Emma's nineteen.'

She explained that Michael had made her happier than Christian ever could have. She said that she just knew for sure that he was the one.

I was full of mixed feelings. I'd settled in whilst I'd been at my mum's, and now I'd been given something else to try to adjust to.

Wednesday 31st August 2011

Me and Jesse spoke about this. We were spending the day with the gang. The eight of us, as Jesse had told me, were going into town, and then over to Portland.

Fred and Natalie had picked us up in Fred's car, which appeared to have had its gearbox fixed.

'How long have you been driving for, Fred?' I'd asked, sticking at my hopes to make things less awkward and proved I'd changed.

'I started learning as soon as I turned seventeen,' Fred said. 'My parents paid for my driving lessons as one of my birthday presents.'

'Is this your present for passing your test?' I asked.

'Yeah, that's right,' said Fred. I noticed he still seemed a bit cagey.

We'd arranged to meet Dave, Lizzy, Ruby-lynn and Scarlet outside the Rock and Fudge, as it was where Lizzy, Ruby-lynn and Scarlet would be getting off of their buses, as well as it being walking distance from Dave's house.

Fred parked in the multi-storey car park. I was keen to get the lift down, as we'd parked at the top, but Fred and Natalie used the stairs, as Fred said he was claustrophobic, therefore didn't feel brave about going in the lift as the multi-story car park does have quite a small lift as well.

We walked through St Thomas Street, to the sea front. Dave was the only one who'd arrived.

'Hey,' he said, when he'd glanced round and saw the four of us.

'Hi,' said Natalie. 'We're so glad you're okay.'

'Thanks. I heard you had to be treated for shock.'

'God, it was so horrible, I was having a major shit fit,' said Natalie.

I saw a number one bus pull over to the bus shelter, and then the doors opened.

'Ruby-lynn!' Natalie yelled to the third passenger who'd departed the bus. I thought I'd go blind at the colour of Ruby-lynn's bright pink hair!

'Hiya,' she'd said when she reached us and gave Natalie a hug.

'This is Jamie, Ruby-lynn,' said Jesse. Ruby-lynn looked round.

'Oh my God, you two look so alike!' she said.

Not long afterwards, Lizzy was walking towards us, shortly before a red haired girl had emerged from the number ten bus shelter. She was introduced to me as Scarlet.

I couldn't help feeling that there was something about Scarlet that I found quite attractive, though I couldn't put my finger on what it was.

Scarlet had behaved slightly like the way Fred and Natalie had, but I promised myself I'd try to make an effort.

We had a nice long walk around town, and then bought ice creams from the kiosk on the beach, and sat on the sand to eat them, whilst we talked, watching everyone in the sea.

It was a nice warm, sunny day, with the slightest breeze. There were quite a lot of people on the beach, but not so much it was packed.

'Mum spoke to me about Michael,' I told Jesse.

'I wanted Mum to tell you sooner,' Jesse had said.

'I know why she waited,' I told him.

'Me and Rochella have never met Michael's children before, but I like to think we'll all get on.'

'Do they still live in California?' I wondered.

'They still do at the moment, but they'll be moving over to England to live with Michael in October, when he moves in with us,' said Jesse. 'Their flight gets into Bristol airport the day after Michael will be moving in with us.'

'Why ain't they living with their mum anymore?'

'It's all complicated stuff to do with this new job she's just got, she feels Amy and Emma will be better off living with their dad in England.'

'Do you know whereabouts in California they live?' I was interested to know.

'You'll never believe it,' Jesse said. 'Los Angeles.'

I jumped back in amazement. *Hollywood*?

'I know, right? How are they able to afford a house in Hollywood,' Jesse agreed. He went on to say that Michael said their house wasn't exactly one like you saw in American movies, or one belonging to a billionaire.

'Pity we didn't bring our swim gear,' said Natalie.

'Yeah,' Dave agreed.

I was beginning to think that myself. The sea looked so inviting. Oh well, I'd been to the beach with the family earlier on in the summer, back in June and July.

We finished our ice creams, then spent another hour on the beach, before we left. I got to know Ruby-lynn quite well. I'd had conversations with Fred and Scarlet, but they still sounded a bit wary, and it was always me starting the conversations with them. Natalie hadn't said anything to me, so far.

After another walk along the harbour, we decided to go over to Portland. Me, Jesse, Natalie and Fred went back to the car to drive there, as Dave took the other three girls back to his place to drive his van to Portland from there. We agreed to meet at Portland Castle.

In the car, I decided enough was enough. I needed to talk to Jesse about how Fred, Natalie and now Scarlet were behaving towards me.

Me, Jesse, Fred and Natalie met Dave and the girls in the car park.

We looked round the gardens first, before entering the castle. When we were in the Tudor kitchen, I tried having a conversation with Natalie, but she didn't seem fully engaged.

'They're still being funny with me,' I said to Jesse when we were alone together in the Gun Room. 'And now Scarlet is as well.'

Jesse sighed.

'Have you tried talking to them?' I asked.

'I'm not gonna pretend it's not making it awkward for me, okay?' Jesse said.

'So talk to them,' I urged him, 'for both our sakes.'

After spending an hour at Portland Castle, we decided to go to Portland Bill.

Fred parked his car at Portland Bill, and then we waited for Dave and the other girls to arrive, before heading over to the kiosk to buy some chips.

'How about you four go and grab a bench, and tell me, Fred, Natalie and Scarlet what you want and we'll get it for you?' Jesse said to me, Dave, Lizzy and Ruby-lynn.

'We will?' said Fred.

'Yeah sure,' said Jesse, giving Fred this look like he was being insistent and trying to hide it, so me, Dave, Lizzy and Ruby-lynn told him, Fred, Natalie and Scarlet what we wanted, before we snagged a couple of benches where we had a clear view of the sea. We moved the benches with some difficulty to join them together, and then me and Dave sat opposite Lizzy and Ruby-lynn.

'So, you enjoy working in Zellweger's, Ruby-lynn?' I asked her.

'Yeah, it's brilliant, and I get a good discount on stuff,' said Ruby-lynn.

'Sounds excellent,' I said. I began asking Lizzy what she'd be doing next year, so she told me about a course she would be doing in Dance and Drama.

'I did do Art and Design before, but I decided it wasn't really right for me,' she'd said.

'I didn't know you were into that stuff,' I said. 'Would you want a career in that sort of thing?'

Lizzy said that there were a couple things she'd wanted to be. She said she'd wanted to be an actress, and was massively into creative writing.

'But if you wanted to act, how come you dropped Drama when you were at school?' Dave asked.

'I know that that probably hadn't been the best idea, but there were other G.C.S.Es I wanted to do, and couldn't fit Drama in, too,' Lizzy said.

Jesse, Fred, Natalie and Scarlet came over with the drinks. Jesse sat down between me and Fred, opposite Lizzy and Natalie.

'Here you go,' Jesse said, giving me my Dr Pepper.

'Cheers.'

We had our drinks and talked whilst we waited for our food.

'Ruby-lynn, don't mind me asking, but when did you decide to dye your hair that colour?' I couldn't help asking.

'Not long after I finished my A-levels at Fleetview,' said Ruby-lynn.

'You were at Fleetview?' I said. 'So you knew Fred and Jesse there?'

'Actually, no, because we were never in any of the same classes,' said Ruby-lynn. 'Anyway, I'm really into bright colours and that. My hair was light brown before. My natural colour.'

'I see.'

I hoovered up my chips and beans as soon as our food had arrived, and then when everyone had finished, we went for a walk around Portland Bill.

'Jamie?' said a voice on my left. I looked round. It was Fred.

'Alright?' he'd said.

'Yeah, I'm cool,' I said.

'Cool,' said Fred. 'Listen, me, Natalie and Scarlet didn't mean to be so iffy around you.'

I blinked at Fred.

'We should've known better than to jump to conclusions, after what Dave told us,' he went on. 'I know Natalie in particular was being a bit distant, earlier.'

I nodded.

'Jesse spoke to the three of us and said we needed to not be so aloof and he was right. I'm sorry,' he said. 'I do want to make friends.'

'That's okay,' I said.

'Okay,' said Fred, looking slightly relieved. 'Good.'

I was grateful to Jesse for talking to Fred, Natalie and Scarlet, as it would make it easier for me to have normal, friendly conversations with them.

Me and Fred joined the others in admiring the view. Over the surface of the dark blue sea, was clear blue sky, sun shining on the cliffs, casting shadows over the rocks below. Everything was entirely pictorial.

Despite everything that Jesse needed to sort out, and what I have next to prepare for, everything is perfect. I've come to a family who love me, and have left my idiot dad forever. And I got my best friend back as well, and made more friends. True friends. Everything is falling into place. At last, I feel like I belong.

THE END

Printed in Great Britain
by Amazon

83166750R00123